HOLD CONTROL

KIM SERRANO

S+S

SWITCH + STERN

CONTENT WARNING

This story contains mature themes including consensual BDSM, emotional intensity, and explicit power dynamics between adults. Every act of violence, restraint, or degradation that appears in sexual contexts is rooted in mutual consent, trust, and negotiation between fictional characters. These scenes are not a guide. They are not real.

If you're looking for safe, sane, and consensual kink, start with research, communication, and a good understanding of limits—yours and your partner's. What's safe for them may not be safe for you.

Read with care.

TRIGGER WARNINGS

- Suicidal ideation and intrusive thoughts
- Implied past sexual trauma
- Workplace harassment (gender-based)
- Homophobic slur (used by background character)
- Pain stimming (non-harmful)

1

Captain Isabel Ventura returned to Heathrow without ceremony.

No announcement. Just four stripes on her shoulder and a walk that held no apology.

The terminal lights were too bright, the floor too polished, and still—people stepped aside. Some recognized her. Most didn't. It didn't matter. There was something in the way she moved: precise and deliberate. Not rushed.

Her boots were black leather, custom-fitted in Milan. Low heel, almond toe, polished to a shine that caught the jet bridge lights. Regulation height—barely. But no one ever asked.

Her uniform fit like a tailored warning. Double-breasted navy, gold trim at the cuffs, shoulders cut sharp, waist nipped just enough. The trousers hit just above the ankle—long enough to be formal, short enough to show off those boots. Crisp collar. No tie. The white shirt underneath was spotless, the top button undone. Just one.

She was lean in a way that read as efficient, not vain. Long lines. Squared posture. The kind you get from being told a hundred times to smile and never once had. No visible jewelry. Her face gave away nothing but precision. Her skin looked expensive. She could've been twenty-five or forty-five. No one ever guessed right.

Her hair was parted clean down the middle, French-braided tight along both sides—sharp, controlled rows that traced just behind her ears and fed into a low, coiled bun at the nape of her neck. No flyaways. Just structure. The braids didn't move. The bun didn't slip. It was a style meant to survive fourteen hours, four time zones, and a full engine failure without needing adjustment.

It had been six months. She looked like she'd only stepped out for coffee.

She moved through the operations center with calm authority—answering no one, asking for nothing. She read the METAR once. Didn't need to again. Fuel numbers—checked, recalculated, confirmed. She pulled the flight plan herself. Didn't trust dispatch to get the alternate right. Not after what she'd seen. A missed detail at a desk could turn catastrophic at thirty-six thousand feet.

Her hands were steady. They always were. But today there was something else—something reverent in the way she handled things. The headset, uncoiled and tested. The printouts, clipped and ordered. The logbook, flipped open with care.

She took her time on the preflight. Longer than most captains bothered with. Nose to tail. She crouched beneath the fuselage, ran gloved fingers along panel edges. Checked for rust. Scratches. Loose rivets. Found a pitot cover still attached. Flagged it. Logged it. Moved on.

Above her, the aircraft waited—massive, still, already hers.

She was almost to the gate when she felt it—that

instinct, that weight. Someone watching, but not with threat. She turned.

The woman was standing off to the side in a navy blazer a half-size too big and new-issue pilot wings that hadn't even dulled yet. Maybe mid-twenties. Pretty. Nervous. Trying not to be obvious.

She gave her a small nod, just enough to acknowledge her and move on.

But the girl stepped forward anyway. "Captain Ventura?"

She stopped. "Yes?"

"I—sorry," she said, already flushed. "I didn't want to interrupt. I just—um, my instructor showed us your JFK approach from years ago? Low vis, crosswind, wet runway. You greased it. I've watched it like...way too many times."

She didn't smile. But she looked at her. Really looked.

"What's your name?"

"Shruthi Aishwarya."

"You flying today?"

"Deadheading to Toronto. First rotation."

She gave her a quiet once-over. Shoes were polished. Shirt tucked. Voice steady despite the nerves.

"You'll do fine," she said.

Shruthi grinned like she hadn't meant to. "Thanks, Captain."

She moved up the jet bridge, boots loud against the floor, her mind already in the cockpit. She didn't expect the noise just outside the galley—a pair of ground crew in vests, half-blocking the entrance with a catering cart and too much time on their hands.

"I thought she was gone for good," one said.

"Yeah but why six months? That's rehab or something."

"She never even took sick days before this."

She didn't flinch. But she stopped.

Cy was already in the galley. Heard it too. Stepped into view—six foot something, salt-and-pepper fade, navy vest over crisp white sleeves, every inch pressed and deadly.

"Run that back a little softer, yeah?" he said. "We're not doing gossip about my flight deck today."

Silence. Immediate. The kind that gets people reassigned to baggage.

She didn't say a word. Just walked past the cart and through the galley like the air hadn't just changed. But as she passed, Cy tilted his head at her in quiet confirmation.

"Welcome back, Captain" he said, low.

She barely made it two steps past Cy before she heard it: Heavy footsteps. No announcement. Just presence.

Then: "You better not make me cry in uniform, Izzy."

André reached her in three strides and pulled her into a hug that nearly lifted her off the floor. Broad arms. Real hold. The kind of grip you give someone who disappeared and didn't explain why.

Izzy didn't brace. She didn't have to. She'd given him this kind of access years ago, after one too many tequila shots and an emergency hair-holding incident outside a private club on King's Road.

"You're creasing my uniform," she muttered into his chest.

"You'll survive."

His voice was low and warm, the kind of deep that settled into your ribs. He didn't move to let go.

"You look good," he said. "Tired, but good."

"I'm here, aren't I?"

He pulled back just enough to look at her. Not a scan— an audit.

"I hated not knowing," he said. "Don't do that to us again."

She nodded, quiet.

He kissed the side of her head and stepped back like he hadn't just reassembled her whole spine.

"I missed you," he said. "Flight deck's clean. Galley's tight. And we stocked the good coffee."

"Good."

She stepped away from André—the weight of his hands still warm on her arms—and turned toward the cockpit.

He hesitated. Just for a second.

There was something in his face. A flicker. The look he got when the galley ovens were broken and he was deciding whether to lie. He opened his mouth like he was about to say something.

But Izzy was already walking.

She couldn't help it.

The cockpit called to her the way nothing else ever had. The low hum of electronics. The glow of the displays. The switch guards. The overhead panel, every circuit and breaker filed neatly somewhere in the back of her skull.

It was home. Her first love. Her longest relationship. She'd missed it so badly it made her chest tight. She stepped through the threshold and breathed in the smell—plastic, coffee, compressed air.

The left seat was right there. Her seat.

Occupied.

She stopped.

The breath she'd been holding caught sharp in her throat. Someone was sitting in the captain's chair. Not just someone—junior. A First Officer. Three stripes. Blond. Polished. Broad shoulders under a new uniform jacket, not yet broken in by red-eyes or galley heat. He was leaning forward, tapping something into the center console with casual ease.

On her fucking seat.

"Breathe," she muttered to herself. This isn't personal. She knew she'd be riding right seat for her first couple of legs. She knew the policy. It didn't mean she was ready to see someone else in her chair.

Your seat doesn't define you, her therapist's voice said.

She almost believed it. Then he spoke.

"Hey—just so you're aware, they changed the STAR. Drops earlier now. Caught me off guard last month. If you wait for the marker, you'll—"

"You'll bust profile. VNAV won't catch it unless you're under 240 before KASIG. If you're still high by DUSMO, you're late. *I know.*"

He turned, smiling—like they'd just shared a moment. Like she'd confirmed something for him.

"Exactly."

Her blood pressure surged.

That word. *Exactly.* Like they were colleagues. Like she hadn't flown that STAR before he probably had facial hair. Like he hadn't just explained it to her from *her goddamn chair.*

Then came the smile—open, warm, and so stupidly handsome it felt hostile.

"Captain Ventura," he said, like the name was a lucky charm. "It's so nice to meet you."

Izzy didn't move. That faint Southern twang she hadn't placed yet—somewhere inland, drawl softened by officer school and good intentions. Tennessee, maybe. Kentucky if she was feeling cruel.

Cy's voice came from behind her, calm and measured. "This is First Officer Nico Farrah."

André added, "Ugh it doesn't look right. You on the right seat."

Cy shot him a look: *Not helping.*

She said nothing.

The FO turned—and she got the full body shot.

Of course he was built like that. Wide shoulders like he was sculpted under duress. Chest stretching the uniform just enough to be obscene. Arms that didn't just fill the sleeves, they tested them—clean lines of muscle so precise they looked digitally rendered. He was defined like he had nothing better to do than master every single iso hold in existence. He probably foam rolled after sex.

He didn't just work out. He disciplined his body. And for what? So he could sit in a flight deck and pretend like he wasn't begging for someone to notice how tight his core stayed when he reached for a checklist?

And of course he had that face.

Green eyes designed for cockpit close-ups and magazine spreads. The kind that made gate agents flirt and captains overlook mistakes. Bone structure that came with a punch-line—cheekbones, jaw, symmetry like an accusation.

He was the kind of beautiful that made people assume competence. The kind that got called "humble" in articles because he smiled once and didn't punch a wall.

She felt it in her molars—this internal grinding—somewhere between fury and a chemical thirst so shameful it felt like betrayal. He was an Adonis in a pilot's uniform and she wanted him gone. Off her plane. Out of her airspace. Preferably into the sun.

Men who looked like him had been undermining her since she was in ground school. Had made her feel unsafe in hotel elevators. Had dismissed her fuel calcs. Had explained lift to her like she was new. Maybe he hadn't done it personally, but his face carried the whole legacy.

And now, after everything she'd clawed back—after the

check-in, the medical re-cert, the silence, the shame, the wait—he was in the seat she lost. The seat she'd protected. The seat she hadn't touched again until she was sure she was still the woman who belonged in it. And the second she came back, it was filled. By someone who didn't have to fight for it.

That was the moment she knew.

Isabel Ventura hated Nico Farrah instantly, entirely, and with purpose.

2

They pushed back on schedule.

He handled taxi. She read the checklist like scripture. Every switch, every callout, every confirmation. His flow was tight. Confident. Not cocky—worse: competent. Smooth hands. Clean inputs. A voice that didn't perform for the recorder. She didn't comment. Just tracked his behavior like she was grading a flight school demo. If he'd screwed anything up, she would've caught it. He didn't.

Then—of course—she bled. Somewhere over Ireland.

It was dull at first—a pressure behind her eyes, low in her hips, like someone was twisting her insides with slow fingers. She blinked hard, ignored it, focused on the upper airways and the perf calc she didn't need to double-check but did anyway. When she shifted in her seat and felt the unmistakable damp bloom beneath her, she froze.

She hadn't packed tampons. She always packed tampons. But she'd been so focused on the headset and the logbook and whether she could still do the damn thing that she'd forgotten the most human thing about her.

She didn't say a word. Didn't ask. She never had. In over

twenty years, she'd flown with another woman exactly once. Maybe twice. She barely remembered. There was no infrastructure for asking. No safe place to say: I'm bleeding and in pain and I need help. So she didn't.

She adjusted in her seat, carefully. Kept her voice level for the fuel update to dispatch. Willed her body to behave.

The relief pilot came in around the fourth hour. She barely looked at him—tall, neutral, inoffensive. She gave him her seat without hesitation, muttered something perfunctory about stable cruise and low traffic, then made her way to the rest area. Eleven-hour flight. Augmented crew. She was required to take at least ninety minutes horizontal. Fatigue risk, insurance compliance, all that.

The bunk was stifling. It smelled like recycled air and polyester and men who didn't believe in double-washing their uniforms. She didn't change—just unbuttoned her jacket, loosened the collar, left her shoes on. She lay down like she meant it, like a body being loaded into a drawer. Back flat against the wall. Right arm bent. One foot hooked at the ankle so she could kick hard if she needed to. No one had touched her in years. That didn't mean she stopped sleeping like someone might.

She closed her eyes and went under in sixty seconds. It was a skill. Like landing in wind shear or threading an approach through microbursts. You didn't wait until you were tired—you commanded your body to obey. She didn't dream.

Back in the cockpit, she slipped into the right seat again like she'd never left it. Nico glanced at her. Not intrusive. Just there. He offered her the rest of his protein bar, the good kind with the almond coating and the smug eco label. She shook her head once. He didn't push it.

He flew in silence. Not because he was nervous—

because he didn't need to fill space. She hated how rare that was.

Most men, given the cockpit and ninety minutes of altitude, took it as an invitation to audition for a TED Talk. Fuel theory. Aircraft preference. She'd been held hostage mid-Atlantic by men who thought silence was a personal attack and conversation was a form of dominance.

Nico didn't do that. He said what mattered and then shut the fuck up.

It shouldn't have felt like a gift.

But it did.

She hated it even more that it made her want to trust him, just a little. She glanced sideways at him as he double-checked fuel flow twice, even though he didn't need to. Monitored the engine temps out loud—not for show, but for clarity. Every time she thought he might say something stupid, he didn't.

And he smelled...fine. Clean. Not scented. Fabric softener maybe, or some nondescript soap that didn't trigger anything in her gut. She caught it when he leaned forward to adjust the panel light. It wasn't attraction. Not really. It was the realization that his presence didn't activate her threat sensors.

She didn't know what to do with that.

Descent started over the Mojave. She briefed the approach like she was defending a thesis. He confirmed every item, matched her tempo, didn't get cute. Final approach. She felt it under her skin—the ache, the insult, the quiet fury of watching some *boy* land her plane.

His yoke. His call. His hands.

He landed clean.

Greased it, even. No bounce. It was insultingly well-executed.

She said nothing. Just logged the block time, noted the touchdown point, and watched him sign his name in her logbook.

The left seat was still warm. She stared at it too long. Tomorrow, she'd take it back.

THE HOTEL GYM near LAX was windowless, beige, and cruel. A slow oven of bad ventilation and worse music—the kind that assumed anything over three hundred beats per minute was the same as motivation. Izzy had looped a resistance band under her sneakers and was midway through a lunge set so punishing she could taste copper.

She didn't work out for aesthetics. She worked out so she could survive. So her body wouldn't betray her mid-rotation with nerve compression or a hip twinge or some slow erosion of her lower back from sitting twelve hours at altitude. She didn't worship her body. She threatened it. Keep going or lose the job. Keep going or die tired.

She adjusted her grip on the kettlebell, rolled her shoulders once, and dropped into another rep.

And then she heard it: the mechanical sigh of the door. Another keycard. Another body.

She didn't look. She didn't need to.

It was him.

She felt it in the shift of the air. In the quiet. He entered without a word—no announcement, no throat cleared, not even the courtesy of a grunted hello. Just Nico Farrah entering her oxygen like he was allowed to. She caught him in the mirror—t-shirt, damp hair, no headphones, carrying a towel like someone who'd been raised right.

She hated that he didn't hesitate. Didn't peacock. Just

picked a station and started his warmup. Rows. Controlled. Measured.

She hated that he never looked at her.

Not in the obvious way. He didn't stare, didn't smirk, didn't glance. Which was, somehow, worse. Like she wasn't even worthy of appraisal.

Except she knew he had clocked her—subtly. Back at the airport. During descent. When she slid into the right seat after rest, and he'd acknowledged her presence without looking away from the overhead panel.

She pushed harder. Dropped into squats, two count at the bottom, letting the burn take over.

In the mirror, Nico didn't break pace. Not once. But she was starting to understand something she didn't want to admit: He was good at watching without being caught.

Not in a predatory way. More like...inventory. He observed the way a pilot reviewed a systems page. Efficient. Quiet. Unapologetic.

She finished her set early, wiped down the mat, and left before he could offer her anything.

FIFTEEN MINUTES LATER, the concierge handed over the package with two hands. Just passed her a shipping box the size of a coffin and jokingly asked if she needed a trolley.

She did not.

She carried the whole thing in her arms—no bag, no disguise, just full Costco shame—through the hotel lobby like she was transporting state secrets.

She didn't see him until it was too late.

Nico stepped out of the elevator in a soft black hoodie and joggers, hair still damp from a post-workout shower.

He looked at the box, then at her. Their eyes met. He nodded once. Nothing else moved—no flinch, no twitch, no trace of amusement. Just acknowledgment.

It was somehow worse than mockery.

He moved aside to let her pass, holding the elevator door open like this was all part of the standard crew experience.

She gave him nothing. Not a word.

Back in her room, she cut the box open with her room card key and surveyed the cargo: one-hundred-and-twenty individually wrapped tampons, various sizes, laid out like candy bars.

She spent ten minutes lining her roller with them—tucking sleeves into zipped compartments, stuffing backups into shoes like she was smuggling product through customs. Every seam packed. Every crevice full. The whole thing looked like a low-rent cartel operation.

She sat down, pulled her hair out of its sweaty tie, and stared at the flattened cardboard like it might accuse her.

Her mind wandered back to him and the way he hadn't looked surprised.

The knock came soft. A triple tap, like a code. She opened the door without checking.

Cy slid in sideways, still in his base layer and compression socks, carrying three dripping plastic bags like a nurse smuggling morphine.

"Couldn't decide," he said. "So I nicked the lot."

He dropped everything on the bed, kicked off his shoes, and collapsed into the corner near the pillows like it was his assigned position.

She passed him a plastic fork with a cracked handle and flipped on the TV.

BBC News. Mute. Subtitles on.

The screen showed footage of a French controller strike. Airport delays stacking like sins.

They didn't speak for the first twenty minutes. The food spread across the bed like a late-stage coping mechanism. Between them sat three orders of pad see ew—because if one was soggy, the others might not be—plus crispy pork belly fried rice with a yolky egg sliding around the container, a twelve piece lemon pepper wing combo swimming in ranch, and an order of cheese fries so aggressively orange it might've been illegal in the EU. There was sushi, too—rainbow rolls that looked like a good idea at checkout and tasted like regret—but they still ate them, because that's what you did with bad choices. A seaweed salad sat untouched "for health," and Cy had brought out a Coke Zero from the galley. They used lids, chopsticks, fingers— whatever worked. The duvet was collateral damage.

Izzy wiped her mouth with a napkin that had been meant for something else and reached for the next container without even looking.

"Thanks," she said. Voice level.

"What for?" Cy asked around a mouthful of rice.

"Galley. Earlier."

He nodded once. "People forget I run that plane when I'm lead. Not you. Me."

She almost smiled. "You do."

"They will learn."

She paused. Looked down at the clamshell container resting on her lap. The seaweed salad hadn't been touched.

"I keep thinking everyone's watching me," she said, quietly. "Like they're waiting for the crack. The mistake. The wrong pause before a callout. Not to catch me—just to witness it."

Cy cracked open the third pad see ew, scooped a bite onto a napkin. "Then don't wobble."

"I know I won't fail. That's not what scares me. It's that someone's hoping I will."

He didn't respond right away. Just chewed. Swallowed. Adjusted the pillow behind him like he lived there.

Finally, he said, "You've been flawless too long. People get curious about miracles."

The TV flickered. A male anchor blinked slowly through a segment about altimeter interference. The subtitles guessed wrong three times.

Izzy leaned back, full and tight and vaguely humiliated by the indulgence.

On the bedside table sat the flattened Costco box from earlier, its barcode barely visible in the lamplight.

Cy gestured toward it with his chopsticks.

"You building a tampon bunker?"

"I lined my roller like I was smuggling cocaine," she said.

"Good. Run it like a job."

He didn't laugh. He just took another wing and passed her the extra ranch. She dipped without comment. They didn't talk after that.

There was no comfort, no dramatic unspooling. Just food, flickering light, and a shared commitment to professionalism so airtight it was practically sacred.

Cy didn't need her to explain. He already had her back.

SIX MONTHS.

Six months of waiting. Of sitting in the right seat like a

ghost of herself, voice steady, hands still, smile tight. Six months of letting men call her "ma'am" with an edge, like a dare. Of nodding politely through sim briefings led by pilots she'd trained, flown with, outranked. Six months of performing stability. Of bleeding in silence. Of swallowing the question: *Do they think I'm fragile?* and replacing it with: *Let them.*

And now, the left seat was hers again.

She didn't hesitate. She sat like she belonged, like the aircraft had been holding its breath for her return. She adjusted the rudder pedals, secured her harness, settled into position like a knife into its sheath. Her hands hovered for a second—just a second—above the panel, before she moved. Fluid. Unapologetic. The checklist wasn't routine tonight. It was ritual. She recited it from memory—her voice clipped, calm, assured. It wasn't for the jumpseat observer. It wasn't for the company, or even the recorders. It was for her. And maybe for Nico Farrah, silent beside her, watching with that maddening, respectful stillness. She didn't look at him, but she could feel his attention like heat. And for once, she didn't mind. Let him watch.

Pushback. Taxi. She took her time—not in delay, but in mastery. Every turn precise. She felt the power building beneath her like breath in the chest of a sleeping giant. At the hold short line, she glanced at the overhead, one last sweep. Tower cleared them for departure. She advanced the throttles with surgical control. The aircraft responded like it remembered her hands.

Rotate. Climb.

It hit her halfway through the initial ascent—the way it always had. That visceral rightness. That low, physical thrum of *yes*. Not satisfaction. Something deeper and more primal. The aircraft moved under her like a body that trusted her touch. Every correction, every pressure, every breath—seamless. Her mind ran ahead of the machine by instinct, anticipating, responding, and leading. She was not regaining a skill. She was reclaiming her place. This was not requalification. This was her resurrection.

At ten thousand feet, she let her hand fall from the side-stick and exhaled. Not a sigh. Something quieter. More final. She stared out at the Rockies—black spines under a bruised horizon. The sun was gone, but the burn still lingered. No need to speak. The climb had spoken for her.

Nico remained silent, and she loved him for it. Not in any romantic sense—God, no—but in the rarer, more dangerous way of respect. He hadn't spoken once since they lifted off. Hadn't offered a single platitude. He'd watched, like someone witnessing a truth confirmed.

Mountain shadows gave way to quiet sprawl—fields, rivers, roads laid out in long straight lines—geometry etched in moonlight. Towns slept and pulsed faintly at the edges. Over the Atlantic, darkness deepened. Time warped. The world quieted.

Then: coastline. Pale green under the edge of dawn. Stone-fenced fields and jagged cliffs rising through the mist like the land was reclaiming itself.

Descent came over Ireland. Smooth vectors. Clean air. She briefed the approach like she was delivering judgment, and the aircraft followed without resistance. Every frequency change, every call, every flap setting—perfect. Final approach into Heathrow lit up like memory. She landed firm. Controlled. Intentional. Not soft. She wasn't here to kiss pavement. She was here to remind it who the fuck she was.

At the gate, brakes set, chocks in, flight complete, she

finally let her hands rest on her thighs. The seat was warm beneath her. Her name was on the logbook.

Nico handed her the clipboard. "Nice work, Captain."

She blinked and swallowed.

Nice work, Captain.

That was it. No soft tone. Just those three syllables, dropped like a coin into her spine.

She felt it hit. Felt her body react before she gave it permission—before she could armor up or look away or breathe through it. A warm flush behind her sternum. The faintest prickle down the backs of her arms. That sharp, electric buzz of *I did well and someone saw it.*

God, she hated how much she loved it.

Six months of being restrained, watched, corrected. Six months of forced neutrality and never once being told she'd done something right, not without a follow-up note about CRM tone or checklist tempo. And now this man—this puppy-faced, allegedly harmless man—had the audacity to acknowledge her competence like it was obvious. Like she hadn't spent the whole goddamn flight bleeding her pride into the yoke just to prove it.

And worse—worse—her body responded. Not just with pride. With want.

The post-flight high was already working through her veins like amphetamine. That pure, vicious pleasure of control. Of performance. Of landing clean. She should've been proud. Satisfied. Cool. Instead, she was buzzing and warm and just this side of reckless—and now he was part of it. Now his voice was in it. His praise, lodged somewhere just south of her lungs, pumping oxygen into a flame she did not authorize.

She didn't look at him. Didn't smile.

Just took the clipboard and said, flatly, "Don't do that."

He blinked. "Do what?"

"Compliment me." She scrawled her signature.

Then she stood and walked out, even though she absolutely did not need to leave the flight deck yet.

She needed cold air. Time.

And to stop letting the words *"Nice work, Captain"* play on loop in her head like a line from a sexy voice note.

3

Six hours in, and her ass was numb on the captain's chair: her kingdom, her prison, her physio's retirement plan.

She shifted—barely. Just enough to get blood back into one leg. The glamorous life of a pilot, they said. Meanwhile, she was strapped into a humming coffin at Mach 0.85, chewing chicken meatballs and holding her bladder hostage.

In the last 48 hours, she'd been in Zurich, Singapore, Sao Paolo and now somewhere over the Atlantic en route to Heathrow. One layover bled into the next. Her phone said Thursday. London said Tuesday. Her skin said please stop. Her La Mer moisturizer was fighting for its life.

Nico hadn't said anything in a while, thank God.

Forty-five minutes taxiing to the gate, crawling behind a line of silver jets inching forward like penitents. The sun rose. Her patience set.

And somewhere in the avionics hum—beneath the checklist, beneath the steady static of altitude—she thought, just for a second, she heard herself breathing twice.

She didn't have time to dwell on it because the bathroom had been a battle—coordinating piss breaks around turbulence, carts, and Nico's golden retriever bladder. The lock didn't always work. Most of the time, Izzy just held it and prayed for descent. Passengers stared like she was a zoo animal someone taught to talk. A petite, biracial woman with four stripes and a command voice didn't fit their worldview. She'd stopped caring.

She hated this job. Every minute of it. And she loved it—deep, violent, and unsustainable.

They parked at the gate like the flight had never happened—like eight hours hadn't just dissolved into the atmosphere. Routine turnaround. Exhaustion baked in. The kind of layover where your body thought it was midnight and the terminal lights said otherwise.

She barely had time to go home, sleep for a few hours, throw on a fresh shirt, and get back to the airport. No point unpacking. No point pretending she'd been anywhere but the inside of a jet.

Now, back on the flight deck mid morning, she powered up the aircraft systems for the next leg. The electronic flight bag blinked awake. One of the dispatch messages lagged. Then another. ACARS stuttered. The release didn't match the fuel plan. Minor. But wrong. She narrowed her eyes and tapped through the screens with surgical intent.

Reset. Reconnect. Wait. Ping.

The error code popped up again. Same one from last week. Same one from Frankfurt. Not critical. Just loud. She reset the datalink again and watched it reappear like it had something to prove.

"Motherfu—" Izzy muttered under her breath.

This was the kind of thing that pissed her off more than actual danger. It wasn't a threat to safety. But it felt like one.

Like something she should be able to fix, except it was outside her control. Everything was functional, but nothing was clean. The aircraft equivalent of waking up with makeup still on—technically fine, but itching in your skin. Behind her, Nico leaned in, all casual posture and concern.

"You good with that message?" he asked, voice pitched careful.

She didn't look up. "Yeah. It's wrong, but it's been consistently wrong. Which is almost comforting. Like a guy who cheats on you at regular intervals."

She heard him choke on his coffee, while she clicked past the alert like it had wasted her time.

"System's trash, but at least it's predictable."

And nothing was more predictable than a handsome white boy in uniform making people feel safe. She could've called it from wheels up. He didn't talk down, didn't leer, and knew how to smile without making it weird. Of course everyone loved him. The flight attendants, the gate agents, the ramp crew. Smiling at him like he'd just paid off someone's student loans.

Days ago, a senior stew had already asked him out in front of her right after the pre-flight briefing. He'd turned her down with that annoyingly gracious tone of his, and Izzy had pretended not to notice the way the FA lingered anyway, still batting her lashes like he might change his mind. It kept happening. Different crew, same choreography. No one even tried to be discreet.

The cockpit door cracked open as Izzy reviewed the brief. A pretty FA walked in, balancing their coffee orders.

Izzy thanked her. Nico grinned—laid-back, easy—and said, "Bless you."

The FA smirked at Nico, a little daring. "You know, if you ever want something stronger than coffee... off duty."

Izzy kept her eyes on the charts. Didn't turn her head. Just shifted her gaze—subtle, sideways. Watched the flush rise up the FA's neck. Watched Nico smile back, effortless, like it wasn't even a choice.

For a microsecond, he caught Izzy's gaze. Not just looked —locked in, eyefucking her so hard she nearly shoved the seat back to reclaim her goddamn space.

Then he blinked and declined a second person in less than a week.

"Appreciate it," he said. "But I don't really do that."

Izzy adjusted her posture, eased the tension, kept her hands steady at the yoke.

AT THIRTY-FIVE THOUSAND FEET, she addressed it. Because she was the final authority on board and apparently now also the HR manager of this flying circus.

"Let me know if I need to speak to anyone on your behalf," she said, eyes forward, voice clean. There was a pause. That irritating silence she noticed he used when he was trying to decide how honest he could afford to be.

"About what?" he asked. She didn't look at him.

"You've been hit on twice. Both in uniform. Both on duty. That's a policy issue. Whether or not it bothers you, it reflects on me if it keeps happening and I say nothing. If I have to write someone up, I will."

As soon as the words left her mouth, she almost laughed.

How rich, she thought, like I'm not ten seconds from writing myself up for impure cockpit thoughts. She watched the horizon. Tried not to think about the way he looked at her before he turned the FA down. Tried not to wonder if he did that on purpose

He finally said, "I'm fine."

She nodded, clipped. "Let me know if that changes."

Then she went back to monitoring systems, resisting the urge to adjust the cooling fan. Not because the air was stuffy—but because her face was warm, and she wasn't about to give him the satisfaction of noticing.

Time slid by. The sky shifted. The cockpit dimmed and brightened again as they crossed latitudes.

And then he touched the dial. Subtle. Like he thought she wouldn't notice. Like she didn't have a goddamn pilot's license and a rage disorder calibrated to Fahrenheit. Seventy-three degrees. She stared at it. Not for long—just long enough to file it under *grounds for divorce*, if they were married, which they were not, thank God.

She waited. Two minutes. Then reached up and turned the dial back to sixty-five with the precision of a woman who had sweat through a bra during December and still didn't complain. He didn't say a word. Just leaned back, arms crossed, body language casual—but she could feel the smug radiating off him in waves.

Of course he ran cold. He was all lean muscle and boyish denial, the kind of body that burned calories in its sleep. He'd grown up in Kentucky where there's a moratorium on jackets and outerwear.

Her blood, on the other hand, ran Florida. Raised in the swamps. Trained in cockpits. Entering the glamorous soft-launch of perimenopause with no fanfare and zero grace. Some days, her body went from normal to inferno in under ten seconds and expected her to continue briefing the SID like she wasn't spontaneously combusting.

The hot flashes weren't constant. Just unpredictable. Unscheduled. Like turbulence but less polite. Today's hit during cruise. No warning. One minute she was fine, the next she was a rotisserie chicken in custom-made ankle boots. Sweat along the spine. Damp between the thighs.

Her skin flushed like she was blushing, but she was not blushing. She was boiling. And Nico, across from her, had the audacity to look cold. He reached for the dial again. She slapped his hand away. His fingers paused inches from the thermostat like it was a relic in a temple and she was the snake guarding it. Their eyes met.

"Don't," she said, quietly.

"I'm freezing."

"I'm molting."

His mouth twitched. "You always run this hot?"

She smiled. Sharp. "Ask better questions, Farrah."

His hand dropped. The dial stayed. Sixty-five. Her domain. He sighed, dramatic, then pulled out a second a hoodie. She took a slow sip of water. Ice-cold.

He was reading something in print, not a screen, because of course he was. Every few pages, he underlined something in pen with steady pressure, then licked his thumb to turn the page. It wasn't seductive. There was no flex, no flourish. It was simply efficient. He used his hands like he knew what they were for.

Her stomach dropped in that way it only did when she was too tired to regulate. She hated that she noticed. Hated more that she cared. And what she hated most—the way her pulse kicked like it hadn't been fed in weeks.

Then he lifted his hand, scratched just beneath his collarbone, and his shirt shifted enough to show a flash of chest—just one line of skin above the clavicle. Nothing dramatic.

But her gaze tracked it before she could stop herself, and her body clocked the shift before her brain caught up. Her throat bobbed once. She crossed her legs. She reached for the harness and adjusted it with unnecessary precision, pulling it half an inch tighter just to give her hands something to do. It didn't need adjusting. She knew that. She still did it.

He didn't react. Nothing to suggest he saw her unraveling beside him with surgical precision. If he noticed, it stayed locked behind his eyes.

She unbuckled with more force than necessary and stood like the cockpit was on fire. She didn't want to leave the flight deck—with him still in it, with her face doing whatever the hell it was doing. But the heat under her collar wouldn't fade, and her thoughts were sprinting ahead of her restraint.

She exhaled once, and said it anyway.

"You have the aircraft."

Not *control*, the way she was trained in the Navy. Just *aircraft*. She wasn't saying that other word to him.

His reply came instantly—calm, steady. "I have it."

She hated the way the response settled her.

The second she cleared the flight deck threshold, she heard his seat shift behind her. He slid into hers without hesitation, already scanning the panel, settling in like he hadn't just been sitting beside her leaking casual temptation.

The galley lighting was harsh and unflattering, which was exactly what she needed. Sterile air. Cheap coffee. Metal surfaces that gave no feedback. She grabbed the carafe, poured herself a half cup just to hold something.

The moment she cleared the curtain, Cy raised an eyebrow without even looking up from his manifest.

"Is it hot in there?" he asked, lazily flipping a page.

"I know you like to set it to frigid temps in there, but

you're giving...tropical." André leaned out from behind a cart, eyes wide, voice fake-innocent.

"Wait. Are you sweating? Girl, why are you flushed?"

"I'm not flushed," she said flatly.

"Oh no, no," Cy said, nodding solemnly. "Definitely not flushed. You just have a—what would you call that, André? A physiological response to—oh, I don't know— airflow?"

André tapped his lip. "Or proximity."

"To whom?" Cy gasped, hand to chest.

André pointed toward the flight deck. "Could it be... First Officer Ken Doll?"

He ducked back behind the cart, where one of the galley ovens was blinking red in passive-aggressive rebellion. The latch had been faulty all week.

Before aviation, André ran the circuit—DJ, fixer, quiet emergency crew. He kept the music going and the collapse at bay. Now he was elbow-deep in a convection unit with the same calm intensity he used to keep the dance floor from tipping into chaos.

A faint click. The red light disappeared.

Izzy stared into her coffee and tried not to think about how many things on this aircraft were currently running too hot.

"He does have those deeply unthreatening good looks," Cy offered, voice mild. "You know. The kind that sneak up on you when your serotonin is low."

"He's very...tidy," André said, leaning in like he was revealing a secret. "The way he stares you down has to be a crime on certain layovers."

Izzy inhaled through her nose, slow and even. She wasn't going to give them the satisfaction. She wasn't even going to blink.

Cy stepped closer, peering at her face like he was checking for heat signatures.

"You look like someone who just saw an ankle in the 1800s."

"I'm fine," she said, tight. André raised both eyebrows.

"Then why did you sprint in here like the cockpit was haunted by a ghost?"

"I needed coffee."

"Sure," Cy said. "Let's go with that."

André tilted his head. "Did the ghost happen to be six foot five and doles out sunshine smiles like candy?"

Izzy took a sip. The coffee was lukewarm and tasted like insult. She was either going to scream or walk out of the emergency exit. She chose neither. For now. Cy reached into a drawer, handed her a napkin she didn't need.

"We support you. Even in your denial."

"I'm not—"

"We know," André said quickly. "You're not. We're just imagining things. Because of the heat. From the cockpit. That you left. Blushing."

Izzy didn't flinch. Just took another sip of the lukewarm coffee and said, cool as pressurized air:

"André, please. You blush more than I do—usually right after falling for someone who says 'conscious-capital consultant' in their dating profile."

Cy choked once, discreetly, behind a napkin.

André clutched his chest. "One time."

"Three cities. Same pitch."

She turned, coffee in hand, and disappeared before he could recover.

She walked back onto the flight deck like nothing had happened. Like she hadn't just gotten dragged in the galley by two men who loved her more than they loved their own peace. It didn't rattle her. Not really. That kind of teasing was mercy. It meant they still saw her. Still expected her to come back swinging.

She sat. Buckled in. The seat was warm.

Nico eased back into his place like they hadn't just traded airspace and body heat.

Outside, the world was blackout. No horizon. Just sky, black and still and done caring.

Then—suddenly—her vision blurred.

No thought or emotion. Just a leak.

She blinked. Once. Twice. Pointless. Her vision kept blurring. Her cheeks were wet. Just tears she hadn't authorized.

Her hands were steady. Her voice, if called, would hold. She was still flying and she was still sharp.

But her body was crying. Quietly. In defiance.

She adjusted the airflow yet again.

Probably the missed dose—two days ago? Yesterday? Hard to track when your pill case didn't speak Istanbul, Doha, Singapore.

Her fluoxetine was legally disclosed, medically cleared, reviewed by two doctors and a lawyer she paid out of pocket. But none of that mattered if someone saw this.

She wasn't scared of losing the jet. She was scared of someone catching her with a wet cheek and deciding she didn't belong there.

That's what the six-figure salary is for. It's for the lie: *I'm fine. We all are.*

And to make it worse, a man can scream at a controller and still get promoted.

A woman tears up once, and every other female pilot has to fly twice as clean just to prove they're not glass.

She wiped her face like scratching an itch. Casual.

Her mind was clear. The aircraft was stable. The passengers were safe.

The danger wasn't the tears. It was who saw them—and what they assumed.

And then, without warning—

"You have control," he said.

Her throat locked.

No. Not that word. Not when her own face was giving her away and she'd just gotten back the captain's seat. But it was standard protocol. He probably didn't think twice.

But she felt it hit—right in the soft part of her chest she'd spent decades armoring.

She blinked. Swallowed again.

"I have control," she said, flat.

And she did.

4

The aircraft powered down like a tired beast giving up. Systems faded, lights dimmed, the cabin pressurization bled out with a sigh. Izzy ran the shutdown checklist with practiced detachment, as if she hadn't leaked emotion mid-cruise. Nico mirrored her every move —flawlessly, infuriatingly—and said absolutely nothing.

Good.

Because if he'd so much as cleared his throat in sympathy, she would've found a clipboard to throw and let HR sort it out later.

He didn't jump up like most first officers, eager to sprint off to the current city's Tinder matches. He lingered, casually and respectfully, which was somehow worse. He just...let her lead.

"I'll take the walkaround," she said, already halfway unstrapped. It wasn't a suggestion.

He nodded.

"Copy that." No sarcasm. Just compliance.

Outside, the tarmac was chaos in high-vis. Reverse beacons strobing, carts circling like confused livestock, someone yelling about a catering mix-up. The night shift had all the charm of a raccoon rummaging through a minibar.

Izzy descended the stairs and hit the ramp like it had personally wronged her. The cold helped. Humidity meant sweat; cold meant control. Her flashlight clicked on. Technically unnecessary—floodlights bathed the fuselage in harsh airport glow—but she wanted her hand doing something useful that wasn't slapping someone for being decent.

She started at the nose. Nav lights: green. Radome: closed and clean. Nose gear: no leaks, no tire trauma, oleo at proper extension. Everything was fine, which of course made her mood worse.

She knew he was behind her before she heard a sound. Three steps back. Quiet as guilt. She didn't have to look. She could feel his perfectly calibrated moral support hovering just out of reach. He kept three steps back, flashlight pointed low, walking when she walked, stopping when she stopped.

He just existed in this perfect little bubble of non-invasive awareness like a goddamn support animal.

And the most enraging part?

It *was* working. She didn't need the help. But knowing he was silently checking everything too made it easier to breathe.

Rear stabilizer, rudder movement, flap seals—everything behaving. Of course. Even the aircraft was being civil tonight.

They looped around the right wing, under the belly. She tapped the drain mast like she hoped it might spit something out just to reflect how she felt. It didn't. Of course it didn't. She clicked off the flashlight.

Then—

"I didn't even think to check the drain mast. Adding that to my flow."

He said it like a weather report. No heat. Just fact.

She squinted at him like he'd confessed a crush. "You miss it once. Then you don't."

He nodded once. Didn't add a single word. Which was correct. And deeply offensive.

They headed back toward the stairs. She walked fast, shoulders tight. He matched her stride effortlessly because of course he did.

"You want me to grab your bag from overhead?" he asked, voice maddeningly pleasant.

"I'm not eighty," she snapped.

"Didn't say you were." He had the audacity to shrug. "Just figured you might want the assist."

She bit the inside of her cheek. It wasn't condescending. It was just him—offering help like it was a sandwich.

The jet bridge stretched ahead—gray, ugly, and fluorescent. She'd never been more grateful for brutal airport lighting. At least it flattened out her emotions to match her cheekbones.

He stayed beside her. Not hovering. Just existing like a quiet disaster.

"I don't need a babysitter," she muttered.

"Didn't think you did."

No change in tone. Just that calm, steady voice that made her want to scream into her jacket. He didn't even look smug. He was just a man who knew she could fly a damn airplane with her eyes full of saltwater and still land it smoother than half the company.

He didn't praise her. Didn't pity her. He just walked beside her like the event was real and survivable.

And that was the worst part.

He saw her cry and he didn't flinch. He didn't run.

He just kept showing up like that was normal. Like she was normal.

God, she hated him.

And she really, really might like him. But she definitely hated him.

THE CREW VAN was over capacity and under-sanitized. Someone's duffel was digging into her calf. The overhead light flickered like a haunted house. And André was holding court from the middle row like he owned the damn shuttle.

Which, to be fair—tonight, he did.

"It's my birthday," he said, smoothing his collar, "and I fully intend to test the limits of both my duty time and my emotional regulation. In that order."

Cy didn't look up from texting his husband the usual evening update. "You've got ten hours off, not diplomatic immunity."

André shot him a look. "Which is why I'm hydrating between drinks and stopping at exactly two cocktails and maybe one regrettable kiss. I'm not a savage."

The rest of the crew chuckled. Even the junior FAs relaxed a little.

Everyone knew the math: ten hours off, eight clean between the last drink and duty required. But the real reason nobody planned to get sloppy?

Captain Ventura was onboard.

She didn't have to say a word. She never did. The woman ran preflight like a military tribunal. If she so much as side-eyed your Aperol spritz, you'd switch to sparkling water and say thank you.

Still, she sank low into her corner seat like she was drafting an exit strategy. She'd tried to skip the party. Claimed she'd rather staple her own hand to the galley wall than be perceived in neon lighting.

It didn't matter.

"You bought me a wallet. From Hermès," André said at debrief, eyes narrowed. "You think that lets you ghost my birthday like some moody Vogue spread? Girl. No."

Okay—so maybe she had panic-purchased an Hermès wallet. It was a long layover. There might have been a break-down and Izzy had no emotional blueprint for friendship. André had once body-blocked a supervisor from seeing her spiral in the jet bridge after a six-hour delay and a call from her ex-husband. That kind of loyalty deserved leather goods.

"You didn't have to get me anything," he cooed, clutching the orange box like a beloved child. "But you can't bribe me with luxury brands to get out of celebrating *me*. You're coming out."

Which was how she ended up here, acquiescing to his demands—squished between a cologne hazard and a jumpseater she didn't remember authorizing.

Nico, of course, was up front by the door. Because of course he was.

Crew van seating had its own unspoken code. Captains took the back for plausible deniability. Juniors huddled near the front for quick exits. FAs claimed the middle—it doubled as catwalk and therapy zone. Whoever sat shotgun was either in trouble, in charge, or deeply annoying.

But Nico? Nico floated past it all like it wasn't even strategy. Like social choreography bent around him without asking. He made looking perfect seem unintentional: relaxed stance, collarbone visible, smile sweet.

She hadn't spoken to him since the walkaround.

And he hadn't said a word about the tears.

She crossed her legs like slamming a file shut.

One of the junior FAs twisted in her seat, already halfway to giggle-drunk.

"Captain Ventura," she asked, "what are you wearing tonight? Like—something vampy, or just keeping it casual?"

It was sincere. Feminine solidarity, extended like a diplomatic handover of lip gloss and trust.

Izzy didn't blink. "Black dress. Heels."

That earned an approving chorus from the middle row.

Then, without turning his head, Cy deadpanned: "You mean that little black dress that says 'I'm a widow and I might kill again'?"

Izzy sipped her water. "Naturally."

The van erupted.

Outside, neon and concrete blurred by. They were close to the hotel now. Nothing fancy—just enough to ruin your circadian rhythm and make you question life choices.

She didn't want to go out. She didn't want to talk.

But she was here.

And she'd brought a two-thousand dollar wallet into a friendship knife fight like that made any damn sense.

So now? She had to party.

IZZY HAD PLANNED to stay forty-five minutes. Just long enough to sing "Happy Birthday," nurse one overpriced drink, and remind André that friendship had terms and conditions. She had one vodka soda and was now on her third mocktail.

The club pulsed like a heartbeat—basslines, strobes, bodies everywhere. Sweat and perfume and every single flight attendant in Europe on their day off. Cy had already disappeared into the crowd like a seductive ghost. André was mid-routine on the edge of the raised platform, mic in hand.

"¡ES MI CUMPLEAÑOS, PERRAS!"

The crowd roared. Someone tossed a speedo on stage.

Izzy leaned against the bar, dizzy and amused and warm in a way she hadn't felt in months. Her dress clung. Her eyeliner held and her shoes hurt. It was somehow perfect.

Then—him.

Nico Farrah.

He wasn't even dancing. He was just there. In the glow of pink light and expensive fog, sleeves rolled, a hint of sweat at his collarbone, smiling like he didn't know how annoying it was to look that good and that gracious at the same time.

He clocked her.

And God help her—he smiled.

He made his way over through the crowd, respectfully dodging three separate men who tried to flirt with him on sight, and landed next to her.

"You look nice, Captain."

Voice soft. Eyes bright. No smugness. Just earnest. Like he meant it.

She blinked once. Twice.

Then took a long, unnecessary sip of her drink.

"Don't call me that in a club," she muttered.

"Sorry. You look nice, Izzy."

Worse. She walked away.

IZZY YANKED the door open with the energy of someone storming a war room, not a unisex club toilet. The music thudded through the wall like a heartbeat. She caught

André in the mirror—mid–lip gloss application, eyes smug and unrepentant.

"You invited him."

André didn't flinch. Just capped the gloss, pursed his lips once, and turned like a man who'd been waiting to be confronted.

"Good evening to you too, Captain Misery."

She closed the door behind her. Hard.

"I told you. I specifically told you—don't invite Farrah."

"You did say that," André admitted, leaning back against the sink like he was preparing for cross-examination. "And I listened. I heard. And then I ignored you. Because it is my birthday."

"André—"

"No. I tried. I really did. I tried not to invite him. But he was talking about the club the whole damn van ride like we'd already sent him an RSVP. What was I supposed to do? Watch him wag his tail like that and tell him he can't sit with us?"

Izzy opened her mouth.

André didn't wait.

"He paid for everyone's cover. He brought snacks. He's out there asking if we need water like a fucking service sub. Be serious, Izzy. Any other FO would've given me a disgusted look and said, 'Not my scene.' But not him. He was already halfway to borrowing my glitter crop top."

She scowled. "He's ruining the ratio. He's violating the social contract. This is a girls and gays zone. No straight men allowed."

André just smiled. "He's not ruining the ratio. You're ruining your own night. Stop acting like we dragged your ex in here."

She was about to protest, but André raised a hand like a preacher.

"And he's not a straight man. He's Nico. He doesn't count. That man is one apology away from joining a lesbian commune."

"Still—"

"Weren't you the one who blushed when he said you looked nice?"

Izzy froze.

"No, I didn't."

"Oh, babe," André said, eyes sparkling with pure malice, "you went pink. It was like watching a strawberry Pop-Tart realize it had feelings."

She rubbed her temples. "This was supposed to be your night. I came for you. I even shaved my legs."

"And now," he said, grinning, "you're tipsy, you're glowing, and you're about to explode."

Cy opened the bathroom door just long enough to stick his head in.

"You two done? He's dancing with a drag queen now. And tipping in cash."

THE DJ DROPPED SOMETHING FILTHY—BASSLINE thick as sweat, vocals like a whipcrack—and Izzy was already moving. Not for show, not for anyone, just pure muscle memory and adrenaline. Dancing was one of the few things that shut her brain up. It lived in her hips, her shoulders, the tilt of her neck. She could get drunk off rhythm alone.

She didn't mean to watch him. But of course Nico was in her periphery, being insufferably charming and loose-limbed, dancing with the drag queen like he deserved to be in her orbit. He wasn't doing that flailing straight-boy thing either. No stiff shoulders, no performative awkwardness. He was good. Fuck.

He dipped the queen with one hand, grinned like sin when she spanked him with her fan, and spun out like it was nothing.

Izzy didn't break rhythm, but she saw it. Saw him.

And then the crowd surged. Bodies pushed in every direction, drunk with sweat and bass, and someone slammed into her from behind. She stumbled back—and hit a wall of muscle.

Nico.

His hands went to her waist instantly. Not possessive. Just reflex. Like he couldn't not.

She didn't move away.

Didn't want to.

She was already dancing.

And now he was in it with her. His body caught her rhythm like he'd been chasing it all night. She didn't look back. Didn't need to. She could feel the tension in him— every nerve tuned to her frequency.

His hands stayed respectful. Barely. One still on her hip, the other hovering like he wasn't sure if he was allowed to lose his mind yet.

Izzy kept dancing.

Let him follow.

Her ass brushed his thigh. Deliberate. The song was too slow, too nasty, and too hot for half-measures. She moved like heat rising, like pressure building, and he didn't just survive it—he matched her.

He was taller. Broader. Solid behind her. And still, he didn't push.

He waited.

Like a fuse waiting to be lit.

The drag queen's voice cut through the beat somewhere behind them, but Izzy didn't turn her head.

She kept moving.

Three songs, maybe four. Time meant nothing. The sweat on her spine was from him now. The air between them was molten.

At one point, he leaned in. Said nothing. Just let his breath ghost over her neck.

She didn't flinch.

She rolled her hips in response, slow and mean, and felt him grip. Just a twitch. Like he was still trying so, so hard not to touch her like he meant it.

She almost respected the effort.

But if he was going to keep dancing like that, like her body was the only beat he cared about—he was going to lose control eventually.

And when he did? She'd let him. Maybe. If he was lucky. If she didn't break first.

Then she caught the laugh—sharp, flirty, familiar from the bar. From the same FA who'd asked Nico out last week. Not inappropriate or predatory—just public and premature, too casual for how new he was. Izzy had clocked it and filed it away. She'd made a silent promise: the *moment* he looked uncomfortable, she'd intervene. Boundaries were her job.

And now? Now she was dancing with him like she didn't have four stripes and a duty of care. Like nothing she did could be misread.

It cut through the music like a blade.

Her spine locked. The second the beat changed, she peeled off the floor.

Nico said her name—quiet, confused, still breathless from dancing—but she didn't look back. She was already gone.

Through the crowd. Past André, who raised an eyebrow but didn't stop her.

He held court like someone genetically incapable of being boring. One hand gestured mid-story—something about a customs officer in Mexico and a very expensive pair of shoes—the other adjusted the club's entire playlist, which he'd hijacked through three fake logins and a geo-spoofed burner, just to loop early-aughts pop girls on repeat.

Cy clocked her exit from the edge of the room but didn't follow.

Outside, the street was humid and too quiet. Her heels clicked against the pavement like a challenge.

She wasn't drunk. Not even close.

But her skin felt electric. Overexposed.

She was grinding. God.

What the fuck had she just done?

There were footsteps behind her. Predictable ones. Longer stride, steady cadence. She already knew them well only after two weeks of rotation.

"Stop following me," she said, not turning around.

He caught up anyway. Cut in front. Didn't touch her. Just blocked her path with that six-foot-something body and the kind of expression that made something in her lower spine pull.

Gone was the easy smile, the open posture, the good boy act.

His face was still. Not blank—composed. Like someone used to assessing threat levels. His mouth was tight. His eyes were quiet.

There was nothing soft in him now.

What she saw instead was discipline.

Coiled. Measured. Capable.

And something behind his eyes—buried, but not gone —flashed sharp and mean.

Not angry. Just... awake.

And for one breathless, stomach-dropping second, Izzy realized he wasn't harmless.

He was just well-trained.

And right now, that training was aimed at her.

"You always leave before the drop?"

"I'm going home," she said, clipped. "Alone."

The silence around him sharpened. "I'm walking you back."

She laughed. Cold. "I've been drunk and alone in cities where they don't even have sidewalks. Where the cab drivers carry knives. You think I can't handle Barcelona?"

He didn't blink. "I'm still walking you back."

Her eyes narrowed. "I don't need a babysitter."

"I'm not your babysitter." His voice dropped. Not louder —lower. More restrained. More dangerous. "I'm walking you because I want to."

There it was. Said plainly—neither nice, nor soft, nor deferential.

Control. A line drawn in calm, capable ink.

Izzy's breath hitched. Her fists clenched. Her thighs did something she was going to pretend wasn't happening.

"You don't get to want things as they relate to me," she said, voice tight.

He stepped closer. Not touching. But the way he stood— grounded, quiet, the weight of him—it landed in her stomach like a warning.

"I do, actually," he said, calm as stone. "You're just used to men who scare easy."

Her mouth parted. Airless.

That heat snapped up her spine like a whipcrack.

She shoved him. Hard, palm to chest. He barely rocked back. Didn't retaliate. Just let it happen.

"I'm going home," she snarled. "Alone."

"Fine."

She turned.

"I'll walk behind you," he said.

She spun around, eyes wild. "You—"

He just looked at her. Like she was a storm, and he'd already decided to walk into it.

She wanted to scream. She wanted to break something.

Instead, she seethed. Turned around. And walked.

He followed. Half a pace behind. Like he'd always known how this would end.

5

The miracle wasn't that the crew showed up. It was that they looked good doing it.

André strolled in first, sunglasses on, lip balm freshly applied, and not a molecule of shame in his body. He moved like someone who'd just finished cardio, communion, and a threeway in a club toilet—and wasn't sure which had been more satisfying.

Two junior flight attendants followed close behind, all bounce and blowout, makeup set like concrete, heels silent on the tile. Their energy screamed walk of shame, but their posture said runway. Whatever they'd done last night, it had been worth putting on false eyelashes for.

Everyone else looked aggressively hydrated. The professional sheen of people who had sinned against both God and duty a mere eight hours ago and were now pretending they hadn't.

Izzy sat at the head of the briefing table, tablet open, checklist glowing. She was dressed for judgment—a neat crown braid, crisp bun, fresh brows, jacket sharp enough to slice through feelings. Not a visual flaw in sight. Still she felt like rot. No one mentioned the club. No one asked if she'd danced.

Nico took the seat across from her, silent and smiling. No eye contact. Just the steady presence of someone who remembered exactly where his hands had been and had the gall not to gloat about it.

Cy did his usual quiet scan of the room—checking hydration levels, spotting hangovers with sniper precision, mentally triaging who'd need a lighter load today, and who might need a firm talk in the galley mid-flight. He met Izzy's gaze for half a second and gave a nod.

Izzy launched into the preflight: med kits, emergency doors, escalation protocols, AED location. She was saying all the right words and not thinking about grinding on someone's thigh.

She wrapped the briefing with a nod toward the man on the opposite end of the table. "Anything to add, Farrah?"

Nico looked up. Met her eyes, finally.

"Let's make this one boring."

Izzy didn't blink. Didn't move. But something low in her abdomen pulled taut like wire.

She gave a clipped nod. "We'll see what we can do."

And just like that, everyone stood. Like it had been a normal briefing. Like the world hadn't tilted slightly off-axis somewhere over Barcelona. Like she hadn't almost—

No.

It was going to be a normal flight.

It had to be.

～

Takeoff was clean. Climbout smoother than it had any right to be.

Nico handled the radios. Izzy handled everything else—systems, checklists, and the creeping urge to think about anything except the night before. Her voice stayed level, posture perfect, performance surgical.

Everything was fine.

Too fine.

The cabin had settled into cruise: dimmed lights, rustling snack wrappers, the low murmur of civilized boredom.

Then came the voice.

Too loud. Too sharp. Not panicked—pissed.

At first, it barely registered. Just another entitled passenger griping about legroom or Diet Coke. But then came the second shout. Louder. Meaner. Words that didn't match the mood of the plane. Words that cracked through the pressurized quiet like a snapped cable.

"You work for me. I paid for this flight. I said now—"

Izzy didn't move. Not yet. But she could hear it.

Cabin noise was different at altitude. It carried. It sharpened. It turned complaints into commands and tantrums into threats. The pitch of a voice—not just the volume—could change the entire frequency of a cabin.

Another shout. A slam.

Cy's voice came through the interphone—low, calm, professional.

"Flight deck, please standby."

And just like that, the quiet wasn't quiet anymore.

She caught it in fragments, carried on the brittle silence that followed.

"—not paying for attitude—"

"That's your job, right?"

Nico looked up. She met his eyes. Neither of them moved.

Then André's voice—measured but tight, the kind of tone that meant he was two seconds from snapping.

"Sir, I need you to lower your voice and take your seat."

The man didn't.

"What are you, some kind of faggot?"

It cut through the cabin like shrapnel.

Izzy froze.

Then—chaos.

A cry. The sound of bodies shifting. A passenger's voice rising: "He grabbed him!" A flight attendant yelling. Something hit the galley wall with a dull, ugly thud.

She didn't need to see it. She already knew.

Assault.

The cockpit door stayed shut—protocol. But her hand was already reaching for the interphone before Cy's voice returned, flat and surgical.

"Flight deck. We have a situation."

Nico was already standing.

At first, it looked like a stretch—casual, unbothered. Arms loose, shoulders rolling back like he was just trying to get circulation moving.

But Izzy saw it.

The shift.

Not in his face—he was still smiling, almost pleasant. But something beneath it had gone utterly still. Precise. Controlled. Dangerous.

The same posture he'd had last night when he stepped in front of her outside the club, told her he was walking her home whether she liked it or not. And she'd let him.

Now, the same stance. The same quiet authority.

She'd seen that kind of stillness before. Back in the Navy.

The ones with dead eyes and steady hands. The ones who didn't raise their voices because they didn't need to.

"I'll check on it."

She didn't say yes. Didn't say no.

She keyed the interphone.

"Cy—Nico's stepping out."

Thirty seconds later, the choreography began.

Cart in the aisle. Cy slid into the cockpit jumpseat. No commentary. Just coverage.

Nico stepped out. The door sealed behind him with a soft click. And the air changed.

Izzy kept her eyes forward. Hands on the controls. She bit the inside of her cheek.

She hated this part.

The waiting.

The not-seeing.

The comm crackled—background noise, shifting voices. Not Nico's.

She keyed it again, sharper now.

"Someone. Report."

A pause.

Then a young voice—breathless, but trying for steady.

"Emma here. Passenger's yelling—he called André a... something. Then stood up and grabbed him. Wouldn't let go."

Her knuckles tightened on the yoke.

A breath. Muffled fabric. A shuffle. The metallic snap of restraint plastic.

"Nico's engaging the passenger."

Izzy closed her eyes briefly.

"Clarify."

Emma's voice returned, slightly steadier, still rattled.

"He asked for restraints. I grabbed the kit. Didn't even

think. He—he just did it. Loop, twist, zip. Like he's done it a hundred times. Oh!"

More background noise. A low, startled "*Shit.*"

"Talk to me, Emma!"

Emma again, softer.

"It's done, Captain. I don't think the guy even knows what happened. He's back in his seat. 32B. Hands and feet restrained. Seatbelt on. He's not talking."

Another pause. "And Nico?"

"Nico—doesn't even look mad. Just...calm."

Izzy's fingers hovered over the thrust levers.

The hum of the engines—steady, familiar—suddenly felt too loud.

The cockpit door clicked open again.

Cy rose without a word, stepping out with the same precision he'd entered. Nico returned to his seat as if nothing had happened. Buckled in. Adjusted his comm. His jacket slightly out of place.

He didn't look at her.

Izzy didn't speak. She wasn't ready to see his face.

Instead, she focused on the interphone as Cy's voice came through.

"All flight attendants—briefing in the aft galley."

Ten minutes passed.

Then: "Passenger is secure. Male crew seated on both sides—Hayden and Leo. Everyone else in that row's been relocated. Last open seat's 56D. He's got no audience now."

A long-suffering sigh came through her headset.

"André's good. Shaken, not injured. Told me to tell you he still looks hot."

Izzy exhaled.

Almost laughed.

Almost.

Izzy finally moved. Checked the clock. Still four hours to JFK. No turbulence forecasted. Enough fuel to divert if needed.

She didn't want to. She hated Atlantic turnbacks. Hated drama. Hated paperwork more.

She clicked over to the ACARS panel. Fingers flew:

UNRULY PAX 32B

PHYSICAL ALTERCATION W/ CREW

RESTRAINED & UNDER MONITOR

SITUATION STABLE — CONTINUING TO JFK UNLESS ADVISED OTHERWISE

She sent it.

Then—finally—looked at Nico.

She had questions. Too many. But this wasn't the time.

And she wasn't sure she wanted the answers.

He sat like he hadn't just restrained a man with muscle memory and a customer service smile. Comms adjusted. Fast, quiet, right.

Now he was waiting.

Professional. Like they were still just flying a route.

"Threat's contained," she said. "We're continuing."

He nodded once. "Good call."

Izzy grabbed her clipboard, flipped to the incident log. Wrote the time: 03:21 Zulu. Cabin disturbance. Restraints used. FO intervened. No diversion.

Then signed her name.

She didn't thank him. That wasn't the job.

ACARS dinged twenty minutes later:

ACK.

FILE SAFETY REPORT IMMEDIATELY POST ARRIVAL

NYPD & FAA WILL MEET FLT AT GATE

HOLD CREW ONBOARD FOR STATEMENTS

ADVISE IF MEDICAL NEEDED

PAX 32B FLAGGED. DO NOT RELEASE

Izzy barely reacted. Just muttered, "Duh," and tapped out a reply:

COPY. NO INJURIES. NO MEDICAL. CREW WILL HOLD.

Nico sighed. Quiet. Long. Didn't complain. Just rubbed his neck like he could already feel the fluorescent lighting of the customs hallway on his skin.

At the gate at JFK, two NYPD officers came up the jetbridge, flanked by a Port Authority rep who clearly hadn't had her caffeine.

The restrained passenger was silent now. Too quiet. A little dazed.

Emma looked two minutes from tears.

Cy was smiling in that way that meant he was fantasizing about quitting again.

The officers cuffed the guy, led him out.

The moment they disappeared, the Port Authority rep turned to Izzy and said:

"Need full written statements from captain, first officer, and any crew who had physical contact. Now, please. Your union's already been notified."

"Right," Izzy muttered. She handed off the flight log and got started on the Captain's Irregularity Report like her pen was an extension of her will to live.

Two hours later, they were still in the terminal, sequestered in a private crew lounge, waiting for the statement review to get signed off.

Nico had stripped off his tie and was sitting on the floor against the wall.

Emma had fully cried and was now eating a protein bar with dead eyes.

André looked fine, of course. He'd applied under-eye balm and was already talking about going viral on TikTok.

"Not sure getting called a slur and wrestling a grown man counts as a branding opportunity," Cy said.

André didn't even blink. "Okay, well, would you prefer I curl up and cry in the aisle instead?"

Cy turned. "I'd prefer you not try to spin assault into content before we've even had a shower."

"Oh my god, it was a joke," André snapped. "Sorry my trauma response isn't British stoicism."

Silence again. Tight, choking silence.

Izzy didn't say a word.

Nico looked like he wanted to.

He didn't.

Eventually, Port Authority released them.

No debrief. No real closure.

Just: you may go.

The hotel van ride was silent. No jokes. No post-shift adrenaline.

Just exhaustion.

By the time Izzy dropped her bag on the hotel room floor, it was almost 3 a.m. local. Her legs ached. Her skin felt like airport air and recycled guilt.

She peeled off her uniform, fell asleep for fifteen minutes standing up in the hot shower, and climbed into bed with the AC on sixty-three degrees fahrenheit.

No high.

No crash.

Just the flatline of aftermath.

There was no reprieve.

Four hours of detainment didn't earn it. Following every rule didn't help either.

The duty desk gave them two hours—barely enough to meet rest minimums, nowhere near enough to reset. No reserves at this hour, not for a transatlantic leg. They were the only option.

The terminal seethed. Passengers glared like they'd personally delayed the flight. Someone shouted about compensation. Izzy didn't react. She twisted her hair into a tighter bun and walked through the boarding door like her bones weren't aching from bad sleep and worse timing.

They were airborne by noon.

The hours passed in a blur—fuel checks, step climbs, dispatch notes, meal service cleared. The galley had gone quiet.

One hour left.

Outside, the sky had collapsed into black. No horizon. Just ocean below and the soft reflection of cockpit lights in the glass. The world had narrowed to this pressurized room and the sound of systems running steady.

Izzy didn't speak until she needed to.

"Where'd you learn to do that?"

Nico adjusted a dial. Didn't look over.

"Army. Combat pilot."

The silence wasn't pointed. Just full.

"Did you see action?"

He shrugged. "Something like that."

She waited.

"Did you ever have to pull the trigger?"

She asked like it was procedural, but it wasn't. She already knew. She just hadn't decided how that knowledge sat.

He didn't answer right away—just stared at the dark like something in it still pulled at him.

Then: "Yes."

Plain. Undecorated.

The quiet that followed wasn't uncomfortable, but it was heavy. Izzy exhaled through her nose. She wasn't sure if her stomach had flipped from altitude or the answer.

He hadn't changed. But the ground under her had shifted.

His hands moved smoothly over the controls. Precise. Controlled. These were the same hands that had restrained a full-grown man like it was habit. He didn't look dangerous. He didn't even look tense.

But there was something alive under the surface. And she felt it radiating from him—constant, unreadable, real.

~

Heathrow, 2300, London time.

A light rain fell—just enough to ruin hair and patience, never strong enough to justify an umbrella.

The crew taxied in silence. When the doors opened, passengers shuffled off in bleary clusters, some grumbling about the delay, others simply relieved to have survived the flight.

The flight attendants looked like something had been exorcised from them.

Cy didn't wait. Before the jetbridge had even finished locking, his phone was out.

"I'm taking annual leave," he muttered, thumbs already typing. "One week. Don't text me. Don't tag me. I'm unreachable."

He offered no goodbyes—just vanished like a magician in black compression socks.

André's phone was buzzing nonstop. He glanced at the screen, grimaced, and avoided even looking at Cy. The argument between them hadn't cooled.

"See ya later, losers," he called out, then gave a pageant wave to no one in particular before heading toward customs.

Izzy and Nico remained behind—not intentionally, just caught in that strange after-state where the flight had ended, but their bodies hadn't caught up.

Outside, London greeted them with its signature drizzle: damp, inescapable, the kind that soaked into your joints and made you nostalgic for things you didn't even like the first time around.

"God, I missed this dump," Nico said as he shouldered his duffel bag.

Izzy gave him a look. "You've been here five minutes."

"I've actually been here seven months," he said, glancing sideways. "Not long enough to like it. Long enough to feel some weird sense of loyalty."

She let out a hum that bordered on amusement. "Six years for me."

His eyebrows lifted. "Jesus Christ."

"Yeah." She looked around, as if expecting the city to object. "I kept saying I'd transfer back. Never did."

"What stopped you?" he asked.

She shrugged. "I think the misery suits me."

He let out a low laugh. "Yeah. It really does."

They slowed as they reached the badge corridor—the crew exit.

Nico didn't touch her. Didn't move any closer. He just watched her with the same focus he used in the air—steady, exact, never flinching.

"Well," he said, voice even. "Have a safe commute."

Izzy gave a nod. "You too."

Neither of them moved.

It wasn't awkward. It was charged—professional above the surface, but something hotter ran beneath.

He didn't make a move. Just gave her a small, unreadable smile.

She turned before she could say something she'd regret, swiped her badge, and stepped into the humid dark as if she hadn't just spent two weeks in a cockpit beside a man who now lived under her skin.

It wasn't fear.

He didn't frighten her because he posed a threat.

He frightened her because something ancient, buried deep in her, had marked him as safe—and that was more dangerous.

Because that part of her—the part she thought she'd buried in therapy, in airport hotels, in every terrible decision she'd made since—was whispering now: *That one. He's the one. Let him carry it. Let him carry you.*

She hated that voice.

But she didn't stop walking.

6

Nico lay sideways across a too-soft crashpad bed, undershirt rumpled, socks gone, headset hair smashed flat and sun-blond at the ends. The room was dim, silent, vaguely haunted by short-term rental air-freshener and regret. His phone rested against a water bottle at just the right angle to make him look like a sad audition tape.

Nico stared at the screen, where a three-pane FaceTime call radiated pure older-sister energy—judgmental, loving, and slightly terrifying.

Samira took the top center, elegant and lethal, framed by the floor-to-ceiling windows of her Battery Park condo like a Bond villain who had SEC clearance and no time for nonsense. She wore black silk pajamas and wireless earbuds, holding a mug that read, I Don't Need Luck: I Have Root Access. Behind her, the Manhattan skyline twinkled—smug and expensive.

Below her, Layla occupied the bottom pane in full chaotic regalia, sprawled in a director's chair, halfway through glam. A makeup artist attacked her under-eyes with

the zeal of a woman trying to erase four hours of bad decisions, while someone offscreen shouted about call times.
Layla ignored it all, sipping a cocktail through a metal straw
like it was a tranquilizer dart.

"Let me get this straight," Layla said, pinning him with
one heavily mascara'd eye. "You've been obsessed with this
woman since indoctrination, and then you went full Bambi-
on-ice the first time you actually flew with her?"

"Indoc," Samira corrected. "Don't make it sound like he
joined a cult."

"It is a cult," Layla said. "You've seen their shoes."

"I'm being emotionally vulnerable," Nico muttered, one
arm slung dramatically over his face. "Why are we roasting
me?"

"Because you deserve it," Samira said calmly.

"Also because you called us," Layla added. "At nine p.m.,
Eastern. To whine."

He groaned. "I tried, okay? I rehearsed it. Sami and I ran
lines. I had a whole professional, casual-but-not-thirsty
script."

Samira arched one perfect brow. "You did. I gave you my
finest Mid-Atlantic aviation queen voice. I even made you
practice saying 'pleasure to fly with you, Captain' without
sounding like a dog trying to hump her leg."

"And I still botched it," Nico groaned. "She walked in
and I just...started talking about descent profiles like a frat
boy with a Jeppesen subscription."

Layla froze. "You mansplained?"

"To a senior widebody captain, yes."

"That you've been lowkey stalking for two years?" she
said.

"Not stalking. Admiring from afar."

"Same thing, minus the restraining order."

Samira sipped her tea like she hadn't just watched him fall into social ruin. "So let me be clear. You disrespected a woman with more hours than God, on an aircraft you're not even type rated on yet."

"Technically, I'm in the sim for it next month."

Samira didn't blink. "And yet."

"Excuse me," Layla interrupted. "You knew she was in your rotation?"

"Yeah."

"And you knew what she looked like before meeting her? And seen her face? The one that says she eats rookies for breakfast?"

"I panicked."

"You're a disgrace," she said, fondly. "Do you know how many men have probably mansplained things to her over the years?"

"That's literally what I've been spiraling about," Nico said. "You think I don't feel like I should launch myself into a canyon?"

"Good," Samira said. "Let the shame drive improvement."

Layla pointed at the screen like she was delivering a verdict. "Next time you fly through JFK, you're staying longer. We want to see your stupid face."

"I'm routed through next month," he said. "I'll have a long layover. I wanna see everyone. I wanna see your show."

"And?" Layla prompted.

He smiled. "I wanna see my nephew. My little habibi probably forgot what I look like."

Layla sighed. "Stop sending him stuff."

"No."

"He has seven Bluey plushes. Seven. Our living room looks like a daycare for repressed Australian dogs."

"I like Bluey."

"You're turning thirty soon."

"Not my fault I have emotional range."

Samira rolled her eyes. "I'm changing your Amazon password."

"You can try," Nico said, smug. "I use two-factor now."

"Oh, honey," Samira said, sweet and condescending. "You think I don't own your second factor?"

Layla wheezed laughter while a production assistant behind her called, "Last looks!"

Nico smiled, real and small. "Love you both."

"Fix your personality," Layla said.

"And your sleep schedule," Samira added.

They hung up.

THE NEXT FEW weeks were a tactical exercise in denial.

And he was losing.

They weren't paired. No explanation, no drama—just a rotation shuffle that dropped Izzy into long-hauls and left him bouncing around Europe like a regional first officer with a decent haircut and nowhere to be.

He wasn't totally alone—plenty of LUMA crew lived nearby. The airline sponsored a cluster of flats just north of Shoreditch, all glass balconies and oat milk gentrification. He'd already run into André at the corner shop, screaming at the card reader and holding two bottles of wine like it was a hostage situation.

She'd been reassigned to the kind of routes that didn't touch the continent. Probably on purpose. Singapore. São Paulo. LAX with a red-eye return. He knew. He'd checked. FlightAware, gate boards, dispatch logs—he wasn't proud, but he wasn't subtle either. He used to track enemy signals from a base that didn't officially exist. Tracking a woman across global airspace? Child's play.

He told himself it was fine.

Casual. Easy. Civil.

It *wasn't* fine. It wasn't even neutral.

It was physically uncomfortable—like something had been removed from his immediate environment and his body hadn't caught up.

He noticed her absence like G-force in turbulence. Like a skipped heartbeat.

It wasn't just that he missed flying with her.

It was that he missed the chance to watch her work. To be near her. To pretend proximity didn't feel like a confession.

Because yeah, he'd been watching her. From the jump.

Not in that loud, creepy way that got junior FOs bounced off rosters.

In the quiet, professional, military-grade way. Controlled. Disciplined.

A well-honed side eye, calibrated for cockpit angles and reflective surfaces.

He had memorized the way her body moved when she stood up from the captain's seat. The curve of her ass in uniform slacks. The way she moved—tight, economical, all precision—like her body didn't waste energy on anything unintentional.

He'd mapped the cadence of her breath during final approach: how her chest, surprisingly full for her small frame—D cups, if he was forced under duress to guess—rose just slightly faster, even while her hands stayed stone-still on the yoke. No tremor. Just mastery.

He'd locked her scent in his brain like it was an ops

frequency. Something cold and unshakeable, like euca-lyptus and jet fuel. Nothing floral. Nothing sweet. Just clean. Expensive. Purposeful.

And he was not proud, but he had already jerked off to the thought of her. Twice.

Hot water. Eyes closed. Her hands in his imagination were just as steady as they were in flight.

He didn't even get to the part where she said his name.

It wasn't infatuation. It was recognition.

The worst part? She hadn't flirted. Hadn't teased. Hadn't said a single thing that could be called an invitation.

Except Barcelona.

She'd been dancing—already loose, already radiant from whatever trance-pop beat the DJ was spinning—and then she'd backed up. Into him. Slow. Deliberate. Her back to his chest. Her body fitting against his like it belonged there.

She didn't look at him. Didn't speak. Just kept moving, rolling her hips like she didn't care who was behind her—and maybe she didn't. But she'd known it was him. He was sure of that.

His hands had hovered—ghosting over her sides, not touching, not quite, not unless she pulled them closer. She didn't. But she didn't move away either.

And for three and a half songs, he lost his entire religion.

Her hair had stuck to the side of her neck. Her breath had stuttered just once. She'd leaned back when the bass dropped.

He'd gotten hard, obviously. No point lying about it. He hadn't even cared. Because she had to feel it. Had to know.

And still, she danced.

Then the lights shifted. Her body stilled. And she was gone—slipped off into the crowd like it never happened.

But it did. He relived it constantly. When he flew. When he showered. When he tried to sleep.

And that was the worst part.

She'd touched him once.

And it was ruining his life.

He wanted to fly with her again. Wanted to earn the right to be in her space.

Not because he thought she'd change her mind.

But because his body had already decided: *That one. That's the one you want. Figure it out.*

So yeah. He was fucked.

And if the airline didn't pair them up again soon, he wasn't sure he could stop himself from flying through her scheduled layovers like it was a coincidence.

7

The sublet had a gym, but Nico didn't trust it.

Any place with carpeted floors and "motivational" decals on the mirror wasn't worth sweating in. He needed something with concrete. Blood in the mat. A trainer who didn't smile. So, between flights—day off, Frankfurt turnaround behind him, muscles twitching for something real—he pulled up the FitPort app and started scrolling. There it was: no-frills MMA studio in *Shepherd's Bush*.

Good reviews. No Instagram thirst traps. Just a steel door and a start time.

Shepherd's Bush. Jesus. How did every damn place in this city sound like either a Victorian euphemism for dick or something you shouldn't Google at work? He'd passed through Cockfosters last week and nearly lost composure on the Piccadilly line.

Still.

Perfect.

He booked it on impulse.

Didn't think. Didn't look too hard. Didn't know what was waiting for him behind that door.

He just wanted to sweat something out.

Not her, though.

He'd given up trying to sweat her out.

She was in his bloodstream now. Permanent.

THE GYM DIDN'T HAVE a sign. Just looked like it had seen some things, wedged between a butcher and a vape shop that probably used to sell drugs more openly.

Nico double-checked the address, then stepped in. Concrete floors. Mat space. The clean, chemical smell of antiseptic and eucalyptus. Real gym energy. Not some chain where the only threat was ego.

He hadn't expected her.

"You lost, love?"

The voice came from the front desk—if you could call it that. The woman behind it was tall, built like the kind of statue you put in front of courthouses to scare people into behaving, and covered in tattoos that weren't decorative.

"Oh. Uh, no, ma'am. I'm—I was told this place had pad work. I just moved here. I fly commercial, but I used to—"

She raised an eyebrow.

"Didn't ask what you used to do. Just asked if you were lost."

He smiled. Didn't mean to. Nerves. Charm reflex.

She narrowed her eyes like she was scanning for structural weaknesses. Then jerked her chin toward the mat space behind her.

"You book through FitPort?"

"Yeah," he said, holding up his phone. "Drop-in. Got the

digital paperwork and everything, so if this turns out to be a front for organ theft, at least my family can track my last known location."

That earned him a twitch at the corner of her mouth. Not a smile. Just a flash of amusement like he'd accidentally passed a test he didn't know he was taking.

"Early bird, are ya? Good. Mornings don't stink of TikTok boxers and cabin crew havin' an identity crisis."

He blinked. "Airline crew?"

"Yeah. Word gets around. We get hosties, off-duty pilots, one dickhead who turns up in epaulettes like it's foreplay. You ain't special."

He nodded, casual, like that didn't register. Like that wasn't already sparking alarm bells in the back of his head.

"You a pilot?" she asked, already knowing the answer.

"Yeah. Commercial. Long-haul mostly. Based here."

"Military before that?"

He raised an eyebrow. "Yeah."

"Yeah," she said again, like it wasn't a question. "You move like somcone who's had to bust a face without leavin' a bruise."

He didn't know how to respond to that. She didn't wait for one.

"Mats are clean. Shoes off. Ego stays at the door. You hit pads, you follow instructions, and if you start peacocking, I'll deck you in front of everyone."

He held up his hands in mock surrender. "Copy that."

She gave him one last once-over—neutral, clinical—and turned to adjust something on the wall-mounted iPad. Nothing about her said welcoming. Everything about her said don't waste my time.

That was when he looked past her.

And he saw the woman upside down.

At first, it didn't register. It looked like just another body on the mat. Quiet. Feet flexed, legs tight, core locked in. She was holding a slow, brutal handstand like it cost her nothing. As if gravity didn't apply to her. As if she was furious at it for trying.

His brain finally caught up.

There was the braid.

The line of her shoulders.

The shape of her body—now perfectly familiar, painfully memorized.

She wore a black tank. High-waisted leggings. Bare feet flat above her head with a kind of violent grace.

His breath caught in his throat—not in some dramatic movie way, just enough to knock his heartbeat slightly out of sync.

It was Izzy Ventura.

No uniform. Just skin, sweat, and a dangerous stillness that made his spine lock.

He didn't move. He didn't speak. He tried to make himself invisible.

She didn't see him at first. Or maybe she did and simply didn't care. She remained inverted, calm as stone, her long spine stacked neatly over her wrists.

Then she dropped.

It wasn't a stumble—it was a landing. Silent. Effortless.

And afterward, she turned.

She saw him.

Her face barely changed. Just the smallest flicker—her mouth pulled down, her eyes narrowed like someone staring down a migraine they'd seen coming all day and still loathed.

"What the hell are you doing here?" she asked.

Her voice was neutral. Dangerous. Like he'd wandered

into her living room and started thumbing through her annotated copy of *The Iliad*.

Nico raised both hands, palms out.

"I didn't know. I swear. I've got a guest pass—FitPort, or something like that? I was just looking for a gym near the company sublets."

She exhaled. One long, exhausted sigh that seemed to deflate the entire room.

"There's no way. I can't have one sacred space in this city?"

She grabbed her jacket with theatrical precision—like someone already halfway to leaving before they did something legally inadvisable—and stormed off toward the locker wall.

He trailed after her like a man condemned.

"I'll go," he said quickly. "Forget I came in. I didn't see anything. I'll uninstall the app—"

"No," came a voice. It was the gym owner. Calm. Final. "You walked in. You train, or you leave through the back lookin' worse."

Izzy turned around, posture loaded like a coiled spring. Ready to scrap.

"Rey. No. He's my colleague. I don't want him in here."

Rey didn't even flinch. "You tryin' to tell me who can and can't walk through my door?" she asked, voice flat. "You rent this place now?"

"No, but—"

"Cool. Then he stays. You go stretch."

Izzy muttered something profane under her breath and stalked off to the far side of the room.

Rey tossed Nico a pair of gloves.

"Pads or sparrin'?"

He barely caught them.

Something deep in his chest ached. He tried to ignore it, but yeah—it hurt.

I don't want him in here.

She'd said it clean. No heat, no drama. Just the truth.

Or at least, her version of it.

He wasn't the type to linger where he wasn't wanted. That wasn't how he was wired. Nico didn't force presence. If someone didn't want him around, he left. No questions. Just grace, a smooth exit, and a practiced smile to make the departure easier.

And yet—

He looked at Rey.

She stood six feet tall, all authority in track pants, her pierced brow raised like a warning flare.

He wasn't afraid of many people. But he wasn't about to cross her.

Also—maybe, just maybe, part of him (the worst part, the one still built for proving things) kind of wanted to stay. Just a few minutes. Just to show he wasn't soft. That he could hold his own. That this gym, this air, this tension—none of it would break him.

And somewhere under all of that, something quieter flickered to life—

An instinct.

Izzy hadn't sounded scared of him. Or disgusted.

She'd sounded like she needed distance. Immediately.

And he knew what that sounded like.

He knew what it felt like when someone pulled away not because they hated you—but because they didn't trust themselves not to stay close.

Which meant one thing.

She'd felt it too. That night.

Barcelona. Her back pressed to his chest. Her ass tight against his thighs.

His hands hovering. Dying.

She hadn't stopped him.

She hadn't looked back.

Just moved against him like her body wanted something her mouth couldn't say. He'd been wrecked. The kind of arousal that humiliated you after. The kind that didn't go away for hours.

And now here Izzy was again—sweaty, glaring, gorgeous—and he was expected to spar like this was normal.

Nico slid the gloves on. Tightened the velcro.

"Pads," he said quietly.

Rey nodded like she knew the whole script already.

"Good."

And across the mat, Izzy was stretching—with her back turned.

But not far enough that she couldn't hear every single hit.

8

The Mat was hers.

Not legally—well, technically yes, she was part owner as Rey needed an investor—but spiritually. Emotionally. Biochemically. It was the only place in London that didn't demand anything from her but presence. No passengers, no scrutiny, no double-takes at the captain stripes. Just sweat, repetition, and Rey calling her a little bitch if she sandbagged her takedowns.

She loved it here—the smell of chalk and eucalyptus, the quiet satisfaction of reorganizing the gear wall even when nothing was out of place. She liked wiping down the mats, hauling pads, counting mouth guards just to be sure. Most of all, she liked helping Rey run drills for the tiny crew of trans women who trained here every Tuesday.

Working the front desk was worth it just to hear Rey talk shit. Scrubbing the sinks gave her a weird sense of control. The stillness in her muscles after hours of movement—that was the part she chased. And the beers afterward, shared with Rey while they lay sweaty and bruised on the mats, felt like a reward. Like they'd fought for the silence and won.

This was supposed to be one of those days.

She'd gotten there early. Worked through her usual flow. Warmed up. Threw herself into balance drills because she hadn't been able to sleep the night before and needed to burn the nerves out of her skin.

She was in a handstand against the far wall when she heard the door open. Footsteps. Male gait. Not a regular.

Whatever. Rey would sort him.

And then she heard his voice.

Casual. A little nervous. Southern vowels flattened by airline polish.

She didn't breathe. She didn't have to.

She knew it was him.

Nico Fucking Farrah, walking into her sacred space in a dry-fit shirt and shorts like he hadn't already ruined her central nervous system from a hundred feet away in a uniform.

Now he was here. Unbuttoned. Relaxed. Dangerous in a different way.

Not boyish. Nothing sweet.

Just tall, still, and divine in the way that burned cities, not saved them.

She didn't drop immediately. She held the pose, listened to him banter with Rey.

Rey. Who hated everyone. Rey, who would rather bench press a man than talk to him.

And she was laughing.

Izzy's stomach turned.

She finally came down from the handstand telling herself it wasn't him even though she already knew.

It was him.

And he looked unfair. The kind of unfair that made her hands itch.

He caught sight of her. Froze.

She gave him nothing. Just a twitch of the mouth. A look that said no. And he immediately looked like he'd been shot. Good.

She turned before she could say anything else and walked to the far side of the mat.

Let Rey deal with it. Let him train. Whatever.

She was fine. She was.

She stretched out, face forward, arms long, trying to loosen her back. And that was when she made the mistake of glancing at the mirror.

He'd put gloves on. And then—he moved.

Clean. Efficient. No wasted effort. No flare.

He wasn't trying to impress anyone. He was just doing it right.

Every punch landed with purpose—snapped sharp from the shoulder, rotation tight, elbows in, breath locked to movement. His footwork was brutal in its simplicity. Weight balanced, stance solid. Not a single unnecessary step.

She recognized it instantly: combat fluency. This wasn't gym-trained, and it sure as hell wasn't learned off YouTube. This was fieldwork. Tactical. The kind of movement that didn't just come from drills—it came from experience. From needing to end something fast.

She didn't turn. She didn't need to.

The mirror showed her everything. His rhythm, his precision. The twist of his torso when he pivoted into a hook. The way he dropped his center without losing posture. His reach—long, lethal, controlled like a goddamn ballistic weapon—and the way his whole body stayed in alignment.

And Rey was holding the pads.

Izzy didn't know anyone stronger than Rey. No one

scarier. Rey was a former MMA champion. She could hold focus through a kick to the ribs without blinking. She was functionally unshakable.

But Nico's hits were making her move.

Nothing dramatic. Just micro-adjustments—Rey shifting her stance between strikes, bracing harder than usual, her mouth tightening when the punches landed with full-body force.

She wasn't annoyed. She was grinning.

"C'mon then, soldier boy. Make me feel it."

He did.

Hook-cross-hook, smooth and surgical. Loud enough to echo. Rey absorbed it, shook out her arms like she was warming up, and barked for another.

It made Izzy's chest go tight.

She'd trained with pros. She'd sparred with national champs. She'd broken a man's rib with her elbow once and hadn't flinched.

But this—this was restraint made physical. This was violence in a well-cut t-shirt, barely leashed, quiet and deliberate.

And worse—he wasn't even trying. He was just focused. Calm. Breath synced. Eyes locked on the pads like they'd wronged him personally.

It was ridiculous.

And yes—some animal part of her wanted that force turned on her. Not as an opponent, but as the object of its focus.

Something buried, unwelcome, and disloyal ached for that kind of intensity.

She could imagine his hands at her sides with that same precision. She wondered what it might feel like, being on the receiving end of that kind of control. That power. That attention.

She forced herself to look away before she started memorizing the rhythm of his fists. Grabbed a towel she didn't need and wiped down a bench that wasn't dirty. Checked the wrap bin. Reorganized gloves by color, then by brand, then by how much she wanted to throw them at his head.

Rey didn't say anything, just raised an eyebrow like she knew.

Nico finished with a final combo that cracked through the space like a threat. Rey absorbed it, smiled with her whole face, and stepped back. He peeled his gloves off—slow, methodical, flexing each finger free—and gave her that fucking smile. The easy one. The one with sincerity and a little Southern syrup.

"Appreciate it," he said. Like he meant it. Like this wasn't a crime scene.

Rey tossed a towel at him. "Better not be a one-off, soldier."

He caught it, still grinning. "Wouldn't dream of it."

Then—he looked at Izzy.

Just a glance. Brief. Controlled. Nothing she could call hungry, or even disrespectful.

Just...direct. Like he saw her and always had.

Rey clocked it and waved a hand. "Don't mind her. She's got resting homicide face."

Nico gave her the most polite nod she'd ever received from a man she wanted to strangle.

Then he picked up his gym bag and walked out, glistening like an apology she refused to accept.

She scowled at his back until the door shut behind him.

She didn't know if she hated Rey more for laughing, or herself for watching.

The rush hit fast after that. Afternoon regulars poured in —stripping off layers, calling for pads, someone asking where the good wraps were. She dove in. Thank God.

She taped hands, ran drills, shouted for hydration, and cleaned up after a girl who got clocked too hard mid-spar. She kept moving. That was the rule. Movement meant she couldn't think.

Rey was in rare form—commanding chaos like a night-club bouncer with a whistle. The Tuesday girls arrived sharp and sarcastic. Someone played trap too loud. Someone else cracked a rib. Izzy ran to the first-aid kit like she was being timed. She was ice in compression pants.

At 19:00 sharp, Rey clapped and hollered, "Wrap it up, weirdos. If you're still on the mat in ten, I'm charging rent."

The stragglers groaned but obeyed. Bags were zipped, pads stacked, sweat puddles wiped up with reverence.

Izzy locked the gear closet while Rey shut the blinds. The fridge hummed in the background. She grabbed two beers—the ones with labels in German.

They hit the mats in silence. Bruised. Satisfied. Still.

Izzy took a long sip of beer and let it sit in her mouth before swallowing. Her body ached. Her skin buzzed. Her brain, mercifully, had gone quiet.

Rey winced, shifted, and rubbed at her side. "Think one of the new dolls cracked something. Caught me dead center during pads. Got no business hitting that hard."

Izzy didn't bite.

She let a breath pass, then asked, "What's actually wrong?"

Rey shrugged. "Tesco. Someone started following me. Bloke in a hi-vis trailed me like I was nicking steak."

Izzy's head turned before she could stop it. "Which Tesco."

Rey gave her a look. Flat. Dry. Almost fond. "Don't do that."

"Rey!"

"Seriously," Rey said. "Put your fists down. I handled it."

Izzy didn't move.

Rey sighed. "I told him off. Loud enough for the manager to hear. He left. I finished shopping. Still pissed, though. Think I'm just gonna start ordering groceries like a hermit."

That landed heavier than either of them said out loud.

Izzy let it sit. She didn't try to fix it. She just stayed there—watchful, quiet, furious in a way she knew Rey could feel.

Rey took another drink. Let the moment hang.

Then—lighter, like it hadn't just hurt to say—she added, "Anyway. Enough about me."

A pause, then a smirk.

"Let's talk about you and your little panic boner."

"No."

"Babes," she said, dry as sandpaper. "You're in the deep end."

Izzy didn't look over. Just drank.

Rey snorted.

"Don't gimme that stoic captain shit. You were starin' at him like he owed you money and dick."

Izzy made a noise like a chair scraping on concrete. "You're disgusting."

"I'm honest," Rey said.

"Look, I was just observing his form. Objectively speaking, he is a good fighter."

"Oh, were ya? That what we're callin' it now?" Rey leaned in, grin sharp. "You was pervin', babes."

"I wasn't—"

"Don't lie to me on my mats," Rey said, wagging her bottle like a finger. "You want him to pin you or fight you, and I don't think you know which."

Izzy stared straight ahead. "I know it's neither."

Rey took another swig. "Liar. "

Rey didn't press it. Just leaned back, let the silence stretch.

Then: "He's coming back, by the way."

Izzy didn't look up, but her whole spine straightened.

Rey smirked into her bottle. "Booked another slot."

Izzy kept her voice flat. "When."

Rey stretched out on the mat, real comfortable. "Client confidentiality."

"Don't be an asshole."

"I'm not," Rey said. "I'm being professional."

"You are not a therapist."

"I'm licensed in pain and suffering," Rey said, tipping her bottle toward Izzy like a toast. "Don't test me."

Izzy exhaled hard. "Just tell me when he's booked so I don't show up."

"No."

"Rey."

"No."

Izzy turned her head. Gave her the full-force, top-gun, do-not-fuck-with-me stare.

Rey grinned, teeth and all. "You think I'm gonna help you run away from your crush? Babe. That's not friendship. That's sabotage."

Izzy muttered something vulgar and drained the rest of her beer.

Rey just sighed, content. "God, I love Tuesdays."

Izzy leaned back against the mat, staring up at the ceiling like it had betrayed her.

She could still hear the echo of his gloves on the pads. Still feel the tension in her molars from holding herself together.

Rey cracked another beer.

Izzy didn't ask for one.

She just lay there, muscles spent, mind loud, trying not to picture his hands again.

She failed.

9

The next couple weeks were brutal.

Back-to-backs. Short layovers. A turn in Marrakesh that felt like someone had personally designed it to break pilots spiritually. His sleep schedule was trash, his knees were clicking like a haunted staircase, and he had a recurrent sim on the books in three weeks.

The big one.

Captain upgrade.

He wasn't saying anything out loud yet—not until the paperwork cleared—but it was happening. Fast.

Faster than it probably should have.

He hadn't even been at LUMA that long. Some of the guys he'd trained with were still on reserve. He'd skipped the line, no question. Not because he was better. Maybe just... less threatening. Familiar.

He looked the part. Moved the part. Said "yes ma'am" and "copy that" with a smile. Didn't make waves. Could outfly half the roster and still get asked if he's shadowing someone.

Sometimes he thought about the guys in his class who

didn't get tapped. Thought about what they had that he didn't—accents, attitudes, edges. Things that made people squint a little harder, double-check the name badge.

He didn't get second-guessed like that. Not often.

He hadn't earned this speed. Not really. But he wasn't saying no to it either.

And in between the sim prep and the bleary-eyed legs and the 4 a.m. taxi calls, he kept going back to the gym.

Not for her.

That's what he told himself.

It was for the routine. The discipline. The part of him that still needed order. Needed to burn off whatever was twitching in his hands before he said something reckless in a flight deck.

Izzy showed up sometimes. Not every session.

They didn't speak.

They saw each other anyway.

And somehow, that made everything worse.

Rey never paired them together—probably on purpose.

Still, they ended up close enough to feel it.

Running drills with two groups between them. Sharing a mat during cooldowns. Reaching the water station at the same time.

They didn't exchange words. They didn't even fake a smile.

There was only breath between them—measured and ragged. Sweat clung to their skin, unavoidable. And the silence stretched, dense enough to choke on.

They haven't flown together in nearly a month. But this felt worse.

In the cockpit, at least, there were rules. Roles. A framework. Here, they were just people.

Just bodies. Just that sound the gloves made when they connected with the pads.

And God help him, he loved that sound.

She hit clean. Sharp. No wasted motion.

He watched her—quietly, expertly. The way a man does when he's done it before. And often.

The way her feet landed—always grounded, always precise. The exhale timed to impact. The tight cut of her back muscles when she extended. The glint of sweat along her collarbone, catching light like it had somewhere better to be.

She was the kind of distraction that didn't ask to be noticed, but ruined you when you did.

He didn't need to stare. He'd already memorized the details.

The clean line of her tricep, leading into her chest like a blueprint for self-destruction.

The shift of her sports bra when she rolled her shoulders.

The way she pulled her thick, damp hair out of its braid and twisted it back up—calm, efficient, utterly unaware that the whole movement looked sculpted for sin.

It didn't feel like leering. Or even lust. Not exactly.

It was obsession dressed in discipline.

Maybe he didn't deserve to look. But he did.

Silently. Steadily. Like it was the only part of his day that made sense.

Sometimes he wondered if she was watching him, too. She never looked long. But he felt it. Just a flicker—like heat, or pressure, or the weight of something just shy of violent.

He wouldn't dare speak to her first. Not here.

But every time he walked in and saw her? It hit him like G-force.

She never smiled. Never said his name. Never acknowledged him at all.

But she didn't leave, either. And he'd take that. He'd take anything.

Because being near her—even like this—was the only time lately he felt fully awake.

ON NICO'S THIRD VISIT, Izzy left early. No warning. Just grabbed her hoodie and vanished mid-cleanup like the room had caught fire.

Nico kept mopping sweat off the mat like it didn't gut him.

Didn't look at the door. Didn't ask.

But Rey was already staring him down.

When the last trainee left, she didn't even pretend to be subtle. Just walked straight over and planted herself in his space, arms crossed, mouth set in that specific way that meant sit down or get knocked down.

"She's not mad at you," Rey said flatly. "So quit sulking like a kicked puppy."

Nico blinked. "I'm not—"

"She's scared," Rey snapped. "Which, for her, is worse. Mad she can handle. Mad means she knows the rules. But scared? That's when she shuts the door and bolts it from the inside."

Nico stayed still. Because movement might make it real.

Rey didn't soften. She leaned in. Just a hair. Just enough.

"Don't push her," Rey added, voice low and sharp. "But don't fucking flinch either."

She poked him sharply in the chest. "You gonna be a coward about it?"

"No," he said. Not loud. Just true.

"Good," she said finally. "Most men like you? I assume they're one bad day from a manifesto."

A pause.

"You, though... you're not useless. Don't make me regret it."

Then she turned and walked off, leaving him there—still sweaty, still wrecked, suddenly aware of just how many ways this could go wrong.

And how badly he wanted it to go right.

Tuesday night was chaos.

Rey had just started the second round of pad drills when one of the girls, Lina, holding focus mitts took a hook square to the nose.

Not hard enough to break It—but enough to gush.

Rey cursed, grabbed a towel, and sent her to the bench with a block of gauze and a Gatorade.

The rest of the group paused, mid-stance.

"Shit," someone muttered. "We're down a holder."

Rey stepped in before the silence turned mutinous. Looked over at Nico, standing near the bag rack with his wraps still on.

"You know how to hold pads?" she asked, clipped.

He nodded once.

"Yes, ma'am. I'm certified on focus mitts and Thai pads. Used to run padwork sessions during flight school."

Izzy blinked. Just once.

"Alright then," Rey said, already turning away. "Group three. Don't fuck it up."

He didn't.

Nico stepped into the group like he belonged there, and five minutes in, he did. He set his stance, offered clean targets, fed combos without flinching. Called counts when needed. Absorbed every strike with quiet efficiency. Corrected one girl's wrist angle mid-cross and made her entire week.

By the end of the drill, all three strikers in the group were looking at him like he'd handed them a signed head-shot and a back rub.

One of them actually fanned herself.

Rey raised an eyebrow from across the mat but didn't say a word.

And Izzy?

Izzy didn't look at him. Not directly. But she didn't correct him, either. Didn't step in.

Later, when the bodies cleared and the sweat cooled, Rey tossed him a beer and nodded at the mat.

"You earned it. Sit down."

The gym had gone still, save for the low hum of old pipes and the faint staleness of dried sweat. Nico sat cross-legged on the mat, beer sweating in his hand. Rey sprawled across from him. Izzy leaned against the far wall, legs stretched out, her bottle balanced on her thigh. She hadn't said a word in twenty minutes, and that was how Nico knew she was relaxed.

"How'd you two meet?" he asked.

Rey cracked a half-smile. "Some dickhead thought he was clever."

She didn't elaborate. Nico didn't push.

"Said the wrong thing, didn't he," she added. "I was about ten seconds from dropping him."

She took a sip of her beer.

"Then she walks in—" Rey jerked her chin toward Izzy, who didn't look up "—and just decks him. No warning. Didn't even put her bag down. Guy flew into the free weights."

Nico's brows lifted. Rey nodded. "Yup. Management asked her to leave. She did. But the next day she shows back up with a business license application and says—dead serious—'Let's open a gym across the street and put this place out of business.'"

She mimicked Izzy's flat tone with eerie accuracy.

"Three months later, we did. Got the permits. Pulled together the funds. It wasn't clean—messy as hell, actually. Council gave us shit, the old gym tried to sue, landlord pulled a bait-and-switch on the lease. But we stuck through it."

Nico tilted his head. "For real?"

Rey smiled, faint and sharp. "She poured real money into it—lawyers, accountants, engineers. Didn't flinch. Just handled it. Clients followed. Eventually."

He blinked. "So the gym was revenge."

Rey took a slow sip. "No. It was survival. The revenge just happened to be lucrative."

There was a pause. Nico turned to Izzy, still silent, still watching the floor like it might try something.

She took a sip of her beer and finally said, deadpan: "Some people deserve to lose."

She pointed across the street, where the old gym used to be.

Now it sold chips out of a window.

10

She'd slept for thirteen hours, then woke up in pain.

Neck. Shoulders. Lower back. All of it aching like she'd been folded into the cargo hold of her own aircraft and forgotten. Her blackout blinds were still down. Her flat was silent—the engineered kind, where the walls didn't breathe and nothing creaked unless you paid extra for it.

She stared up at her ceiling: concrete, exposed, aggressively curated to look "unfinished." The kind of apartment that came with a private gym, floor-to-ceiling windows, and LED panels that could simulate sunrise, except hers were still stuck on Bangkok at Noon from a week ago and she couldn't be fucked to reset them.

She rolled over, groaned, and reached for her phone. Four notifications.

One from LUMA scheduling (nope).

One from Cy. A photo of a tray of raw macarons and "Guess who's advancing to biscuit week 😊"

And one flagged Priority from the CTO.

She opened it. Regretted it.

Subject: Exciting AI Initiative Coming Soon!
Team—
As part of our ongoing innovation strategy, we'll be piloting a new AI-assisted cockpit system designed to streamline workflow, reduce pilot workload, and optimize route decisioning.
Think of it as your new copilot. 🌝
More to come—
Russell

She closed the app without breathing and opened Messages.

Izzy: If you don't come back to work, the robots win.

Izzy: You think Paul Hollywood is gonna pay your mortgage?

Izzy: Come back to work, coward.

Izzy: NO ONE LIVES OFF A HUSBAND'S TEACHER SALARY, CY.

Cy sent back a laughing emoji. No words. She hoped he felt guilty.

She'd been spamming André with memes for days—cursed TikToks, blurry bootlegs, a photo of them passed out on a layover hotel bed with the caption "Fame killed Judy Garland. You're next." He finally relented yesterday.

Lunch in Soho. A matinee of *Six*. André cried during "Heart of Stone" and tried to say it was allergies. She didn't press it. She didn't cry either, but her stomach turned when one of the queens pointed at the crowd and said, "You're still here. You made it." Her circadian rhythm was so mangled she almost stood for a standing ovation at intermission.

She had a week off. One whole week. She'd spent most of it unconscious, half-naked, or in the gym. Sometimes all three. She still didn't know what time zone she was in.

By the time she made it back there again, it was near closing time. Her trainers were still tied wrong from the last time she put them on. She pushed the door open with her shoulder, hair still damp from the world's fastest shower.

Rey was already halfway out, keys in hand, braid slicked back, wearing that look that said don't ask.

"I gotta go. One of the girls needs me. I don't want to get into it."

Izzy just nodded. "Want me to lock up?"

"Yeah. He's still in there," Rey added, with a tilt of her chin toward the main floor. "Tell him to piss off before I've got to put him on payroll."

"Copy."

Rey looked her up and down for a second. "Get some real sleep."

"Hire an assistant," Izzy shot back.

They threw the middle finger at each other at the same time.

Izzy exhaled. Rolled her shoulders. Walked onto the mat.

And there he was.

She should've told him to leave. She could have walked away without a word, stepped back through the door, and acted as if she hadn't seen him standing there—sweating through his T-shirt like some simmering hallucination. But she didn't. She dropped her bag by the front desk, took a long swig from the half-dead water bottle inside, and leaned against the wall.

He didn't acknowledge her at first. Just kept moving—footwork drills, punch combos, long lateral pivots. His form was near perfect.

Her body was still sore. Her spine still hated her. But her

hands wanted something to do, and watching him move was irritating enough to count.

When he finally slowed and turned toward the pad stack, she pushed off the wall like it meant nothing. Like her heart wasn't still hammering from watching him move.

"You drop your elbow too far on the inside hook," she said, not looking at him. Her voice came out clean, sharp. Not breathless. "That's why it bounces."

Nico blinked, sweat sliding down his neck. "I absorb it just fine."

"Sure," she said, walking past him like she hadn't noticed how he suddenly stood very still. "If you're into wasted movement and getting clocked by someone half your size."

He didn't take the bait. Just followed her toward the mat, that maddening calm wrapped around him like armor.

"Show me."

It stopped her cold.

No hesitation. Just that voice—low, even, entirely sure of itself. He didn't raise It. Didn't lean forward. He just said it and waited, like he already knew she would.

She turned. Deliberate. Chin first, then shoulders. Her expression sharpened as she faced him fully, gaze narrowing with the kind of precision that had ended careers in cockpits and relationships in kitchens. He took it. No flinch, no smirk, no defense. Just that steady posture, like his feet were already planted for impact.

Worse than cocky. He looked calm.

She stepped onto the mat.

"Fine," she said. Her voice had no weight behind it. Just function. "Southpaw. Open stance. Pivot off the jab."

She didn't wait for agreement. He followed, of course. Still in gym clothes, shirt darkened with sweat, posture loose but present. She was barefoot. Ankles aligned. Blood still moving from the last round. No warm-up. Didn't need one.

She reached for him without ceremony. One hand closed around his wrist. The other braced at his elbow.

"This is your block," she said. Flat. Functional. "You're muscling it. You need to angle. Intercept on the outside."

He nodded once. Nothing performative. Just attention. His body adjusted, mirrored her exactly, weight shifting without resistance.

They began.

Slow at first. Measured. Drills, resets, contact. Her voice cut in only when necessary—correcting a foot position, adjusting a breath. He followed each cue, exact and unbothered. No flair. He let her lead.

The rhythm arrived before she admitted it had. They moved with tempo now. Jab, pivot, catch, recover. Their shadows crossed and split on the mat, both of them moving clean.

Then she set it up.

She launched the jab. He stepped to meet it. She angled, hips rotating, and hooked his balance from the outside. It happened in one trained sequence. His center of gravity disappeared. He dropped.

No theatrics. Just the sound of his breath leaving him as he hit the floor—hard and clean. Her body followed, not from hesitation but because the motion demanded it.

She landed straddling him, one knee pressing down beside his hip, the other foot grounded, spine aligned. Her palm braced over his sternum. The other still held his wrist, thumb firm across the tendon. She was steady without thinking.

His eyes found hers.

No embarrassment. Just focus. Like he was still parsing what had just happened, like he hadn't expected to end up underneath her but didn't mind being there.

His hand rose—slowly—and came to rest at her waist. Not controlling. Just a quiet point of contact. As if anchoring himself in the moment.

They didn't move.

She could feel his chest beneath her palm. The rhythm of his breath. Slower now. Tighter. Not nervous—something else. Something measured. Heat lifted off him in pulses. Her body registered every point of contact: hips, thigh, the brush of his shirt.

Her heart wasn't composed. It fought like it had something to prove. She could feel it. Loud. Wild. Betraying her.

She should've pulled back. Should've stood. Should've taken the win and put distance between them.

She didn't.

His thumb moved. Just slightly. It traced the seam of her waistband, no pressure, no demand.

Her breath hitched.

She felt the floor under her knees, the air between their mouths, the electric silence of a boundary crossed without a word.

"Let go," she said.

It came out raw. Not a command. Barely audible. She wasn't sure which of them she meant.

He didn't flinch. Didn't fumble. He just released her—hand sliding off her waist with exact control. No drag, no grasp, no trace of regret.

She got off him too fast. Like recoil. Like a mistake. Her limbs moved before she had time to decide what story to tell about what had just happened.

He sat up slowly, then stood. Rolled his shoulder once. Picked up the mop from the wall, grip casual but firm.

"I'll get the floor," he said, tone too smooth, too easy. "If you want to wipe down the mats."

Like she hadn't just knocked the breath out of him. Like she hadn't held him there long enough to memorize the texture of his skin through his shirt.

She didn't answer. She turned and walked to the spray bottle. Each step too exact. Each movement too restrained. Like stillness was the only way to keep from unraveling.

They worked in silence.

And every motion was practiced enough to look meaningless.

But none of it was.

When they finished, he dumped the mop head in the bin, rinsed his hands in the utility sink, and dried them on the hem of his shirt.

"I'll call us a cab," he said.

She blinked. "I'm fine taking the Tube."

He didn't turn.

Didn't even raise his voice.

Just said, low—deeper than usual, stripped of charm, of patience: "We're not doing that again."

That hit her square in the gut, sharp and hot, blooming low like her body already knew what it wanted.

That voice. The edge of it. The certainty.

She swallowed, throat tight, and didn't argue again.

Because they both knew—

She wasn't walking home alone.

And he wasn't asking.

And God help her, part of her liked that he wasn't.

∾

HE DIDN'T WALK her to the door. He didn't try anything.

Just leaned forward in the backseat, eyes flicking up to the building as the cab slowed down. Concrete, glass, and engineered stillness—the kind of building where every flat came with a Peloton and a psychological void. Private security. Keyless entry. A concierge desk that probably did more background checks than MI5.

He let out a low whistle.

"Damn," he muttered, mostly to himself. "This you?"

She didn't answer. Just opened the door.

He didn't reach for her. Didn't lean out.

Just said, quiet and warm, "Good night, Captain."

And she slammed the door in his face.

It wasn't because he deserved it. It wasn't even because she was angry.

It was because he said it like he meant it—like he saw her. And the postcode hadn't scared him off.

And now he knew where she lived.

That sent a bolt of something sharp and low and entirely the wrong kind of good straight through her.

Once in her concrete box, she didn't even turn on the lights. Just dropped her key fob and kicked off her trainers. She stripped in the hallway—shirt over her head, bra unhooked, tights peeled down in sharp tugs. Skin flushed. Nerves live. Core clenched like her body hadn't gotten the memo that it was over. That it hadn't happened.

She took care of it.

Quick. Focused. Leaned back against the tile of her shower, hand between her legs, and eyes closed.

She didn't think of his name. She didn't have to. Her body knew who it was for.

It rolled through her sharp and fast. A full-body clench,

her free hand braced against the shower wall, her lips parted on a ragged exhale.

When it was over, she exhaled like she'd finished a sprint. Shook out her arms. Gave herself exactly four seconds of guilt, then moved on.

Toweled off. Pat dry, not rubbed.

Thirty-minute skincare routine, aggressive and exact.

Serum. Ampoule. Barrier cream.

Silicone eye patches she'd kept in the fridge.

No thought. Just ritual.

She dropped into bed like someone had knocked her out. Face clean, legs bare, silk sheets crisp under her. She opened her email on reflex. New message.

Subject: New Rotation Assigned
Captain: I. Ventura
First Officer: N. Farrah
Duration: 14 Days
Start Date: Monday
Base: London Heathrow (LHR)
New rotation now live in CrewPortal.
Route: LHR–SEA–JFK–LHR-BOM-LHR
Total duty days: 8
Rest/layover locations: SEA, BOM, JFK
Please review itinerary and confirm within 24 hours.

She didn't touch the screen. Didn't blink. Just stared. Chest still faintly damp from the shower. Thighs still warm. Her heartbeat did a slow thump against her ribs.

Two weeks. Alone. In the sky. With him.

She dropped her head back against the pillow. Exhaled.

And then, quiet at first, then louder—like something breaking open: "Shit."

11

The flight was smooth.

Too smooth.

The aircraft was doing what it was supposed to, but everything else felt off. Dispatch notes were sloppy. The METAR didn't match what she'd gotten from ATIS. The EFB had lagged just long enough during preflight that she'd clocked it, marked it, and pretended it hadn't irritated her.

And during cruise, her name had autopopulated in a system field she hadn't touched.

It was probably a glitch. A cached credential. Muscle memory.

But something about it felt... too knowing. Too fast.

She cleared it. Logged the moment. Didn't say a word.

She'd barely spoken to Nico during climbout.

Now, mid-cruise, she reviewed the route again for the third time. Her face was carved from restraint. Eyes hard. There was nothing wrong, technically—but nothing about it felt clean either.

Nico glanced over once. Then again.

"You keep reading the same line like you're hoping it gives you a reason."

She didn't look at him.

"You keep breathing like it's useful."

The words hit the air and immediately tasted wrong.

Too sharp. Too mean. Cheap.

She didn't need to look at him to know it landed.

She felt it. In the shift of the silence. In the way her own stomach turned like she'd thrown a punch she hadn't meant to land.

Before she could take it back, he spoke.

Calm. Quiet. No smile. No softness.

"Don't talk to me like I'm a rookie just because you're pissed at something else."

Her head turned. Fast.

"I'm not—

"You are," he said. Still not looking at her. Still steady. "And you can keep doing it. But I'm not gonna pretend I don't notice."

He went back to his tablet without a word.

No dramatics, no visible attitude—just calm precision.

He was a man who knew exactly what line she'd crossed, and he wasn't about to let her pretend it hadn't happened.

And the worst part?

She respected the hell out of it.

Her chest tightened. Her hands itched. Her body wanted to fight, but her brain already knew she was losing something else entirely.

"If you're gonna try to get in my head, you'd better know how to get back out."

"Count on it."

The plane had landed clean.

Taxi was smooth. Gate agent slow, but tolerable.

The fight began at door disarm.

It nearly reached its boiling point by the time they hit the jetbridge.

They were arguing over protocol—specifically, how she'd double-checked a clearance call he had already made.

Their voices stayed low but cut sharp, like knives hidden in velvet.

The last thing she'd said was, "Then maybe next time, don't wait for me to clean up your decision."

And the silence that followed? Nuclear.

Even the flight attendants didn't say a word.

Now they were in the crew van.

Ten minutes into the ride to the layover hotel.

No one was speaking.

The driver had tried once—something about traffic on I-5—and then never again.

It was a brutal route. Heathrow to Seattle.

Ten hours in a metal tube punching west into head-winds, with nothing but recycled air, caffeine, and sugar keeping everyone upright.

The time zone swing was unforgiving. You landed in daylight with your body screaming for sleep and your brain stuck somewhere over Greenland.

Everyone in the van had that wide-eyed, dead-inside look of professionals being held together by salt, spite, and overpriced hydration powder.

Uniforms rumpled. Eyebags violent.

The junior FA looked like she might cry if someone breathed wrong.

Even Cy and André—back on roster, finally speaking again after the fight they'd had post Barcelona—sat in total silence. No banter. No "Galley Confidential" voice. Not a single play-by-play.

Which was hilarious, really. Because they didn't scare easy. They had mocked turbulence, smoke alerts, and a crew meal labeled 'experimental.'

But this?

This was a pilot cold war.

And even they knew better than to poke two nuclear powers mid-standoff.

Izzy hadn't said a word since the door closed.

Her chest rose, then stilled. Her fists clenched in her lap like she could strangle the tension out of her own body.

Her eyes kept darting to the window, then back to the floor.

Not because of the scenery.

Because of him.

Nico was sitting diagonally across from her.

Elbows on knees. Forearms tense.

Not looking at her, but definitely not not looking at her.

He'd stayed silent after touchdown—offered no defense, no apology. And somehow, that made it worse.

She could still feel the way his voice had landed in the cockpit, flat and unbothered: "You can keep doing it. But I'm not gonna pretend I don't notice."

He was supposed to back down. He didn't. He met her at altitude and held.

Now they were thirty minutes from the Westin, and she didn't know if she wanted to bite his head off or demand he touch her.

12

The hotel restaurant buffet was a purgatory of linoleum and trauma bonding.

Gray chairs. Beige food. Light jazz playing like it hated itself.

It was the kind of dinner that came with the room and somehow still felt like punishment. A few crew were scattered around the space in activewear and thousand-yard stares. No one was really talking. Just the low hum of exhaustion and the quiet clatter of utensils against plates that weren't quite clean.

He walked in late, after a long shower and a failed nap.

Still damp behind the ears. Still pissed.

Izzy had barely looked at him since landing.

Not during the walk to the terminal.

Not during debrief.

Not even in the van, where the air had been so thick with tension he swore someone was going to suffocate on it.

She'd been silent.

Cold.

Controlled in a way that made him want to knock something off a shelf just to see if she'd flinch.

And now—there she was.

Across the room.

Sitting with André and Cy, dressed down in black joggers and a hoodie, hair in a fresh braid, face clean. No makeup, still perfect. He didn't let his eyes drag too long, but it didn't matter. His body already had the image burned in: her mouth drawn into a hard line, her eyes hard, her entire posture saying *don't test me*.

And yeah—he still wanted to. Badly.

He was halfway to a table on the other side of the room when he heard it.

"Nico," Cy said, waving him over like they were old friends. "Come sit."

Izzy didn't say anything. Just kept slicing into her reheated chicken breast.

But Cy kept waving. André raised an eyebrow.

So Nico walked over.

Smiled like a professional. Said, "Hey."

Pulled out a chair.

And that's when she stood. Not rushed. Just clean and final.

She picked up her room key, said "Excuse me," in that clipped voice she used when she couldn't afford to feel anything, and walked out like sitting beside him would've cost her too much.

Nico sat anyway. Didn't say a word.

Watched her walk out with that natural sway of her hips that drove him insane.

He took a breath. Inhaled the frustration. The ache. The buzz of adrenaline that hadn't left since descent.

André huffed a breath like he'd been holding it in. "If you're gonna fold, better do it now."

Cy leaned in. Whispered, not unkindly: "I've known the girl ten years. She is always watching to see who holds steady when it gets ugly."

Nico didn't answer. Just dropped his fork and went after her.

THE SECOND she opened her door, he knew she wasn't going to make this easy.

She was fresh out of a quick shower, robe knotted tight, hair wet and dark around her collarbone. And that same fucking wall in her eyes she'd been building brick by brick since London. He could have walked away. Sleeping it off would've been smarter. Giving her the silence she wanted might've spared them both.

But he didn't. He pushed past her.

"What the hell is your problem?" he snapped, already halfway into the room.

Her voice was ice. "Come again?"

"You've been biting my head off for the past day," he said, turning to face her. "And not because I did anything new—because something shifted, and you're too scared to look at it."

Her temple ticked with restraint. "You don't know what the fuck you're talking about."

"I do, actually," he said, stepping toward her. "You just hate that I'm not afraid of you."

She crossed her arms like a drawbridge. "Well maybe you should be."

That did it. He felt his patience burn out like a fuse.

"Why?" he demanded. "Is it the rank? The age gap? The

fact that you broke six glass ceilings to get here and I'm just the hot idiot riding shotgun?"

She flinched, and for a second, he hated how much he liked it.

"I know who you are, Izzy," he said, voice low now, teeth clenched. "You don't break me. You sharpen me. And maybe that's what's pissing you off."

She shook her head, pacing like a caged animal. "This isn't some fantasy. I'm not your fucking prize. I don't have space in my life for bullshit right now."

"Who said anything about bullshit?" His voice cracked open. "You think I'm trying to drag you into some mess? I'm trying to show up right now. You want real? Let's talk real. You're burnt out. You're tired. You're circling the drain and flying like nothing's wrong. You want me to stay away because you're scared I'll see it."

"You don't know what I've been through," she spat.

"No. But I've been trying to," he said, stepping closer. "And you keep pushing me out like that's noble. It's not. It's cowardly."

Her eyes snapped up to his. "*Cowardly*?"

"Yeah," he said. "You'd rather blow this up than let me carry even a little bit of weight"

"I don't need anyone and I like it that way. And I don't want to be in another goddamn situation where I disappear myself."

He stared at her. "Then don't. I don't want less of you. I want all of you. That's the whole point."

"You don't know what the fuck you're asking."

"Then tell me," he said. "Or hit me. But stop acting like I'm too dumb or too young to handle this."

She made a sound. Sharp. Almost a laugh.

She looked like she was done.

That dead-calm kind of done that meant: I will not cry, I will not break, I will walk away before either of us sees too much.

She stepped forward—not toward him, past him. Like she was heading for the door, like she meant to end this whole thing with silence and space.

He didn't move.

So she pushed.

Not a shove. A forearm to his chest, high and deliberate, pressing into his clavicle like she was clearing him from the cockpit door. Tactical. Measured. It was her saying move. Not please. Just move.

He didn't.

She tried to slide past him on the left. Quick, clean, planned.

He caught her.

Elbow to palm, soft grip, trained reflex. He turned with her momentum—not yanking, not punishing—just redirected her. Spun her just enough to back her against the wall. His hand caught hers mid-motion. The robe shifted.

Now they were too close. Her chest brushing against the base of his sternum with every breath. Her pulse a live wire under his fingertips.

The tension crackled in the inch of air between their mouths.

"Say stop," he said.

She didn't say anything.

She just looked at him—with the kind of hatred that could turn a man to dust. A look sharp enough to flay. Like he'd cornered something wild and brilliant and unforgiving, and it was about to bite clean through the trap.

So he kissed her.

Like it was a dare. Like the moment he backed off, she'd land a punch.

And maybe she would've.

But she didn't pull away.

She kissed him back like she hated him for it. Lips rough. Teeth scraping his bottom lip like she wanted blood, or maybe just proof. Her hands went to his chest—not to touch. To shove. But he didn't budge.

God, her mouth.

She tasted like salt and tension, her breath shallow and sharp. Every inch of her skin was telling him to fuck off, and every muscle underneath was leaning in.

When she broke the kiss, it wasn't to breathe. It was to glare.

He was panting. She wasn't.

She looked up at him like she wanted to rip his face off. Like he was the reason she couldn't keep the line between self-control and surrender clean anymore.

"Tell me to stop, Izzy," he muttered, voice raw.

She didn't answer. Just grabbed the front of his shirt and yanked him back in like she was starting round two. The kiss was worse this time—hotter, dirtier, reckless. Her nails dragged down his chest, catching fabric. She stood there in her robe, half-covered, daring him to look.

Her breasts were pressed against him now, bare under the robe, and he could feel everything. She gasped when his thigh slotted between hers, then bit it back like it was weakness. He wanted to press again, harder, just to see what else he could drag out of her.

She tried to push him again. Not out of fear. Out of instinct. Out of sheer dominance.

So he caught her wrist.

Pushed it gently, deliberately, above her head. One arm pinned. Then the other.

She stared at him, wide-eyed, unafraid. Not fighting. Waiting.

He leaned in, lips brushing her earlobe. "Lie to me. Go ahead. Say stop."

She didn't.

Instead, she shifted her knee between them, like she might try to reverse the pin. He blocked it, held her tighter, and felt the shift.

Not anger.

Not resistance.

Permission.

And then—her robe fell open.

Her nipples were tight, peaked from cold or rage or both. Her chest rose and fell like she'd just finished a sprint.

Nico didn't breathe—couldn't. Her breasts were out. Just *out.* Like the universe had decided to throw him a live grenade and see what he'd do with it. His brain fried on contact. Static. White noise. Full body shutdown. They were perfect. Round, soft, unreal in that mythological, tits-on-a-statue kind of way. He wanted to bite something. He wanted to scream.

Time went sideways. His knees actually buckled. He was going to die in this hotel room, and this would be his legacy: a man felled by tits.

He didn't think. Couldn't. The moment his mouth found her breasts, everything short-circuited—no language, no thought, just need. He kissed them like he was starving, bit and sucked like possession was a biological imperative. Her skin was soft and fever-hot, and he swore he could feel her heartbeat against his tongue.

She was cursing. Loudly. Viciously.

"I hate you," she spat, over and over, like it hurt to say and hurt worse not to. "I fucking hate you."

He still had her wrists pinned above her head. She squirmed, tried to twist free—but it was half-hearted. Performative. She didn't want out. Not yet.

His free hand slipped down, cupped her between the thighs—and fuck. She was soaked. Dripping. His fingers slid through heat like he'd just reached into her soul.

"This how much you hate me?" he said, low and ragged, half-laugh, half-threat.

She bucked, tried to knock him off, but all it did was grind her against his palm. He let her. Watched her hips chase the friction while he took her breast back into his mouth, tonguing and biting like he wanted to ruin her there too. She moved faster, breath catching, body taut.

It didn't take much time. She came hard. Shuddering, gasping, but not softening. She went still for half a beat—then snarled something so filthy, so venomously mean, it felt like a dare. A demand.

He didn't wait.

Still holding her wrists, he shoved his sweats down with one hand, kicked them off just enough to get free. Then he let go of her arms, grabbed her by the hips, and hauled her up like she weighed nothing. Her legs wrapped around him, and before the next breath hit the air, he had her pinned to the wall and was inside her, hard and deep and fucking gone.

13

She didn't mean to say it out loud.

It came out of her as a snarl, sudden and sharp—a slap across the moment. The worst version of herself, breaking loose from where she'd kept it caged for the past two months. She didn't even recognize her voice when it landed—low, venom-laced, and final.

He froze. For half a second, just enough for her to see the flicker of shock in his eyes.

Then he moved.

The robe was already undone, useless. Her back hit the wall again, not hard, not soft—just final. And then he was yanking his waistband down and—Jesus Christ.

She looked.

Too big. Too much.

Fuck.

Her breath hitched in her throat like it was trying to reverse course. The part of her brain not slicked over with hunger and fury screamed, *You're out of your fucking mind.*

But the rest of her—her hips, her mouth, her goddamn heart—was past the point of giving a shit.

She wanted him like a wound wanted pressure. Like she needed to feel something so sharp, so consuming, that maybe it'd drown out the war inside her head. She clung to the adrenaline, rode it straight into recklessness.

She didn't get a warning. There was no breathless whisper, no quiet check-in, no chance to brace herself.

He thrust. Once. Brutal.

The sound she made wasn't human. White-hot pain cracked her in half. The world blinked out. She saw nothing. Felt everything. Her whole body locked like a live wire, her mind a static burst.

Then: black.

Half a second. Enough time to wonder if this was how her stupid story ended.

But her body—traitorous, hungry thing—readjusted.

The pain didn't leave. It just melted. Blunted at the edges. Made room.

And then he moved.

She gasped. Her legs locked around his waist without her permission, and he held her up like she was weightless. One big hand gripping her ass, the other anchoring her thigh, and she didn't know who was fucking who anymore.

She was just—being used.

Used, held, split open, driven against the wall like she was something to be taken.

And then, god help her, it started to feel good.

Too good.

She whimpered, arms flying up, curling around his neck. It wasn't surrender. Not quite. It was desperation. Her fingers dug into his nape, then softened, pulled him closer. She kissed him this time—different now.

There was want in it.

Stupid, aching, terrifying want.

He didn't slow down. He didn't speak.

He just fucked her through it.

Each thrust knocked the air out of her lungs. Her teeth clicked. Her ribs jarred. She could feel him—Jesus, she could feel him all the way up. Every time he bottomed out, her spine lit up, cervix singing, please no, please more. But on the pullback—

Oh.

He hit something on the way out. Something sharp and electric that made her knees lock and her eyes roll back and her hands claw into his back like she was holding on for dear fucking life.

Her orgasm crept up like a freight train. Inevitable. Furious. Unfair.

She couldn't stop shaking. Couldn't stop kissing him. His mouth was rough, then gentle, then rough again—like they didn't know what they were doing, like they were making it up as they fell apart.

She came like it was being ripped out of her.

Violent. Messy. A scream into his mouth and nails down his back and one last, frantic grind of her hips against his.

He followed—fast. Hard. A choked sound against her shoulder.

They didn't speak. Couldn't.

Just breath and blood and skin and the echo of everything they'd broken just to get here.

And the worst part?

She still wanted more.

14

They separated without words. She staggered to the bathroom—shaking, dripping. He stayed slouched on the floor, back to the wall, head in his hands, breathing like he just survived combat. She closed the door quietly. He huffed out a silent disbelieving laugh, like a man finally lost the war with himself.

Twenty minutes passed. Nobody moved. The only sounds were the drip of the faucet and the breathing.

Then she emerged, barefoot, her skin flushed and glowing under the hem of a T-shirt too big for her frame. It hit mid-thigh. She held a little travel first aid kit in one hand. Her eyes met his—glassy, dazed, like her brain had been fucked right out of her skull—but there was something sparking behind the haze now. Something raw and lit and awake. He could've stared into that look for the rest of his life and never felt full.

"Sit on the bed," she said.

He tilted his head—half-cocky, half-testing, like he was trying not to hope too hard. She nodded past him, subtle as a signal flare, and he turned to look.

His reflection stared back from the mirror behind the bed. His back looked like a wild thing had danced there—faint red welts crisscrossed with pinpricks of blood, as if her lust had a physical cost and this was the receipt.

"Oh," he murmured, and sat.

She opened the kit with the same steady precision as when she adjusted dials mid-descent—calm, focused, every motion efficient. When she reached for him, he caught the shadows blooming along her wrists—blue, green, ghost-purple. He couldn't help but wonder if the rest of her—her chest, her hips—was painted in the same palette. He had the urge to strip that shirt from her and take inventory. But then she dabbed at his shoulder blade, and the sting lit him up like fire.

She worked methodically, lip caught in her teeth, gaze flicking between wound and cotton. A couple of Band-Aids for the deeper lines. From the reflection, he watched her wrists move, delicate and battered.

When she was done, he caught one hand in his, turned it palm up, and pressed a kiss to the bruised skin. Then the other. One kiss became two. Her breath hitched, and then her mouth found his again—slower this time, aching, tender.

But just when he thought she might retreat, fold in, tell him to get out—she shoved him. Not away. Down.

He hit the mattress with a grunt, but before he could think, she was touching him. Her hand wrapped around him like she'd been born to do it—no fumbling, no hesitation, just precise, reverent strokes that made his brain short-circuit. It was better than any sick little daydream he'd had of her. Her hands moved with the instinct of someone born to mastery—like anything she touched, she could learn, command, and make hers.

Suddenly, he believed in something again. God, fate, karma—whatever force had landed her hands on him. And God help whatever man came after, because Nico wanted those hands inked into his story forever.

Then her mouth.

She kissed along his length, slow, wet, teasing—tongue licking with almost scholarly attention. His head fell back. She worked him in, deeper, deeper, until her lips kissed halfway through his length and her throat clenched around him. It didn't all fit—it couldn't—but she was damn determined to try. Her eyes brimmed with furious, beautiful tears, her cheeks flushed, and he realized: this wasn't suffering. This was pleasure. She loved this. He fisted her hair and rocked his hips just enough, and she preened. She glowed under it. She touched herself while he whispered filth like prayers, and when he growled for her to take off her shirt, she did it without hesitation.

That's when he lost his mind.

Her chest. It was all bloom and ruin, a violent garden of bruises inked by his mouth, his teeth. Not delicate. But breathtaking in its wreckage, as if her skin had been marked by something half-mad.

And yet as she put her mouth back on him again and her lips started to slide up and down his cock, those breasts bounced, and he thought he'd die from the beauty of it.

"I'm close," he gasped.

She moaned like she was daring him to be.

When he came, it was thunder and light. She swallowed all of it—but not before she pulled back to show him the last drop on her tongue. Then she licked her lips like a fucking starlet and he nearly wept.

"Sit on my face," he rasped.

And she did. She lowered onto him like a gift he hadn't

earned, thighs trembling around his jaw. Her first orgasm took no time at all—sharp, sudden, electric. She tried to pull away, breathless, whimpering that she was too raw—but he locked his arms around her thighs and kept going. Torturous. Unrelenting. Worshipful.

After a time, she came again. And again. Violent, gasping, helpless. Until her legs gave out and he finally let her go. She collapsed beside him, boneless.

They stared up at the ceiling. The room stank of sex, hot skin, sweat, and saliva. She didn't touch him. Didn't speak. But she didn't tell him to leave.

She shifted onto her side, curling into herself, knees drawn up tight. Fetal position. He recognized it instantly. He'd seen her sleep like that once on a long-haul—tucked into the narrow bunk behind the cockpit while the jumpseater took the yoke. Back then, it had seemed like a habit. Now it felt like armor. And it gutted him just the same.

She was still catching her breath. Her gaze found his, no longer sharp or guarded, no trace of the earlier edge—just something quieter, undone, like a door cracked open. It almost broke him.

He reached out, thumb brushing her bottom lip, then smoothed a loose strand of hair from her face. He hadn't realized how long it was until now, half her braid unraveling, the rest spilling around her shoulders like dark water. She looked like some sea creature washed up in his bed—mythical, too tender to touch, with hair like wet bark and moonlight, draped across her breasts.

When his hand passed over her again, her eyes fluttered shut. Her breathing slowed. Sleep came fast, heavy. He kept stroking her hair, slow and aimless, until his own exhaustion finally claimed him too.

15

He woke to the sound of silence—too much of it. The clock read 6:38 am. No light filtering in from under the bathroom door. Just the cooling imprint of her body on the bed and a sour twist in his gut.

He sat up fast. Her phone was still charging on the nightstand. But her key card was gone.

She walked.

His heart kicked. He didn't think. Just threw on sweats, grabbed his own phone, and bolted.

Only one place nearby made sense. The 24-hour pharmacy two blocks down.

He spotted her through the glass. Alone at the front of the store, arms crossed over her chest, staring down a locked plastic case with a tiny lavender carton inside. The kind you had to ask for. Like it was liquor. Or ammo. Like shame should be built into the design.

Her face was carved out of stone. Beautiful, pissed-off stone.

He walked in. Quiet steps on linoleum. She noticed him

just as a teenage clerk shuffled out from the stockroom, keys jangling like he hated his job.

Her eyes narrowed. "Are you kidding me?"

He held up his hands. "Not here to make a scene."

The clerk unlocked the case, slotted the pill onto the counter with all the drama of stocking gum. Nico slipped in beside her and tapped his credit card on the reader before she could say anything.

"I had it," she muttered, but there wasn't heat behind it.

"Yeah, well," he said, voice low to her ear, "I should've had it yesterday. Let me have this."

The kid bagged it. Nico took it from him, didn't look at the price, didn't look at the receipt. Just waited until she followed him out into the cold morning air and handed her the bag.

She didn't thank him. But she let him walk beside her.

And that, somehow, felt like more than he deserved.

They didn't speak. The silence between them was taut, practiced, professional.

They walked two blocks like that. Then she slowed. Tilted her head toward a dark window like she was running a threat assessment.

The Starbucks wasn't even fully open. Lights half on. Chairs still upside down. The girl behind the counter looked barely conscious.

Nico didn't ask. Just placed a hand at the small of her back and guided Izzy in—light, firm, like he'd done it a hundred times.

She didn't flinch. Didn't look at him. Just let him.

He waited for her to order. She didn't.

"I'm fine," she said, eyes on the pastry case.

He nodded, unfazed. Stepped up to the counter.

"Grande mint tea. And a croissant, warmed."

Izzy gave him a look—flat, surgical—but didn't argue.

They took the booth in the back, near the restroom, where no one would see them unless they went looking. She sat, still in last night's clothes, legs crossed like a drawbridge.

He placed the tea in front of her. She didn't touch it.

"You should eat something first," he said, quiet. "It hits softer with food."

"I said I'm fine."

"Cool. Croissant's still coming."

She exhaled hard. Not quite a sigh—more like a warning shot.

They sat in silence until the cup stopped steaming. His knee bounced once, then stopped. He watched her fingers, clenched tight around the table edge.

Then she said it: "You've done this before."

Not a question. No heat to it, just the sterile edge of data collection. Still made his chest tighten.

"Yeah," he said.

That's it. No deflection. Just acknowledgement.

She didn't look at him, but he felt it—the tiny shift in her posture. Like she's reevaluating him. Not surprised. Just annoyed to be right.

He didn't take it personally. If he were her, he'd judge him too. She didn't strike him as someone who let herself make the same mistake twice. And here he was. Mistake number...whatever.

He waited for a breath.

Finally, he added: "But not like this."

She looked down at the tea like it just said something offensive.

She picked it up, drank it anyway. Ate half the croissant

that just arrived like it was a calculated risk. Still didn't speak.

Then, without fanfare, she reached into the plastic bag, pulled out the box, and took the pill.

She didn't look at him while she did it. Just peeled back the foil, swallowed it with the rest of the tea, and set the cup down like it was any other morning. Like it didn't cost her anything to let him see that.

He didn't speak. Didn't blink. But he noticed it. That she let it happen. That she let him be the one to hand things over. That, somehow, settled under his ribs like warmth. Wrong place, wrong time, entirely fucked context—but still. She accepted what he offered. That was the only win he was getting, and he took it. Quietly. Selfishly.

Then her phone buzzed. Not the usual crew ping—he could tell by the way her posture shifted, like someone had tapped her between the shoulder blades.

She unlocked it. Scrolled. Froze.

Her fingers hovered over the screen, not moving. Eyes scanning too fast. Then she leaned back—just slightly— looked down and blinked too fast

He watched her.

"Something wrong?" he asked, low.

She didn't answer right away. He thought she wouldn't. Then—

"The tickets I opened last month," she said. Still staring at the screen. "About the new interface errors. The LNAV misalignment on climb-out?"

He remembered. Back then, she'd sounded annoyed. Now, she sounded...constrained.

"What about them?"

"They're gone," she said. "Closed. Marked 'resolved' with no logs attached. I never signed off."

That pulled his attention sharper. He leaned in slightly, voice quiet. "Who closed them?"

She shook her head. "No name. Just IT systems. And now my access to the feedback channel is restricted."

That registered—that was bad.

But he couldn't help it. A flicker of something else twisted through him. Not fear.

It was the fact that she was telling him.

Not Cy. Not André. Not someone vetted and neutral.

Him.

She finally looked at him then. Not to check his reaction, but to read him—like she wanted to see if he understood just how fucked up this was.

He sobered fast. "Want me to look at it?"

She blinked. Once. "Not yet."

Then, softer: "Just...keep your eye on it, okay? If anything feels off on this leg—I want to know."

He nodded. "Always."

She stood. That was it. Moment over.

But he didn't move right away. Just sat there, watching the space she'd left, stupidly wired on the fact that—for one breath—he wasn't a mistake. He was a variable she chose to keep in the equation.

"YOU SHOULD WAIT five minutes before you go in." They were standing around the corner of the hotel.

He blinked. "What?"

"I'm not walking through the lobby at six a.m. with you behind me like we're arriving from prom."

Right. Of course. No witnesses. Not even the front desk.

He nodded. "Got it."

She didn't look back. Just walked off with that same

precision she used in the flight deck—shoulders squared, hair tied, stride clean. He watched her cut across the street and slip through the revolving door like the whole night hadn't happened. Like he wasn't still wearing the same clothes, trying not to smell like her.

From where he stood, Nico could see André and some baby flight attendant lingering by the elevators right as she walked in—he caught the flash of André's expression, the slight tilt of his head. Thank God they hadn't gone in together.

He exhaled, leaned back against the wall, and tried to reset.

The pharmacy run was done. He'd held it together long enough to get through the logistics, to stay upright in public. And then it hit—the comedown.

Yeah, okay. He was wrecked. Emotionally, physically, and something worse—fixated.

The adrenaline had carried him through the night like it was a mission: focus, execute, stabilize. Now there was nothing left to do but feel everything else.

Because what the hell even was that?

He'd gone in to talk. That was the plan. Clear the air. Offer her a way forward that wasn't full of tension and petty bullshit. He hadn't brought the condom he always kept— left it in the travel kit in his bathroom—because he hadn't gone in there expecting to fuck her. He sure as hell hadn't gone in expecting her to say, *fuck me or get out of my room.*

So yeah, no protection. Not his usual style. Pilot stereo- types were real—he'd flown with guys who were known to leave STDs like airport lounge reviews. One in every time zone. All one star. But that wasn't him. He had standards.

But the second she looked at him like that—like she was daring him to flinch—it was over.

He could still feel the imprint of her nails on his back

And now he was just...standing here. In dirty sweats. Hair fucked up. Pulse still slow from whatever that was.

He had no idea how the hell he was supposed to be wheels up with her in a few hours—like he wasn't still a little high off the scent of her.

BACK AT THE AIRPORT, they didn't speak until they hit the gate.

Izzy handed him the flight plan folder without looking at him.

"You're flying today." No inflection. Just the facts.

He blinked. "Seriously?"

"You need the hours," she said, already turning toward the jet bridge. "Sims are soon, right?"

They were. He was technically supposed to be observing today. Sitting back, taking notes, shutting up. But she was handing him the takeoff leg like she was ticking a box—like this wasn't generosity or mentorship, just logistics.

"Cool," he said, matching her flat tone. "Love a challenge. Seattle departures are fun."

She didn't answer. Just arched one perfectly shaped brow in a way that said: *Don't get cocky.*

And yeah—Seattle was no joke. Departure out of SEA was unforgiving—mountains on both sides, margins narrow, and ATC expecting you to thread through like you weren't hauling forty tons of fuel between hard limits.

Morning thermals could kick your ass. The crosswinds weren't any kinder. And the controller? He sounded like he hated his life and took it out in clipped vectors and attitude.

But he didn't flinch. Didn't smirk. Just filed it away.

There was a job to do. And right now, they were back in the cage. Two uniforms, one stripe between them, and a thick sheet of ice laid over everything that had happened in that hotel room. And the pharmacy.

He took a step beside her. Something about her was different.

Not softened. Captain Ventura didn't soften—she depressurized. Slightly. Like some internal valve had opened just enough to keep her from cracking. The edge was still there, but today it hummed instead of hissed.

It was nothing most people would notice. But he wasn't most people. He'd spent enough hours watching her to know the architecture of her silence. This version—loosened by a fraction, brushing up against leniency—was new.

And because he was ninety percent discipline, ten percent reformed degenerate, the thought surfaced, uninvited: *four orgasms and she's letting me fly a plane again. Got it.*

He immediately wanted to slam his head into the overhead panel. *Grow up,* he told himself. *Fly the damn jet.*

But the truth stuck. She'd handed him control. Quietly. Like it cost her something.

And he'd taken it. Carefully. Reverently. Like it meant more than it should.

16

Izzy slid into the left seat, fingers steady on the overhead switches, posture exact. Every movement had its place. Every breath belonged to the checklist.

Nico settled beside her. Right seat. His domain, technically. His assessment flight. He was composed—still—but there was something different about the silence between them now. It wasn't performance anymore. Just quiet, and the memory of heat.

She didn't look at him. Couldn't. Not yet. The world was still too loud inside her skin.

"Moderate chop after departure," she said. "Reported at five thousand. Gusts up to twenty-three."

"Copy that."

"And the MFD's been freezing on climb. Saw it twice this week. You?"

"Same," he said.

"Watch it," she said. "Departure's yours."

He took it without pause. No delay. No comment.

He was flying from the right seat—standard. Both sides had full controls. Most passengers didn't know that.

He almost said thank you. She could hear it. Pressed behind his teeth, held back with effort.

But he didn't. Good. She wouldn't have known what to do with it.

She handed him the aircraft anyway. It wasn't nothing. It felt like nothing. It should have been. But she hadn't given up control to anyone since before the leave.

Now she had it back. And she was choosing, deliberately, to let go of it. Not all of it. Just this.

She didn't pretend it wasn't related. Whatever he'd done to her body that night had dislodged something deeper. And it hadn't settled since. But she'd rather crawl naked through a Known Crewmember line than say that out loud.

Taxi. Line-up. Clearance.

She said nothing else. Just monitored. Let him fly.

He handled the sidestick like it was a test. It was. Not one she intended—but one they both knew he was taking.

Takeoff roll. V1. Rotate.

Nose up. Crosswind from the left. Correction decent—strong, maybe a little too forceful. Then the turbulence hit, sharp and sudden. Not dangerous. Just inelegant.

Still, she watched. Logging everything. The way he flew through it, not around it. The way he kept the plane upright and himself composed.

"Positive rate," he said.

"Gear up."

She kept her voice even, her hands motionless. Only her heartbeat refused to cooperate.

They climbed through eighteen, then twenty. She engaged the autopilot and let it settle.

That should've been it. Time to reset. Let the aircraft take over. Let the moment pass.

Then the MFD blinked.

Three seconds of static. Then it came back. No error code. Just...clean.

She caught it. So did he.

He didn't speak at first. Just stared. Quiet. Present. Then: "And that makes it the third time this week now."

Her eyes stayed on the screen. "File it."

"What's the point? They keep deleting your reports. Like you said."

And then—without fanfare—he reached into his flight bag, pulled out his phone, and raised it.

She turned. Eyebrow already lifted. "Are you fucking serious right now?"

This was a gamble. Everyone knew her stance on personal electronics in the flight deck. She'd once chewed out a training captain for checking WhatsApp before top of descent. There was a story—part myth, part warning—about her slapping a phone clean out of someone's hand at cruise.

"It left a shadow on the status page," he said, already lifting the camera. "I've been trying to get a clean shot since last time."

"Oh."

She told herself it meant nothing. The warmth in her chest. The way he remembered what she'd said. The fact that he listened. Cared. Risked a procedural flag—on his assessment flight—just to back her on something everyone else ignored.

She didn't respond. Just held out her hand.

"Give me your phone."

He blinked. "What?"

"I'll put my number in. That way I have the photo too."

He handed it over, cautiously. Like he wasn't sure if this was a favor or a setup.

She typed fast. Just digits. She passed it back like a checklist item.

"There."

He looked down at the screen. Smiled. Barely. "You always enter it yourself?"

"Only when it's evidence," she said, voice dry, pulse not behaving.

He sent the photo. Just the image, clean and time-stamped.

She didn't smile. But something in her mouth betrayed her, and she knew he caught it.

They returned to silence. The cockpit settled around them again—structured, sterile, still.

But she'd typed her number into his phone.

And handed him the aircraft.

And—for the second time this week—she didn't have regrets.

17

Izzy wasn't used to feeling full—at least, not like this. It wasn't hunger she'd fed, but something deeper. Something that loosened her shoulders and slowed her breath.

They'd eaten their way through the market like they were on a mission: roti prata, char kway teow, fried carrot cake, mango sago. André nearly passed out over a bowl of laksa. Izzy had barely spoken for twenty minutes, just stood there chewing, sipping from a sweating glass bottle of barley water, and letting her nervous system recalibrate under the glow of hanging lanterns.

Singapore smelled like spice and sugar and asphalt that never cooled down. The air wrapped around her like soup. She didn't mind.

Every time she stood on a different continent and looked around like she belonged there, it still caught her off guard. This life. This view. Her body in uniform. She'd grown up in a half-collapsed house on a forgotten naval base in Florida, duct tape on the windows and roaches in the cereal. Now she walked through night markets in Singapore with coworkers who felt more like blood than anyone she was actually related to. She'd flown a plane here. She'd wake up in another country in two days. And then again. And again.

Cy grew up in council housing in the UK. André didn't talk about his childhood at all. He had an American passport and a voice that could shut down a rowdy galley with one syllable. That was all anyone needed to know.

They were sitting now, crowded around a folding table too small for their appetites, and Cy was picking at a final plate of durian like he was trying to see God through texture.

Izzy leaned back in the plastic chair and sighed, hand resting on her stomach.

"This is what happiness feels like," André declared, stretching with drama. "I'm calling it. This exact moment."

"You say that every layover," Cy said.

"Yeah, but this one has laksa."

Izzy laughed—quiet, surprised. She'd forgotten what it felt like to laugh without checking herself first.

Cy noticed. Of course he did.

"You're different," he said. Not a question. Just a surgical observation.

"I'm full," she replied, deflecting.

"You're glowing."

"I'm sweating."

Cy leaned in, eyes narrowed, voice low. "You've had sex."

André nearly choked on a rice cake.

"Cy," she hissed.

"Oh my God," André said. "Don't tell me it was—"

"Don't."

Cy grinned. "That First Officer. What's his name. Sunshine McJawline."

"I don't know what you're talking about," she said, reaching for her drink like her legs weren't out here doing reconnaissance. "And if you don't stop, I'm going home."

"You're not going anywhere," André said, slapping the table. "You're going to tell us everything. In order. Alphabetical if possible."

Izzy groaned and pressed her forehead to her hand.

"I hate you both."

Cy passed her a napkin. "We missed you."

André rested his chin on his hand. "Seriously, though. Is he nice?"

Izzy didn't answer. Which was an answer.

Cy raised an eyebrow. "Is he helpful?"

That got a twitch from her mouth.

She exhaled, finally. "There's something wrong with the MFD. He's been logging it. Helped me get photo evidence today."

Both men stilled. The mood shifted—quiet, focused.

"What kind of wrong?" André asked.

"Freeze mid-climb. Then it resets—like nothing ever happened. No error logged. Just gone. Frankfurt first, then today. I can fly without it. But you know these new kids." Her voice tightened. "If it hits them at the wrong time—"

Cy nodded slowly. "Yeah. No, that's serious."

"I just got back and of course I'm the one spotting tech issues. God forbid I let something slide—I'm constitutionally incapable of looking the other way."

"You'd be suspicious of a light switch," André said.

"But you're right to look into it," Cy added. "Honestly, I'm surprised you're not more riled up."

Izzy shrugged. "I'm tired."

"You're different," Cy repeated. Then smiled. "In a good way."

The plastic tray between them was almost empty now—chopsticks askew, sauce clinging to paper plates. The market noise blurred into a low shimmer, distant and unbothered. A breeze moved through the corridor, not cool, just enough to remind them they were still outside.

Izzy stretched her legs under the table, spine loose.

She glanced over at André. He was staring into his drink, the condensation collecting under his fingers. Quiet. Present. But the edges of him were too smooth, like a story with the conflict edited out.

"You okay?" she asked.

It was the same voice she used when she asked a fellow pilot if they'd reviewed the NOTAMs. Neutral. Professional. Just enough space to opt out.

André looked up. Something passed across his face—not defensiveness, not shame. Just weariness.

"I'm tired too," he said.

She nodded, slow. "I know."

He looked away. "I don't want hookups. I want...I want to come home to someone. I want a name on my mailbox that's not mine. I want groceries for two."

Izzy didn't say anything. He wasn't asking her to.

"I meet someone, and then I'm in Barcelona, or Seoul, or stuck on a delay in Cairo. And they get tired. Or I stop trying. And it falls apart before it starts."

"Yeah," Cy said. No fluff. Just truth.

André exhaled. "I'm starting to think the problem's me."

Izzy shook her head. "The problem is the job. The schedule. The fact that none of us live in one place long enough to build anything solid."

"But you did," André said. "You had Miles."

She hesitated. "And now I don't."

He nodded. "Right."

They went quiet again. The kind that didn't rush to fill itself.

Cy shifted in his chair, slow and sure, and said, "You're not the problem, Dre. You're just...exhausted. From trying."

André looked up. That was the part that hit.

"You want something real," Cy continued. "Doesn't mean you're broken. Just means you're not built for surface-level anymore."

Izzy's gaze flicked to him. Then to both of them.

And felt the old ache rise again—not regret. Just the weight of how much love they all carried, and how little space this life left to put it down.

She reached across the table and rested her hand over André's. Just for a second. Just enough.

He didn't pull away.

"Come hang out with me next week," she said. "Long layover. Bring snacks. We'll watch trash and not speak."

André gave a half-smile. "Yeah. Okay."

Cy arched a brow. "Am I invited to this sacred silence?"

"Aren't you busy manifesting Bake Off again?" André asked.

Cy grinned. "Always."

"He can swing by after and force-feed us samples if he must," Izzy said. "God knows my kitchen's empty enough to simulate the judging tent."

André leaned back in his chair, let his eyes close for a breath. "Thanks, you two," he said.

Izzy didn't answer. Just stayed there, hand on her tea bottle, full for once. Not with food.

Just with them.

~

THE HOTEL ROOM was too quiet. Izzy sat cross-legged on the edge of the bed, hair still damp from the shower, night market food sitting heavy in her stomach in the best way. She should've felt good. Grounded. Even happy.

Cy and André had peeled off twenty minutes ago, still arguing about checking in on the junior FAs. She'd taken the long way back—three detours, one unneeded 7-Eleven stop, a walk through a street she knew was safe but dark.

She wasn't avoiding Nico. Just delaying contact long enough to pretend she hadn't been

The air-conditioning in the room was too strong. She should've turned it off, but she didn't.

Then her phone buzzed.

MILES.

She stared at the screen long enough for it to stop. Then watched it ring again. She picked up. "Hey."

"Hi." His voice was soft, hesitant. Like he didn't know if he should be calling. Which meant he definitely shouldn't be.

"I saw a photo on social media," he said. "Of you. Back in uniform. Looked recent."

"It is."

"You look good."

"I probably look tired."

"You always did. That was part of the charm."

She didn't laugh. But she didn't hang up.

There was a pause.

Then, carefully: "I didn't know you were cleared."

"Few weeks ago."

"I mean... fully? You're flying?"

"Yes."

Another silence.

She could feel it happening in his head—the timeline

math, the six-month blank space, the dots not quite connecting.

"You didn't tell me."

"No."

"I guess I thought I would've... known. I thought maybe someone would've said."

"Miles." Her voice was soft, final.

He let it sit. Then he let out a sigh, like he was steeling himself.

"I wasn't trying to check up on you," he added. "I just... got this thing in the post. Something weird. From the NHS, I think. Billing summary, or... I don't know. Not addressed to me, but I guess I was still on some record from before."

Her whole body went still.

"Said you were under observation. Last autumn. Something clinical. I don't know what the wording meant," he added. "I didn't— I just thought you took some time off. I didn't know it was—"

"Bad enough for three days?" she said. "Yeah."

Another breath. She could hear the guilt calcifying in his throat.

"You didn't do anything wrong," she said.

"I loved you."

"I know."

"I would've helped."

"I know." That was the worst part. He would've. He really would've. And she would've taken that help and resented him for it. They both knew that.

"I'm glad you're back," he said. "I hope you're happy."

"I'm working on it."

And that was the end of the call. She didn't cry. But she also didn't sleep.

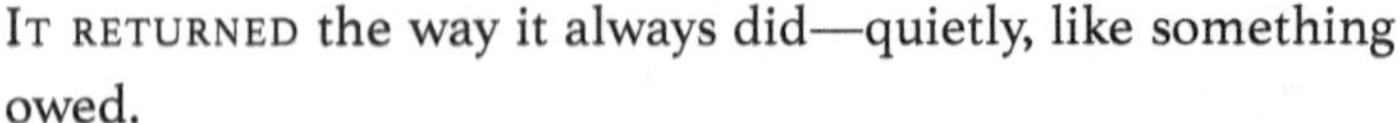

IT RETURNED the way it always did—quietly, like something owed.

The chair. The room. The silence that settled after the question: *Are you thinking of harming yourself?*

She hadn't blinked. Her eyes were swollen from a week of tears—steady, silent, dehydrating grief. The papers came back from Miles—signed, unchallenged, final.

She thought about lying. She wasn't naïve. She knew what happened when pilots told the truth.

Technically, yes, antidepressants were allowed now. But that kind of vulnerability came with a cost. Wanting to be taken seriously meant staying guarded. Being a woman in the cockpit meant walking a line no one else even saw. And doing it alone meant there was no one to catch you if you slipped.

She worked for the most progressive airline in the world. LUMA practically branded itself on mental health advocacy. But it had barely been a decade since pilots were even legally allowed to be treated for depression. And between the paperwork, the requal process, the silent doubt in people's eyes—was it worth it?

She could have lied.

But she didn't want to die. And she didn't trust herself not to.

Miles was her only family. Her friends were scattered and struggling in their own ways. And she was tired of performing.

So she answered the therapist truthfully.

"Yes. I am."

It wasn't a cry for help. It wasn't a spectacle. It was just the truth.

The therapist didn't react.

She nodded once, then reached for her iPad.

"I can initiate a Section now," she said, even. Measured. "Or you can go voluntarily. You'd be admitted within the hour."

Izzy remembered the way the water pitcher caught the light. She remembered staring at her trainers, calculating how long they'd take to lace.

She nodded. Voluntary. Just barely.

The place wasn't bleak. That would've been easier.

She liked it more than she wanted to admit.

The quiet. The softness. Being around people who didn't need her to be competent. Group sessions where nobody interrupted. Art therapy that gave her something to do with her hands. Music therapy where a man with sleeve tattoos sang Velvet Underground like it meant something.

No one asked what she did for work. Nobody pressed her to explain why she hadn't slept. Not a single person looked at her like she was supposed to be holding it together.

And when the bridging medication finally took the edge off—when she thought she could stand on a train platform without thinking about jumping—she asked to go home. The care team believed her.

They booked the discharge appointment that same afternoon. She was lucid. High-functioning. Respectful. She knew exactly what she needed—and what she couldn't afford to need for too long.

She never told anyone except Rey.

Not André. Not Cy.

And now—Singapore.

Five-star linens. Silk robe. Healed skin. Wrecked mind.

She stared at the ceiling and tried not to cry over a man

she barely got to know and a life she'd left behind on a folded NHS intake form.

18

Izzy was quiet in the van. Not her usual quiet—something was *off*. She didn't look at him. Didn't say a word. Not even when the driver clipped the curb hard enough to jostle her. Just stared ahead, hands folded too neatly in her lap.

Maybe it was jet lag. Long rotation. He wanted to believe that.

But when they reached the aircraft and she started the walk-around like it was a requal sim, he knew better.

She briefed the flight attendants with textbook precision. Said only what had to be said. Nothing more.

In the cockpit, it got worse.

She flew like she was being watched. Every checklist perfect. Every callout tight. No sarcasm. Just cold, clinical flying.

It wasn't her.

Izzy flew like she didn't care what anyone thought—but this? This was different. This was her flying like she had something to prove. Like if she got everything right, no one could ask her anything.

Nico sat beside her and tried not to mess it up. Matched her energy. Kept it professional. But the whole time, he was watching her out of the corner of his eye, trying to catch a flicker of whatever was going on behind her silence.

He waited until they were at cruise. Lights low. Cabin calm.

Then he tried. Just a little.

"You briefed that like the CEO was on the jumpseat."

Nothing.

Not even a glance.

"Don't start," she said. Flat. Like she wasn't mad—just didn't have room for anything else.

He shut up. Looked down at his knees. Swallowed hard.

That hurt more than if she'd snapped at him.

He didn't want her angry. He wanted her alive. Wanted the version of her who rolled her eyes and muttered insults under her breath and made flying feel like something he got to do with her, not just near her.

It was quiet for a long time after that. Hours, maybe. He couldn't tell anymore. Time didn't make sense somewhere over the Pacific. Everything felt like floating.

Eventually, he said it.

Low. Careful.

"Tell me what you need."

She didn't move. Didn't blink. Just kept looking out the windscreen like the dark sky was something she could disappear into.

Then she said: "Nothing."

And somehow, that was worse.

Because he believed her.

And because it meant he couldn't fix whatever was breaking her up inside.

The second her rest break started, she was out of the

seat—no jokes, no small talk, not even a glance back. Just unbuckled, unbothered, gone.

Nico stared at the empty left seat.

The headset still hung where she left it, the cord wrapped one coil too tight. Strangled, almost. Like even the sound of the air traffic control feed had become too much.

For a moment, he just sat there, listening to the silence she left behind. Still. Dense. Almost deliberate.

He waited. Five minutes. Then ten.

No footsteps from the galley. Just the steady hum of cruise altitude.

She hadn't even taken her tablet and water bottle. Just vanished.

Something in his gut twisted.

He pulled out his phone—quiet, intentional. Not like he was sneaking anything. Just careful. Like he didn't want the gesture to speak louder than the reason behind it.

He opened WhatsApp—barely clinging to signal on the crew WiFi—and scrolled to the chat with Cy and André.

He'd had their numbers since the end of their last rotation together.

Izzy hadn't given him hers until a few days ago. And only then under the duress of a cockpit software bug and an emerging avionics conspiracy.

He hesitated. Switched from the group to just Cy. Typed. Deleted. Tried again.

Nico: *She's not okay. Flying like she's trying not to feel anything. I didn't ask. Didn't push. If you know something—or if she needs anything after landing—I figured you should know. No need to reply.*

Three seconds. Sent. He set the phone down like it was evidence.

This wasn't a plea. It wasn't drama. He wasn't looking to

be the guy who swoops in and saves the day. He just recognized the look. The kind of quiet that wasn't peaceful—it was barely held together.

His phone buzzed.

He ignored it at first. Checked the overhead panel. Confirmed heading, fuel, engine readouts. Took his time. Then flipped the phone over.

Cy: *Yeah. I know.*

Cy: *She talked to her ex. Miles. He told me he called. It went sideways.*

Cy: *You did the right thing not saying anything. Just stay by her side.*

He read it twice. Then again.

Cy didn't waste words. That's why Izzy trusted him.

But that last line—stay by her side—hit low. Like a prayer and a command all at once.

He started typing. Stopped. Rewrote. Deleted.

Then finally:

Nico: *Copy. Anything she needs, I'm here. You or André say when. That's it.*

Phone down. Again.

Eventually, she returned. Hair knotted too tight. Face unreadable. The faint scent of crew hotel soap still on her hands. Not scrubbed. Just...removed. Like she'd tried to reset something.

She didn't look at him.

He adjusted the rudder trim so she wouldn't have to.

THE SKY OUTSIDE WAS STEEL. Stainless and flat. They'd left Singapore just after 6 a.m., local time—the city still blinking awake beneath them.

But in New York, it was the night before. Sunday

evening. Golden hour clinging to the skyline of a place they hadn't reached yet.

Two cities. Two clocks. Two truths at once.

Somewhere over the Pacific, his body gave up trying to parse any of it. His watch said one thing, the cockpit clocks another, and his phone—when it flickered back to life on cruise WiFi—acted like time was a rumor.

He didn't know what meal he'd eaten. Breakfast? Dinner? Emotional betrayal with a bread roll?

He drank coffee like it was communion. Just something to keep his hands moving. Something to keep his brain from spiraling.

The cockpit was quiet.

Izzy flew like a ghost. Clean. Professional. Efficient. But off.

She wasn't present. She was maintaining. And he knew better than to comment.

Let her fly. Let her land. Then figure out if she still wants the world when they get there.

HE WAITED until the last passenger deplaned, until the cabin crew had packed up and waved goodnight, until the jetbridge door hissed shut with that smug little sigh.

Izzy hadn't said more than ten words since touchdown. She was standing near the flight deck door now, checklist in hand, lips in a line so tight he could barely tell if she was breathing.

He moved slowly. Deliberately. Casual.

Step one.

He logged the times—*almost*. Then, with great ceremony, he reached for the IRS switches.

Shutting them down too early would wipe the nav data

and screw up the logs. Rookie shit. He knew better. He did it anyway.

She didn't even turn her head.

Just said: "You want to try that again after writing down the hours?"

He froze, finger hovering. "Oh, we write them now? Wild."

She let out a slow breath through her nose.

Step two.

He turned to leave. No bag. Just sauntered off like his entire flight kit wasn't still buckled behind his seat. The one with his logbook, his EFB, his headset—everything short of his goddamn passport.

Izzy didn't look up right away. But she caught it.

"You forgetting something?"

He turned, blinked innocently. "What?"

She stared. Cold. Blank.

"Your bag, Nico."

"Oh. Shit." He snapped his fingers like it had just occurred to him. "Right. That thing."

She didn't answer. Didn't roll her eyes. Just watched him go retrieve it like she was updating the mental ledger of his idiocy.

No smile. Not yet. But her voice was less empty. Progress.

Step three.

He pulled the nuclear option. Adjusted his jacket, slung his flight bag over his shoulder—and kept his lanyard on. Proud. Visible. Dangling just a little too freely.

Yes, IDs were required in the terminal.

But no one wore them like that—full swing, front and center, like he was auditioning for a recruitment poster.

Veterans clipped it tight or tucked it subtle—just enough to flash when needed, never enough to catch wind. He wore his like it was part of the damn uniform. Like it belonged in a company portrait.

Izzy always noticed.

He walked halfway down the jetbridge like that—ID badge flapping against his chest, full cringe-mode activated.

And right on cue: "What the hell are you doing?"

He stopped. Looked down. Gasped, quiet and horrified. "Oh no!"

She caught his eye, one brow lifted, arms crossed. "Are you fucking with me?"

Nico tilted his head. Smiled. Soft. Just a little smug. "Yes."

A huff.

Then—finally—the corner of her mouth twitched. A barely-there exhale. Not a laugh. But the tension in her shoulders dropped a half inch.

He didn't press it. Didn't gloat. Just walked beside her toward the elevators, slightly too close, quiet and calm.

She didn't move away.

Didn't speak again either—but he could feel it. She wasn't locked up anymore. Not fully. And that was enough.

HE ALMOST DIDN'T LOOK out the window. He was mid-FaceTime logistics with his sisters—Layla was talking about brunch outfits, Samira was threatening to ghost them both —and he was just wandering toward the hotel window to stretch his legs when he saw it.

Stopped mid-step.

Tilted his head.

"I think something's happening," he said to no one in particular.

Down in the main tower's parking lot, the entire LUMA crew was outside. Doing things.

This was what happens when a crew's been awake too long and trusted with too much sky: they start to spiral in perfect, coordinated chaos. Like moonlit cult vibes, but unionized.

One of the junior flight attendants had a bath towel draped over their head like a ceremonial veil. Another had her arms spread wide and was doing slow, stomping laps around the flagpole, chanting something. A third was trying to braid a hi-vis vest around the pole like it was a maypole at a Midsommar-themed air disaster.

Someone else was barefoot and holding a bag of ice like it was a sacred relic. Another was laying facedown on the grass.

A vaguely familiar FA—Marisol, sweet, quiet, wore enamel pins—was now fully in a standoff with a front desk employee and speaking at a decibel that implied legal action was pending.

And through all of it—through the noise and the stomping and the spiritually unhinged energy of flight attendants three meals past sanity—Izzy stood completely still. Watching. Glowing. Untouched. Like she'd summoned it all on purpose just to punish the building.

She was in a floor-length silk robe, black, with thin straps that gleamed under the parking lot lights. Her skin glowed. Her arms were crossed.

She looked like someone who had been dragged into hell and came back angrier.

He stared.

"I gotta go," he said, already ending the call. "Emergency."

.   .   .

By the time he made it across the parking lot, the chaos had escalated to full weirdness. One FA was throat singing. Another was crying and saying she was going to submit her resignation and apply to clown school.

Izzy didn't acknowledge any of it.

Just turned her head slightly when he walked up beside her.

Her voice was flat. Quiet.

"They said it's going to be at least an hour."

"Electrical issue?"

"Who knows."

He looked at her. She didn't return it.

Her robe was almost iridescent up close. It clung to her in a way that made his brain lag two full seconds before catching up. Her nails were painted a dark wine color. Her skin glowed as if she'd just finished exfoliating all her rage.

He swallowed.

"My room's in the garden suites," he said. "No alarms. Thermostat works. You could crash there if you want. It's... just quiet."

She didn't answer right away. Didn't move. Just looked out at the crew like she was trying to decide if the planet was worth saving.

Then, finally: "If anyone asks, you begged."

She didn't talk much on the walk over. Just tugged that robe around her shoulders and stepped around a sprinkler like it personally offended her.

He let her into the room first. Stepped back. Gave her space.

She looked around like she was checking for faults.

"Already set to sixty-five?" she asked.

"Yeah some freak set it to your exact preference."

She narrowed her eyes but didn't respond. Just walked to

the bed, pulled back the blanket, and slid in with the kind of efficiency that told him she'd made her decision back in the parking lot.

He grabbed his collapsible puffer from the closet.

"What are you doing?" she asked, already turning out the bedside light.

"Not freezing to death."

"Dramatic."

He didn't reply.

Just got in next to her—puffer zipped halfway up, heart thudding like it was trying to make a break for it.

They didn't touch. Didn't speak.

But she was there. And the silence wasn't loaded anymore. It just was.

19

She woke up in a bed that wasn't hers, in a room that smelled like hotel soap and Nico Farrah—and worse, he was wrapped around her.

His chest pressed against her back. One arm snug around her waist. One leg slotted between hers like it belonged there.

Her hand was resting on his forearm. Not gripping. Just...there.

She must've reached for him in her sleep. Not for comfort—she didn't do that—but for relief. Her body ran hot. Always had. And his was the inverse: steady, grounded, almost unnaturally cool. Like her nervous system had gone looking for equilibrium and picked him.

The blanket had slipped. The room was freezing. But she wasn't cold.

He was. That was the sick part—he'd kicked off the puffer sometime in the night and used her body heat instead, like she was his personal furnace.

It made no sense. Except it did.

Because even in the cockpit, they could never agree on a

temperature. She'd blast the fans to keep from sweating through her uniform, and he'd just sit there, jacket on, like a long-suffering human icepack. Now she knew why.

This was the compromise. They had to touch. Otherwise, one of them would freeze and the other would combust.

She hated how good it felt.

He didn't move. Neither did she.

So she stayed still. Breathing steady. Letting him think she was still asleep. Wrapped in the kind of quiet intimacy she didn't believe in—until her body betrayed her and wanted more.

She felt it before she opened her eyes—the slow drag of breath against the back of her neck, the weight of his arm at her waist, the way their bodies had slotted together like it was inevitable.

God.

Her thighs ached. Her skin felt tight. Her heart beat in a place she couldn't name.

Of course she was turned on.

This was exactly the kind of betrayal her body specialized in—waiting until she let her guard down, then lighting her up like a fuse.

She didn't think. Didn't plan.

Just moved—slow, instinctive, a tiny shift of her hips against the heat of him behind her. Deliberate enough to count. Lazy enough to pretend it wasn't.

He didn't say a word.

But she felt it.

The way his hand flexed. The way his chest caught on the next inhale. The way he got hard—fast, full, impossible to ignore.

Her breath hitched.

That should've been enough. A warning. A line.

But instead she turned.

Rolled over into him, into the hard plane of his chest, the sharp scent of skin and sweat and whatever soap he packed like it didn't matter.

Her eyes met his. Barely open. Heavy with sleep and hunger.

No shame.

He kissed her like he hadn't stopped dreaming.

Deep. Messy. Mouth open and demanding, tongue sliding past her lips like he already knew exactly how she tasted.

His hand gripped her thigh, dragged it up around his hip, and she followed. Clung. Let him press her down into the mattress like they didn't have history or consequences or flight duty in twenty-four hours.

Her breath came out in pieces. Caught against his mouth.

His hand slid under the hem of her slip, fingers grazing her hip, her waist, her ribs—everywhere but where she wanted.

She moaned—soft, desperate. Not performative. Just real.

His other hand tangled in her hair, pulled just enough to make her gasp—

And then his phone went off.

Shrill. Stupid. Daylight crashing in all at once.

He jerked back. Swore under his breath.

"Shit," he muttered. "Shit, I'm late."

Pressed his forehead to hers like that would undo it.

She blinked. Breathless. "For what?"

"Brunch. My sisters. They'll kill me."

Izzy let out a quiet laugh, shook her head, and slipped out of his grip with practiced ease.

He exhaled sharply—half groan, half plea—like her absence had physically hurt.

She didn't look back. Just padded toward the bathroom, bare-legged and unbothered.

"Sounds like you've got a busy day ahead of you, Captain Social."

"Yeah," he said. "After brunch, I'm taking my nephew to the Bluey experience at CAMP. He's gonna lose his tiny mind. I've been watching clips to prep."

She'd stopped in the doorway of the bathroom. Gave him a look.

"You're studying for Bluey."

He nodded, dead serious and put on a pair of jeans from his suitcase. "I need context. I can't just walk in blind."

She stared. "You're not flying a leg, Nico. You're taking a toddler to what is essentially an overpriced merch store."

He shrugged. "Same thing. High stakes. Limited snacks. Unexpected turbulence."

She rolled her eyes so hard it was a miracle she didn't sprain something. "You're a dork."

"And prepared," he said, already checking train times like this was a military op. "But what about you? Any plans?"

She stretched. Casual. Not entirely decent. "Workout. Then I might swing by that pilot mixer later in the evening. See if I can dig around about the software issue."

He paused mid-button. "That thing the CTO emailed about?"

"Yeah. Fancy apartment by Columbus Circle. Skyline views, overpriced canapés, some kind of all-hands post-meeting for pilots and engineers. You get it too?"

He nodded. "Yep. Same invite."

She adjusted her slip in a way that made him visibly swallow.

He made a soft sound. Half laugh, half groan. But he didn't look away.

Just stood there, halfway dressed, watching her like something unspoken had just changed.

She glanced over at him, catching the look. "What?"

He shook his head. "Nothing."

She pursed her lips.

"I've survived worse sausage fests. I was once one of two women at some niche avionics summit—a hundred men, all deeply committed to explaining systems like I hadn't taught half the LUMA fleet how to run a sim failure."

And that—that—was when it flickered.

Something low and dark in his face. Quick. Animal. Gone as soon as it surfaced.

She didn't comment. But she noticed.

She grabbed his room's complimentary water bottle and drank half its contents. Casual. Unbothered.

"Cy and André are coming. They'll get their skyline pics and keep me from strangling anyone"

Nico nodded from where he was jamming feet into clean white sneakers. "You think you'll get anything useful out of this thing?"

She glanced over her shoulder. "Maybe. If the ego fog clears long enough for someone to admit the software's broken."

He winced. "I could go too."

She turned, suspicious. "It's not mandatory."

He blinked. "I could also go as support? Wingman. Quiet muscle?"

Her look could've burned a hole through the floor.

"You're volunteering to be background noise so I can inter-
rogate half the room?"

"Exactly," he said, hopeful. "I'll stand near the snacks
and pretend to be normal."

She folded her arms. "And if some captain starts talking
about his time on the triple-seven and tries to bond with
you over flap schedules?"

He shrugged. "I'll fake a phone call. Or start speaking
Arabic. Throw him off."

That one earned him a blink. Not approval, exactly. But
a consideration.

"So I can come?" he asked again, like a dog who'd
brought his own leash.

She sighed. "Fine. But don't come crying to me when
André makes you take his next round of thirst traps on
portrait mode."

He grinned. "Deal."

20

The apartment defied gravity and good taste.

Top floor of a skyscraper on Billionaires' Row, one of those residential monuments to generational theft that jutted into the Manhattan skyline like a middle finger made of glass. The entire north wall looked down on Central Park—an aerial view of old money, curated joggers, and other people's children.

You didn't *live* in a place like this. You staged it. Curated it.

Hosted summits for the morally flexible and hired freelance models to fill the frame so no one noticed the actual gender ratio.

Inside, the air smelled like polished chrome, expensive failure, and Louis Roederer Cristal Brut. Bottles chilled in brushed steel buckets, lined up with military precision near the open bar. Every flute poured by staff in crisp black vests who had clearly been instructed not to make eye contact, but had also collectively decided they were one comment away from pushing a billionaire over the balcony and calling it praxis.

The crowd was a split ecosystem:

Pilots—clustered in groups, too loud, too rich, too smug. Mostly retired, mostly male. The kind of men who'd flown widebodies across oceans for decades, racked up international pay and divorce alimony like frequent flyer miles, and now consulted at outrageous rates to feel important.

They wore their dress uniforms like medals. Braid at the cuff, silver wings shining. Some had jackets unbuttoned, ties loosened just enough to seem casual, but the flex was clear: *we still run the sky.*

Tech—younger, thinner, hungrier. Some still clinging to the hoodie-and-sneaker mythos, others overdressed like they'd Googled "old money" and landed on loafers and attitude.

The aviation start-up crowd tried to blend, but you could tell the ones who'd actually built something from scratch—their eyes flicked to the exits every time a pilot raised his voice.

Even here, survival instincts stayed sharp.

Then Izzy walked in.

Dress uniform. Rank bars sharp, collar pressed. No wings—she didn't need the introduction.

She crossed the threshold and the temperature shifted. Not visibly. Just enough.

People noticed.

Men turned.

Some recognized her. Some weren't sure. But the sharp ones—the ones who paid attention when power walked into a room—clocked the ring finger. Bare. For the first time in six years.

Their gaze landed the way it always did—possessive, practiced, and boring.

She'd assumed, somewhere around thirty-eight, that it would taper off.

It hadn't.

If anything, the absence of a ring made it worse—sharpened their interest, made her a possibility again.

Not a woman. A vacancy.

She registered them all. Didn't break stride.

She wasn't here to charm anyone.

She was here to dig.

About the software. The glitch. The silence around it.

She had Cy and André working the perimeter.

And now—Nico, trailing somewhere behind, trying not to look like he was tracking her every move while absolutely doing that.

The lighting was gold and glass. The noise was laughter and ambition. The stakes were quiet but nuclear.

Izzy stepped into the center of it, heels soundless on marble, eyes hard.

THE FIRST GROUP was already clustered near the terrace doors—half-circle formation, champagne and blazer buttons tight, talking shop in that low, smug register that never really invited interruption. All of them older than her.

Izzy let them notice her gradually. Not with a grand entrance—just a quiet drift into the periphery, a half-smile at Captain Frears, a nod at Monroe, an offered hand with the same touch she used to disconnect autopilot at high altitude: precise, barely felt.

"Ventura," Frears greeted her, eyebrows arching. "Didn't think you came to these anymore."

"I don't," she said, warm enough to pass for sincere. "But it's been a while. And you all clean up nice."

They laughed. She took a sip of champagne. Just waited. Listened. Let them make room.

It wasn't until the conversation turned to fleet upgrades that she slid it in, casual, like a stitch through silk.

"I heard they're accelerating rollout on the new suite," she said. "Couple of the FOs noticed some odd behavior on the MFD out of SFO."

Monroe shrugged. "Yeah, we got that one. Glitchy UI, nothing serious. They're patching it."

"I've seen it too," she said. "Slight lag on mode transitions. Doesn't trigger ECAMs, but it's... noticeable."

"Teething issues," Frears replied. "They'll work it out. Flying's 90% automation now anyway."

Another pilot chimed in—someone she'd flown with back in Madrid. "You worried it'll mess with your hand-flying?"

She smiled without showing teeth. "I didn't learn to fly on cruise control."

She didn't say Annapolis. Didn't need to. The way she said it—controlled, grounded, lethal—was enough. Military-trained, not commercial. She didn't come up through some sanitized simulator pipeline. She learned it with G-forces, stall warnings, and men who didn't care if she made it back.

It landed—but gently. Enough for one of them to pause, then shake his head like she was just being charming.

Hal spoke up then—of course he did. "Maybe it's the younger crowd getting jittery. No one taught stick-and-rudder like they used to."

She didn't look at him. Just turned to Frears instead, like

Hal hadn't spoken. "I've logged the bug with tech ops. Just thought I'd see if anyone else had seen it."

Frears offered her the kind of smile men give their daughters when they're wrong but trying. "Appreciate the thoroughness. They'll figure it out."

"Of course," she said, setting down her glass. "Just doing my part."

"That's our girl." Again, from Hal.

SHE LEFT them before they could dismiss her twice. Not in a huff—just a pivot, efficient and frictionless, like a well-executed turn in clear air.

The next cluster was easier to look at—tailored suits, better shoes, newer watches. The next-gen captains. West Coast-flavored, buzzword-fluent, men who thought being married to women made them feminists. They greeted Izzy like they were proud of her, which told her everything she needed to know.

"Captain Ventura," one of them beamed. Mattson. Flew 787s. Hosted a podcast about leadership. "Heard you're on the Singapore-JFK rotation. That's a beast."

"It is," she said. "But I like the long haul."

"Of course you do. You've always had range."

She let that hang. A smile, no commitment.

They made space like they were doing her a favor. Offered her a drink—declined. She already had enough bubbles in her system and bullshit in her ears.

They talked fleet upgrades. Buzzwords stacked like Jenga blocks: systems architecture, cross-functional input streams, user-centric design.

She let them talk. Waited.

Then, lightly: "Has anyone been flying with the new suite in live ops?"

Three heads turned.

"Oh, we haven't been assigned it yet," Mattson admitted. "But I've been in the briefings. It looks solid."

She nodded. "We've seen some screen behavior out of SFO and SEA. Minor, but... glitchy."

They stilled. The mood shifted.

"Tech will get ahead of it. Growing pains."

"Maybe," she said. "But we're flying it now. It's not hypothetical."

The silence cracked, just a little.

One of them forced a smile.

She gave a nod so small it barely counted. Then left, efficient as ever.

She was gone before they could suggest inviting her on their podcast.

IZZY FOUND her near the bar, alone by choice. Captain Delaney. Atlantic routes, nearly four decades deep, doesn't touch social media, still uses a paper logbook because it "helps her think." Her gray was blunt-cut and her blazer looked older than Izzy's flight career, but her presence was untouchable—like a ship that had weathered every storm and now refused to dock.

Izzy approached with less armor. A nod. A quiet hello. Respectful.

Delaney raised her glass. "Ventura. You still scaring the men?"

Izzy snorted. "Only the useful ones."

Delaney smirked and took a sip. "Good."

They stood for a moment in silence. The air between

them was easy. Then Izzy, because she still hadn't learned to let go, asked, "You flown with the new suite yet?"

Delaney exhaled. "God, not tonight."

Izzy waited.

Delaney set her drink down. "I'm not getting into it. I log what I see. I file what I have to. Beyond that? I'm two years out. I'm just trying to pay off the Alaskan homestead."

Izzy blinked. "I'm not asking you to blow anything up."

"I know. But you've got that face on. Like you're building a case." She turned and looked at Izzy directly. "I'm not your exhibit."

That one stung. Not sharp—just blunt.

Izzy drew back slightly. "Okay. Fair."

Delaney softened by a millimeter. "You're not wrong, by the way. About the software. About all of it. But I fought those fights in the '90s. They nearly ate me alive. You want to jump into that meat grinder again, be my guest. But don't look at me like I owe you backup."

"I wasn't," Izzy said quietly.

Delaney raised an eyebrow.

Izzy sighed. "Okay. I was. That's on me."

Delaney shrugged. "You'll get smarter about it."

Izzy was already turning to go when Delaney added, "For what it's worth, I like your odds better than mine ever were. You don't flinch."

Izzy paused. "Not in public."

"Good girl," Delaney said. Then picked her drink back up and turned toward the terrace, already out of reach.

A voice behind her.

"Captain Ventura. Mind if I borrow you?"

She turned. Not slowly—deliberately.

Another man in dress uniform. Another vague smile. Her whole body prepped for a sales pitch or a compliment she'd have to pretend not to hear.

But the man was older. Crisp, understated, handsome in that aviation royalty kind of way—the kind of face that had been in cockpits since birth and in lineages since Pan Am. No drink. Just the quiet confidence of a man born into the sky and raised to command a room without raising his voice.

Kieran O'Hara.

Captain. Married to Morgan Delgado, CEO of LUMA US.

He didn't need to perform. He'd already won the only arms race that mattered.

"I heard you've been asking about the software," he said.

"I have."

"Good," he said. "So have I."

He didn't lower his voice. Didn't scan the crowd like a conspirator. Just stood there, calm and weathered, like he'd been in worse rooms with better lies.

"I've been reading up on the rollout schedule," he said. "The Airbus installs are coming faster than the Boeing ones. They're not saying why."

Izzy tilted her head just slightly. Testing. Not for truth—for nerve.

"The diagnostic tool," she said. "It's not flagging standby reversion failures. I've seen two. Uncommanded logic flips. Nothing on ECAM."

Kieran exhaled through his nose. Not surprise. Just confirmation. Like he'd been waiting for someone else to say it out loud.

"I haven't flown the new package yet," he said. "But I've

looked at their patch notes they are burying under layers of documentation."

She nodded once. Small. Controlled.

He leaned in, fractionally.

"If this goes wider—if you take it upstairs—it can't come from the CEO's husband."

"I know that," she said. Flat. No flinch.

"I'm not asking for cover," she added. "I'm asking if I'm the only one seeing it."

"You're not," he said. "You're just the only one saying it in daylight."

The tension was quiet. Not hostile. But real.

He didn't offer comfort. Didn't tell her she was brave. Just watched her—like a pilot checks a holding pattern, measuring fuel and risk.

Then, clean as a checklist item, he reached into his blazer and handed her a folded card.

"I want to help off-record. If it escalates, you didn't hear anything from me."

"Copy," she said.

There was nothing performative about it. No fist-pump alliance. Just two people in uniform, acknowledging a crack in the system they weren't allowed to name.

He was already slipping away when she almost said something—thank you. But he was gone.

Blended perfectly into the wallpaper of respectable men.

She looked at the card in her hand. Then she put it in her pocket.

And then Russell Cayne, Chief Technology Officer of LUMA Air US, arrived.

She felt him before she saw him. That instinct that

precedes turbulence—the slight shift in air pressure, the heat of something about to cost you.

"Captain Ventura."

She turned again. Slower this time. Composed.

He was all polish and pitch. Impeccable suit, too-white teeth, the calculated relaxation of someone who knows he has leverage and enjoys pretending otherwise.

"Glad I caught you," he said, smiling like this was a friendly reunion and not a perimeter check. "We haven't had a chance to talk, have we? In person, I mean."

She turned. Slowly. Professional face on. Hands calm. Heart not.

"No," she said. "We haven't."

"Well, first—welcome back. You look well. Really...well-rested."

Her face didn't move. But her fingers curled tighter around the stem of her glass.

The rest wasn't spoken. Didn't need to be.

They both knew what was really being said.

That her absence wasn't a secret. That her file had been read, probably passed around.

That one wrong set of eyes on the wrong line, and she'd be grounded for good.

Not just here. Anywhere.

Russell took a sip of his drink, then tilted his head—mock concern, polished to perfection.

"I did want to mention—just so you're in the loop—we saw a few of the tickets you flagged. About the software. The ones that were... overwritten."

Izzy didn't answer. Just held his gaze.

He smiled like he was being generous. "I think the concern came down to tone, really. Not the content. But, you know, with the rollout, marketing's been a little sensitive about optics. Having reports that sound…volatile—it doesn't help confidence."

He said "volatile" like it was a diagnosis. Like it came from a risk matrix already circulated behind closed doors, her name highlighted in red.

"I completely understand why you logged them," he went on. "But sometimes these things land differently when they come from someone still transitioning back into operational status."

There it was.

Her health. Her leave. Her credibility, subtly yanked out from under her and handed back with a smile.

"If you're still seeing interface issues," he added, tone light, "I'd suggest routing them through flight ops. Let them triage. No need to escalate anything directly."

The word *escalate* landed like a door slamming shut.

"We just want to keep things running smoothly. For you. For everyone."

And then he smiled again. Close. Warm. Like a noose made of velvet.

Then he was gone.

Izzy stood still.

The rooftop noise surged around her—cutlery, jazz, champagne laughter, the wet clink of ice in tumblers. Someone nearby misquoted a flight hour stat. Someone else laughed too loudly at something that wasn't funny.

But she didn't hear it.

Not really.

Her glass was empty. Her pulse was not.

And for the first time all night, it wasn't anger pooling behind her ribs.

It was dread. Cold and precise. Like pre-stall buffet. Like watching a red fail light flicker on and knowing you can't say anything.

21

What struck him first—every time—was her voice.

The uniform was polished. The way she held her champagne, deliberate. But her voice—low, raspy, feminine but edged—that cut deep. It held rank. It carried weight.

Nico leaned back, bourbon in hand, pretending he wasn't tracking every syllable. But he was. God, he was. Because he knew the other version of that voice. The one she made when her breath caught. When she was underneath him, just unraveling.

And no one else here knew that sound.

It mattered more than it should've.

She stood with the senior captains. Not smiling. Just letting them orbit. The stars of old aviation, dripping legacy and pension. She was sharper and more dangerous. And still, somehow, the one they underestimated.

He stayed by the terrace railing. Bourbon low. Posture easy. Watching without looking like he was watching.

He'd been to a few of these events now, and they still felt

like a setup. Suits. Polished glass. People with yachts and clean fingernails. Before LUMA, the fanciest thing he'd ever been invited to was a bachelor party in Lexington that ended with a fight over who stole the bottle service. And once, during his deployment rotation, he flew an Iraqi diplomat to Riyadh and stood beside the car in full dress blues while someone else gave the speech. He was the driver. Not the guest.

And now?

New York City rooftop. Billionaire view. His name on a badge. A uniform that fit too well. A body honed to pass checkrides and notice shifts in cabin pressure like they were omens.

She tilted her head at something Frears said. Laughed once. Not a real laugh—a deployment laugh. The kind you make when someone says something off but you're at work, so you just log it for later.

Nico caught himself watching her throat when she swallowed.

Get it together, Farruh.

He shifted his stance, smoothed his mouth. Tried not to think about how, twelve hours ago, his hand was under that silky black thing she wore—Izzy half-asleep, moaning into his chest—right before his phone lit up with a *Where are you???* from his sisters.

Brunch. He'd promised his sisters *brunch*. Weeks ago. With Layla and Samira and his nephew.

He had nearly fucking blacked out.

Now Izzy was thirty feet away, in full uniform, lit by skyline and disdain. She looked like authority. And the men here didn't know what to do with her except pretend they weren't rattled.

He knew better.

He knew what her hands felt like when they stopped holding restraint. He knew how she fought—how she surrendered. He knew the part of her voice that cracked when she couldn't hold it back anymore, and how quickly she rebuilt it.

She turned, just slightly, and scanned the room. Not making eye contact. Just... assessing. Like a soldier checking her perimeter.

HE WAS HALFWAY through his drink when someone stepped into his space—LA beauty aesthetic, skin like a filter, all angles and ambition.

"You're LUMA, right?" she asked—not a question, a flex.

Soraya Vale. He clocked the poster board near the bar—some branded tequila she was selling upfront. Travel influencer. Reality TV star, maybe? Brand deals for luggage, skincare. A portfolio, not a resume. She sized him up like he was a prop.

Behind her, two guys in loafers and no socks were already half-talking over each other about "the branding potential of lifestyle aviation."

Soraya's smile didn't reach her eyes. "Tell me you're not just a First Officer."

Nico blinked, bourbon in hand. "Guilty," he said. "I'm the backup dancer. The captain's the star. I just smile and nod and try not to get sued."

Her eyes swept over him—slow, appraising, like she was calculating a bid.

"Oh, come on," she said, blinking up at him through heavy, exaggerated lashes—falsies so long they could swat flies. "You *look* like a captain. That uniform doesn't wear you —you wear it."

That's when pastel-suit-guy launched into the pitch—Love Island meets Top Gun, pilots as lifestyle content, "confessionals at thirty-five-thousand feet."

Nico tilted his glass, slow, as the guy spoke.

Then he moved. Subtle, efficient. Shifted his stance by a hair, just enough to make the guy nearest him adjust, unconsciously. A ripple of movement, like a chess piece nudged mid-game. The guy's glass wobbled—Nico's hand flicked out, steadying it without a word. A quiet, practiced intervention. The guy muttered a thanks, slightly off-balance, and Soraya glanced away, distracted by a sudden burst of laughter across the terrace.

Nico used the angle—stepped around, tracing the perimeter like he was just stretching his legs. Never in a straight line, always slow, fluid, blending into the flow of bodies.

By the time she turned back, half a question on her lips—he was already gone.

The other side of the balcony was cold glass and city light. Nico wanted to find a quieter spot to take a picture to send to his sisters. Izzy was still inside, mid-conversation with a Bombardier pilot. Figured that was going to take awhile.

Then he heard her name.

"Ventura," said the man with the scotch. Hal. Delta now. LUMA exile. "Still walks like she owns the airspace, huh?"

Nico turned, slow.

Hal leaned back in his chair like he thought he was funny.

"I flew with her a few times back in the day. Back when she still had that fresh-outta-training shine. Bright-eyed and sweet. Still pretending not to know we were all watching her."

A LUMA FO—mid-30s, good rep—set his drink down and stepped away from the group.

"I'm gonna head in."

Didn't say why. Just left. Shoulders stiff.

Another LUMA pilot, older, stayed.

"Hal," he said quietly. "You're out of line."

But that was it. No escalation. Just that stunned, heavy freeze.

And Hal kept talking.

"What? All I'm saying is, she's the kind that makes you work for it. All polish, all performance. Bet under all that attitude she's just waiting for someone to shove her up against a bulkhead and remind her she's not in charge."

No one laughed. But no one stopped him either.

And that's when Nico turned. Walked back inside.

Not in a rush.

Just recalibrating the rest of his night.

THE HALLWAY WAS QUIET. Dimmed lighting. One of those luxury condo corridors no one was supposed to linger in.

Nico walked like he belonged there and no one questioned it.

Hal had peeled off from the rest of the group a few minutes earlier, half-drunk on mixer booze and his own ego.

Nico didn't say anything at all.

He just waited until the moment was quiet enough to follow him without looking suspicious. Until the two of them were alone.

Then it was just a matter of timing. He cut the corner, closed the distance, and—

Contact.

A sharp step in, elbow forward, driving into the kidney

line with precision. Not full force. Just enough to make the man seize up, stumble, and make that low, ugly noise people make when their organs get surprised.

Nico caught him by the shoulder as he collapsed.

"Shit," he murmured, just loud enough to pass for concern. "You okay, man?"

The guy couldn't speak. Nico helped him to a bench. Smiled. Took a glass of water from the catering table nearby and handed it over like a medic.

"Could've sworn that corner was tighter. Watch your footing."

The guy gasped, trying to speak, bent over with both hands on his knees.

That's when Nico leaned down, real close to his ear. Low enough that it wouldn't travel. Low enough to change a man's behavior.

"Say her name like that again, and I'll make sure you piss through a bag for the rest of your life."

Silence. One breath. Two.

Then Nico straightened, patted the man's shoulder like nothing had happened.

"Back spasms? Been there, man."

He stood back, checked his sleeves, and turned to leave.

That's when he saw her.

Izzy. Standing ten feet down the hallway, arms folded, eyes locked on him like he'd just grown a second head.

Nico didn't stop walking until they were in the elevator. She cut him off before he could slip past. The elevator closed behind her.

"Are you serious right now?"

He raised an eyebrow. Played it cool. "What?"

Izzy stepped into his space, not backing down. Her voice

wasn't raised—but it was surgical. Furious in that quiet, devastating way she did best.

"Do you actually want to make captain, or are you just out here handing LUMA legal reasons to skip you? Because I don't care what he said—this isn't a combat zone, and you don't get to pretend it is just because your ego's twitching."

Nico didn't blink. Just held her gaze.

"If that's all you're worried about," he said, voice even, "then don't."

A breath. He could feel it land. The way her expression shifted—confusion at first, then something heavier.

"I was trained to end fights without leaving fingerprints," he added, softer. "This didn't even register."

She stared at him. Full stop. No expression. Then—

"What the fuck."

He shrugged. Not cocky. Just honest.

"It wasn't for you. Not really. It was for me. Because I've been letting people say shit my whole life. And tonight? I didn't feel like letting it slide."

She stepped back half a pace. Looked at him like he was made of something she couldn't categorize yet.

"You're out of your mind."

"Probably."

"You think that's comforting?"

"No."

They stood there in the glow of the elevator. And Nico thought—she's still here. She hadn't screamed and tried to get off at the next floor. She was still looking at him like he was a problem she might not want to solve.

"Izzy," he said, voice quieter now, "I know how to fly clean. I know how to fly dirty. I know how to fight and make it look like breathing. But I'm not reckless."

She didn't respond. Just looked at him like she was reading a checklist.

"I'm not going to ruin this," he said. "I want it too much."

The job, the title—sure.

But it was her. That was the part he couldn't afford to lose.

She shook her head slowly, exhaled like he was giving her heartburn.

"You're a fucking lunatic."

He smiled, just a little. "Still here though."

She rolled her eyes. Bit the inside of her cheek.

Then walked past him, toward the opening door.

But he heard it—the click of her boots slowing just before she turned the corner.

And he let himself breathe again.

22

They were standing in the wind tunnel of Midtown, that cursed intersection of glass and ego known as Billionaires' Row, and Nico Farrah looked like he was about to throw up.

Which was strange.

Because five minutes ago, this man had threatened another senior pilot so quietly and so precisely it had sounded like a bedtime story. Izzy had watched him fold a man's organs in with a casual elbow jab, then deliver a whispered promise that would've made an interrogator sweat. And now he was standing next to her on the sidewalk, shifting from foot to foot, like he wasn't sure how to operate in open air.

Izzy narrowed her eyes.

They were technically done for the evening. The event had ended. Cy and Andre hopped into a yellow cab to meet the other FAs for drinks. The other pilots had scattered. The sky was bruising into late twilight, the city humming with dinner plans, resentment, and Uber surge pricing. She was just about to hail a ride when Nico spoke.

"So—" he started, then stopped. Cleared his throat.

She looked at him. He didn't meet her eyes.

There was a tightness in his expression, the kind of tension that only showed up when he wasn't flying. On a flight deck, he was calm. Composed. A little too composed, sometimes, like it was all muscle memory and stillness. But here, with no instruments to monitor and no checklists to distract him, he seemed suddenly, wildly human.

Izzy waited.

Nico exhaled through his nose. "Okay, um. I had a plan. But I forgot it. Because you looked at me like that."

She blinked. "Like what?"

"Like you were about to grade me."

"That's just my face."

He gave her a helpless, lopsided smile. "Yeah, see, that's the problem."

It was so earnest she didn't know what to do with it.

He ran a hand through his hair. "Right. Okay. What I was trying to say was that I, uh, I have a thing tonight."

"A thing."

He nodded, rapidly. "Yeah. A non-creepy thing. Totally safe. Normal. Not weird. Just—it's in the Lower East Side. My sister's taping her Netflix special. It's kind of a big deal."

Izzy narrowed her eyes. "Wait—you're telling me your sister's a stand-up comic with a Netflix deal? That's real?"

Nico winced like he knew how it sounded. "I swear to God. She's funny. Like, professional funny."

"Right..."

He inhaled again. Hands in his pockets now, like that would hide how tense he was. "Look. I'm not asking for, like, a big thing. You don't even have to stay the whole time. Just —you want to come? With me? It's kind of short notice. And we're still in uniform, but it's casual, and she won't care. And it's not drinks or anything, because I know we have to fly in less than ten hours, and—"

"Nico."

He stopped. Like she'd thrown a switch.

She watched him. His cheeks were flushed, and not from cold. His tie was crooked. He looked so uncomfortable. It was disarming.

"I'm just going to make sure I have this straight," she said slowly. "You just delivered a credible medical threat to another pilot—without blinking. But asking me to a comedy show is what's breaking you?"

He groaned, low and guttural. "God. Yeah. I know. It's— look, I'm not trying to be—"

"Deranged?"

"Exactly."

"You already failed."

"Yep."

She paused.

It *was* deranged, honestly. He shouldn't be able to pull this off. She should have said no. For every professional reason, for every boundary she'd spent her whole adult life carving into stone.

But instead—

She exhaled. Tucked a flyaway strand behind her ear.

"It sounds like the setup to a weird lie."

"It's not. She's—Look, you'll see. If it sucks, we can pretend it never happened."

"You're really selling this."

He winced. "Yeah, I'm not great at this."

She crossed her arms. Looked him up and down. "You're trying to ask me out to your sister's Netflix taping while we're both in uniform and still sweating from a pilot mixer."

"When you say it like that it sounds completely horrible."

"And insane."

A breath.

"But sure," she said. "Why not."

He blinked. "Wait. You'll go?"

They stood there for a moment, the traffic noise thick behind them, the skyline flexing like it knew it cost ten million a square foot to exist.

"I'll go."

Then he offered her his arm. Playfully. Nervously.

And she—God help her—took it.

They didn't look like a couple. They looked like pilots who'd walked off shift and accidentally wandered into each other's gravity. But when she felt the tension in his body start to ease under her hand, she didn't let go.

Not even when she realized what she'd just agreed to.

A date.

With Nico Farrah.

Who had just threatened permanent catheterization for her honor then had the nerve to blush about a comedy special.

She didn't know whether to commit to this or call a cab.

But the warmth in her chest was already making the decision for her.

23

It was stupid how much fun she was having.

Worse, it was easy.

Somewhere between Billionaires' Row and the Lower East Side, the edge she kept in her shoulders had started to fall. Not all at once—more like a careful unzipping. Nico had kept pace beside her like he was trying not to spook a wild animal, throwing out dumb jokes and weird facts and self-deprecating one-liners like he was auditioning for her trust and didn't want to admit it. Which, apparently, he was nailing.

She hated how often he made her laugh.

She hated more how much she liked the sound of it when he joined in.

It was late, and the city was blooming in that reckless way it only does after ten—humid air thick with exhaust and cheap perfume, streetlights bleeding gold into puddles, people everywhere, alive like they'd never have to sleep again. Nico tugged her gently by the hand through a side alley she never would've walked alone, murmuring, "This way," like he had a map in his blood.

There was a door. A clipboard. A guy with a headset who barely looked up before nodding and letting them in.

Apparently, Nico Farrah was on the list.

Inside was organized chaos—people shouting into walkies, a flurry of makeup brushes, cables, camera rigs, snacks laid out next to LED panels and security tape. Izzy didn't know what she'd expected, but it wasn't...this. It wasn't production. There were comics wandering around in hoodies and Crocs, stagehands in black cargo pants, a woman covered in rhinestones rehearsing into a hairbrush. Izzy was pretty sure she clocked two people she'd seen on Comedy Central, but no one else was acting impressed, so she swallowed it.

Then Layla walked in.

And everything clicked.

The voice. The face. The perfectly arched eyebrow.

Izzy had seen her—on TikToks in crew vans, on flight attendant group chats, stitched into viral takedowns that made even the pilots laugh. Layla Farrah wasn't just famous. She was loud. Dangerous in the way only women with nothing left to lose could be.

She was also holding a half-asleep toddler on one hip and barking into her phone while a glam team tried to fix her eyeliner.

"I swear to fucking God if he's not here in sixty seconds I'm making Ahsan open the show."

Then she turned, spotted Nico, and lit up with the particular joy of someone who lives to humiliate her siblings.

"You're late," she announced, dumping the kid into his arms without ceremony.

"Sorry," Nico said, already bracing, catching the toddler with practiced ease. "Subway delays."

Layla wasn't listening. Her eyes had already shifted—locked onto Izzy with the sharp, delighted focus of someone connecting a very satisfying set of dots.

"Is this who I think it is?" she asked, already grinning.

Nico hesitated. "This is Izzy."

Layla lit up. "Oh captain, my captain," she sang, waggling her eyebrows. "I get it now."

Izzy didn't even have time to react before Layla took her hands—firm grip, glossy nails, no hesitation—and said, "It's so nice to meet you," with the kind of syrupy tone that made Izzy's brain short-circuit.

She flinched.

Because Layla was looking at her in that way—sharp-eyed, delighted, like she'd just unwrapped a surprise she hadn't ordered but was absolutely keeping.

Her grip was warm. Two hands, not one. The kind of greeting that lingered a beat too long.

Izzy's pulse spiked for reasons she didn't want to examine. She wasn't used to being seen like this. Definitely not by beautiful, famous women in full glam with toddlers on their hips. Layla hadn't even blinked. Hadn't hesitated. She'd sized her up like a pattern she'd cut before.

And beneath all of it—the handshake, the grin, the obvious amusement—was something heavier. Not dangerous, exactly. Just alive. Like Layla was turning a dial Izzy didn't know she had.

It was destabilizing. Unfair. And weirdly...kind.

Nico was still standing there, holding the sleeping toddler like a hostage and staring at the wall like maybe if he didn't move, this whole moment would go away. She glanced over at him for support, but he looked like his soul had left his body ten seconds ago.

Izzy didn't have time to decide how to feel about it,

because a headset-wearing producer popped in and barked, "LET'S GO LAYLA, you're on in two, stop being weird!" and Layla just winked at both of them, and vanished toward the wings.

They were hustled into a VIP side room with a couch, a monitor, plates of snacks, chilled water, and a gift bag that had Layla's face on a bottle of hot sauce.

Izzy blinked. "What the hell did you bring me to?"

Nico grinned, adjusting Ahsan without waking him. "You said yes."

Then the lights went down.

Layla's entrance was nothing short of surgical. The crowd roared before she spoke.

And then she did—opened with a single, devastating line about growing up Arab in Kentucky after 9/11. The kind of line that cracked open a room.

"Y'all remember Brandon?" she asked, pacing the stage in thigh-highs and a blazer dress. "He called me a slur every single day in third grade. I'd like to thank him personally for the trauma that landed me this Netflix deal. Eat shit, Brandon."

You could feel the air rearrange itself. Someone in the back gasped. The audience didn't know whether to laugh or cheer. So they did both.

Izzy howled.

It didn't stop there. Layla kept landing blows—sharpened jokes about being brown and invisible and then suddenly a threat. About how her little brother joined the military to "prove he was patriotic enough to not get body-checked at airports," and how white Americans were obsessed with being scammed by brown people while simultaneously scamming them with the myth of the American Dream.

"And the irony is? Nico never got pulled into secondary. Not once. Me, my littler sister, our dad—we all got the "random" searches. But Nico? Green eyes, dirty blond hair, cheekbones like a recruitment ad? TSA saw him and probably offered him a job."

Izzy nearly choked on her water. The irony was nauseating—and so completely real it hurt.

Next to her, Nico turned and stared at her like she'd just committed a hate crime. His mouth was open in theatrical betrayal.

"You're laughing?" he whispered. "At our trauma?"

She stiffened slightly. "Jesus. Should I not be?"

His face cracked into a grin. "Relax. We workshopped that one together."

She looked back at the stage, trying not to let it show how much that eased something in her chest.

They didn't just survive it. They'd weaponized it.

And they were letting her laugh too. And she couldn't stop. It was not polite. It was from her gut. From somewhere she hadn't heard in years. She clutched her stomach. She wiped her eyes. She couldn't remember the last time she felt like this—alive and absurd and just happy to be exactly where she was.

Nico looked over at her. Still holding the toddler. Still glowing with secondhand sibling panic.

"She's making you laugh more than I do," he said, mock wounded. "I'm jealous."

"Maybe you should be," Izzy said without thinking.

He turned a little pale. She pretended not to notice.

When the set ended, Layla came offstage like a rockstar—sweaty, radiant, vibrating with adrenaline. She didn't pause to bask. She was already scanning for her son.

Nico stepped forward without a word, shifting Ahsan more securely in his arms.

Layla reached them, pressed a kiss to each of Nico's cheeks like it was ritual, then brushed a palm gently over the sleeping toddler's hair. She murmured something soft, just for the two of them, and then turned sharply toward her handler to bark a command about traffic and car seats.

Izzy found herself moving without needing direction. She slung the diaper bag over her shoulder, followed Nico out to the curb, and helped as they loaded Ahsan into the VIP SUV waiting to whisk Layla and her kid back to her Brooklyn apartment.

It wasn't glamorous. It was quiet. Fluid. The three of them moving in sync like they'd done this before.

Once Ahsan was strapped in, Layla turned to Izzy, expression unreadable for half a second.

Then:

"This boy's a gem," she said, nodding toward her brother. "Hope you're not blind."

And with one last flying kiss, she was gone, the car peeling off.

Izzy didn't speak for a minute.

They walked. Up the Lower East Side, past bodegas and twenty-four-hour pizza joints and a street performer doing bad magic for a tourist couple in matching denim jackets. They walked through the pressurized quiet that only New York offered at 2:30 in the morning—when the chaos had cooled just enough to let the city breathe.

They didn't talk about the show.

They didn't talk about the fact that Nico had held her hand the entire way out of the venue and hadn't let go.

They just talked. About dumb things. About food. About flying. About how hot dogs were legally not food, and which US airport had the worst coffee, and which flight attendant at LUMA definitely had an OnlyFans—and was probably paying off a mortgage with it.

They both agreed this FA was the most competent person on the entire fleet and that they'd miss her desperately once she hit millionaire status and quit on a Thursday with zero notice. Which, honestly, she could do any day now.

She didn't realize they'd walked all the way to 14th Street until they passed the bodega that only sold gluten-free snacks.

By the time they got back to the hotel, there were maybe four hours left until duty.

They walked in just before dawn. The lobby was empty, still humming faintly with whatever expensive air systems kept everything sterile and still. Neither of them spoke in the elevator. Neither of them needed to.

By the time they reached her floor, the toddler drool had dried on Nico's shirt. Her boots hurt. Her shoulders ached. But she wasn't ready for the night to end.

He walked her to her door. Hands in his pockets. That same look on his face like he was holding back twelve different impulses. She had the same ones. Maybe more.

They didn't escalate.

Not because they didn't want to.

But because—stupid as it sounded—this had been a first date. A real one.

A beginning.

And somewhere between Layla's trauma jokes and the

way his hand had held hers like it wasn't a casual thing, it had become obvious that if this turned into something physical right now, it would short-circuit whatever fragile restart they'd just earned.

So he kissed her—softly, just once—and pulled back like he meant it. Like he wanted her to remember it.

She stood there, stunned.

Then she turned, stepped inside, and shut the door before she could change her mind.

Pressed her forehead to the door.

And whispered, "Oh, fuck."

Because he had her. And she knew it.

24

The morning after the best night of her year, Captain Isabel Ventura grounded a transatlantic flight.

Weather was fine. Crew was ready. The problem was something else entirely.

Her eyes were locked on the multi-function display, where the aircraft's navigation data was telling her a quiet lie.

The route across the Atlantic looked normal—until you zoomed in. Somewhere between their final U.S. waypoint and the first fix on the oceanic track, the aircraft's system had quietly skipped a step. It was tiny. A gap just wide enough for something to go very wrong at forty thousand feet.

If they lost comms, or had to divert with an engine out, and the nav system followed a route that didn't exist—

They wouldn't show up as off course. They'd just vanish —no transponder, no position report, only silence.

By the time anyone realized, they'd be out of fuel and out of sky.

And worse: the alternate airport she'd filed wasn't showing at all. Gone. As if Bergen didn't exist.

She tapped through to the fuel prediction page. The numbers looked clean at a glance—but they were off by four percent. Not huge. But enough. Enough to put them outside the safe window if anything went sideways mid-crossing.

"LUMA 604 holding at gate," she said into the mic. "Stand by."

Nico looked over. "What's up?"

She didn't answer. Her headset chimed again—Dispatch, calling through ACARS.

"Captain Ventura," said a man with a customer service voice and zero interest in listening. "Got your flag. What's the issue?"

"The route's broken," she said. "It's skipping a leg. Bergen isn't showing. Fuel prediction's off by four percent. Terrain overlay won't show past sixty nautical miles."

"Yeah, that's the patch from last night," he said. "It's just a visual thing—UI bug. Doesn't affect the actual flight."

Her whole expression retracted inward.

"That's not how this works," she said. "If I can't see where we're going or prove the fuel math checks out, I can't legally cross the Atlantic."

He huffed. "The plane's airworthy. MEL doesn't list this as a no-go item."

"MEL doesn't cover oceanic diversion procedures," she snapped. "You want me to launch an ETOPS flight with missing alternates and hope it doesn't matter?"

Another chime. New voice. Female. Professional. Polished in that way that meant trouble.

"Captain Ventura, this is Carla from Ops Control. We're hearing your concerns. Engineering has confirmed it's not a system failure—just a display issue. You can refer to your paper backups."

She didn't look away from the screen.

"The printouts don't match," she said. "They're based on the same corrupted software. Our dispatch plan is invalid, and I'm not flying over the Atlantic on faith."

There was a beat of silence.

Then: "You're within your discretion, of course. But this will be recorded as a pilot-initiated delay."

Izzy didn't flinch. "Good," she said. "Put my name on it. Make sure you spell it right."

She felt, more than saw, Nico freeze beside her.

"You see it too?" she asked without turning.

He nodded once. "Yeah. You're not wrong."

Her headset chirped again. Ground control this time.

"LUMA 604, confirm you're still holding?"

"Affirm. Flight's grounded. We're waiting on maintenance and re-dispatch."

"Copy. Holding at Gate 57."

The interphone buzzed again, sharper this time. The kind of buzz that meant they were running out of time.

"Captain," the forward FA said. "We've got passengers yelling, recording. One guy's standing in the aisle saying he knows a pilot at Delta and this would never happen on their fleet."

Nico snorted under his breath.

She didn't smile.

"They want answers," the FA said. "I've got crew getting overwhelmed. You want us to hold the door?"

Izzy looked at the screen one last time. Bergen was still gone. Fuel was still wrong. Terrain still cut off at sixty miles like the earth ended there.

They weren't flying.

And they weren't going to pretend they were.

She keyed the mic. Her voice was steady. "Start a controlled deplane."

There was a pause on the line. Even the FA wasn't ready for it.

"Confirm?" the voice came again, quieter now.

"Confirm," Izzy said. "Open the door. Let them off."

She heard the cabin explode—seatbelts unclicking, carry-ons yanked from overhead bins, voices shouting about missed weddings, connections, court dates. The usual cocktail of entitlement and panic. Someone slammed a bin shut with enough force to rattle the bulkhead.

Izzy didn't move.

She watched Nico instead. He didn't speak, didn't question her. He just nodded once again, like: *Yeah. You're doing it.*

Behind them, chaos reigned.

In front of her, the screen still showed a broken map.

And she could live with angry passengers. She could live with delay codes and union complaints and whatever bureaucratic hellstorm came next.

But what she couldn't live with?

A black box that told a different story than she did.

She could've flown it. Of course she could've flown it. She could've hand-flown that aircraft all the way to Heathrow on raw data and instinct, no automation, no displays. She knew that plane better than she knew most people.

But this wasn't about her.

It was about the system. About trusting software she knew was wrong, and being asked to fly anyway. And when something failed—because it always failed eventually—

they wouldn't ask if she had the skill. They'd ask why she didn't stop it.

So she did.

She opened the delay report, typed in the notes. Entered the code. Signed her name.

Clear. Final. Unapologetic.

25

She waited until everyone else was gone. Passengers first, then cabin crew, then ground. Last one off, like always. That was the job—you stayed with the aircraft. You walked off secondhand, used up, and calm.

Except this time, calm felt like a lie she didn't know how to perform anymore.

She stepped into the jetbridge and hit the wall of noise before she even saw them.

Passengers hadn't dispersed. Not all of them. A crowd had clustered near the gate podium—phones out, arms crossed, pulsing with that specific, ugly entitlement that air travel brings out in people who think turbulence is a conspiracy.

And someone must've pointed.

Because the moment she came into view, it started.

The booing.

Low at first. Then sharper. Scattered claps of derision. Someone muttered "took you long enough," and someone else, louder, said "hope you're proud of yourself." A teenager near the gate turned around and fake clapped like it was a fucking comedy roast.

She didn't flinch.

Didn't break stride.

Just walked straight through it—jacket on, eyes forward, expression blank. She didn't look for Nico. She didn't need to. He was already there.

She barely heard him say, "This way." Just felt the shift of air as he fell in beside her.

He guided her off the main concourse with quiet precision, down a hallway marked Authorized Personnel Only that no one stopped them from using. Just a corridor lined with vending machines and industrial beige, far from the cameras.

She didn't say a word until they stopped near a service elevator.

He handed her a bottle of water. She didn't drink it.

Eventually, they emerged back into the public side of Terminal 4. The departures board still showed their canceled flight like a scar.

She sank into a seat beneath it, skin crawling inside the fabric of her uniform.

Nico hovered just behind her. Out of frame. Silent. Solid.

No one was telling them to leave, but no one was giving them a flight either. LUMA was polite like that—purgatory in uniform.

Ops didn't call.

They emailed.

Not even the decency of a phone call or a rep looped in. Just corporate tone dressed up as concern: *We'll be reviewing the incident with Captain Ventura once she's had time to reflect.*

Reflect on what? That the cockpit display glitched? That they didn't die?

She re-read the email, slouched under a departure board.

Nico was next to her, inhaling a pretzel like it was a sport.

The concourse buzzed in its usual way: fluorescent, indifferent, laced with too much perfume and not enough ventilation. They stood near the standby list like they were waiting for God to clear them.

"Mom," a small voice whispered nearby. "That's a lady pilot."

Izzy turned. A six-year-old in glitter sneakers had clocked her. Half-hid behind a roller bag. Eyes wide like she was staring at a Marvel character.

The mom smiled, hesitant. "I'm so sorry to bother you, miss. She just—she wanted a photo. You're the first woman captain she's seen."

Izzy blinked. That brittle muscle behind her cheek tried to soften. "Of course," she said.

The mom fumbled with her phone. The girl crept beside Izzy, grinning like she was posing with Captain Marvel. Nico stepped out of frame without a word. The shutter clicked.

"Thank you so much," the mom said. The girl waved. They walked away.

Then—

"She looks like my pilot Barbie," the girl said, quiet, almost to herself.

Izzy didn't flinch. But she heard it. Nico definitely heard it. He was chewing again, slower now. Watching her.

"Yeah, well," she said, not looking up. "Hope Barbie came with lumbar damage and a thousand-yard stare."

He snorted. "Jesus. You always do that?"

She sipped her water bottle. "Do what?"

"Shoot it down before it can land."

She didn't answer, letting the cool liquid settle on her tongue before swallowing.

"You think that kid wants to be a pilot?" she asked after a moment.

"I think she saw something she didn't know was real."

She didn't mean to start talking. But the words came anyway—like they'd been queued up behind her teeth all day, just waiting for someone dumb enough to listen.

And Nico—sitting there with cinnamon sugar stuck to his cheekbone—was exactly that.

"I wasn't born destined for shit."

Her pulse was still up from the grounding. Not adrenaline. Residual rage.

"I was good. Smart. Whatever. So were five other girls in my class. The only difference? A calculus teacher who kept me in school long enough to graduate valedictorian. A neighbor who let me sleep on her couch when things got weird with my stepdad. A base chaplain who pulled strings to get me into Annapolis before I even knew what an officer was."

Her voice cracked—not from tears, just exhaustion—and she hated herself for it. Hated that she couldn't shut up.

"I wasn't a prodigy," she said, sharper now. "I was prepared. I studied. I did the hours. And it didn't matter. None of it mattered. Not until someone vouched for me."

She could feel him watching her. Not pitying. Just— present. And that made it worse.

"That's the thing nobody likes to admit," she muttered. "It doesn't matter how smart you are if nobody opens the goddamn door. I had a priest that felt sorry for me and made one call. That was it. That was the hinge."

She laughed, once.

"I didn't join to salute a flag. I joined because the Naval

Academy had free food, no tuition, and I could afford a Greyhound to get there. They gave me a bed. I gave them my twenties."

She knew she was ranting. She knew it sounded messy and ungrateful and cracked at the edges. But she couldn't stop. The day had already wrung her dry, and that little girl with her glitter shoes and plastic-hero worship had cracked something open in her ribcage that she didn't have the energy to seal.

Silence stretched. Nico didn't fill it. Of course he didn't. He just stood there, pretzel demolished, watching her like she was a cockpit warning he'd been trained to respect.

"That kid," he said softly, "she's still gonna remember you."

Izzy exhaled like it hurt. Shook her head once. And said the ugly part out loud.

"I almost hope she won't."

EVENTUALLY, standby cleared. Not even an interline jumpseat, just two regular economy seats on metal that didn't belong to them. Different branding, tighter pitch, indifferent crew. She still had her blazer on. Her blouse had sweat-stained through at the spine. She hadn't showered in twelve hours and hadn't changed in almost sixteen.

He didn't try to sit next to her. She didn't try to find him. They both knew there wasn't going to be small talk. Just the shame of being seen and the comfort of being invisible.

London met them with gray light and customs queues. She made it to the curb first. Pulled out her phone, not to check messages—there were none—but just to look like she had a purpose.

Then Nico stepped beside her. No words, no delay.

He said, quietly, "I don't think you should be alone tonight."

She didn't answer. Just shrugged—barely. A flick of the shoulder like a reflex she forgot to mask.

He nodded. Got into the cab with her.

SHE WOKE UP IN PIECES.

For a second, she didn't know where she was. The room was too quiet to be a hotel, too dark to be a crew bunk, too still to be moving. Her sheets smelled like her detergent, but it felt like someone else's bed.

That happened, sometimes—after too many flights, too many time zones. Your own home turned strange. Objects misplaced themselves. Light switches defied memory. Muscle remembered more than mind.

Her heart was pounding. No sound had woken her. Just the kind of panic that didn't come from outside. The kind that surfaced from the chest up, like a tide rolling backward.

The light in the kitchen was on.

She didn't check the clock. Didn't want to know how little she'd slept. The floor was cold under her feet as she padded out, still in a t-shirt that smelled like stale deodorant and her own exhaustion.

He was there.

Standing at the counter like he belonged to the room. Same black hoodie. Same unshakable quiet. Water just starting to boil. Mug already out.

She didn't say anything.

Neither did he.

He moved slow, precise. Poured the water. Dropped the tea bag. Set it in front of her like a ritual.

Then leaned back against the counter and stared at the floor.

She didn't say thank you. He didn't expect her to.

They just stood there. The silence between them not comforting—pressurized. The kind that filled the lungs too fast.

She couldn't feel anything clearly. Just the thick sediment of shame. The slow throb of her skull. The ache behind her ribs that might've been grief or rage or both.

He started to move—slow, careful, like he didn't want to wake whatever version of her he'd just seen.

He was headed for the couch. The one he offered to sleep on when they arrived hours ago—bone-tired, drenched in jet lag, stepping into her space like it wasn't sacred.

It had cost more than her first car. Custom Italian leather, curved like a question mark, zero back support. Her interior designer insisted. It looked incredible in photos. It felt like punishment in person.

"It's not comfortable," she said. Voice flat. Almost inaudible.

He paused mid-step.

"You don't want to mess up your back before the next long-haul. Just—" she swallowed. "Sleep in the bed."

He looked at her. Not long.

"Okay," he said.

She turned before he could follow. She just got back in bed and faced the ceiling like she hadn't said anything at all.

He joined her a minute later.

The mattress dipped under his weight. He lay on his back, body motionless except for his breath.

They had shared hotel beds. But this wasn't that.

This was her bed.

Her bed in her flat, her sanctuary, the one place no one touched. Not even after the divorce. Especially not after the divorce. She didn't go through a phase. No apps. Just silence. She hadn't wanted anyone.

Until Nico, of course. And that had made her furious.

And the memory of it—the charge, the way he touched her like she was something he'd studied—flickered through her so fast and so hot it left her breath shallow.

She shifted once, too fast, thighs pressing together like she could outrun it.

She didn't touch him. She didn't even move toward him. But he turned his head at the exact moment she did—eyes open, fixed on her like he'd been waiting.

Of course he had.

He didn't say anything right away. Just looked at her. Not with hunger. With that same unblinking attention he always gave her at cruise altitude, like she was the only thing in the sky that mattered.

"Stay still," he said—low, steady, like it cost him to speak.

A pause. Just breath between them. Then: "Let me take care of you."

Something about the way he said it made her body go still for real. Not obedient—activated. Her pulse surged behind her teeth. Not just arousal. Something lower. Older. A part of her that didn't have language for this but still knew exactly what it meant.

She hated that it worked.

Hated how fast her body fell in line like it had been waiting for permission all this time.

He wasn't touching her yet, but her breath had already gone shallow, legs loose with anticipation she couldn't disguise. Not lust. It was that thing. The way he took control like it was his to hold. Like he knew she needed to be told what to do, even when she swore she didn't.

She nodded.

"Okay," she breathed.

He didn't reach for her like she was something to be coaxed or cajoled. He just moved.

First, the blanket—peeled away slow, deliberate. The air on her skin made her inhale without meaning to.

Then her shorts. The little silk ones she'd half-changed into, not expecting company, not expecting to be touched. He slid them down her thighs like he already knew how little fight she had left.

Her underwear followed. No performance. Just quiet, practiced removal, like she was something delicate that needed unwrapping—not because she was fragile, but because she was his tonight, and he wanted it done right.

She didn't stop him.

She didn't help him either.

He left her bare and half-on her back, then reached for a pillow. Slid it beneath her hips like that was a normal thing to do in the middle of her exhaustion. Like her body was something he already knew how to arrange.

She could've protested. Could've told him to stop, to slow down, to fuck off. But her mouth didn't work. Her limbs didn't care. Her body—traitorous, tired, and keyed all the way up—had already decided it didn't want mercy. It wanted him.

And then he was there. Between her thighs. No teasing. No hesitation.

His mouth was devastating.

Not eager. Just exactly right. Like he'd read every tell,

mapped every nerve ending, and decided tonight was about precision.

She came once. Then again. The second left her breathless, furious. The third made her bite down on the inside of her wrist to stay quiet.

It was unbearable. How good he was at this. How known she felt. It was the kind of good that made her hate him a little—because she'd tried to lock this part of herself away and he'd picked it open without even trying.

When he was done—when her body had nothing left to give—he didn't say anything.

He just lay beside her, breathing normally like it hadn't cost him anything, and let her come back to herself.

But she didn't.

She slept. Hard. Like she'd survived something.

Because she had.

And he was the only one who knew what it took.

26

It started with a text.

People are saying you panicked in the cockpit.

She read it sitting on the locker room floor at the gym, phone still plugged into a charger that didn't reach the bench. No greeting. No sender name she cared about—just another number in the industry, someone who had probably never said a full sentence to her in person.

She locked the screen. Unplugged the phone. Went back to bag drills like nothing had happened.

She didn't wrap her hands. Not properly. The gloves went on bare. No tape. Just skin against leather, knuckles unprotected.

By the end of the first round, they'd split open—just enough to sting. By the second, the seams of the gloves were wet. She could feel the stick of blood when she curled her fingers. It hurt. Not enough to stop. Just enough to make her feel something she could control.

She didn't wipe it off. Let it soak in.

The gym always had airline people around. FAs who trained off-duty. Ground staff with FitPort codes. A few other pilots, mostly newer, mostly men. She heard things—little things behind her. Not directed at her. Never to her face. But it was audible.

"Isn't that her?"

"The one from JFK?"

"The screensaver glitch lady."

She didn't ask questions. She didn't need to. Rumors didn't need volume to spread. Just open space.

Rey clocked the blood before she even reached the bag.

"What the fuck've you done to your hands?"

Izzy didn't stop right away. Threw one more punch, then another, like quitting was worse than pain.

"Oi. Off. Now."

She pulled the gloves off like it didn't matter, even as the lining stuck. Her knuckles were wrecked—split open and smeared with sweat, blood dark in the creases. Rey grabbed her wrist.

"For fuck's sake."

"I'm fine."

Rey snorted. "Yeah, and I'm a fuckin' ballerina. Come on."

She hauled her toward the office, already reaching for the med kit under the bench. Didn't ask. Didn't wait. Sat her down like a bouncer throwing someone out of a pub.

"Don't be thick," she muttered, cleaning the worst of it with disinfectant. "You wanna bleed, fine—but don't waste my gloves on it."

Izzy didn't flinch. Not even when Rey rinsed the blood off with peroxide and taped her up with short, efficient movements like she was lacing a boot.

"I didn't notice," Izzy lied.

"No?" Rey raised a brow. "Just forgot how bones work, did you?"

She tied off the last wrap with a little too much tension.

"Next time, tape up or piss off."

Izzy stood. Didn't thank her. Didn't meet her eyes.

"Thanks for the lecture," she muttered, grabbing her bag and walking out.

Rey leaned back against the desk.

"You're not the only one bleeding quiet, love. Get over yourself."

Izzy left.

Didn't slam the door.

Didn't look back.

At home, her apartment felt too clean. Glass windows that didn't open. Light she couldn't dim without an app. She stopped sitting on her couch. Started eating standing up.

No one from LUMA contacted her.

No schedule updates. Just her roster disappearing from the app, one day at a time. Like she'd never existed. Like the system had just quietly unassigned her.

An old friend from training sent her a message: *Did you see the thread on PPRuNe?*

She didn't reply. She didn't need to.

She saw it two hours later. A post with the subject line: Captain Overreaction? The details were vague enough to be deniable. Specific enough to be her.

"She grounded a transatlantic flight over a minor display issue."

"Leave history—shouldn't that disqualify command?"

"Wouldn't have happened to a male captain."

"FO tried to calm her down. She wouldn't listen."

Nico's name wasn't in the thread. Neither was anyone else's.

It wasn't even rage she felt. Just a kind of professional nausea. Like being seasick in your own skin.

The next day, a flight attendant she knew from her old Frankfurt rotation pulled her aside in the gym entrance.

"Someone mentioned you and your FO. Like...together-together."

Izzy blinked. "Excuse me?"

"They said they saw you in New York. Holding hands."

She laughed. Just once. Not because it was funny—because it was pathetic.

That night she got an email from HR.

Captain Ventura, in the spirit of transparency and support, we invite you to a confidential conversation regarding any personal circumstances that may be relevant to your current duty status.

She didn't reply.

She closed her laptop. Stared out the floor-to-ceiling windows like she was waiting for something to happen. Nothing did.

That night, someone posted on Reddit: *Saw a captain and FO leaving a pilot event together—looked cozy.*

The comments did the rest.

"She's sleeping with her FO."

"No wonder she lost it mid-flight."

"Women aren't stable enough for left seat."

'Looked cozy'—what does that even mean?

Means she's fucking him, dude.

Typical. FOs trying to upgrade the easy way.

She kept seeing the word emotional. Like it was a stain. Like they were diagnosing her with femininity and calling it a safety hazard.

Miles texted the next morning. *Saw something about you online. Are you okay?*

She left it on read.

What stayed with her wasn't the rumor—it was the silence. Morgan Delgado hadn't said anything. Freja, the international CEO who usually commented on weather disruptions, hadn't acknowledged it. Not a single leadership voice above base manager level had reached out.

And that wasn't incompetence.

It was strategy.

Someone was keeping them out of it.

Someone was managing the optics at the top.

Someone like Russell Cayne.

And for a moment—brief, foolish, human—she thought: *I have Kieran O'Hara's number.*

She remembered him handing it to her. No fanfare. Just a card, passed quietly at the cocktail hour. She'd tucked it into the pocket of her uniform slacks without thinking.

Now she fished it out—creased, sweat-softened. Started to dial.

Then stopped.

Not because she didn't trust him. She did.

Kieran O'Hara had survived thirty years of aviation politics without selling his soul. He'd done it clean. And now he was married to Morgan Delgado, the U.S. CEO of LUMA. Their relationship was public, fully disclosed, bulletproof.

But that was exactly the problem.

Morgan could have a husband on the line. She could declare it, sign the ethics paperwork, and carry on. Because she was a CEO. Because her proximity to power was the structure.

Izzy didn't have that.

She wasn't protected by policy. She was trapped by it.

A captain sleeping with an FO was gossip. A captain whispering to the CEO's husband was a liability. It didn't matter that there might not be much between her and Nico except silence and bad timing. It didn't matter that Kieran offered help in good faith.

She couldn't afford to be seen pulling rank through marriage—someone else's marriage—when they were already calling her unstable.

So the number stayed in her notes app, unsent.

She didn't text. Didn't draft. Didn't ask.

Just went to the gym. Wrapped her hands.

And hit the bag until her wrists ached and the rumors felt farther away than they were.

27

He should have gone to the gym. His real one in Shepherd's Bush. The one that smelled like mat burn and blood and eucalyptus. The one where Rey would ignore him and Izzy would pretend not to watch him wrap his hands. His favorite place in the world, and now he couldn't walk through the doors.

Not after this week.

Not until she looked at him again like he belonged there.

Maybe not even then.

So instead, he had come here. The sublet's gym.

He hadn't run into anyone. It was empty. Dead. No music this time. Thank fuck. Just his own breath and the thud of rubber plates hitting the platform as he dumped the last set of cleans without finesse.

His lungs were burning. Sweat slid down his spine. Wrists ached. And he still didn't feel like he'd done enough to stop thinking about her.

Izzy.

The silence around her was louder than anything else that week. She'd gone quiet. Not completely gone—just sharp with silence. It was worse. Nico could survive cold. Cold had edges. Cold gave him something to push against. But this? This was like trying to hold onto smoke.

He sat on the bench and braced his elbows on his knees, forehead in his palms. His phone buzzed on the ground near his foot. The sound sliced through the quiet like a bone crack.

He ignored it.

It buzzed again. And again.

He reached down, unlocked it, and everything went still.

A work chat screenshot. A redacted document. Blurry, like it had been taken fast and without permission. Intentionally. A name was missing. But the details weren't. The medication was circled.

Fluoxetine.

Leave of absence: November to April. Six months.

And then, the comment underneath: "Captain grounded a working triple-seven. I'd spiral too if I couldn't trust my own brain."

His stomach dropped. The kind of drop he felt in his teeth.

He kept scrolling. Now it was in WhatsApp. Screenshot after screenshot. A friend of a friend's group thread. The same language. The same smug, slanted cruelty.

He found one that tagged the Chief Pilot.

"Sending love. Always proud of our pilots."

Which was code. Death by a thousand emojis.

She was being gutted in full view. Not by the company—at least not anymore, not on record.

This was worse.

This was what the industry did when it wanted you to quit without firing you. The slow bleed of reputation. The shadow campaign. The nudge and wink version of character assassination.

And he couldn't do a fucking thing about it.

He stood again too fast, legs stiff, pulse roaring in his ears. Grabbed the loaded bar and jerked it into a deadlift just to feel something in his hamstrings. He held it until his grip gave out.

He racked the bar. Stared at the wall. Tried not to throw his phone against it.

His chest tightened.

They hadn't spoken—not really—since the grounding. A few texts. Logistics. The kind of sterile professionalism that should have been fine, except that before, she would've let him stand next to her, even if she didn't say anything. Now she wasn't letting him do anything.

And honestly? She was right not to.

He scrolled up to Layla's last message. It was still unopened.

The preview hit like a punch in the ribs:

You're running out of time to be honest.

He didn't open it. Didn't answer.

She wasn't wrong. But what was he supposed to say? What the hell did you say to someone who was being flayed alive in real time—someone you were falling for hard—and the only thing you had to offer was another cut?

He couldn't stop it—gossip spreading, the algorithm shoving her name under strangers' thumbs, over and over. He'd tried reporting things, flagging posts. Nothing stuck. The trolls were getting faster. Meaner. Smarter.

And Izzy? She wasn't the type to explain herself. She would let it stand. Let people assume. Let them eat the version of her they wanted. And he knew—he knew—that was the worst part for her. Not that it had happened. That it was public. That they knew.

The woman who controlled everything she could—her voice, her posture, her fucking skincare fridge—had just been exposed in the most intimate way a pilot could be: her own mind, laid out like evidence.

He wanted to burn something.

Instead, he opened her text thread. Typed: *Let me know if you need anything.*

Deleted it.

Then, impulsively, he dropped in a meme. Something stupid. A dog in a flight deck. Harmless.

And two seconds later, he unsent it.

Coward.

He leaned back against the mirror. Wiped his face with his shirt. He was shaking. Not from exertion. From guilt.

It wasn't even coherent guilt. It was just this constant, gnawing churn in his stomach like he was wearing someone else's name tag and waiting to get caught.

His flights that week had been clean. Smooth. No snap decisions. The kind of flight they wrote brochures about.

He'd hated every minute of it.

Because she should've been there. And she wasn't.

Because things were happening. Quietly. Around him. To him. Because of him.

And the only thing he knew for sure was that whatever was coming next—he didn't get to feel good about it.

HE HADN'T TURNED on a single light since walking back into the flat. Just dropped his bag, kicked off his sneakers, and landed on the couch like his body had given up before his brain did.

He had been scrolling for hours. Same three apps. Same four threads. The silence in the pilot WhatsApp group had a shape now. Not just quiet—avoidant. Controlled. Something had been brewing. He could feel it in the way people stopped typing.

Then the link dropped.

A podcast clip. Grainy studio. LED lights set to male rage. Two men in snapbacks pretending to be intellectuals. One of them talked like a used car. The other leaned into the mic like he thought it was foreplay.

"You think I'm getting on a long-haul flight with some emotionally unstable female on Prozac? Bro, that cockpit's got a tampon in it."

Laughter.

Nico didn't move.

Not at first.

Not when the second guy jumped in with:

"I don't even care if she's logged ten thousand hours. Women can't emotionally handle command. That's science, bro. Hormones."

Not even when the fake applause kicked in, some sound-board shit that made it worse.

But his chest started to burn.

Not rage. He wasn't there yet, but it was something colder.

Something sharp.

He watched the clip again.

And again.

Not because he needed to—but because he was waiting. Waiting to see if they'd say her name. If they'd show her picture. If they'd make it real.

They didn't. But they didn't have to.

The comments did it for them.

"Bet this is about that LUMA chick."

"Didn't she ground a plane because she had a panic attack or something?"

"I'd rather die than let an old-ass lady with anxiety fly me over the ocean."

The air got thin. His vision narrowed.

He put the phone down. Picked it up again. Locked it. Unlocked it. Like maybe the screen would load something different if he stared long enough.

He ran a hand through his hair. Stood. Walked to the sink. Came back. Didn't remember doing it.

The thing crawling under his skin wasn't just fury. It was impotence. He knew how to fight. He knew how to handle threats. But this? This was a virus. A smear campaign in podcast form, weaponized by algorithm and misogyny.

And she was alone in it.

He should've texted her. But what would he even say? *Saw a podcast insult your existence. You okay?*

No. He couldn't. Not when her texts were down to one-word logistics and radio silence.

She wasn't shutting him out. She was bracing for impact. He knew that posture. It was the same one he used to take behind the yoke in a warzone.

It meant: *don't come closer unless you're prepared to bleed too.*

He stayed like that for a while. On his feet. Muscles locked in a holding pattern, breath stuck somewhere between inhale and detonation.

Then he sat back down.

Phone in his hand. Thumb hovering. The screen was still on that smug face, paused mid-laugh like the man thought he was untouchable.

Nico opened his messages.

Scrolled past the unread group chats. Past the check-ins he hadn't answered. Stopped at a contact with no name, just a lightning bolt emoji.

He typed one sentence and linked the podcast audio.

Nico: *Just listen to the clip. Do what you always do.*

He sent it. Locked the phone. Put it face down like it might bite. Then leaned back and waited. Not for a reply. For a reckoning.

28

Izzy didn't cry. She didn't scream. That would've made it real.

She read the transcript. Watched the clip. The smug inflection on "a certain female captain with a known history of instability." They didn't need to name her. They didn't need to say unstable. They knew the audience would do the math. She deleted the flight crew group chat. Left Nico on read. Cy brought cake. She didn't touch it.

She trained like her body owed her something. Burned through drills until her vision fuzzed. Rey walked in and found her almost passed out on the mat, cheek against the vinyl, drenched in sweat like she'd tried to outrun her own nervous system and lost.

"You're not dying on my floor," Rey said, dropping a protein shake like a threat.

Izzy drank it. Slowly. Silently. Like penance.

Now she lay flat on the mat, cheek against rubber, sweat drying into salt. Her wrists ached from drills she didn't need. Her knee was pissed, but she couldn't feel it yet—not through the slow burn across her shoulders.

Rey had left an hour ago with a grunt and, "Try not to pass out either. It's bad PR."

The gym was quiet. Not peaceful. Just empty.

Her phone buzzed.

She ignored it. Then it buzzed again. She reached for it without lifting her head.

A video. Sent by Rey.

The thumbnail was grainy, badly lit. She tapped it.

It opened on a shaky vertical shot of a train platform. Lina was in frame—Tuesday night crew, same oversized hoodie she always warmed up in, sleeves chewed at the cuffs. Her posture was casual but alert. A man off-camera was yelling. Slurs, probably, though the wind made the audio patchy. Lina didn't flinch. She tracked him with her eyes, not her feet. Textbook stance. Calm.

He lunged.

She moved.

A sharp parry, clean elbow to the clavicle, open-hand redirect. He went down hard. She stepped back immediately. Defensive posture. Centered weight. No extra movement. Just breath control and quiet fury.

Someone—maybe the person filming—shouted, "She didn't touch him until he touched her!"

The video cut off as the police arrived.

Izzy stared at the screen. She didn't move. She didn't replay it. Not yet. Her throat felt like sandpaper. Her spine throbbed from where she'd crashed on a takedown earlier. She played it again.

This time, she saw it: Lina checking her own pulse after. Two fingers to her neck. A slight frown, like the number was inconvenient.

The clip ended.

She scrolled down and found the post.

It was a photo. Lina's bruised knuckles. Nails still glittery.

The caption read: "I didn't win a fight. I ended a situation. Tuesday nights pay off. Thanks, Rey and Izzy. That's it."

In the comments:

"Where do you train?"

Lina: "You can't afford it. Good thing I didn't have to."

Izzy's chest pulled tight, like something in her ribs remembered how to ache. She didn't smile. She didn't repost it. Didn't send it to Cy or André or anyone. Just opened a new message to Rey.

Izzy: *She moved like you.*

Rey's reply came fast.

Rey: *Nah. She moved like you. Don't get soft about it.*

Izzy sat there for a while, legs sprawled out, phone loose in her hand. The mat was starting to cool under her spine.

Eventually, she stood. Pulled her hoodie off the wall hook. Picked up the bucket and rag from the corner where they always lived. The gym needed to be cleaned before she locked up, and the mats were still streaked with sweat and chalk.

She dunked the rag, wrung it out, dropped to her knees, and started wiping in long, steady strokes.

That silence, with no cost and no witness, was the only win she'd get this week.

29

The HR rep had a therapist's voice and a recruiter's teeth. Smooth as laminated empathy. The kind that made you feel like a burden for surviving.

Izzy sat upright in her kitchen, camera on, a loose-fitting cashmere sweater dress on, jaw locked.

The flat around her was steel, tile, matte fixtures—clean like surgery.

"Thanks for making time today," the rep began, with a practiced smile and a tone so light it could float away.

Izzy didn't smile back. "Sure."

"We just wanted to... check in," the woman said. "No pressure. Just follow-up."

Follow-up. Like the leak hadn't set off an internal audit. Like someone didn't whisper about her mental health through LUMA's teeth.

"How are you holding up?" the rep asked.

"I'm ready to get back to work."

A pause.

Izzy caught it—the slight shift in eye contact, the diplomatic inhale.

"Burnout is real," she said carefully. "Especially for women. Especially for women of color in fields like this."

Izzy blinked. "Right." She held back from saying, *Wow, what an insight. You should publish.*

The HR rep smiled like a paper cut. "We're just asking you to think about the long term. Maybe give yourself some space."

"I don't need space. I need a plane."

"I understand. But until the investigation is finalized, we can't clear you to fly."

"Because I refused the software?"

The rep gave a helpless laugh. "Well, we're still figuring out what to do with that, honestly. The rollout is fleet-wide. So long term, there won't be a way around it."

"Jesus Christ," Izzy muttered.

"We take your concerns seriously, Isabel. That's why we're asking you to take a step back. Let us do our due diligence. In the meantime, rest. Take care of yourself."

Izzy stared at the screen. She felt caged in widescreen HD. Her mouth was dry. Her temples were starting to pulse.

"We really do value your voice. Especially your mentorship of First Officer Farrah—your report on him was incredibly detailed. Your recommendation was a key factor in his promotion. You must be proud."

The breath didn't leave her body so much as vanish.

"I guess it's Captain Farrah now, huh?" the woman added with a chuckle.

It was said like small talk. Like the weather.

But her breath cinched on the inhale and didn't come back.

Captain.

He made captain.

He made captain and didn't tell her.

The HR rep kept talking. Her mouth moved like a puppet behind glass. Izzy smiled. Nodded. Did all the appropriate woman-shaped things.

Apparently, the promotion went through the same day she grounded the aircraft—same timestamp, different consequences. She lit the match and he got the wings.

Onscreen, the little window in the corner showed her face: underlit, too pale, mouth clamped shut. She looked like someone trying not to flinch.

She closed the laptop lid before the call even ended.

The room reabsorbed the silence.

She sat for a long time in the kitchen chair, the one with the cold metal back that left no room for comfort. She stared at the blank screen like it owed her answers. Captain. He'd made captain. The day she grounded the plane. He stayed with her that night. Sat on her couch. Slept in her bed. Told her she shouldn't be alone, when he already knew.

He knew—and said nothing.

Before the leak. While she was fighting for oxygen inside a cockpit that had turned against her, he was being promoted behind her back.

Her chest didn't hurt. It hardened.

Every long silence in the crew van. Every laugh in the gym. The way he'd pressed his mouth into her neck like prayer. It all rewrote itself in real time, refiled under manipulation.

Of course he didn't tell her.

Why would he?

Information was currency. And she'd been free with hers.

Izzy didn't text him.

Didn't call.

Didn't even re-open the chat thread, though she knew exactly where it sat.

This wasn't silence.

This was sediment.

She felt herself fossilizing by the hour. Not withdrawing. Just becoming rock.

Becoming something he could break his new captain's wings against.

30

She didn't even spar.

The gym had nothing for her today. Rey didn't say it outright, but the way she tossed her a towel and nodded toward the showers was enough. A mercy call. Go home. You smell like anxiety.

The Tube was humid and fluorescent. She scrolled out of habit—half conscious, trying not to notice her own reflection in the train window.

Some dumb thread. Aviation thirst-posts. A picture of a pilot's hands on the yoke with a caption like "I want him to ruin my credit score."

She should've swiped past it.

But then her name showed up.

Someone tagged her. A list of favorite landings. The tone was fawning—"quiet professionals," "women who fly like killers." She would've rolled her eyes, but one line caught her:

"Ventura in Lima, March 2023. Crosswinds 24 knots. That final was god-tier."

She blinked at the screen. Read the line again.

"Ventura in Lima, March 2023. Crosswinds 24 knots. That final was god-tier."

It didn't make sense.

That flight hadn't been recorded. It wasn't even on her resume of professional flexes. Just a routine, ugly-weather approach she happened to grease under pressure.

She hadn't told anyone.

And yet this stranger—some handle with eight followers and a name like @gearupgirl94—had named the airport, the month, the crosswind component.

Not just the surface winds, not a vague direction or speed—she had the actual crosswind value. Twenty-four knots.

That number didn't come from guessing. It wasn't something you could just pull from FlightAware or a METAR archive. Twenty-four knots wasn't the surface wind—it was the crosswind. The actual component. To get that, you'd need the exact runway, the landing time down to the minute, and a working knowledge of vector math. Nobody was calculating that unless they'd been there.

She wasn't tagged in a tribute. She was tagged in a breach.

Something cold settled under her skin. The kind of cold that came not from fear—but recognition.

They hadn't just been watching.

They'd been inside.

By the time she got back to her flat, she'd convinced herself it didn't matter.

The lights were already on. Something was baking.

For one awful second, she thought maybe she'd left the oven on and was about to burn the place down. But no.

There was music—Billie Holiday, vinyl-scratch soft—and someone had cracked the kitchen window.

She dropped her bag.

Cy stood at the stove. Apron, socks, brows drawn.

André was curled into the corner of her couch with a bag of crisps and a mug of something pink and suspicious.

Five days. Five days since she'd spoken to either of them. Five days since HR. Since that tight, surgical call where someone said "non-punitive" and "temporary grounding" and she pretended to nod like she was fine. She wasn't.

She'd only seen Rey. And Rey didn't count. Rey didn't ask questions.

Izzy blinked. Her hands were still clutching her phone like a weapon.

"What's going on?" she asked flatly.

"A wellness check," Cy said, not turning from the quiche.

"I'm your emergency contact. I will crawl through this window if I have to. And I don't care if you're mad at me. You can burn sage later."

"You promised me Selling Sunset," André added. "You said we could watch a whole season and trash every man in LA with facial filler. You owe me."

She opened her mouth to tell them off—to say thank you, to scream, to collapse.

Then the door opened again.

And Nico walked in.

He looked so good it pissed her off.

His honey-dark blond hair had dried in those loose waves that never quite behaved—longer now, slightly sun-touched at the ends. He'd probably run a hand through it outside, trying to flatten it down and only made it worse. His face was flushed from wind or walking, she couldn't tell, but it lit up the sharp angles of him—those unfair cheekbones, the straight, stubborn line of his jaw.

He still had his uniform on. Not the full display—no four-stripe jacket, no shoulder boards in sight. Just the shirt, the trousers, the tie half-loosened like he'd been pretending not to make this look intentional. His ID badge was in his pocket. She saw the outline of it behind the fabric. Still had his flight bag on his shoulder, like he'd just come straight from Heathrow.

He looked like sex and safety.

She hated how fast her body clocked him.

Hated how her gut twisted at the sight of him in that shirt.

Hated that despite everything, despite the silence and the lies and the fact that he was part of this ambush, she still missed him.

She wanted to crawl into his lap.

She wanted to knock his teeth in.

"Why are you here?"

She didn't yell. She didn't even raise her voice. She just stared at Cy like betrayal had a name and a stove and access to her locks.

Cy met her eyes.

"Because we were scared you wouldn't let us in."

A pause.

And then André, quiet for once: "And we knew he wouldn't leave."

Her lips pressed into a bloodless slash. The walls of her flat felt too close, too warm, too fucking occupied.

"The door's reinforced. You couldn't have kicked it down."

"You went dark. We made a plan."

She nodded once. That was all she gave them.

"I need to get extra milk and eggs for this," she said, pointing at all the baking ingredients laid out across her marble countertop.

"We have everything—" Cy started, but she was already gone. Shoes still on. Wallet in one hand, humiliation in the other.

She wasn't gone long.

Just walked to the corner shop and back.

She opened the door slowly. Quietly. No reason to announce herself. The bag of groceries was sweating through her fingers—eggs, milk, some tarragon she didn't need. She pushed the door shut with her hip.

They didn't hear her.

Cy was still at the stove, back turned. André sat on the counter, legs swinging, glass in hand. Nico was leaned against the wall like he belonged there—like she hadn't walked out mid-sentence and left him standing in her flat with nothing but guilt.

She didn't mean to listen.

But she didn't mean not to.

The TV was still on—plastic surgery, Range Rovers, someone shrieking about prenups.

But their voices cut underneath it. Low. Controlled. Like they'd already been talking about her for a while.

Nico's voice, quieter than the rest.

"She doesn't owe me anything," he said. "I just wanted her safe."

Izzy blinked. Her body froze, but her face didn't move.

Cy sighed. Not annoyed—tired. The kind of sound you make when you've argued every angle and finally gave up.

"You should've told her," he said. "About the upgrade."

"I know," Nico answered. "I just—I didn't want to make it worse."

"You didn't want to make it worse," André repeated flatly, like he was taste-testing the phrase and didn't care for it. "So instead you let her find out like a stranger."

Nico didn't say anything.

"She's not fragile," André added. "You don't get to decide what she can handle."

"I wasn't trying to decide," Nico said. "I was trying to give her a minute to breathe."

"By lying to her?"

The silence after that was ugly.

Then Nico, voice stripped down: "If she never talks to me again, fine. I just needed to make sure she was okay."

That's when her blood stopped moving.

Because it didn't sound noble.

It didn't sound selfless.

It sounded familiar.

Izzy's vision went soft around the edges.

She'd heard this conversation before. Not these voices—but this tone.

Low. Regretful. Selfless.

The performance of a good man explaining his pain to people who had already decided it was her fault.

That wasn't love. That was optics.

She was back in Oxfordshire, standing in the too-clean drawing room of Miles's parents' estate, still in her boots from the drive, still smelling faintly of the flight she landed twelve hours ago.

His mother's hand on the rim of a teacup. Bone china. Shaking slightly—but not with nerves. With control.

"We know your work is demanding, Isabel," she said, like she was offering a towel to someone bleeding out. "But Miles has been so patient. Surely you could take some time. He's trying so hard."

His father didn't even pretend.

"He comes home alone every night. We hear him pacing upstairs. Is that really how you think marriage should be?"

And his sister. Silent. Watching her from the corner of the room with that glassy, brittle stare like Izzy had walked in holding a gun instead of her overnight bag.

Not one of them raised their voice. But they treated her like a bomb someone had stupidly invited to dinner.

She'd stood there, back straight, spine tight, listening to them turn Miles into the victim. He never spoke a bad word about her. He just wanted her to be happy. He waited. She never came home. She was the career-obsessed one. The absent one. The selfish one. The woman who didn't deserve that kind of love.

And now here she was again—watching it unfold in her own kitchen. Nico hadn't meant to rewrite the story, but by softening himself, he hardened everyone else against her. And once again, she didn't even get the dignity of being the villain by choice.

She stepped forward.

And just like that—everyone flinched.

André almost dropped his glass. Cy turned too fast and hissed from a burn. Nico straightened like he'd been caught stealing.

Izzy just smiled.

"You're gonna need more eggs," she said.

She put away the groceries. Sat down in her own kitchen like it wasn't already occupied by a story she didn't consent to.

Hours passed.

The sky was low and silver outside the thirty-second floor windows, streaked with the reflection of the Thames— wide, indifferent, glinting like brushed metal.

Cy was outside on the balcony, speaking in patient but exasperated South London lilt to his husband about a "back garden tap issue that should've been handled last year," which Izzy had learned was their love language.

André was a sprawl of limbs and designer loungewear across the couch, mouth slightly open, dead asleep with one sock half-off like a passed-out Greek god.

Nico was at the dining table, back to her, engineering some kind of culinary atrocity using Cy's homemade currant biscuits and American peanut butter.

"This is either a cultural bridge," he said over his shoulder, "or a minor diplomatic incident."

Izzy didn't answer. It was a running bit—him calling them cookies, Cy muttering about colonial vocabulary, and the Americans in the room always outnumbering the British just enough to be dangerous.

She stood at the sink, head angled just so, pretending to rinse a glass. Really, her left hand was submerged in the ice bucket. It was meant for drinks—she'd prepped it hours ago, forgot about it, never offered it around. Just left it there. Cold comfort.

The pain was surgical. Controlled. Not dramatic—just a reminder she was still in her body.

But of course Nico saw it.

He always did. The master of not looking directly, of making you feel unseen until he came in with the kill shot.

She caught his reflection in the microwave door when his head turned—only a little. A twitch. A register. His voice didn't change.

"Sami used to do the same thing," Nico said quietly, almost to himself.

His eyes stayed on her hand. André was dead asleep, the

TV still going like white noise, but Nico spoke like someone guarding a secret anyway.

She froze.

"My older sister. By two years. Rubber bands. She kept them high on her wrist so her sleeves would cover the marks. Started in high school, back in Kentucky."

Izzy said nothing.

"Literal genius. She rewrote the admin settings on the school network once—just so my name disappeared off a suspension list. No one ever figured it out."

He scratched the back of his neck, like the memory still made him nervous.

"But she was—"

He paused, like selecting the exact weight of the word.

"Sensitive. Too much love, nowhere to put it."

Her fingers twitched in the water.

"What happened?" she asked, low.

He didn't answer right away. She slowly lifted her hand out. The skin was red, almost purple, stiff, wet as glass. He was already walking toward her with one of her linen hand towels, folding it like muscle memory.

"It was a guy," he said, gently wrapping the towel around her hand like he'd done this before.

"Different guys. All of them wanted to try her out like a flavor. The worst was her college boyfriend."

There was something in his voice now. Hollow. Familiar. Like the sound of rage buried under snow.

Izzy didn't ask. But she saw it. That flicker behind his eyes. That one second where the restraint cracked just enough to show the monster behind it.

"Is he—?"

"Alive?" Nico didn't even look up. "Yeah."

Her pulse kicked. Heat climbed the back of her neck. Not from shock—from the way he said it.

Quiet. Flat. Like it barely mattered. Like he'd already made peace with it.

"He ended up in the hospital," Nico said. "But yeah. Alive."

She studied him. Sharp profile, soft voice. No apology.

"How the hell are you not in jail?"

He just shrugged. Casual. Loose-shouldered.

"Some people," he said, "you only have to explain once."

Her pulse faltered—barely. A low heat stirred beneath the stillness. Not from the story, but from the restraint beneath it.

He had answered cruelty with precision, not fury. Not for pride. For protection.

And that caused something in her—quiet, long-dormant—to give way.

He was still so calm. So composed. Wrapping her hand like it mattered. Like she mattered.

And then—

A gust of wind. Cy emerged back from the balcony, phone in hand.

"He wants to know if we own a wrench or if we should just burn the flat down and start again."

Izzy flinched. The moment shattered. The towel slipped.

Right.

The show was still on. The baked goods were flawless.

And the fight was coming.

But not yet.

Not while the meringue still held its shape.

She swallowed the bile rising in her throat.

She smiled at something on the TV.

Laughed at the wrong moment.

At least Cy's baking was absurd.

Coconut tart with a rum glaze that could silence a room. Currant rolls, tight and perfect, dusted with powdered sugar like it was a finishing school. Guinness ginger cake so dark and sticky it bordered on sinful.

There was a cassava pone he served in slices like gold bars, still warm in the middle. Pineapple chow turned into miniature hand pies. Sorrel-glazed donuts.

And the showstopper—a bread pudding laced with condensed milk and bitters, topped with brûléed bananas and just enough nutmeg to make you behave.

Cy pulled it from the oven, set it down like a trophy, and barely had time to admire the caramel crust before his phone buzzed. One glance, and he was already grabbing his keys—his husband had apparently tried to "fix" the kitchen lights and was now texting from beneath what might become an electrical fire.

"You don't have to be okay," he said on the way out, letting her slip his jacket over his shoulders before turning back and folding her into his arms.

Cy kissed her forehead, and added, "But you don't get to disappear."

"Okay," she said as she closed the door behind him and turned around.

Outside, the London skyline was going gold.

Her window framed it perfectly—the Eye turning slow and delicate in the distance, lit from beneath like someone had set a halo under the river.

André, Nico, and Izzy went to the window and watched the light come on. The first pinprick. Then another. Then the whole wheel glowed.

It was stupid how beautiful it was. Like the city was apologizing for what the people in it couldn't say.

When that was done, André made the moves to head out, keys in hand.

"Next week," he said. "You're mine. Season two. No excuses."

She nodded.

And then he was gone.

The air was too still. The fridge hummed like it knew something.

She didn't look at Nico.

Not yet.

But the fight was already building in her throat.

31

They sat across from each other in silence. Two glasses of water untouched on the low table between them. The air was still. Not dead—held.

The only illumination came from the city itself: windows in other buildings, sodium glow from traffic far beneath, a red beacon blinking from the top of the Shard like a distant warning. Planes blinked overhead, invisible unless you were looking.

Inside, it was shadows. No one had turned on a single light. They hadn't noticed. Or maybe they had, and it felt wrong to break the dark.

No overheads. Just two people in a luxury flat that felt like an observation deck for grief.

Izzy wasn't raising her voice. She didn't need to.

"You made captain," she said, quietly. "And you didn't tell me."

Nico didn't blink. He'd hope this would come later. Or not at all.

His mouth opened. *I didn't want to hurt you. I didn't know how. I thought it would break you.*

But none of it sounded like enough.

"I wanted to," he said, throat raw. "But I knew it would feel like a knife."

She nodded once. Not forgiveness. Just acknowledgment.

"You watched me get grounded," she said. "And you just stood there."

He flinched.

"I didn't know how to be near you without making it worse," he said. "You were drowning and I—every time I reached for you, it felt like I was stepping on your chest."

Her jaw flexed. Nothing else moved.

"I don't think you meant to hurt me," she said. "I really don't."

She paused. Just long enough to decide if she was going to say the next thing. Then she did.

"But that's the part that keeps happening to me. Men who think sparing me the truth is some kind of kindness. Like I'll fall apart if they let me see the whole thing. Like I'm this fragile little crisis they have to manage while they carry the emotional load."

His throat tightened. He already knew where this was going.

"Miles did it too," she said, flat. "White lies. Soft omissions. Acting like I was the storm and he was the one holding it all together. When really, he was just scared of having a hard conversation with a woman who knew more than he did."

She looked at him then. Not angry. Just done.

"You don't get to lie to me to protect me," she said. "I've survived worse than the truth."

She wasn't done and kept talking.

"I've diverted on fumes. I've landed without instruments.

I've signed off body transfer forms and sat with the remains until someone came to claim them. I've flown into places people didn't come back from. And I've survived men in uniform who were supposed to have my back and didn't. I've survived my own fucking family."

She wasn't crying. She wasn't shaking. She was just done.

"I don't need anyone softening the truth for me."

She looked away again. Not for effect. Just to stop herself from saying more.

"I know," he said. "I didn't pay for the seat the same way you did."

His voice was low. Not apologizing. Just there.

"But I see it now. I know it's fucked. And I'm not gonna pretend I earned what you had to survive to keep."

"But you still got to move forward," she continued. "The system made sure of that. Two years in. Two."

Her voice was calm. Steady. Not angry. That was the worst part. She wasn't yelling.

"While I spent ten. After the Academy. After two wars. After flying with men who wouldn't look me in the eye unless they were asking if I was lost."

Nico pressed his palms into his knees.

"Believe me, I kept waiting for someone to tell me it was a mistake. Like I'd skipped a line and they were coming to collect."

Her eyes met his. She didn't blink.

"It took me over ten," she said. "And I came in with more hours than you. More command time. More combat. More fucking life."

"I know," he said.

She leaned forward slightly, elbows to her thighs, fingers laced tight.

Nico's mouth parted, but "You made widebody captain at twenty-nine," she said. "I didn't make it until thirty-six."

She didn't say it like an accusation. She said it like math.

"I've been flying commercial since I was twenty-four. Regional captain by twenty-seven. Major airline by twenty-nine. Narrowbody command by thirty-two. Widebody by thirty-four. And they still made me wait."

Her eyes stayed on him. "You got there faster. But I was always ahead."

She didn't pause to let it land—just kept going.

"Combat. Carrier landings. Medevac in blackout zones. I flew transport out of war zones before you were even done with basic."

Her voice was steady now, deadly calm.

"I've flown in places the GPS refused to acknowledge. I've landed with no radio contact, no tower, no backup. I had wings before you had a callsign."

She leaned forward slightly. "And it still took me longer."

He didn't say anything—just breathed out, like the weight of it all finally landed.

"Because they looked at you and said 'he's ready'—and looked at me like I was in the wrong room."

Nico's mouth parted, but couldn't argue. He wouldn't.

"You're not the problem," she said. "You're the proof."

It hit him like a blade between ribs.

"I hate that you're right," he said, voice low. "I hate that I'm proof."

"You didn't have to fight for every hour. Every seat. Every cockpit. You didn't have to smile through evals just so someone wouldn't flag you as 'intense.' Or 'negative.' Or 'difficult.'"

He closed his eyes.

"No. I didn't. And I knew it. I've always known it. Even when I pretended I didn't."

"I was always more qualified," she said. "But the world still picked you. Smiled while doing it."

He swallowed.

"I didn't get it because I earned it more than you," he said. "I got it because the timing was fucked. Because—"

He let out a bitter breath.

"Because COVID decimated the seniority list. Half the airline retired. They were desperate. They weren't looking for the best pilot. They were looking for the safest bet. And I looked like one."

He didn't look away.

"I look white enough. Military pedigree. No HR flags. I walked in and they saw a man they already trusted. I didn't have to prove anything."

His voice cracked on the last part.

"You had to prove everything. And they still held it against you."

She nodded once. Her expression was unreadable. Beautiful, as always. Unreachable, now.

"I recommended you because you deserved it," she said. "But the moment you made captain, I stopped being a peer. I became the comparison. The cautionary tale."

Her voice didn't break. It didn't need to.

"You were the success story. I was the problem they quietly solved. The crazy woman they kept out of the cockpit."

She held his gaze, the words landing heavy between them.

"That's the optics," she said, voice low, firm, "and no matter how hard you worked, no matter what you earned— it still looks like you played me."

Nico sat back against the cold leather couch.

"You didn't stop being anything," he said. "You—" He cut himself off. Swallowed the rest.

"I became the one they measured you against," she said. "Not because of anything you did. Because that's what this system does. It elevates men like you, and examines women like me."

He nodded, slow and ashamed.

"It gives you the benefit of the doubt," she said. "And gives me—process."

His breath caught.

"I would burn it down if I knew how," he said. "I swear to God, I would."

But she just looked at him, tired.

"This system was always going to pit us against each other," she said. "But I'm not going to let it pit me against you. Not like this."

"Then let me fight it with you," he said. "I'll follow your lead. I'll—"

"You can't fix this," she said, gentle but final. "You are this."

His chest went hollow.

"I don't hate you," she added. "But if I stay, I will. Because every time I see you, I'll see the version of me they never let exist."

Silence.

The lights outside blinked faintly, aircraft skimming sky, city pulsing on without them. He could feel the floor of the building beneath him, solid and endless. And useless.

"So I'm ending it," she said, rising, "before I start hating you for getting what I earned first."

He stood too because sitting felt pathetic. She didn't

even look at him. He searched her face anyway, hoping for a sign she hadn't meant it. There wasn't one.

"Is this really what you want?" he asked.

She didn't answer. She turned instead, crossed to the door, and opened it without ceremony.

"It's what I need," she said, eyes fixed on the hallway beyond.

She didn't look back.

He didn't move right away. He didn't say anything at all. She hadn't asked him to. That was the part that gutted him the most. She had given him room to speak and then made it clear that no answer would matter.

So he walked.

He stepped past her into the hallway—quiet, pale, spare. Everything in place, nothing harsh. The kind of clean that cost money. Cool-toned walls, soft lighting that didn't hum or flicker, a stillness that made his footsteps feel too loud.

He didn't look back. She didn't watch him go.

The door closed behind him with the softest possible click.

That was the last thing she gave him. Not a word. Just silence and the sound of something final being locked away.

32

Five minutes passed. Then ten. She was quiet, miserable, furious at herself for it—until she looked up and saw the badge.

The one he'd worn all wrong that one morning in what felt like ages ago just to make her laugh.

Resting half-under a baking sheet, like it had every right to be there.

She called him because she couldn't stop looking at it.

She could've mailed it. Could've told herself it was nothing. Could've gone to bed and ignored the ache in her throat that had nothing to do with being alone and everything to do with how quickly he'd walked away when she told him to.

But something in her wanted to hear his voice break before she let it go.

The call was short.

"Hey," she said flatly. "You left your badge."

A pause. Then his voice, soft and already guilty, almost boyish: "Shit—I'm sorry. I wasn't trying to—God, I wasn't thinking. I wasn't trying to leave something, I swear—"

She could hear it all, even in those few rushed words. The embarrassment. The mortification. The fear that she thought he'd done it on purpose. Like some men do, like the ones who leave a sock behind or a toothbrush tucked in the medicine cabinet as if that grants them rights.

But Nico had never done that. Not once. He was always meticulous about retreat—folding himself out of her space like he was trying not to leave fingerprints. So of course this small mistake humiliated him. Of course he thought she'd think it was a ploy.

She let the silence spool out until she could almost hear him biting the inside of his cheek on the other end of the line.

"I know," she said.

And then, lower. Almost like an afterthought, but not: "Nico?"

"Yeah?"

Her breath came ragged, shaky at the edges.

"Make me regret making you leave. Don't hold back."

It wasn't a request. It was a line drawn.

She never wanted gentleness. That was a lie: measured hands, polite silences, men who smiled too easily.

It was never gentle when it ended.

She wanted ruin. The sharp edge of hunger. The bite of something that could hurt.

Nico didn't answer. He just hung up.

And when the lock turned barely five minutes later, she didn't need to look up to know what version of him had walked back in. The air shifted. Dense. Charged. It was the kind of silence that arrived with a storm.

Her body responded before her thoughts did—heart hammering, lungs high in her chest, hands twitching with the muscle memory of a takedown. She could've floored him now if she wanted to. Had, once at the gym. Hard. He knew it. That was part of why he moved so carefully now.

But none of that mattered. The pain had settled low, deep, insistent, radiating outward like something physical. She could feel it in her molars. That cold, ringing pressure that used to send her reaching for the freezer, for ice held to skin until it stung enough to cut through the noise. Pain had always been the cleanest thing—honest, controllable, sharp where everything else was messy.

When her mind slipped, it was pain that pulled her back. If she could bruise, she wouldn't have to tear herself open. If she could break, she would.

And tonight, she would.

She turned slowly, deliberately, and there he was, standing in the doorway like a man who knew there would be consequences. His mouth was drawn, but not tight. His eyes—those impossible, kind eyes—looked like someone had put a match out in them.

"If you want this to stop," he said, voice low, careful, steady, "say it. Otherwise, I'm going to do exactly what you asked for. You're in control, Izzy. I won't touch you unless you tell me."

She stepped closer. Not to touch him. To be sure he could hear her when she spoke.

"Touch me. Slap me. Tie me up. Use me. Call me names. Do it like you'll never be allowed to again," she said, her voice stripped bare. "Because you won't. This is it. So take everything. Leave nothing good behind. You have my consent. And when I want you to stop, I'll say stop. I want this. *I need this.* Do you understand?"

He nodded. "I do."

The silence that followed didn't feel victorious. It felt like a vacuum.

The second the words left her mouth, her stomach dropped—clean and sudden, like turbulence in a clear sky—and her body went cold with the shock of what she'd just handed him. A goodbye she couldn't take back. Something in her blood protested, like it was trying to reverse time. Like it was warning her, *You are not built for this kind of silence.*

She could feel it now: this might be the last time she saw him. Not out of drama, not out of ego, but because she'd just burned the bridge while still standing on it. And he hadn't said a word.

His fingers drummed once, then curled.

Then he shut the door behind him.

He didn't speak when he reached her.

Just lifted his hand to her throat with terrifying calm.

It wasn't theatrical. It wasn't sudden. It was precise—fluid in a way that didn't belong to a man making it up as he went. This was someone trained, someone who knew—intimately—where the softest places on the body lived.

His palm rested against her windpipe—not pressing, not yet. Just a promise. That he could.

And that promise was a blade, drawn slow and silent.

She had seen him like this only twice before, in glimpses so fast and so sharp they'd left her nauseous. Once, with that entitled passenger threatening André thirty-five-thousand feet over the Atlantic. Another time in Manhattan when that pilot said those things about her. Both times, Nico had moved with that same impossible stillness—trained stillness—like violence wasn't a choice but an option stored just beneath the skin, accessible and ancient.

And now his hand was on her neck.

And she was wet.

She hated herself for it.

No. That wasn't true. She recognized herself in it. That

sick, spiraling corner of her brain where intrusive thoughts echo. Step into traffic. Pull the fire alarm. Jump onto the train tracks just to feel something before the world goes black.

This wasn't suicidal. It was sensational. Alive. Her pulse, deafening.

She reacted without thinking, training kicking in. Rey had drilled it into her a hundred times—turn the head to relieve pressure, drop the shoulder to shift her center of gravity, trap and twist his wrist to break the hold.

But he countered it. Effortlessly.

His hand locked around her wrist, stepping in just as she shifted—center of gravity gone, balance gone, all of it taken.

He threw her like it was natural. Like she'd meant to fall, and he'd just shown her how. She landed on the couch like a sigh, but he was already on her again.

Pinning her down, his hand back on her neck, the other on her wrist.

The grip shifted—firmer now. Her lungs adjusted on instinct, each inhale a measured thing.

His weight was distributed perfectly. Controlled. Practiced. Like he'd done this in drills. Like this was a language his body had always spoken.

Her skin prickled.

And still, she arched up against him.

Her arm twisted again, on instinct. A real twist, not a real fight.

He didn't entertain it.

Didn't flinch.

Just leaned in closer, voice venom-low.

"You call me back," he said into her ear, "just to pretend you've got second thoughts? Don't insult both of us."

His grip tightened. Her vision sparked.

"I'm not having second thoughts," she bit out. "I'm waiting for you to catch the fuck up."

He drew back, his eyes wide like he'd been slapped. Then he smirked.

"Fucking slut," he said—not cruel, not admiring. Just naming it like she'd made him believe it.

With anyone else, that word would have been their death sentence. She had laid out men twice her size for less. But he said it like a truth he owned, and that made her want to give it to him. It was not about control. It was about being something wild. Owned by no one but herself.

Then he grabbed her robe.

She cursed when the fabric tore.

It was the same goddamn robe as before from the hotel during the New York layover—soft, black, too vulnerable. He ripped it open like he hated it for what it reminded him of.

And then her underwear—simple, cotton, too easy to destroy.

He didn't hesitate.

She was bare. No bra. No barrier.

His fingers were inside her before she could inhale properly. Precise. Brutal. Perfect. He knew her body too well already. Knew what angle made her hips jump, what rhythm made her bite her lip hard enough to bruise.

And just as she started to climb—just as her spine began to curve, her mouth opening around a sound she didn't recognize—

He stopped.

She whimpered. Then choked on it.

"Nico—"

"Shut up."

The words were cruel. But the slap came first.

His palm across her face was clean, deliberate. Not too hard. Just enough to sting. She froze just for a second like she was deciding between moaning or lunging at him. Nico saw it. The flicker. The sin and shame of it. And he smirked like he'd just found her favorite pressure point.

He continued working her with his fingers, slow and merciless, dragging her to the edge and yanking her back just as her body began to coil. He started and stopped over and over, the rhythm maddening—two fingers curling inside her, then gone, then back again, twisting, thrusting, pausing with obscene precision.

She was keening through gritted teeth, her hips chasing every withdrawal like she could force him to finish it. "Please—Nico—please, fuck, please—"

"Quiet," he said. "You don't get to beg and then pretend you hate what it does to you."

And only when she was soaked, shaking, nothing but raw nerve and ruined pride beneath him—did he let her come. Only when she was moaning and ruined and breathless—only then did he let her fall over the edge.

She shattered like she had nothing left to lose.

And he watched.

Watched her come apart with the same dark calm he'd entered the room with.

"You like my hand around your neck," he said, almost with contempt. "You like being slapped. So why are you acting surprised, Izzy, when you're getting what you asked for?"

She bit her lip. Couldn't think of a smart retort. So, instead, she bucked him—wild, desperate, furious—off of her.

"Fuck off."

He hit the floor with a grunt, caught off guard just

enough to let her scramble up, heart pounding like it wanted to punch through her ribs. Her thighs were still shaking as she backed away from him. Her jaw ached. Her throat burned.

He rose slower than he should've, but it wasn't hesitation. It was calculation. She could see it in his eyes—that terrifying, glassy stillness that overtook him when he slipped into this other self. The good man was gone. This version didn't ask if she was okay. This one punished. This one moved like he enjoyed the geometry of domination, like there was pleasure in the math of her surrender. He was activated, cold and in control, savoring the precise calibration of pain and obedience. And she needed it more than she could say.

He was on her again before she could even take a full breath.

He grabbed her wrist, spun her back to face him, and shoved two slick fingers into her mouth—deep, fast, unrelenting.

"Taste yourself," he said, voice low and dark with heat. "Since you're so fucking proud of what a mess you are."

Her lips stretched wide around his fingers as he pushed them in to the knuckle. She tasted salt and skin and shame, and still she licked—reflexively at first, then deliberately, like she was trying to prove something. Her tongue curled around the pads of his fingers as he pulled them out slowly, a thin trail of saliva stringing between them.

He paused for half a second. His expression flickered— something visceral, possessive flashing across his face.

"Fucking filthy," he muttered. "Look at you."

She moved—not to escape, but to tempt. A flicker of motion, all muscle and mischief. This was the game. Her sick little fantasy: not just to be chased, but to be hunted. By him. The only one who could keep up, who could push her without shattering bones or breaking her overpriced furniture.

He leaned in, too confident, voice soaked in mockery—and that was her window. She dipped under his arm, a flash of bare skin and calculated power. One pivot, weight shifted, balance stolen. She spun out of his grip like smoke and bolted.

Three strides. That's all she got.

His hand tangled in her hair like a noose.

She gasped, her head yanked back hard enough to wrench her spine, and he dragged her down to her knees like it was nothing. The floor slammed against her shins. Her robe was half-torn, slipping off one shoulder. Her thighs were still wet.

They were by the floor-to-ceiling window now.

Thirty-second floor. Panoramic view. London glittering behind the glass like a jury.

He cornered her there, braced her back against the freezing pane, one hand still in her hair, the other pressing against her collarbone, keeping her exactly where he wanted her—caged, on display, breathing hard against the skyline.

"You run," he said, voice thick with amusement, "but you want this. You want to be pinned. You want to be used. That's what you called me for, right?"

"Yes."

His grip in her hair tightened. She winced, breath catching.

"Then it's my turn," he said, lips brushing her ear like a dare. "To use you. That's what you are, isn't it? Mine to use?" He kissed her neck once, not sweet, but claiming. "And maybe I won't even fuck you. Maybe I'll just make you ache and leave."

Something in her broke open.

"Try it," she hissed. "See what happens."

Slap.

"Shut up," he growled.

Her head whipped sideways, the crack of it sharp in the charged air. For a moment, everything stalled—like her brain short-circuited, stunned into silence. Then the heat hit. It bloomed fast, wild, rolling through her core like wildfire. Her breath caught. Muscles locked. She squeezed her thighs together on instinct, helpless against the pulse low in her gut.

He leaned down again. "You want it? Prove it."

His voice dropped further, into that dark, terrible place she only heard when he stopped trying to hide it.

"Show me," he said. "Show me that you deserve it."

Her hands shook, but she moved fast.

Her fingers found the buckle of his uniform belt—rough, LUMA-issued leather—still snug from the flight. She tore it open, unzipped him with trembling urgency, and took him into her mouth without hesitation nor a shred of pride.

She'd never been particularly fond of giving head—always felt like a chore, a favor, a gesture more than a desire. But him? He was different. Aesthetically profane in the best way, like something hand-sketched by a depraved artist with a God complex. The shape of him was almost elegant—smooth skin, a subtle curve, not excessive but absolutely audacious in girth. He tasted clean, good. Familiar and electric.

Her jaw was already aching, barely managing half of him, but that didn't stop her. She pushed herself further, tongue dragging along the underside from base to hilt.

He inhaled through his teeth.

And then—moved.

His hand tangled back in her hair, guiding her rhythm with deliberate, punishing control. He fucked into her mouth like it was his right, bracing one forearm on the window, the other gripping her skull, using her throat like a weapon he'd earned.

She gagged. Moaned. Drooled. Her back arched from the pressure, shoulder blades pressing into the cold glass.

Outside, the city blinked on like a thousand silent voyeurs.

"You like getting your face fucked?" he hissed, breath hitching. "Like letting the whole city see what a whore you are?"

She moaned around him, loud and needy, one hand moving between her legs—

Slap.

He pulled her off him with a sharp tug to her hair. She gasped around the loss.

"Did I say you could touch yourself?" he asked.

She shot him a look of defiance, panting, something slick smeared across her lips.

"Hands behind your back."

She obeyed. Slowly.

He dragged her mouth back to him and thrust again, deeper this time, relentless. She choked again, harder, her whole body shaking now, nothing grounding her but the pain in her scalp and the glass at her back.

When he finally tensed—shoulders drawn, jaw locked— he groaned like it hurt to hold it back.

Then, at the last second, he yanked her off him with a wet, brutal pop.

He jerked once, twice—hot, violent—and came all over her chest.

She flinched but didn't wipe it off.

He looked down at her—ruined, panting, kneeling in front of the city.

"You don't get to swallow," he said, voice flat.

She knelt there, his release cooling across her chest, her breath catching unevenly.

"Fuck you," she rasped, voice shredded and bitter.

He laughed.

She knew his laughs—easy ones, private ones. This wasn't either. This one was cut glass. A sound made to wound, not share.

"Oh," he said, that smile in his voice like a hook in flesh. "You'll pay for that."

He stepped back just enough to reach down and pull the belt from the slacks puddled at his ankles. He hadn't taken the rest of his uniform off—still wore the LUMA button-down, crisp-white, now creased and untucked, and the navy tie hung loose around his neck like a noose not yet drawn tight.

She watched the belt slide free through the loops—slow, unhurried. He didn't rip it off like a man drunk on impulse. He unthreaded it. Like it was sacred. Like it was something he'd used before in another life, not for pleasure, but for precision.

He folded it once in his palm. Then again, doubled over, heavy. The leather looked dark in the dim light, the buckle glinting once as it turned in his grip.

She swallowed. Hard.

He hadn't used the belt before. But she'd always felt that potential in him. That edge. That knowledge. The possibility coiled beneath the kindness. She'd wanted to ask.

Tonight, she would.

"Use it," she said, her voice steady. "Make me feel it."

And she knew—knew—he would stop if she said the word. If she looked up with anything close to fear, he'd drop the belt and hold her instead. She had that power. She just didn't want to use it. Not when she needed pain to dull her heartache.

Because this wasn't punishment. And it wasn't vengeance. This was what she'd asked for, explicitly, body-first. A balm she could only admit to him that she needed. A way back into her skin.

"Fine."

He reached down, wrapped his hand around the back of her neck, and dragged her up to stand.

She didn't make it easy.

She kicked. Twisted. Tried to drop her weight and break his hold, planting her feet and yanking sideways—but it didn't matter. He overpowered her like she weighed nothing. It was a struggle, yes, bodies crashing and straining—but never cruel. They weren't trying to win. Not really. No one here was aiming to injure. The restraint between them was just as deliberate as the violence.

Nico pinned her arms flat against her breasts, his forearm locking her in place, her back crushed to his chest. It was the first time she felt the scale of him.

She had known, abstractly, that Nico was tall. That he was strong. But up close—contained by him like this—she finally understood the size of him. Over a foot taller. Seventy, maybe seventy-five pounds of clean muscle over her. And none of it wasted. None of it unsure.

She forgot, sometimes. They spent most of their time side by side in the cockpit—seated, leveled, and uniformed.

And outside of it—he was steady. That was the word.

Not small. Never that. He didn't try to disappear. He just didn't encroach. He didn't loom or claim space like it was owed to him.

He stood like a tree. Quiet. Unmoving. Something you could lean against if you needed to. Something that gave shade without asking for anything in return.

And now she felt all of him. And none of it backed down.

He picked up her bathrobe sash with the same hand that held the belt, adjusting his grip once as if assessing weight and balance—like he was carrying weapons, not accessories. Then he walked her to the bedroom.

She stumbled. Refused to move cleanly.

The room was serene.

Lavender and eucalyptus from the diffuser curled in the air like mist. Pale wood floors. Soft cream rug. A tall, minimal rail-style headboard wrought in brass, warm and elegant. The bed itself was plush, luxurious, immaculately made.

But the painting above the headboard gave everything away.

A large canvas, moody and visceral, soaked in shadow and contrast, like someone had bled darkness into velvet and then tried to scrub it out. Not abstract. But too emotional to be neutral. No one could look at it without feeling something curl in their ribs.

He didn't spare it a glance.

He turned her, pushed her gently toward the bed, and had her kneel on the mattress, facing the brass railings. Her knees sank into the softness.

Without speaking, he took her arms and guided them up, wrists crossed, and looped the bathrobe sash around them with an efficiency that made her gasp.

Not haphazard. Precise.

The knot was beautiful. Elegant. Two loops over the rail, cinched with tension, pulling her forward just enough that her back arched and her arms were stretched. The pressure was perfect. There was no slack, no wiggle room—but she wasn't in pain.

Yet.

He stepped back and let her feel it. The restraint. The helplessness. The silence between them like a tide.

Then—

He held the belt where she could see it.

Let the leather skim along one arm, down to her shoulder blade, the curve of her ass, the backs of her thighs. Not a warning. An invitation.

She closed her eyes.

Her breath caught in her throat.

And she nodded slowly once. Twice. "Do it, Nico."

Sharp. Controlled. Like it would've broken her ribs to say more than she already had.

The leather slid away. She felt the air shift as he stepped back, as he adjusted his grip again, folding the belt tighter, testing the weight, the angle. She couldn't see him. The position kept her facing the brass rail. Her arms stretched high, back curved, knees sunk deep into the down comforter that smelled like eucalyptus and some faint trace of herself.

She exhaled—once, slow—and tried not to brace.

Tried not to chase it.

And then the belt landed.

It was clean. A strike measured and placed with intent—catching just enough of her upper thigh that the shock radiated outward, blooming bright beneath the skin. Her whole body jolted, a gasp ripping free before she could swallow it.

Heat flooded the spot instantly. A sting, yes, but also something else—something heavier. A slow, burning awareness. A reckoning.

It rewired everything inside her in a single second.

And she cried out—not loud, not theatrical. Just the sound of something breaking loose. Something not allowed to be felt in daylight.

Pain was a scalpel. It cut through the fog. It reminded her that she was a body. That her skin could still speak. That her mind didn't get the final word.

He waited. Didn't strike again. Just stood behind her, breathing slow, watching her breath catch and recalibrate.

She clenched her fists against the rail, wrists bound tight.

Tears stung her eyes yet again. She wasn't crying. Not really. But the heat was there. The want was there. That sick, bone-deep hunger for something to mark her and make it real.

Her thighs trembled. Her breath stuttered. Her heart hurt so fucking much it made her dizzy.

He stepped closer. The bed shifted.

"Good girl," he murmured, voice like a cut wrapped in velvet. "Still with me?"

She nodded. Fast. Too fast.

"Say it," he said, the belt trailing over her again, teasing the same spot, threatening it.

"Don't stop," she whispered, the words catching on the edge of something she didn't want to name. "I'm still here."

"Good," he said again. "Then we keep going."

The second strike came lower. Aimed. Precise. Beautiful in its brutality.

And Izzy let herself shatter.

Not from the pain.

From the relief.

Because for the first time in days, in weeks, in months maybe—she knew exactly what she was feeling. And there was no room left for anything else.

Only the heat. Only the sting. Only him.

The next three strikes came with a rhythm. Almost meditative. Almost merciful. One across the swell of her ass —sharp, clean, placed with exacting cruelty. Another lower, slicing across the back of her other thigh so sudden it cracked a sound from her throat she didn't recognize. The third blurred into light. She didn't feel it so much as hear it, a muffled thud swallowed by the distance building behind her eyes.

The world blinked out for half a second—like surfacing from under cold water—and when she looked around, he was already on his knees behind her.

His hands, rough and cool, slid across the welted skin he'd just marked. Not soothing exactly—firm, clinical, a slow inspection. He touched her like he was checking his own work. Stroking gently where the skin pulsed hot and furious, dragging his fingers through the mess between her thighs like it belonged to him.

And then—

His mouth.

She gasped before she even processed it. He licked her with the flat of his tongue, brutal and wide and slow, and she buckled forward against the restraint. Her wrists tugged at the knot. The rail creaked faintly under the strain.

He didn't ease her into it. Didn't give her warning. Just devoured.

She couldn't see him. Couldn't see anything.

Only the painting.

That dark, unnamed sprawl of shadow and blood and

memory above her bed, the one she'd stared at so many nights. Now it was all she had—vision fixed on the void, while someone she couldn't see used his tongue like punishment.

There were no thoughts left. Just sensation. Just the violent dichotomy of pain and pleasure flooding her in waves.

She pushed back against him, shaking, unable to control it, her body chasing the rhythm like it was the only law that still applied. But he held her still. One hand gripping the side of her thigh. The other reaching around to roughly palm her breasts.

He licked. And sucked. And circled her clit with sickening precision. Not teasing like before—not withholding. Just cruelly thorough.

Her first orgasm came fast, so fast it frightened her. The second followed before she'd finished breathing. She moaned into the mattress, the softness of the duvet taunting her, and still he didn't stop.

Even when she whimpered. Even when her thighs flinched. Even when she throbbed from overstimulation, he kept going. Not out of sadism. But because she hadn't said stop. And she didn't want to.

She was raw. She was wrecked.

She was his.

"Nico—" she gasped, voice barely a thread. "Please, I need you now."

He moved.

She heard the sound of clothing hitting the floor. The heat of his body behind her now matched hers. His shirt was gone. His skin on her welts sent sparks across her spine.

Her wrists were still bound. Still stretched forward

against the brass. The knot hadn't loosened—not even a little.

And when he grabbed her by the hair again, pulling her head back so sharply the back of her skull nearly kissed the space between her shoulder blades, she moaned.

He stroked himself against her—long, slow drags against her slick, swollen folds—and she gasped like he was flaying her open.

"Fuck's sake, Nico," she gritted out.

He didn't answer.

She heard the soft foil of a condom wrapper tearing.

She looked over her shoulder, eyes wet. Her gaze darted between the condom and his eyes and she shook her head.

"Wait," she said.

He stopped and immediately dropped his hands.

"Finish inside me."

"Are you sure?"

"Yes."

And that was it.

He dropped the condom. Grabbed her hips. Then drove into her without mercy.

It was an impossible angle—her head yanked back by her hair, her arms outstretched in front of her, body arched like a bow being snapped. He held her there, used her there, fucked her like he had something to prove to her body, not her heart.

Each thrust was a bruise.

Each pull of her hair a lesson.

Her scalp burned. Her hips ached. Her ribs trembled. She had never felt anything like it—so much pain and pleasure in the same breath, crashing through her until all she could do was gasp through it.

He whispered things in her ear as he used her, things so filthy they made her clench harder around him.

"Fucking ruined," he hissed. "You like being used like this, don't you?"

She moaned. Nodded.

"You're mine."

She wanted to agree. She wanted to say, *Yes, I'm yours,* but she only shattered again.

The orgasm this time didn't feel like pleasure. It felt like relief.

Like her body couldn't carry it anymore and had to break open to let it out.

He groaned behind her, his breath catching as he finally let go—thrusting deep, deep, deeper, and filling her. Until she felt the impossible warmth flood her, thick and real and so final she could barely breathe.

She trembled.

And for one quiet moment, she didn't feel sad.

Just full.

And that, she thought dimly, was close enough.

Izzy didn't move.

Couldn't.

She felt high.

Not the sleek, glossy kind of high that made people dance or laugh or float. This was something deeper. Thicker. Like being wrapped in wool. Her nerve endings were humming. Her muscles were mush. Her pain receptors had gone quiet in a way that only happened after everything had been used.

The endorphins were eating her alive.

She floated in it. That heavy, golden quiet that only came after ruin. Not joy. Joy had long since stopped returning her calls. But this—this heat blooming low in her belly, this ache threaded through every muscle, this ragged, aching fullness—it was something older. Truer. It lit up the dark corners of her mind like a match held to a damp page.

This wasn't happiness. This was pain so clean it felt holy. It was heroin. Slow, warm, and mean.

She didn't hear him move until the bed dipped.

Nico was behind her again, silent, warm.

"Still here?"

"I'm still here."

He untied her wrists with a gentleness that somehow hurt more than getting slapped. His fingers moved with care, not hesitation, loosening each loop like it was sacred. She didn't thank him. Didn't speak. Her arms dropped uselessly once they were free, too weak to hold their weight.

He didn't try to hold her. Didn't press against her back or gather her into his chest. He just reached for a corner of the pillow and pulled it under her head—slow, deliberate. Touched her shoulder once with the backs of his knuckles. Then disappeared.

The bathroom light clicked on down the hall. Water ran. A washcloth was soaked and wrung out.

He returned a minute later. She still hadn't moved.

He didn't say anything. Just knelt beside the bed and cleaned her chest and thighs, gently wiping between them, catching what dripped, what smeared, what he'd left inside her like a brand. The cloth was warm. Then cold. Then warm again.

Her legs twitched. Her hips flinched. She let him do it anyway.

"Izzy," he murmured, once, not as a question. Just her name.

She didn't answer. Couldn't.

Her throat felt like it had been scraped raw from the inside out. Her scalp ached where he'd held her. The side of her face pulsed from where he slapped her. She still felt him inside her.

And she didn't want to forget it.

He helped her shift. Helped her sit up slowly, one hand behind her spine. She moved like a puppet—pliable, detached, some part of her hovering above it all, watching the scene unfold with fascination.

He fetched her a new silk slip from the closet and pulled it over her head and helped her loop her arms through the straps.

He placed a glass of water and a bottle of paracetamol he found on the nightstand. Sat beside her but didn't reach for her again.

The silence between them wasn't cold. It was surgical.

When she finally looked up, he was already watching her. Half-dressed. Still breathing heavy like he hadn't recovered.

Then he said it. Quietly. No anger. Just gravity.

"You'll be okay. But I won't be here when you are."

She didn't answer. Didn't flinch.

She nodded once. "I know."

She bunched his half-buttoned shirt in her fist and pulled him down for a final kiss. It hurt more than anything he'd left on her skin. She laid back down on her side with a wince and faced the opposite direction.

He didn't stop her.

He stood. Put his uniform back on in silence.

She listened to the sound of the front door unlocking.

He didn't slam it. He didn't linger. No goodbyes.

And when the lock clicked back into place behind him, she didn't cry. She just laid there, emptied out, like something had been carved from her and carried away.

33

The chemist was too bright. Flat white light hummed above Izzy's scalp like judgment. Everything smelled like plastic packaging and wet receipts.

She bought the morning after pill like she was picking up gum.

No plastic alarm box. There was no one eyeing her like she was about to steal the Crown Jewels. In the UK, they didn't treat emergency contraception like contraband. Just a short conversation with a pharmacist who asked, "How long ago was the unprotected sex?" and didn't flinch when she said, "Seven hours."

It was only a few months ago she'd once had to press a call button at a Walgreens in Seattle just to look at the damn box. Waited ten minutes while a teenage employee fetched a manager with keys like she was trying to boost a PlayStation.

Here, they slipped it into a paper bag and said, "Take it with food."

That was it. Transaction complete.

She added it to her internal archive of modern romance: the comparative accessibility of morning-after pills across international metropolitan areas.

She popped the blister pack in the stairwell, washing it down with a chocolate protein bar she didn't want. It stuck halfway down her throat like guilt.

The mirror on the wall was hung too low, probably meant for children or people who hadn't aged ten years in one month. She looked anyway. Hair in a ponytail. Loose white dress tied at the neck. Cheekbones more gaunt than usual. Her expression said nothing.

The bruises bloomed under her dress—purple and green, sharp and blurred. A mouth-shaped mark behind her knee. Fingerprints on her arms. Belt stripes across the curve of her ass that stung when she walked. The linen brushed against them, a whisper of fabric that made her skin hum.

They weren't the kind of bruises she could laugh off as "MMA sparring." These were deliberate. Intimate. These meant something.

She shifted her weight, and her thighs ached.

Last night had been madness, but not the accidental kind. It was deliberate. Chosen. She wasn't drunk. She wasn't pressured. She made a request.

And he'd listened.

Her mouth twisted. She felt—what was it? A flush of pride, maybe? A little preening hum beneath the ache.

He did that because I demanded it. Because I could take it.

But it coiled with something else: *Jesus, Izzy. Who the fuck are you becoming?*

She didn't feel violated. She didn't feel regret. Not really. But there was something about bruises on the backs of her arms that made her want to hide. And something about the one behind her knee that made her want to stand taller.

God, last night had been reckless.

She adjusted the tie on her dress and stared into the mirror like it might hand her a verdict. But it only reflected what she already knew: She had let him say goodbye with his hands.

And she had let him leave with her name still raw in his mouth.

She walked home.

Her flat was quiet. Not messy, not clean. There were still piles of cakes, cookies, and tarts from Cy's visit the day before. Her fridge was a battleground of skincare and oat milk. She put the empty foil packet on the counter, poured herself a glass of water, and didn't drink it.

Bake Off was on. Someone was crying about custard. She turned up the volume and curled up on the sofa in the linen dress, pulling her bruised knees into her chest. She didn't text Cy. She didn't want to bother him.

She just watched sponge cake fail and drank water that didn't taste like anything.

Then her email pinged.

It was from Cy. No subject line. Just her name.

She opened it.

Two hundred names. Crew. Ground. Fellow pilots. Even some instructors. All of them saying she was one of the finest captains they'd flown with. That she was sharp, generous, immaculate, precise. That if LUMA didn't clear her to fly again soon, they'd have a union nightmare on their hands.

Put her back in the sky or you will have hell to pay.

Her phone slipped from her hand.

She didn't change. She just took the elevator down, walked out onto the street and hailed a cab. No bra, no coat, nothing in her bag but her phone and a key.

BRICK LANE WAS loud with attitude that night—fried dough, faint bass, girls in platform boots pretending not to shiver. The air stank of sugar and ambition, cigarettes and bergamot cologne. Past the curry houses and record stores and the shop that only sold disco vinyl, the pavement narrowed near Spitalfields.

When she got to the crooked little Victorian walk-up with too many flower pots and one aggressive tabby in the window, she rang Cy's bell.

He opened the door in a hoodie that smelled like cloves and lavender softener. She collapsed against him, arms locked around his waist like she might break if she let go.

"I've been a shit friend," she said, into his chest, into the soft part of his shoulder, where her voice wouldn't echo.

"No," he said, arms already around her, hands warm on the knobs of her spine. "The world's just shit. But we'll get through it."

He let her in without a word more. The flat smelled like brown butter and nutmeg. She kicked off her boots and stepped into a life she'd been part of for nearly a decade. They'd met back when LUMA was still a Europe-only operation and she was flying out of Heathrow, back before the mergers, before widebodies, before everything. She'd known Mas just as long—handsome, silver-fox energy, with kind eyes and matching salt-and-pepper hair to Cy's that had gone white at the temples. Persian, raised in South London, and so infuriatingly serene she sometimes fantasized about shaking him just to see if he'd flinch.

He was grading homework at the dining table, red pen in hand, glasses perched on the tip of his nose. "You look like you haven't eaten," he said, standing to give her a hug. His arms were softer than Cy's but just as steady.

"I haven't," she muttered into his shoulder.

"Then you should stay for dinner."

There was a whole meal ready—lamb and pumpkin stew, basmati with saffron and crispy onions, a salad that had no business being that good on a weekday. She picked at it, barefoot and exhausted, until finally she said, "Thank you. For the letter."

Cy nodded, refilling her wine. "Nico got a bunch of the pilots to sign it. Most of the long-haul boys."

She didn't respond to that. She took another bite. Her jaw was tight. The tension never really left anymore.

Cy gave her a moment. Then cleared his throat—not gently. The sound was deliberate, theatrical, and just short of a sigh.

"Anyway," he said, dragging the word out like a silk scarf, "since you've barged into my home and stolen my lamb, I assume that means you're morally obligated to help me become a national treasure."

He slid the folder across the table like he was handing out customs cards down the aisle. She flipped it open and found a typed recipe list, some headshots, a half-written bio that started with "I bake like I dance: chaotic, Trinidadian, and always with a little rum in the sauce."

Right. The Bake Off campaign. That was still happening.

He aced the phone interview a few days ago. Apparently

someone from production had said he was charming, honest, and "classically Cy"—which could mean anything or everything.

They worked into the night—emails, paperwork, mock-ups for Cy's submission packet. She helped him pick through outfit options for the in-person audition: not too coordinated, not too boring. Something that looked like a man who knew how to fold a fitted sheet and deliver a one-liner that ruined your day. Understated, pressed, maybe a little floral. The kind of thing that said I'm not trying too hard. I just look like this. Something that wouldn't melt under the lights.

The house was absolutely saturated with baked goods. Every surface held a tray or a cooling rack: coconut buns, guava pastries, an experimental mango-tamarind babka that Mas had vetoed as "too funky for British taste buds." Her favorite was the condensed milk pound cake with a touch of rum in the glaze—sticky, tender, and scented like home, if home had better lighting and someone who knew what mise en place was.

The technical bake for the audition was a choux pastry challenge, so he'd been practicing: cream puffs filled with spiced custard, pâte à choux infused with cardamom and bay leaf, one batch dusted with cocoa and chili sugar, another filled with sorrel curd and topped with a candied hibiscus petal. The Carribean influence was subtle but specific—sweet and sharp and precise. You could taste where he came from. You could taste who raised him.

They filmed a little test segment on Mas's DSLR. She held the cue cards. Gave notes. Cursed when the audio lagged.

Around midnight, she curled up on the couch under the

same quilt they'd had since their Frankfurt days. Cy kissed the top of her head, Mas passed her a hot water bottle, and the tabby cat climbed on her ribs like he always belonged there.

No one said it aloud, but the quiet was safe. And for one night, that was enough.

34

Nico had made it exactly halfway through folding a pair of his own boxer briefs when the knock came.

Not a polite one. A Farrah one. Precise. Steady. Like a countdown.

It had been three days since Izzy ended it, and he hadn't felt anything since—just the dull hum of systems failure. Grief, maybe. Or just shock. He couldn't tell.

He opened the door to a triple threat: Layla in tinted sunglasses and a giant green faux fur coat, Samira in her architectural trench, and Ahsan half-asleep on Samira's hip, clinging to her like a decorative barnacle in a leopard print hat with ears. All of them looked judgmental in different fonts.

Layla's gaze flicked to the boxer briefs in his hand. "Still folding your shame, I see. Charming."

Samira walked straight past him without a word. Ahsan barely stirred—just blinked at Nico with that eerie toddler focus that knew no boundaries, no social grace, no mercy.

Then he let out a long, almost pitying sigh and face-planted into Samira's shoulder.

Layla followed, her boots clicking like a threat. "We took a red-eye. I gave up a Netflix wrap party and Samira skipped a board meeting. Ahsan's technically unconscious. That's how worried we are."

Samira opened the fridge. "Two protein bars. Three takeout containers. No vegetables." She turned to him. "Do you want to die?"

"I'm fine."

"Delusional," Layla muttered, flopping dramatically onto the couch. "You look like a widowed Boy Scout."

Ahsan stirred just enough to lift his head at Nico. Then, eyes still barely open, he mumbled, "Sad."

Nico ran a hand down his face.

Layla raised an eyebrow. "Read for filth by a jet-lagged toddler. You've officially hit rock bottom."

Samira shut the fridge. "Where's your phone?"

"Dead."

She pulled out her own. "Then I'm charging it. And going through your texts. I need to know when the spiral started."

"I didn't tell you to come," Nico said. Weakly. Uselessly.

"Right, and I didn't need to tell mom about the nipple piercing when I was sixteen," Layla said "But some things need to be known."

She stood. She just grabbed his wrist like it was a leash and said, "You know what? Shoes. Jacket. Let's go right now. You look like you've been crying into dry pasta."

Before he could protest, Samira had already scooped the toddler into her arms and walked out the flat.

They did not stay in his depressing sublet. Obviously not. They took him to The Lanesborough like he was a divorced pop star on the verge. The staff already knew Layla by name. There were flowers in the suite.

By the time he sat down on the velvet sofa in a room that cost more per night than his last bonus, Layla had already ordered a full high tea service and was explaining to the baby that "uncles get sad sometimes but then we bully them into drinking oolong with cookies the size of their heads."

The tea tower arrived. Nico didn't even like scones, but they were warm and the cream was the kind of decadent that makes you question democracy. He ate two, then three. Ahsan threw a jam-smeared spoon. Layla caught it mid-air.

They went to Fortnum's and Harrods. Nico tried to be normal. He tried to just walk and be grateful and absorb the love bomb without collapsing.

But then he saw the toddler-sized duffle coat with toggle buttons and matching hat.

He bought it.

And then the tiny Chelsea boots.

And then the fucking corduroy overalls.

Layla wrestled him away from the baby department like she was dragging a drunk out of a casino. She was five feet tall and looked like she'd blow away in a strong wind, but she nearly got him to the floor by tickling behind his knees like a gremlin assassin.

"Say you yield," she said.

"I will not—" he gasped, laughing for the first time in a week, full-bellied and unguarded.

"Say it!"

He collapsed. "Fine. I yield. Jesus. You're evil."

"Correct. And Ahsan already has three coats."

Back at the suite, she set up her ring light like it was a crime in progress. Ahsan napped in a silk toddler bed. Nico nursed a chamomile tea like he had a choice.

Layla hit record.

"So apparently," she began, full mascara and murder in her eyes, "this bald-ass podcaster—who looks like if a thumb had a YouTube channel—said women shouldn't fly planes because 'our emotions make us unreliable in emergencies.' Sir. You cried during *Dune* and said Paul Atreides reminds you of your inner child. Shut the hell up."

The delivery was vicious. The lighting was flattering. The captions were accurate. Nico could already hear the stitch edits coming.

He slipped into the next room with the baby monitor and sat near Samira, who was typing with the calm of a sniper.

"He tried to hide his metadata," she said without looking up. "But his Discord server logs show IPs from six different scam funnel sites. I traced them to two Swiss holding companies and a fake charity in Dubai."

Nico blinked. "Jesus."

"He's running crypto-funded MLMs targeting kids. If I leak it, the FBI will hit him from one side, and Interpol from the other."

Nico looked at her. No hesitation.

"Do it."

Samira nodded. "Done."

He walked home hours later, alone. The box of ma'amoul was warm in his hands, its paper corners soft with butter.

He didn't open it right away. He just sat on his couch and stared at it like it might answer something for him. Then he took one out and ate it slowly, powdered sugar clinging to his lips. It tasted like Beirut, like his grandmother's hands, like softness from people who loved you even when you didn't ask for it.

His phone buzzed. An email from the MMA gym. A newsletter. He didn't usually open them. But this time he did.

The top image was a group training photo. Izzy. Him. The girls. Her hair pulled back, her smile sharp and real.

He could still feel her body against his. His chest cracked open.

He unsubscribed. Then closed his laptop.

35

Izzy didn't believe in hope. She believed in spreadsheets. In backups. In dry-run drills for things no one else thought to prepare for—cockpit fires, legal ambushes, a text from her ex-husband at 2 a.m. So when Cy told her he'd made it to the audition round for Bake Off, she didn't say congratulations.

She opened a shared Notes file and titled it: **[CLASSI-FIED] Operation: Rise & Slay**

Then she texted it to André: *Get in. We're weaponizing pastry.*

What started as a joke—a way to kill time while grounded—turned into a recon document so detailed MI6 would've taken notes. It had contestant surveillance, coded recipe strategies, emotionally manipulative talking points, and a full psychological profile of Paul Hollywood. No one asked her to make it. But Cy was family. And this was how she loved people: quietly, obsessively, and through encrypted shared files.

Because if the BBC wanted vulnerability, he'd give them precision. If they wanted tears, he'd give them torch sugar. If they wanted narrative, he'd have one, courtesy of one unhinged flight attendant and a pissed-off captain with time on her hands.

[Classified] Operation: Rise & Slay

Subject: Cyrus Yorke

Objective: Get into Bake Off. Win.

Profile

Codename: Starbaker Zero

Strengths: Laminated doughs, citrus layering, hand confidence.

Weaknesses: Cries when praised. Refuses sabotage (coward).

Audition Strategy

Signature Bake:

- Nostalgic but elevated
- TV pretty, not influencer ugly
- 8 words or less

Suggested: "Granny's Coconut Rum Tres Leches Cake—but make it vengeful."

Video Tips

- Say "my granny" even if it's a lie
- Don't say "fun"—say "flavor supremacy"
- Bake like you've survived loss. (You have. Retail.)

British Bake Token:
- Treacle tart, Victoria sponge, hot cross buns
- Reinvent it. Respectfully. Aggressively.
- Do NOT touch spotted dick. Ever.

<u>Enemy Intel</u>
Name / Weakness / Take
- Rupert / Weak wrists / You're what he wishes he could whisk
- Ellie / Cries near heat / Smile sweet. Then crush.
- Jayden / Aesthetic only / Serve substance in matte finish

<u>Prep Answers</u>
"Why now?" → "Because I stopped making myself small."
"What if you fail?" → "Then I'll still taste better than the rest."

<u>Final Note</u>
If you need a courier for your bake, Izzy has two passports and dry ice. Don't test her. She will fly to Madagascar and back for you if you need single-origin hand-cured vanilla beans.

∼

THE GYM WAS QUIETER than she remembered. Late-night hours hit different. The playlist was softer, older. The clang of weights less competitive, more meditative. No loud drills, no crowd-pleasing strikes. Just the regulars—the real ones.

The loyal crew who'd followed Rey from the old gym, the kind of people who didn't care about branding or lockers that locked, who showed up because they knew Rey would actually teach them how to fight.

Izzy wasn't sparring. She hadn't even changed. She wore a cream cashmere set—loose trousers and a long-sleeved top that made her look like she didn't belong here anymore. She didn't care. She was helping Rey with the mail. Sorting forms. Tagging invoices. Entering emergency contact updates into a spreadsheet like it mattered.

She liked doing the small things. The quiet things. The things no one could say she did wrong.

She was halfway through labeling a stack of shipping boxes when Lina pushed the door open.

"Is your boyfriend coming by?"

Izzy didn't look up.

Lina leaned in the doorway with the exaggerated ease of a twenty-something who knew she was hot. "What? He hasn't been around. Did you break up? Is he single? Should I get his number?"

It was a joke. Everyone in the gym flirted like it was a warm-up drill. But Izzy's body betrayed her before she could come up with something snide. Her hands stilled. Her face went blank. Not cool, not chill. Just—absent.

Rey didn't miss it.

"Oi," Rey snapped from the back of the office. "Out."

Lina blinked. "What? I was just messing—"

"Time and place, mate," Rey said. Her voice was flat, but her accent sharpened like a knife against tile.

Lina raised her hands, still smiling, but she backed out. The door shut behind her with a soft clack.

Rey didn't look up from her clipboard. "You want me to stab her or you want to do it?"

Izzy exhaled, tension spilling out slow and hot through her nose. "You'd get caught. I'd be too thorough."

Rey made a noise that might've been approval.

They were quiet a moment longer. Rey flipped a page.

"I'm not saying anything about him," she said finally, like she was picking up a conversation they'd never started. "But the good ones—if you let 'em go—they'll circle back when they're supposed to. And if they don't, it's 'cause they weren't real."

Izzy didn't answer.

Rey looked at her then, just once. "You're allowed to be wrecked. Just don't bleed on the mats."

Then she went back to the clipboard like she hadn't just said the smartest thing Izzy had heard all week.

"And anyway," Rey added, pen between her teeth, "get out of my office. You're making me nervous, sitting there in that cashmere like some high-value shareholder."

Izzy stood. Took the mail. Didn't say a word.

But when she walked out of the office, she almost felt— if not better, then steadier.

And that would have to be enough.

She met André for lunch the next day in Marylebone, at one of those aggressively charming brunch spots where the ceiling was covered in fake wisteria and every table came with a ring light. The menus were spiral-bound like novellas. The drinks had names like Grapefruit Manifesto and

Emo Recovery Smoothie. Every other table had a girl in pastels pretending not to take a selfie.

They sat outside under a linen parasol that did absolutely nothing about the heat. Izzy had dressed for shade, not sweat, but was already regretting the long sleeves.

André ordered soup.

It was thirty degrees Celsius, and they were sitting outside. The bowl arrived in a matte ceramic mug that hissed like dry ice, steam curling up like it had a special effects budget.

Izzy raised an eyebrow.

He ignored it. Took a dramatic sip and said, mid-crouton, "So. I'm not saying the aircraft's haunted, but... is the cockpit supposed to be pinging high-frequency signals between crew devices like it's trying to hook up with someone?"

She blinked.

André shrugged like he was debating which toast to post. "I was syncing my Fitbit—don't start—and the damn thing kept jumping signal in the galley. I figured it was the ovens. But it's not heat. Then I checked again after we landed—same spike. Weird little EMF echo. And my smart mug was pinging too. Like, legit interference. Weird, right?"

Her spoon stalled just before her mouth. Half-lifted. Hovering.

He gave her a look. Not alarmed. Just expectant. Like she was taking too long to laugh.

She didn't laugh.

His smile slid off, slow and exact. "Wait. That's not normal?"

She didn't move. Not externally. That would've given her away. But inside, her instincts tucked in tight, curled like something trying not to be seen.

God. He was terrifying when he did this. Not showboating. Just quietly, casually two steps ahead of every system he touched. The kind of man who made a Fitbit perform recon and a smart mug scan for spectral interference like it had clearance.

She remembered different flights. Different glitches. André, not rated for tech repair, still fixing things the moment they failed. Tablets that updated mid-cruise without the mechanics even knowing. Quiet miracles that looked like coincidence—unless you knew better.

"I keep forgetting you're not just a menace," she said, voice flat. "You're a fucking oracle with unlimited data."

He beamed. "It's true."

It should've clicked sooner. That night at the club in Barcelona—André hijacking the audio system mid-set with a spoofed signal like it was nothing. She'd laughed.

But she should've *asked*. Should've realized what kind of tech literacy she was really playing with.

She'd brushed it off because it didn't *fit*. Because he was charming, and flirty, and dropped one-liners like it was a condition of employment. Not the kind of person you expected to breach encrypted comms with the same ease he applied lip gloss.

That was her mistake. Bias. And now it might've cost her intel she could've had three months ago.

She told him so. Flat-out. "I should've clocked this months ago. You spoofed a whole sound system at a night club in thirty seconds and I just...laughed. I underestimated you. I'm sorry."

André blinked, a little thrown. "I—uh. Wow. Okay. I mean...thank you?"

"I mean it."

He grinned, a little bashful now, fiddling with his spoon like it had betrayed him.

She exhaled hard. "Then when it came to the cockpit, I ignored the signs. All of it. The static pops. The overhead flickers. The times the comms glitched like they were trying to confess something. I chalked it up to stress. Fatigue. Phantom data. The kind of haunted bullshit you stop noticing when you're not allowed to name what's wrong."

Her eyes flicked back to his. "But *you* noticed, Dre. You always do. You listen to what's off in the galley, in the jumpseat, in the cracks between systems where the shit actually starts. You turned this *brunch* into a surveillance op and I'm still sitting here with my thumb up my ass like I don't have command clearance."

He raised his eyebrows. "So what do we do?"

"We start small," she said. "Quiet."

And with a napkin, a borrowed pen, and a voice like cut glass, she began to diagram the kind of plan that didn't make noise until it was already too late.

36

She hadn't meant to stay over.

One glass of wine became two. One episode became four. And then she and André were wrapped in throw blankets, half-asleep on opposite ends of his LUMA-sponsored sectional, watching a finale neither of them had followed. She remembered the screen casting purple light over the kitchen tiles, her feet tucked under her, André muttering something about how no one on Selling Sunset had a real license. After that, nothing. Just the kind of sleep you can only get when your body's too emotionally wrung out to dream.

When she woke up, the flat smelled like espresso and organic cleaning spray. André was gone—probably at Pilates —so she showered in the guest bath, grabbed her bag, and made her exit looking exactly how she felt: puffy, under-slept, and completely unbothered by the fact that she hadn't braided her hair for the first time in public since...maybe ever.

Her hair hung down her back in a straight, heavy curtain, still damp from André's conditioner. She'd left it untouched—no styling, no pins, nothing to hide behind. Just her.

She stopped at the hip sandwich shop around the corner—the one with the menu printed in lower-case serif and a line out the door. Got something with fennel she wasn't in the mood for. It cost seventeen pounds and the man behind the counter called her "my darling" like it was a spell. She didn't even taste it. She just stood there on the sidewalk, blinking in the midday light, remembering why she didn't like this neighborhood.

Then she saw him.

He was coming out of the Pret next door.

Uniform sharp. Sunglasses on. Shoulders back.

Four stripes.

She stopped moving. Didn't breathe.

He stepped onto the curb like someone had choreographed it. Like he belonged to the street. Looking fresh, holding a fucking green juice like his organs weren't made of pre-workout.

He looked unfairly good.

Like he was built for a cinematic universe. His wheat gold hair was still faintly damp at the roots, already dry at the ends—freshly washed, neatly styled, like he'd just finished his morning routine with time to spare. Clean-shaven. Hydrated.

Heads turned when he stepped out.

Not just turned—*snapped.*

Two baristas from the shop behind her visibly paused mid-conversation. A cyclist nearly clipped a bollard. Someone muttered *"Jesus Christ"* under their breath.

And the worst part? He didn't notice.

Didn't preen. Didn't wink.

She stared at him.

Then: "Hey."

He shifted his weight, stepping aside like he expected her to walk past him. Like maybe she would do what she always did—refuse the moment. Choose pride over discomfort. Distance over ache.

But she didn't move.

And he didn't stop looking.

Her hair moved slightly in the wind.

Her mouth opened before she could stop it.

"You never said you lived in LUMA housing."

It came out harsher than she meant—clipped, almost accusatory. Like his proximity was an ambush and he'd planned it.

He blinked. Sunglasses still on. Shoulders still perfect.

Then, simply: "You didn't ask."

No edge. Just fact.

That's what landed the hardest.

Because he was right.

She hadn't asked. Not where he lived. Not anything.

She'd been so busy holding him at arm's length she'd never even thought to look past it.

The shame bloomed sharp and fast.

Because of course he was here. Of course he lived near André in LUMA's corporate housing. Of course she'd practically slept under his roof without knowing it.

She looked down at her sandwich. Whatever dignity she had left was leaking into the aioli.

He just watched. Steady.

Not mad. Maybe already forgiven.

His mouth opened. Then shut.

Then, softly: "You okay?"

She should have said yes. Should've kept walking.

But instead she stood there, sandwich and all.

"Not really."

He stilled. Just for a second. Like he hadn't expected honesty.

"You want to come up?" he asked. "I've got coffee."

No.

No.

Absolutely not.

She was not doing this.

Not after her little monologue about ending things, about how this wasn't good for either of them, about how it was over. She meant that. She'd meant all of it. Even the cruel parts. Especially the cruel parts.

This would be a bad idea. A sloppy, backsliding, coffee-scented mistake.

But his eyes didn't move. His voice hadn't twisted. He wasn't asking her to fix anything.

Just come up. Just coffee.

She hated herself for it.

"Okay," she said. "Just for a minute."

SHE FOLLOWED him up the stairs, already regretting it. She should've said no. She had said no—five times, in her head, before her mouth betrayed her. Just for a minute. Famous last words.

The door opened.

She stepped inside.

It was quiet. Not just soundless—quiet. Like the space itself didn't need to prove anything. The lights were soft. The air smelled like clean cotton and something citrusy— probably whatever he used to wipe the countertops.

She didn't want to like it.

But the couch was deep and worn in. Real wood floors.

Books on the shelf that had spines. A kitchen with sharp knives and heavy pans that had been used, not displayed. His shoes were lined up by the door. There was no framed motivational quote, no tragic beanbag, no frat boy vibe. Just order. Not performative. Just... lived in. Lived in by someone who gave a shit.

Which was, frankly, offensive.

She moved through the room slowly, half-expecting to find the tell. A Red Bull can. A stack of unopened mail. A dumbbell in the hallway.

Nothing.

His plants were alive.

Succulents on the windowsill. A row of cacti in mismatched terracotta. One stubborn Hoya hanging by the kitchen light—trailing vines like it had something to prove.

Nothing showy. Just the kind of greenery that endures.

Like him.

Quiet. Contained. Still here.

And then—the final insult—he said:

"I have that Catalan roast you like. From that café in El Born? You said it tasted like your spite."

She turned.

He was in the kitchen, holding up the tin like it meant nothing.

Like he hadn't just revealed he remembered her favorite obscure roast—only sold in one alleyway café in Barcelona she barely mentions.

Her throat went dry. She hated that her chest hurt. She hated the little pull in her stomach, the muscle memory of safety.

"That'd be great."

He set the mug in front of her. Coffee, steaming. The light through the kitchen window was soft and unfair.

Morning light. Honest light. The kind that didn't let you lie about how tired you were.

She sat. Only because he'd pulled the chair out.

He didn't sit yet. Just leaned back against the counter, watching her the way he always had. Like she was going to say something dangerous. Like he wanted her to.

So she did.

"I think they're spying on us."

He doesn't laugh. Doesn't blink. Just leans forward slightly, like he's listening to a checklist.

"In the cockpit?" he asks.

"Everywhere." She swallows. "Cockpit, tablets, possibly SIM cards. I don't have proof, not really, but—things aren't adding up. And I think it's connected to Russell."

"With the airline's approval?"

Calm. Like she'd said it was raining.

"Maybe not them directly. A vendor. Someone partnered with them. I don't know yet."

She curled her fingers around the mug. Didn't drink.

"But I think they've been monitoring pilots. Flight deck, tablets, even our phones if they're on the crew network."

Now he blinked.

Then he reached for his own mug—coffee, no sugar—and took a sip before responding.

"Okay."

Just that.

No suspicion. Just immediate alignment. Because of course he believed her.

And that was somehow worse.

"You're not gonna ask if I'm sure?" she said. "Or if I'm crazy?"

"Are you?"

She shot him a look.

His mouth twitched—almost a smile. Like something about her exasperation knocked loose a memory he'd been holding onto too tightly.

She was still absorbing the coffee and the plants and the fact that none of this was falling apart, when he said: "I've been looking into it too. After we stopped talking."

She stilled. Slowly set the mug down.

"Define looking into it."

"Flight data. Sync logs. Inconsistencies across firmware updates. A few anomalies Sami flagged when she was poking around. After... after your medical information got leaked."

That landed like a body hit. Low and clean.

She stared at the wall, shame prickling up the back of her neck—cold and sudden.

She shook her head. Focus.

"Samira? The same sister who hacked your school records to wipe a suspension?"

"Yep."

She hadn't realized Samira was that kind of smart. Or that kind of dangerous.

Izzy looked at him. "What does she do, exactly?"

Nico hesitated. Then: "She builds threat detection systems for governments and banks. They pay her to break in before someone else does."

Silence.

Izzy sat with that.

With the fact that he had people like that.

Not just dangerous—loyal. Quietly pulling strings while she'd been coming apart at the seams.

Jesus.

She hadn't wanted help. But help had happened anyway.

"You didn't think to tell me?" she asked, quieter than she meant to.

He shrugged—but the timing was too careful. Like he'd been bracing for that exact question.

"Wasn't sure what the post-breakup protocol was on sharing classified conspiracies. You said we were done. I figured that included data breaches."

She stared at him.

"This isn't a mixtape, Nico. It's a fucking crime."

He met her eyes. "I wasn't keeping it from you. Also, she just sent me the encrypted link last night."

She didn't answer.

He took a sip of his coffee, like that could cushion it.

"But you're here now," he added. "So. Here."

He slid the laptop across the table, screen lit. No ceremony. Just the truth, handed over clean.

She opened the file.

The screen filled with charts, logs, raw code—chaotic at first, then horrifying in its pattern. Metadata timestamps pulled from cockpit inputs. Location tracking tied to SIM IDs. Entire message trees marked for extraction.

One flagged note from Samira: cockpit voice data mirrored, corpus appeared in dark web dump two weeks ago.

Another: Firmware update included third-party packet routing. Monetization suspected.

And then—

Pilot behavioral indexing.

Sold.

Sold.

She scrolled, and it just kept getting worse. Crew comms. Cabin audio. Personal devices. A spreadsheet full of anonymized performance scores that weren't anonymous at all.

Somewhere in the data, she recognized herself.

"Pause there," Nico said, leaning in.

She froze—not at the screen, but at the nearness. His hand braced on the table beside hers, shoulder just brushing her arm.

He smelled like soap. Clean cotton and sleep. Like a quiet morning she'd tried not to miss.

"See that cluster?" he said, pointing. "That's a repeat pattern—same flight number, same aircraft, but different crew. Same anomaly spike."

She nodded, eyes locked on the screen—but her body registered the warmth beside her like a second betrayal.

"It's a full database," she murmured.

He didn't say anything.

He didn't have to.

It was all structured. Efficient. Meant to be forgettable. But she saw it—beneath the version control and scrubbed filenames, beneath the metadata and firmware patches.

They'd tracked her.

How often she checked systems. How long she paused before answering ATC. Her reaction time. Her eye movement. Heart rate variability. Micro-expressions, probably. Stress indicators, logged and exported. Her first day back? It was there. The minute she touched the yoke? Logged.

The involuntary tears. Recorded. Not anonymized.

Just harvested. Labeled. And sold.

And suddenly, it wasn't abstract. It wasn't "everyone's data is compromised." It wasn't about algorithmic advertising or Instagram knowing you broke up before you did.

This wasn't passive.

This was weaponized proximity.

She was a pilot. Nico was a pilot. They weren't consumers—they were infrastructure.

And someone had turned that into content.

"Morgan and Freja would never sign off on this," Nico said. Quiet. Certain.

Izzy didn't answer. Not right away.

Because he was probably right.

And somehow, that was the worst part.

Morgan hadn't known.

And still—this happened.

Right under her.

Izzy's fingers curled around the edge of the table.

So what the fuck else don't they know?

The silence held, just long enough for her to start feeling it in her teeth.

Then he glanced at the clock on the wall. That careful, guilty kind of glance that already had regret folded into it.

"Shit. I've got to get to the airport."

She didn't look at him.

"Must be nice," she said flatly. "Still being allowed to fly."

That landed. Harder than she meant, maybe. But not untrue.

He didn't say anything. Just looked like he'd been slapped without warning.

She stood, sweeping her hair back over her shoulder in that instinctive way someone does when it falls to the wrong side—except hers was too long, too heavy, too lush to move without drawing attention. It slid like silk down her back, a curtain re-drawn.

She didn't have to look to know he was watching. She could feel it—that quiet, helpless focus of a man who had already memorized the shape of her and was being punished for it now.

"I'll head out first," she said. "Send me the link."

"Done."

She moved toward the door. He followed—not close. Just near enough to feel the weight of everything unspoken.

"What are you gonna do?" he asked, voice low.

She paused at the threshold.

"I don't know yet," she said.

Then added, quieter: "But someone's going to wish I stayed grounded."

And then she was gone.

37

The guy's name was Connor. Because of course it was.

Walk-in. Day-pass. One of those FitPort power users who showed up to real gyms like they were club appearances. Loud. Built like a fridge. Not fat, not ripped—just that steroid-bulked stiffness that came from too many mirror reps and not enough sparring. The type of man who shadowboxed in the lobby and asked Rey if the girls here sparred "with contact."

He was Nico's exact height. Which would've been fine, if he'd had even one percent of Nico's quiet. But he didn't. He had mouth. He had hands. And he didn't know what to do with either.

Rey had tolerated him for one day. Just one. She let him bungle his way through mitt drills, corrected his stance once, ignored the "but I saw this on YouTube" comment. She gave him the standard three chances.

Fourth chance, he tried to "demonstrate" a rear naked choke on a teenage girl—unprompted.

"Oi," Rey said, standing up slow. "Izzy. You feel like stretching your legs?"

Izzy was already unwrapping her wrists. "Sure. You want him vertical or horizontal?"

Rey shrugged. "Dealer's choice."

They called it sparring. It wasn't.

Connor was all testosterone and top-heavy enthusiasm. He walked into the ring like a man preparing for a photo op. No mouthguard. Full swagger.

Izzy stepped in silent. No warmup, no tape, no fanfare. She was five-three on a good day, lean as a bone-handled blade, in a sleek Lululemon tank top. She tied her hair back in a secure bun.

Didn't speak.

The bell rang.

He led with a lazy jab, trying to feel her out. She didn't flinch. Didn't even blink. Just slipped it clean and pivoted. He smirked like she'd missed.

She hadn't.

Second pass, he swung wider. Sloppy. She let him get close enough to smell her shampoo—then stepped inside and slammed an elbow up under his chin. Not full force. Just enough to rattle the wiring.

"Alright?" she asked, deadpan.

His ego said yes.

Third pass, he tried to clinch.

Mistake.

She ducked under, twisted, and dropped him with a leg reap so clean it looked like choreography. He hit the mat hard. She didn't let him breathe. Followed fast. Mounted. Posted. Sunk a forearm across his throat—not choking yet, just informing.

"You ever touch someone here again without asking,"

she said softly, "I'll break your jaw first and apologize to Rey after."

He bucked. She didn't move.

"Tap or nap, sweetheart," she said. "I'm not your mama. I won't coddle you."

He didn't.

So she adjusted her hips. Increased pressure.

He tapped. Fast. Like a man who'd never been toyed with before.

When she stood up, the room was quiet. Rey was grinning like Christmas came early.

"Izzy's strong—for her size," someone said as she passed, towel slung around her neck.

Rey didn't even glance up. "No. She's strong. Period."

Izzy smiled, quiet and sharp. Let them talk. Let them need qualifiers.

The guy she'd just laid out had Nico's build—same reach, same easy strength, just unearned. Undisciplined. He'd grunted through the drill; Nico would've adjusted his stance and asked for another round.

It made her think of him.

And how, when she gave up power behind closed doors, it wasn't surrender. It was a decision. A risk she only took with someone who knew exactly what it meant when she let go.

Nico had earned it. That was the difference.

And if he ever stopped deserving it, she could put him on the ground before he realized she'd moved.

THE FLUORESCENT LIGHT in Rey's office was making her eye twitch. One of those overhead tubes with a dying ballast, buzzing like a fly in her skull. She could've left. Showered. Gotten food. But instead, she was still in her sports bra and leggings, knuckles raw, the sweat drying cold in the small of her back. Her body ached like it always did after a good grapple—but it was her head that was working overtime.

She'd finished Rey's admin thirty minutes ago. Receipts logged, membership forms scanned, invoices tagged in the system. Done and dusted. But her laptop was still open.

Because she wasn't here for admin anymore.

The files weren't hers. Samira had sent them through Nico. Encrypted, scrubbed, legal-adjacent. There was no folder name, just a timestamp and a smiley face emoji in the subject line, which made Izzy want to scream.

Now they were spread across her desktop—PDFs, screenshots, data logs, internal comms she wasn't supposed to see. The kind of shit that made her stomach twist. Line by line, she was walking through it. The version history of a software update, timestamps that didn't match, error reports quietly deleted from the official logs. A test flight rerouted through Seattle the week before her MFD glitched on before take-off.

She wasn't doing anything fancy. She was a line pilot. But she knew how to read a flight log, and she had a pretty solid bullshit detector. And this? This stank.

She was past furious. Past scared. Just methodical now. Clicking, highlighting, saving to a secure folder in case someone got cute.

She pulled on Rey's hoodie, not because she was cold but because the smell of the gym grounded her. She blinked at the screen, mouth drawn into a hard line, wrist tense from holding the mouse.

Not quite a smoking gun. But enough to raise the eyebrows of people who matter.

. . .

THE PING CAME SOFTLY—HARMLESS, almost pleasant—but it broke the air like a warning shot. Izzy didn't look up right away. She finished the line she was highlighting, reread a log entry with a time discrepancy that hadn't bothered her until now, and only then let her eyes drift toward the corner of the screen. New mail.

Subject: Wellness Concern – Immediate Review.

Timestamp: 22:47.

She blinked once. Clicked. And then she sat still.

It was from HR, sent through the usual compliance portal, but the CC list dragged a slow chill up her spine. Legal. Flight Standards. A manager she didn't know well. And buried several replies down—Russell. Of course.

There was no accusation, not in so many words. Just language so polite it could bruise. The kind of email that pretended to be about care and concern while circling like a drone strike.

We are following up on a post-flight observation entered through the confidential wellness reporting protocol. Concerns were raised regarding unexplained emotional behavior during standard flight operations. We appreciate your commitment to safe operations and want to ensure all pilots are able to self-regulate effectively under pressure. As part of our proactive oversight initiative, we'd like to schedule a conversation at your earliest convenience.

Izzy read it twice. Then again. Slowly. The phrasing was neutral, like they'd hired someone to make it sound like help. But it wasn't. It was a warning dressed as wellness. A muzzle disguised as empathy.

Unexplained emotional behavior. Pilot self-regulation. Proactive oversight.

Her pulse spiked—not in fear, not yet—but in something colder. Sharper. Because now she knew exactly what they were going to do. They weren't going to challenge her outright. They weren't going to address the software, or the bugs. They were going to paint her unstable. They were going to lay a paper trail she couldn't outrun.

And the worst part was, she knew exactly what they were talking about.

What was it two, no, three months ago? It had been an easy flight. Boring, even. No turbulence. The kind of crossing that lulled the cabin and let the flight deck go quiet in the best way. They were somewhere over the Pyrenees when it happened—just past top of descent, checklist tucked, hands idle for a breath too long.

And then—barely a thing. A single tear. Not even a breath behind it. She'd wiped it away like it was nothing, because it was nothing. Just a hairline crack in pressure. A release valve. Her body reminding her it was still running on something volatile and human.

She hadn't looked over. But she didn't have to. She knew he saw.

Nico hadn't moved. No reaction, no kindness offered, no tension in the air. Just continued like nothing had happened. When they landed, smooth as silk, he'd said it the same way he might read out flap settings: "Textbook."

That was the part that stayed with her. It was a flawless flight.

Which is why this email—this cold, too-late thing blinking on her screen now—didn't make any sense at first. Nothing had gone wrong. There were no delays, no deviations, no missed calls or unstable approaches. She hadn't made a single operational error. She hadn't raised her voice. She hadn't hesitated.

All that had happened—if you even wanted to call it something—was a tear. One. Slipped loose at cruise, wiped away before it even cooled. It wasn't dramatic. It wasn't visible from the cabin. It hadn't touched the flight path, the workload, or the sterile tone of the rest of the flight.

So why flag it?

The only thing she could think of is that the plane had noticed. Or, at the very least, the system riding shotgun. One of those quiet new patches they were told was still in beta. Nothing official, just backend tools to "support pilots." Another passive net cast under the language of care.

She stared at the screen for a long time. Then she shut the laptop. Waited. Opened it again.

There was no sense in waiting anymore. No sense playing quiet while the ground was already shifting.

They weren't trying to help her. They were trying to get ahead of her.

So she opened a blank email and began to type. Sent a few texts. Made phone calls.

If they were going to move first, she'd make damn sure they weren't the only ones in motion.

38

It had been a month since she grounded the plane.

Nearly three weeks since they clipped her wings for it. Since the system flagged her as a risk.

She told herself it wasn't punishment—just oversight. A formality.

But every day since had been quiet. Too quiet. The kind of quiet that says: We're watching you.

And now?

Now she was standing in her flat, staring at a sushi tray so extravagant it looked like it belonged at a state dinner.

It came in a matte black box the size of a carry-on suitcase, layered like a lacquered banquet tray from a Shogunate archive. Gilded dividers. Real flowers. Dry ice. Individual servings of otoro fanned like petals. A handwritten card in brushstroke calligraphy, addressed to Captain Ventura, with respect.

Twelve servings. Twelve.

She'd invited maybe seven people. Maybe. And hadn't been convinced even one of them would come.

The total had crossed four digits, and she'd winced

when she'd approved the charge—but she hadn't changed her mind. She never could, not when it came to this kind of thing. Hosting made her feel like she had to prove something: that she was worth showing up for. That if people came, they'd be met with more than she ever got. That she could feed them something beautiful, even if the whole night fell flat.

Now it was twenty-five minutes past the time she'd set, and the tray sat unopened on the table. Not one chopstick wrapper disturbed. The soy sauce came in handblown glass vials. The wasabi was fresh-grated and arranged like moss. It looked like an exhibit.

She paced to the kitchen, poured herself half a glass of wine, then stared at her phone again. No new notifications. She almost texted André. Almost.

But he was already on his way. She knew that. At least— she hoped so.

She set the phone down. Smoothed the edge of a linen napkin. Told herself she'd go over the notes in front of the mirror. Just in case.

She hadn't dressed up. Not really.

Just a black column dress—silk, soft but sharp. High neck, v-cut front, a row of small buttons running down the center like it mattered. There was a front slit, barely enough to move in, but it shifted when she walked and made her feel like she still had a spine under all the doubt. The dress held her in place. Made her look composed, whether or not she felt it.

No earrings. Just a gold chain and the good watch. Her hair was down. Clean.

The silence pressed in. Familiar.

Then—uninvited, sharp, and ancient—the memory came.

The mall birthday.

She hadn't thought about it in years—not really. She'd buried it with everything else from that era: clumpy mascara, AIM away messages, and the year she thought silence would make her likable. But now it surfaced clean, surgical. She was fourteen. Or fifteen. One of those ages that mattered more than it should've. A group of girls had asked her what she was doing for her birthday, and when she'd said nothing, they'd insisted—*We should all go to the mall.*

She'd picked the time. Told her mom. Showed up early. Wore lip gloss.

No one came.

Not one person. She'd walked the whole mall twice and bought herself glitter eyeliner. Spent the rest of the day pretending it was fine. That she'd misunderstood. That maybe she had said the wrong date.

The worst part wasn't the silence. It was realizing later that they'd never meant to come. That they'd set it up just to watch her believe it.

Because a boy on base—one she liked, one she trusted —had spread something cruel about her. A rumor that made her easy to want, and easier to punish.

She blinked. Swallowed.

That was a long time ago. Different hemisphere. Different stakes.

Still.

She looked at the door. Then at the food. Then at the door again.

And waited.

The buzzer startled her. Sharp, electric, too loud in the hush of the flat.

She crossed to the intercom expecting André, already composing some dry remark in her head—*Told you I'd be eating this sushi alone*—but when she hit the button and heard the voices layered on the other end, her brain snagged.

It wasn't just one voice. It was several. An assortment of British accents. A couple she didn't immediately recognize.

By the time she reached the door, five people were already stepping out of the elevator. Pilots. Uniforms half-undone, jackets folded over arms, that LUMA swagger softened with awkwardness. She recognized every one of them. Some she'd flown with in long-haul silence over the Pacific. Another had once spilled tomato juice across his EFB mid-flight and looked at her like she might throw him out the door.

She hadn't invited them.

But they were here.

Seven, by the time they'd all made it up—five based in London, the others on rotation. One was Captain Sato, who she hadn't seen in years. Cheerful, loud laugh, always brought back candy. They'd only flown together for a month —CDG to Haneda—and got along better than she expected. Then he rotated onto the LAX–Tokyo line and disappeared to the far side of the world.

Two of the quieter British junior pilots stood just behind him—pilots she'd flown with when they were FOs, barely spoken to, and always assumed didn't register her beyond checklist calls. One of them rubbed the back of his neck, sheepish.

"Sorry," he said. "Security downstairs held us up. Said you never have visitors, so they weren't sure."

"I don't," she said, before she could think better of it.

They all laughed—too loud, a little nervous.

"I was surprised to hear from you," one of the older ones said, lingering near the kitchen. "Didn't think you liked me.

But I figured...if you were saying something, it had to be real."

She opened her mouth. Closed it.

Another pilot smiled. "Ventura. Nice place you got here."

Then, quieter: "Heard about what happened. It's not right."

She blinked.

Someone offered to uncork the wine. Another hovered by the sushi box like it might bite. They started talking—familiar things, ops things, rumors and rosters and the weather over Dubai—and suddenly, the space wasn't so quiet anymore.

Then came André and Cy, fashionably late and carrying bags like saints. André dumped a bottle of Prosecco into the sink and said, "Oh, babe. You've got that look. We brought fruit and plausible deniability."

Cy stepped in behind André, balancing a covered tray and already scowling at the dramatic swirl of dry ice fog curling off her sushi box like a stage effect.

He didn't even say hello. Just: "Why is there vapor coming out of the takeaway you swore would be chill?"

André snorted, already halfway to the kitchen. "She said 'for just a few people,' Cy. I walked in and saw enough toro to bankrupt a tech startup."

Cy ignored him, setting his tray down with surgical care. "Three cheesecakes. Coconut cassava, rum-soaked guava, and one with a ginger crust. I brought dessert because I knew you'd panic and forget." He lifted the tea towel like a magician revealing his final act.

Izzy stared at the sushi box, then at him. "It's not that much."

He looked at the gold foil. Then the soy sauce in glass vials. Then at her.

"You spent a grand on an anxiety response," he said calmly.

She laughed. It burst out of her. Sudden, unguarded. It almost startled her more than the buzzer.

And then the door buzzed again.

Flight attendants this time. Ten of them. All familiar. Some with messy buns and coffee breath, some already taking off their shoes at the door. They were led by Emma—handles-business-Emma from that nightmare passenger incident in what felt like ages ago, who hugged her one-armed and said, "I brought everyone I could get to answer a text."

The flat filled fast.

It wasn't crowded—yet—but the corners were gone. There was nowhere quiet to stand. Someone was putting on music. Someone else had taken over her kitchen and was slicing fruit with frightening efficiency. Her windows glowed with London's skyline, but no one was looking out. They were looking at each other. At her.

Then: a dispatcher she'd only ever had drinks with once. A Heathrow station manager she barely knew, standing near the door like a sentry. More people. More jackets on the rack. More shoes by the door.

Izzy moved to the edge of the room. Tried to count. Lost track.

She'd never had this many people in her home.

And they'd come for this—not to eat, not to network, not for her wine or the view.

They'd come for her.

Her fingers curled around the edge of the counter. The air felt thinner than it had a moment ago—like the room had risen in altitude while she wasn't looking. Everyone was moving, laughing, talking. The space pulsed around her.

Her eyes dropped to the sushi. Still pristine in its gold-lined tray.

Twelve servings.

Twelve.

There were almost twenty people in her flat.

Her brain slid sideways—dislodged from feeling, snagged on numbers. On etiquette. On supply.

There's not enough.

Her pulse picked up. Not with panic—just that tight, humming edge that came when systems didn't align. She could fly a plane through a monsoon, but God forbid someone leave her place hungry.

She reached for a linen napkin. Smoothed it flat. Thought about calling someone. Ordering more.

André caught her eye from across the room, already shaking his head.

He mouthed, *Don't you dare.*

She exhaled.

Her thoughts quieted on their own.

No one rang a glass or made a speech. The room just settled. One by one, voices dropped, movement slowed, and eyes turned toward her. Izzy hadn't asked for silence, but she felt it circle around her like a cockpit door sealing shut.

She stood at the center of the living room—slippers firm on the hardwood, shoulders square in the black silk dress she hadn't meant to wear for war—and held a slim stack of folders. Printed, stapled, heavy with the weight of evidence she never thought she'd be the one to present.

"All right," she said. Her voice carried more than she expected. "You're not here to be impressed, so I'll skip the soft sell."

She handed out the packets—one at a time, deliberate.

No digital copies. She'd had them printed off the network, scrubbed twice by Nico's sister. Just paper. Just ink.

"You're holding everything I could confirm without setting off alarms," she said. "There's been a breach. Multiple, actually. The aircraft are recording more than we were told. Not just the cockpit voice recorders, not just the flight data. They've patched in secondary monitoring—passive biometric scanning, behavioral data tracking. It's running under the newest software suite. Most of us didn't get briefed because it was labeled as a beta oversight tool."

Someone swore under their breath.

She continued. "It's not just surveillance. It's sloppy. It's unsecured. There are signs the data has been scraped by third-party systems, possibly cross-referenced with external identity platforms. Some of that data includes personal device metadata—Fitbit sync logs, smart watches, even phone accelerometers. Nothing connected to the aircraft should be that porous."

Murmurs now. One pilot checking his watch. Another pulling out their phone like it might bite.

"That kind of breach isn't just a privacy issue," she said. "It's a safety one."

She let that land, then kept going, voice steady and hard.

"You're all used to the black box. The voice recorder, the FDR, the paperwork—yeah, we know we're recorded. We accept that. That's post-incident review. That's about safety.

But this?" She lifted the packet, tapping the pages like they were burning her fingers.

"This is different. This is predictive profiling. It's not about what we did—it's about who they think we are. They're building models of us. Micro-expressions. Heart rates. Reaction times. Fatigue patterns. Emotional tells.

They're using that data to decide who's fit to fly—before we've done a thing wrong.

And you can't second-guess yourself at 37,000 feet." Her voice dropped, sharp and clear. "You hesitate in a cockpit, and you could kill four hundred people.

That's not safety. That's control. That's a kill switch you don't see coming until they pull it."

Again, she let the words hang there, just long enough to feel them tighten the air.

Then André—sprawled on the arm of her sofa with his usual posture of elegant contempt—chimed in.

"If you've got a smartwatch or a fitness tracker that hasn't been hard-disconnected from Bluetooth since you started your trip, assume it's still pinging," he said. "Same with any app that tracks your heart rate, your sleep, or your 'stress index.' They love that shit. Makes it easier to build a behavioral profile."

Someone asked how to check.

"Airplane mode doesn't do anything," André said. "You've gotta go full device settings, turn off location services, then shut off background app refresh. And turn off any 'predictive' health feature. That's the flag most of these third-party systems latch onto first."

Izzy nodded. "You don't have to do anything with this packet. But if you've felt like someone's been watching, or if your schedules started shifting for no reason, or if you've had flights flagged that didn't make sense—it's not in your head."

She scanned the room. Faces she knew. Faces she didn't. No one laughed. No one rolled their eyes.

"If you want to do something about it," she said, quieter now, "you're not alone."

And for the first time, she believed it.

One of the junior pilots was flipping through the packet too fast. Another hadn't touched it yet. Someone else—mid-forties, Welsh guy, solid stick—finally said it:

"Isn't this... like—" he hesitated, "—bigger than us? If someone's got this level of access—this much personal data on pilots—"

He didn't finish.

But she knew what he meant. The air tightened.

"Yes," Izzy said. "It's not just about wellness flags. Or schedule manipulation. This much data in the wrong hands is a threat to international aviation security. You can build entire psychological profiles. Identify pressure points. Medical history. Fatigue patterns. Family connections. All of it."

The room went still.

She didn't raise her voice.

"Over two decades ago, they hardened cockpits to keep terrorists out. But now? Someone doesn't need to break in. They just need to know enough about us to fly right through the gaps."

A long silence. Even André was quiet.

Then someone said it, low: "You don't need to hijack a plane if you know the entire crew's weak spots."

Izzy nodded. "Exactly. Locked doors will not be enough."

No one had to explain the rest. That there was now a way to dismantle cockpit integrity without ever opening the door

André stood—easy, neutral. Like he'd stepped into the version of himself meant for safety, not notice.

"You want to help? Great. Most of you are flying tomorrow. Here's what you do. Don't write this down."

The room quieted again.

"Before and after each leg, check your EFB. Settings. Battery usage. If the beta software is running in the background without being open, that's a problem. If it's using data when you're not connected to Wi-Fi, huge problem."

He pointed vaguely, like someone would dare write it down anyway.

"Next—your phone, your watch. Put them in airplane mode at the gate. Mid-cruise, glance at them. If they reconnect to anything, log the time. After landing, check background app activity. If anything health-related was still working in airplane mode, that's your flag."

A pause. Then, dry:

"Airplane mode is polite. It's not secure."

Someone shifted, uncomfortable.

"If you've got a portable EMF reader, bring it. Or—" He nodded toward the sideboard, where a neat row of identical black devices sat lined up like favors at a haunted wedding. "Just take one. Courtesy of Captain Ventura, who apparently moonlights as the Resistance."

A few people laughed. Izzy didn't.

"They're real," she said simply. "And calibrated."

"Run a sweep near the flight deck wall during cruise. If it pings—log it. Timestamp it. Do not mention it on comms."

He looked around.

"If your pairings change last-minute or you get a flag after a clean flight—tell us. If someone gets pulled, or your schedules don't match anymore, flag it."

Then: "Send nothing until you've landed. Use the secure folder Captain Ventura sent you. Not your cloud. Not Slack. Not text."

Another pause. Then quieter, meaner:

"They are counting on your professionalism making you too obedient to notice."

He sat back down. Took another bite of cheesecake.

"That's all. Burn it into your brain."

The room stayed quiet after André finished. No one reached for their phones. No one moved toward the door.

Izzy looked at them—pilots, flight attendants, ops staff —crowded into her flat like they'd all somehow taken the same wrong turn and ended up at the center of something bigger than they meant to be part of.

She stepped forward. No podium, no ceremony. Just her voice, and the stack of folders almost gone from the table.

"I don't expect all of you to act on this," she said, level. "You don't owe me that."

She let her eyes move across the room, anchoring where they landed.

"I was the first one to make noise, and you've all seen what happened to me. Some of you can't afford to take that risk. I know that. I respect that. Your jobs, your reputations —they're not abstract. They're your means of survival."

She reached for the EMF reader and held it up. The soft blue light blinked once, waiting.

"So take what's useful. Leave what isn't. If you choose to do nothing, that's still your choice. But if you choose to do something—know I'm trusting you with more than just my data. I'm trusting you with my name. My job. My life."

She placed the reader down with the others.

The room stayed still.

Then, one by one, people stepped forward. No rush. Just motion—careful, solemn—as they picked up a device, tucked it into a pocket, nodded once, and stepped back.

By the end, the tray was empty.

And Izzy, still standing, said only this:

"Clear skies."

39

Nico had noticed the pattern.

A cluster of pilots disappearing from crew housing mid-evening. Plain clothes, empty hands. A real crowd, not a layover team. Then the flight attendants—four of them leaving together, Emma in front, carrying what looked like a laptop bag.

It wasn't gossip. It was movement.

And movement like that meant coordination.

Which meant someone was pulling threads.

Now Kerrigan was across from him on the shuttle, trying too hard not to squirm. Mid-thirties. London base. The kind of FO who flew solid, filed quiet reports, and didn't get involved in anything.

Except he looked like he hadn't slept. And he kept checking his phone with the screen brightness turned way down.

Nico didn't look at him. He didn't need to.

"You look like shit," he said mildly.

Kerrigan gave a little laugh. "Rough night."

"You were on rest."

Kerrigan hesitated. "Yeah. There was... a thing."

Nico said nothing. Just kept his eyes forward. Let the silence press in.

They stepped off the shuttle. Walked the glass tunnel toward the terminal.

"Just a thing," Kerrigan said again, softer this time. "At someone's flat."

Still no reaction.

"A gathering."

Nico stopped walking.

Kerrigan froze mid-step.

Nico turned his head. Not his body. Just enough to let his voice move sideways when he said, "Whose flat?"

Kerrigan cracked. "Izzy's."

Nico blinked once. Not a twitch of surprise.

For a moment, Nico had the intrusive thought that he could push this man down the escalator they were on. Just one clean shove. It was early. No one around. Long ride down.

Then he reminded himself: this FO was newer, even if he was older than Nico. One of the ones who still forgot to refer to captains by their last names. And—critically—he hadn't gone to Izzy's flat on his own. It was for the thing Nico already suspected. The spyware. The data breach. Her grounding.

Not that it mattered. She had the right to invite any man she wanted into her home.

But still.

He adjusted his grip on the railing. And when the escalator reached the top, Nico walked off. Silent. Steady.

"I didn't know it was supposed to be quiet," Kerrigan said quickly. "No one said it was classified or anything. I wasn't even going to go, but someone texted, and then it was—"

"But you knew not to say anything," Nico said, calm as a clean kill.

Kerrigan swallowed. "I guess."

"What was it."

Not a question. A directive.

"She gave us...intel. About the beta software. Surveillance. A whole list of things to check mid-flight."

Nico said nothing.

He didn't need to.

Once, a man had confessed to a plot to bring down a field hospital with a wired corpse, just to make Nico stop being quiet—because the quieter Nico got, the worse it got.

Kerrigan glanced at him. "You're not going to—?"

"You didn't say anything."

They reached the jetbridge. Nico stepped past him like he hadn't spoken at all. But his mind was already writing the briefing.

Izzy had moved.

And she wasn't moving alone.

HEATHROW TO JFK was smooth enough to be boring. No jetstream to ride, no systems drama, just seven hours of air he didn't need help managing. Kerrigan kept trying to bond. Nico replied in clipped monosyllables.

A minor nav sync blip cropped up near Gander. Nico caught it first, ran the fix himself, and double-checked the logs before Kerrigan could touch anything.

He flew clean. Professional. Untouchable.

He didn't mention Izzy once.

He didn't need to.

Even with four stripes on his shoulder, he wasn't the only captain in the cockpit. The training captain sat behind him, silent, shadowing his moves. Until probation was over, Nico still had to prove he could fly alone.

Layla's loft in DUMBO looked like an architectural hallucination. Floor-to-ceiling windows framed the Brooklyn Bridge like a mood board. There was a disco ball above the kitchen island. A clawfoot tub filled with plush toys. A vintage Mustang had been cleanly cut in half and repurposed into a couch—polished chrome, buttery leather, working hazard lights. Nico was sitting on it now, legs slightly spread to keep a toddler from rolling off.

Ahsan was draped across him like a weighted blanket with opinions. Grumpy. Possibly fruit-sticky. He was clutching the remote with both hands and refusing to blink. Nico didn't dare take it back. The two-year-old was built like a linebacker and fought like his mother.

On the TV, the news was playing the downfall again—footage of a raid on some marble monstrosity in Puerto Rico. Tactical teams. Flashing lights. A man in sunglasses being led into a black SUV with his hoodie over his head.

Influencer compound dismantled. Extradited to Miami. Awaiting trial for money laundering, trafficking and assault.

Same man who once went viral saying he wouldn't board a plane if the pilot was a woman. Quoted a psychiatric case with just enough detail to set aviation forums on fire. Didn't name Izzy. He didn't have to.

Samira sat nearby, not watching the screen. She was scrolling something encrypted on her phone—thumbs moving fast, face locked down that particular Farrah angle that meant someone in a government building was about to have a bad day.

Layla was leaning against the kitchen counter, barefoot, drink in hand, the picture of maternal ease with full revolutionary undertones. Her curls were up, her eyeliner was criminal, and she looked entirely unbothered that the man she'd spent a month publicly humiliating had finally been brought down by a combination of subpoenas, Wi-Fi, and divine feminine rage.

"They're playing it again," she said.

Nico glanced up. "What?"

"My clip."

The chyron changed: COMEDIAN'S TIKTOK TAKEDOWN GOES GLOBAL: 5M VIEWS AND COUNTING.

Then the footage rolled. Layla, on stage, mic in hand, eyes sharp as ever.

"You're not an alpha, you're a tax shelter for weak men with a victim complex."

The audience lost it. Drink toss. Applause. Someone screamed.

Layla sipped her water mid-set and finished:

"If my son ever talks like that, I'll ground him until he's thirty."

Ahsan made a disgruntled sound and tried to launch himself sideways. Nico caught him, one arm secure.

"Chill," he muttered. "Your mom just ended a man's empire."

Ahsan responded by headbutting his chest and sighing deeply.

Samira finally looked up from her phone. "Interpol picked up one of his finance guys. It's falling fast now."

Layla grinned. "Justice looks good on me."

Nico exhaled through his nose, heart still running a half-step behind the room.

Nico looked down at Ahsan, who had gone slack against his chest, warm and heavy like a weighted vest. On the screen, the compound was crumbling. On the couch, Samira was tanking state secrets. In the kitchen, Layla was glowing like a prophet.

He'd been benched. Babysitting while the real operators moved.

Unacceptable.

"Alright, little man," he murmured, easing Ahsan into Layla's arms. "Back to base. Uncle's got some recon to run and a few egos to detonate."

He grabbed his jacket off the chair, pulse already recalibrating.

THE PILOT HOSTING the post all-hands get-together lived in a bland luxury condo on the Upper East Side—doorman, perfumed lobby, a wine fridge no one knew how to use. The furniture was nice, in the way that West Elm catalogs were nice: personality-free, vaguely masculine, prohibitively beige. Someone had a Peloton. The air smelled faintly of aftershave and ambition.

They were in their mid-thirties, most of them. Clean-cut, polite, loud in groups. Into expensive boots that never touched dirt, single-origin pour-over, podcasts about startup culture hosted by men named Bryce. They all had the same unlined face, the same easy laugh, the same gleaming white confidence that came from never being told no in a way that stuck. Nico didn't like them. But he knew how to make them like him.

He brought good beer—imported, but nothing too niche. He laughed at the right stories. Threw in one of his own about a bird strike over the Turkish border in Syria that made them go a little quiet, a little impressed. Let his Kentucky drawl stretch out like a dog in the sun. One of them chuckled, called him corn-fed like it was a compliment. He smiled anyway. It was working.

When the topic shifted to their upcoming Kilimanjaro trip, Nico let his eyes go wide just enough.

"Seriously? That's sick. What gear you bringing?"

"Actually," one of them—Andrew or Drew or something equally irrelevant—grinned, "VortexAero hooked us up. They're beta testing some altitude-readiness plugin for smartwatches—kind of slick, actually. We didn't even pay."

Nico tilted his head, feigned casual. "VortexAero?"

"Yeah," said another, plopping onto the couch. "They're behind that new cockpit software—the beta release? The one LUMA's been testing on the 787s."

Nico blinked, once. Let the silence do the work.

"Oh," he said, with a laugh just this side of dismissive. "That's where I know the name from."

He smiled like it was trivia. Like it hadn't just locked something into place behind his eyes. Just another little perk of having friends in high places. Just a cute story. Not a breach.

"Dude," said another, already one beer over the line. "It tracks recovery time, sleep quality, oxygen adaptation—like, all this quantified-self shit. Feels pretty Iron Man."

Someone else called out from the kitchen. "Yeah, Elliot says it'll help pilots manage fatigue. Like, long haul stuff. Honestly? I hope LUMA rolls it out. I'm always jetlagged coming back from Tokyo."

. . .

"OH, TOTALLY," Nico said, easy and warm. "I'll have to ask him about it."

He said it like he might text a buddy. Not like he'd be flipping the chessboard. Not like every word they'd just said confirmed exactly what he came to hear.

One of them passed him another beer and asked if he'd ever thought about getting into glacier climbing. Nico smiled, said maybe.

THE HACKATHON WASN'T LOCKED down. Open-floor "tech sprint," technically invite-only, but no one was checking. The space was pure start-up delusion—cold brew on tap, branded yoga mats stacked in a corner, someone giving a talk on "flight deck neuroplasticity" in a voice that sounded like a TEDx hostage video.

Nico didn't RSVP. He didn't need to. He wore a bomber jacket, black jeans, no name badge. Just confidence, cologne, and that glide-walk military had drilled into his spine. Everyone else looked like they'd slept under their desks. He looked like he'd sauntered out of a cologne commercial to commit espionage for fun.

He scanned the room until he spotted her. Late twenties, maybe thirty. Blazer over a T-shirt, conference badge flipped backward, Apple Watch tan line. Hair tied back like she gave up halfway through. The power ponytail of someone who used to give a shit.

Project manager. He could tell by the way people funneled toward her without realizing it. Like iron filings to a magnet that wished it was dead.

He recognized the type—Samira built her cybersecurity firm from a spare bedroom and a grudge. He worked for her once. Could only stomach the tech industry for a month. Hated everyone. Never went back.

He made a slow approach. Gave her time to notice him. Not enough to prepare.

"Hey," he said smoothly, nodding toward the nearest screen. "Which one of these is gonna replace me?"

She snorted—an inelegant, involuntary sound. Covered it too late. "None of them. Unless you're deeply mediocre."

"Ouch." He smiled, unbothered. "I fly widebody international. Should I be nervous?"

"Not unless you're scared of decision trees and 4 a.m. Slack threads."

He made a thoughtful face. "Terrifying."

She squinted at him. "Do you work here?"

"Nope."

"Are you a pilot?"

"Depends. Are you gonna report me?"

She gave him a long blink. "God, I'm too tired for this."

"Then don't waste energy. Just tell me what the killer app is."

Her lips twitched. "Killer app?" She scoffed. "Everything's still in beta. The flight behavior tagging model's a joke. We trained it on sim footage and like—three real flights. It predicts erratic stick inputs if you so much as sneeze. Half the devs don't know what a rudder is."

Nico let out a low whistle. "So... not exactly FAA-certified."

"It's vaporware," she said flatly. "Wrapped in AI buzzwords and sent to pitch. The execs want it to look like innovation. It's really just surveillance with better fonts."

He tilted his head. Let that land. "And yet... here you are."

She didn't rise to it. Just rubbed her temple with two

fingers and said, "I had PTO last week. Spent it migrating dashboards."

Nico whistled low. "Living the dream."

She cracked a smile, dry and dangerous. "You here to leak something? Or just vibe?"

"Little of both."

"Figures."

He leaned in slightly, just enough to lower his voice. "You always this honest with strangers?"

"I'm too tired to lie attractively."

He laughed—short, surprised. "That's a shame. You'd be great at it."

She looked at him then. Not impressed. Just flat. "You don't work here. You're not an investor. And you haven't pitched me anything. So what do you want?"

He smiled. Sharp. "The truth. And maybe your name."

"Why?"

"Because I'm polite."

Her eyes narrowed, but she gave it to him anyway. "Leah."

He thanked her. Didn't linger. Didn't ask for her number. Just turned and left—confident she'd be thinking about him the next time the model failed. Or the next time she tried to sleep and couldn't.

Either worked.

~

His next target had a badge, a brand deal, and a very public calendar. He'd met her once—briefly—at that rooftop circus on Billionaire's Row. Now she was head-lining a travel-tech expo in Midtown, and he was walking in not in uniform, but in a perfectly tailored suit Layla's stylist had handpicked with the words "look expensive, not available."

Soraya Vale. Brunette. In a skin-tight halter dress. Laugh like a marketing pitch. Not a pilot. Not crew. Someone's plus-one, maybe. Or someone who didn't need an invite at all.

She'd flirted. He'd smiled. Filed her under "harmless." Forgot about her.

Until now.

Her name came up in a branded TikTok ad that auto-played while he was researching LUMA's recent PR partnerships. He saw her again in a Reel a few slides later—press junket in Mexico City. Flight tagged. LUMA collab. Same laugh. Same face. Gold status influencer.

Finding her in person was easy. Industry pass. Sponsored by half the airlines on the Eastern seaboard. She was doing a panel on the "future of guest experience in high-tier cabins."

He let her see him from across the open bar.

She recognized him instantly. Her smile widened like she'd vision-boarded him into existence.

"You're the hot pilot from the rooftop."

He didn't correct her.

He let her talk first. Let her brag. Let her think he didn't already know her last name and her engagement metrics. He asked her questions—soft, leading ones—until she offered up Elliot's name without prompting.

"Oh, that party was Elliot's. He's trying to make pilot training sexy again, poor thing. Cassandra funds half of it—her dad's a CTO for one of the boutique airlines or some other boring shit. I don't pay attention."

"Russell Cayne?" Nico said casually, like it was trivia.

She blinked. "Yeah. That's it."

He asked a few more questions. About who else had been there. How long the company had been in beta. If she'd seen him pitch. She told him everything. Names. Funding rounds. She even mentioned that Elliot's next pitch deck was going to include biometric performance metrics "borrowed from active flight crew."

"Anonymized, obviously," she added with a wink.

Nico smiled like she'd said something funny.

He thanked her. Told her he had to run.

But she stepped in front of him as he turned to go. Leaned in close. Her voice dropped to something low and hungry.

"I've got a minibar, a split-level shower, and zero gag reflex. You look like someone who would appreciate all three."

He didn't flinch. "That's kind of you. But no."

She blinked. Then laughed. But when he moved to leave, she grabbed his arm—tight, nails sharp.

"You really gonna walk away? After all that nosy little digging? You don't think I'll say something?"

And that's when the smile dropped.

Just for a second.

The version of him that used to get answers in windowless rooms surfaced in the stillness behind his eyes.

He didn't say anything. He just looked at her. Stared for long enough that the expression drained from her face like air from a cabin at altitude.

She let go.

He stepped back.

"Enjoy your panel," he said, smooth as silk.

Then he walked out, already assembling the next move in his head.

～

IT WAS A BRIGHT, brittle morning in Central Park. Samira wore boots that made no sense for the grass, but she moved like someone who dared the mud to try her. Ahsan was dressed like a French cartoon—striped shirt, tiny scarf, the works. Nico had curated the outfit himself and was now jogging backward across a path near the Balto statue, trying to catch the exact moment his nephew pointed at a pigeon like it had insulted the family.

He crouched, framed the shot, and took three rapid photos. Not because Layla had asked. She hadn't. He just needed her to see it.

"You're insane," Samira said, without glancing up. She had the kid's backpack slung over one arm and her phone in her hand, thumbs flying.

"He looks amazing. This outfit deserved real light," Nico replied. "I planned it around the scarf."

"You what?"

"It's called style, Sami."

They stopped at the swings. Nico pushed Ahsan gently, one hand on the plastic seat, the other still texting Layla new photos like he was on contract. Meanwhile, Samira had stopped pretending this was recreational. Her phone was open to a secure notes app, lines of text reading like a classified indictment.

He glanced over and caught a glimpse of the screen:

- Elliot = Cassandra Cayne's husband. No tech credentials. Just optics.
- Russell Cayne approved Q1 cockpit software trial. Circumvented internal oversight.

- *Startup valuation inflated through media manipulation. No working prototype. All "vision."*
- *Patent filings nonspecific—AI training language, but nothing executable.*
- *FAA waiver secured with language like "assistive performance layer." No definition.*

They headed toward the zoo. Ahsan shrieked in joy at the sea lions. Nico lifted him onto his shoulders, handed Samira a snack pouch without speaking, and kept walking.

"What's the verdict?" he asked, eyes ahead.

"I've got three attack vectors. Pick one."

Nico didn't even turn his head. "Go with the one that gets them investigated but doesn't trace back to us"

Samira nodded, already adjusting the phrasing in her draft. "Anonymous tip to LUMA's internal safety board. Enough heat to trigger review. Framed like it came from inside the startup."

"Perfect," he said.

They found shade near the meadow and laid the blanket out. Ahsan collapsed across his chest, soft and warm and vaguely sticky. Samira continued typing—no wasted movements, no hesitation.

"I gave you her number," Nico said. "And her encrypted contact. Can you send it to her the way you send things when it matters?"

Samira's hands stilled over the keyboard.

"Excuse me?"

"Everything. The file. The findings. The risk trail. It's Izzy's call."

"You're not going to charge in and save the day? Interesting. I guess some of us grow out of that phase."

"Don't start."

She turned, fully this time, eyebrows raised. "You're actually going to defer to her."

He nodded once. "Yes."

Samira studied him for a long moment. She wasn't looking for sincerity—she was looking for stability. Something she could trust not to combust under pressure.

"Huh," she muttered, and started typing again. "You might be salvageable."

"Thanks, I guess?"

Ahsan was chewing on half a baguette, eyebrows furrowed like he was working out an economic theory. Nico's sunglasses were perched in his hair. He was texting Layla a burst of toddler modeling shots while Samira typed what amounted to a digital death sentence for a billion-dollar startup.

"You're dangerous when you believe in something," Samira said, eyes on her phone. "Most men need someone to stop them from going off the deep end. You? You need someone who can drag you back after."

Nico didn't respond. Just watched Ahsan toss bread crumbs at a pigeon and then clap like he'd caused a miracle.

There was a silence—not dramatic, just weighted.

"You remember," she said, without heat, "when I came home for fall break with a black eye?"

His nostrils flared, barely perceptible.

Her face remained impassive.

"You didn't ask questions," she continued, peeling the foil off a sandwich like she was listing groceries. "Didn't call baba. Didn't wait for me to decide what I wanted. You just...handled it."

Nico didn't look at her. He watched Ahsan clumsily feed a piece of cheese to a pigeon and muttered,

"He put his hands on you."

"He needed a jaw wired shut and six months of PT for his shoulder."

"I didn't hit him that hard."

She let out a dry laugh.

"You told him something. Even now, I don't know what you said. Just that it caused him to drop out of school and move to Alaska."

Nico wiped his fingers on a napkin like he was trying not to break it.

"What's your point?"

Samira finally turned to face him. No judgment—just a quiet assessment, like she was reading schematics for a volatile machine she helped build.

"Izzy? She's your weight class. That's why I'm helping."

That hit home.

"You were never going to end up with someone soft," she said. "Not someone who'd flinch if she saw what you're capable of. You need someone who doesn't just survive the way you are—but matches it."

Ahsan yelled something incoherent at a goose. Nico didn't move. His jaw twitched once—barely there—but Samira caught it.

"So yeah," Samira added, back to her phone. "I'm writing your little anonymous leak and not invoicing you because if she's what I think she is? You might finally not be a liability."

Nico exhaled once, slow. A single breath. That was all. Then he finally looked over.

"You're real sweet."

She typed one last line and hit send.

"Don't get used to it."

The email arrived midmorning.

Subject: Notice of Review – Pilot License Inquiry

She opened it before she was fully awake, still in a towel, still tasting mouthwash. The language was formal, exact, and unmistakable. Her license was under review. She was to report in person to LUMA International Headquarters. A charter had already been arranged.

She read it twice, then again. Nothing changed. No incident reference. Just a date, a location, and a tone that felt too final.

For a few seconds, she stood still, locked in the doorway between the bathroom and the rest of her flat. Her skin was cold. Her heart had gone somewhere lower in her chest.

She moved mechanically—got dressed, made coffee she didn't drink, stood by the window with the cup in her hand like holding it could help her think.

If she couldn't fly, there was nothing left to return to. Not really.

She could work the gym. She would help Rey expand,

maybe open a second location. They'd talked about it before, joking over post-training drinks.

But that life wasn't this life. And she'd built this one from scratch. Flying was the only thing she had ever been certain about. Every certification, every hour, every exam—she had earned it. And she knew how fast it could all be taken.

There had been a time, years ago, when someone tried to bury her.

She was still in the military. Twenty-four, overqualified, already flying solo when most of the guys her age were still learning how to taxi. Her evals were sharp. Her hours were solid. She'd just passed a sim with near-perfect scores.

He was her superior. Mid-thirties. A little too confident around her. He cornered her one night in the hangar after drills. Told her he liked the way she handled pressure. Said she "carried herself different." Asked if she wanted to grab dinner, off base.

She said no. Clearly. No apology, no excuses.

A week later, the paperwork started. Not disciplinary—he wasn't stupid. It was quieter than that. A flagged notation in a wellness review. A vague reference to her "reaction to feedback." Whispers that she struggled with team cohesion. No formal accusations. Just enough to stall her progress.

Her next assignment didn't come through. Her hours dropped. Her CO called her in and asked if she was "managing the stress well."

When she pushed back, they framed it as attitude.

She filed a complaint. Nothing came of it. He got promoted the following spring.

She never flew with that unit again.

No one told her she was done—but she knew. They

closed the door slowly, and by the time she noticed, it was already locked behind her.

She hadn't thought about him in a long time. But the fear came back easily. Like muscle memory.

Her phone buzzed. A message, encrypted. No sender. No visible origin.

She unlocked it. The document inside was clean, organized, annotated. A breakdown of everything wrong. The nepotism. The manipulation of internal review protocols. The signatures. Russell Cayne's name. His son-in-law's startup peddling the bad software. A map of intentional misdirection laid out in bulletproof clarity.

There was no signature. No watermark. No hint at the source. But she knew. The shape of the data, the order of the facts, the ruthless efficiency—it could only be him. It had come from Nico.

It had the quiet competence of someone who had done worse things in better uniforms. But it also had a little flair, dry wit tucked in the footnotes—just enough that she could feel one of the sisters' hands on the edges.

She let out a breath. It didn't steady her.

She remembered André, yesterday, looking smug over lunch and saying, "Your ex lover's sister just destroyed a podcast bro's career for you. Which one of the love languages is that one you think? Gift giving? Or acts of service?"

Izzy hadn't asked him to repeat it. She hadn't needed to.

She closed the document, locked her phone, and stood there for a while.

The hearing was real. The threat was real. But someone else had moved first.

And it wasn't just someone. It was Nico.

She could feel it in the precision. In the way the data was

sequenced—clean, surgical, war-ready. He hadn't flooded her inbox. He hadn't made a scene. He hadn't tried to "handle" it for her.

And that, more than anything, told her how hard he was holding back.

He could've sent it to the press. He could've blown up the board. He could've gone full ballistic ex-military revenge fantasy and brought the whole house down.

But he didn't. He sent it to her. Privately. Quietly.

Because even in his panic, even in his need to fix it, he still understood: It had to be her call.

And for a man like Nico—that was restraint that bordered on violence.

41

The jet hit the runway like a dropped sofa.

First bounce, hard. Second, worse. Nosewheel slammed down with all the finesse of a toddler with a toy plane. Izzy's teeth clicked. Her arm braced against the seat before she realized she was doing it.

Whoever was flying this leg had no business being near a yoke, let alone type-rated on anything with calfskin-lined cupholders.

She didn't say a word. Just checked her watch, adjusted her collar, and silently added the name to a mental burn book she hadn't opened in a while.

This day was already going to hell. Might as well start on impact.

Izzy unbuckled before the cabin door even opened. The air outside was cold and painfully clean, the kind that made your teeth ache. Her phone lit up with a message from André—"Don't make that face. The one that makes you look like a wanted criminal in every country."

Copenhagen looked surgical. No loose ends. Even the cars moved like they knew they were being watched. The ride from the private airstrip to LUMA's Nordic headquarters was short, silent, and insulated. She didn't speak to the driver. Her hands were shaking.

The building stood like it had never made a mistake in its life. Frosted glass, unbothered steel. She stepped through the doors and tried not to flinch at the scent of ozone and sterilized fear. Security badges scanned. A woman in black led her to the elevator. No conversation. Just a nod and the kind of silence that suggested: *You're expected.*

The ride up was slow. Intentional. She could see her reflection in the brushed metal paneling—shoulders squared, face unreadable, except to anyone who knew what to look for. This wasn't a debrief. It was a diagnosis. They were going to dissect her. See what broke.

The doors opened.

Pilots. Everywhere. Not in uniform—worse. Off-duty. Civilian clothes, but deliberate. Familiar. Leather jackets from old fleets, battered LUMA backpacks, travel-minded with purpose. No one wore wings, but everyone had earned them. And most of them? Long-haul. Heavy metal. Transatlantic command.

Captains and senior FOs who usually didn't speak unless they had to. Now packed into a hallway in Copenhagen like they'd gotten the same message: *If they go after her, they go through us.*

Delaney was posted near the back like someone had dared her to attend and lost. Arms folded. Sunglasses on indoors. She didn't glance at Izzy. She didn't move.

"She's not walking in there with a target on her back while the rest of us pretend we didn't see it," Delaney said. Grudging. Like she'd rather be at home but showed up anyway, because this was one of those moments where silence was cowardice.

"We're here so you remember you're not on your own, Ventura."

Someone shifted. No one spoke.

Izzy's chest went tight. She hadn't asked for this. She wouldn't have. But they came anyway. All the captains who'd kept their distance. All the ones who used to look through her. Now standing in the hallway like they belonged to the same side.

And for the first time in years, maybe ever, she didn't feel outnumbered.

When she walked in, there were seven people physically present. Five were lawyers. One was Russell Cayne, seated like he still owned the room. And one—one was Morgan Delgado. US CEO. Legend. Unkillable corporate dominatrix in the flesh.

Izzy had seen her at company events, sure. Shook her hand briefly at a Women in Aviation summit in Doha. But standing across the table from her now, as prey, not colleague, was a different type of exposure. Morgan didn't look at her. She was reading a folder. Her lipstick was the kind of red worn by women who expected to be obeyed. Her charcoal suit was cut so sharp it could've drawn blood.

Izzy had tried to match the energy. She wore a sleeveless black turtleneck dress that hugged her shoulders and fell to mid-calf. Small gold hoops, and she made the decision to keep her long hair down. Her boots were polished. Her nails were bare. The watch on her wrist was a Vacheron Constantin Overseas, black dial, steel bracelet. She bought it the day she made widebody captain. She didn't wear it often. But she wore it today. Because it told time better than any of these bastards.

She stood behind her chair, refused to sit. No one told her to.

No one offered water. Not even coffee.

The room was arranged like a courtroom without a judge. Two more lawyers were on Zoom—faces beamed onto the mounted flat screen like prophets from the HR cloud. Behind them, through the floor-to-ceiling windows, the waterway cut across the Copenhagen skyline like a slow wound. Nyhavn. That was the name. She couldn't remember the last time she saw it from a place that didn't feel like exile.

Morgan stood. Closed the folder. The air pressure in the room changed.

"Captain Isabel Ventura," she said. "You are here today under review for the following violations."

The charges came like scalpel cuts.

"Circumventing proprietary software policy."

"Obstructing a vendor's beta test."

"Noncompliance with internal comms protocol."

"Creating reputational risk to LUMA via unofficial channels."

Izzy's pulse pounded behind her eyes. Her fingers twitched. She opened her mouth. She'd memorized it: *I am the best pilot in this fleet. I have given this company more of myself than anyone here would dare admit. And I will be damned if none of you have the backbone to defend me, so I will do it myself.*

But Morgan lifted a single hand.

Izzy stopped breathing.

"These," Morgan said, "are the accusations made by a man who used your trauma as a test case."

Silence.

"Who installed surveillance on your cockpit. Who flagged your ID. Who made you the control variable for a system you never opted into."

She turned to the room like she was pivoting on a West End stage. Her voice had edge, not volume.

"Captain Ventura, you are not here to be terminated."

Morgan paused and let out a deep breath.

"You are here because you refused to break."

Izzy didn't move. Didn't breathe. Couldn't. Her palms were sweating. Her legs were locked. The windows gleamed like a threat.

"When the software glitched out," Morgan continued, "you refused to fly a plane across the Atlantic to prevent a worst-case scenario where an engine failure mid-route would leave you with no diversion data, no coordinates, and no fuel strategy—just a metal tube, over cold water, with no one coming."

Someone shifted in their chair. The lawyer on the left blinked rapidly. Russell was turning red.

"When every legal department failed to stop the leak of your protected health information—you said nothing."

Morgan walked to her. Unhurried. Deliberate. She stopped one step too close.

"You were never the risk, Captain," she said, quiet and clean. "You were the firewall. And you held."

No one exhaled.

Izzy's hands stayed flat on the table. She didn't move. But somewhere beneath the surface—beneath the nerves, beneath the conditioning, beneath the years of being watched and judged and written off—something gave.

Last night, she'd thought it was a trap.

She'd seen Morgan only twelve hours before. Not in a boardroom. London. A cocktail bar so curated it didn't have a name, just velvet curtains, deep red lighting, and bartenders who looked like former models turned disgraced

Michelin apprentices. No one ate. The drinks had names like Emotional Labour and Exit Strategy.

The second she ordered Unresolved Issue, André bailed—twenty minutes in, trailing cologne and chaos.

Izzy stayed with her half-melted ice and a headache she didn't want to take home. Her phone was face down. Her second drink was a mezcal thing called Second Shift. It was working.

Morgan Delgado appeared without warning. Just materialized beside the booth like she'd been waiting for a cue.

"This isn't a company bar," Izzy said.

"No," Morgan said, slipping into the seat across from her. "But you're a company problem."

She looked stunning. Dangerous. Like someone who wrote severance packages in red ink. Her trench was draped over the booth, collar sharp. Her shoulder-length hair was in loose waves that dared someone to touch it.

She scanned the menu with mild amusement.

"Do you recommend 'Terms & Conditions' or '*The Patriarchy Isn't Real, You're Just Hungover*'?"

"They all just taste like trust issues and orange zest," Izzy said.

Morgan nodded. "Terms & Conditions, then." She waved down the bartender and ordered one. "And another of whatever she's having."

The drinks came fast. Of course they did. The entire staff had clocked Morgan five seconds in and collectively decided not to fuck around.

Morgan sipped. Smiled faintly. "That's good. That's very good."

Izzy took a long pull from her own glass. No ice this time. She wasn't flying, wasn't on duty, wasn't responsible for anything but getting through the night.

"I read something interesting this morning," Morgan said. "A report that didn't come through Legal."

She took a slow sip. It didn't soften her expression.

"It names Russell. Details the breach. Lists surveillance tools—never FAA approved, never disclosed, never consented to. And it tracks the people: pilots, crew, engineers. Many of whom have been collecting receipts for weeks."

She looked at Izzy over the rim of her glass. Squinting—half amused, half lethal. A pause, just long enough to let the silence press.

"Someone's been mobilizing."

Izzy didn't flinch. Didn't blink. Her face turned impassive, eyes empty, spine straight. She looked exactly like a woman who'd never seen the document in her life.

Morgan placed her glass down, unhurried.

"I was in Chicago when I finished reading it ten hours ago. Took the first available jumpseat to London."

A breath.

"It's not an incident report, Captain. It's a war file. And it's going to burn a very expensive bridge."

Izzy looked at her. No fear. Just a low-grade burn behind her eyes.

Morgan met it. "I don't do warnings. But I do reconnaissance."

A pause. The bar hummed around them. Morgan set her drink down with quiet finality.

"And I need you calm tomorrow."

"I am calm."

"No," Morgan said, not unkind. "You're operational. That's different."

She didn't press. Just leaned back, one ankle crossed over the other.

"I believe you," she said. "And I believe we owe you."

Then she stood. Finished her drink in one smooth motion. Slipped on her trench. She didn't say goodbye, didn't offer comfort. Just nodded once and disappeared through the curtain like she'd never been there.

When Izzy asked for the check, she was told the tab had already been settled.

Now, in the light of morning, the woman from the bar stood ten feet away and drew blood with a single sentence.

Morgan turned. Her voice dropped two degrees and ten IQ points to address the man across the table.

"Russell. You are relieved of all duties as Chief Technology Officer, effective immediately. Security has your badge. Legal has your laptop."

There was a pause.

Then he laughed. A deranged bark of disbelief.

"Oh, you've got to be fucking kidding me."

The room froze. A lawyer on Zoom went pale.

Russell surged to his feet so fast his chair screeched back into the wall. His tie was askew, hairline sweating, the kind of man who thought he was indispensable because no one had slapped the delusion out of him yet.

"You people—" he spat. "You think this airline runs on your little feminist speeches and brand values and fucking ESG checklists? You're nothing without me."

Morgan didn't flinch. She didn't blink.

Russell jabbed a finger toward her like he'd finally lost the last of his leash. "You cold bitch. You don't even know what half the code does—I kept this place from getting sued every quarter!"

He pivoted, wild-eyed, toward the table. "That patch? The one you all think is spyware? That wasn't even the bad one! You want full transparency?" He slapped the table. "I rerouted the beta test so it wouldn't trigger in Dubai. Because their Civil Aviation Authority would've buried us in fines. I've been cleaning up your fucking messes for months."

No one moved.

Except Morgan, who turned slightly—just enough to angle her body toward the door.

"Do you know how much I've protected you people?" Russell shouted, voice cracking. "Do you have any idea what we buried to keep the FAA happy after the Atlanta incident? Ask your golden boy developers why the A350 update had six ghost alerts, not two. Go ahead. ASK."

He was sweating now. Veins in his neck visible. Something about him had collapsed inward—desperation dressed up like dominance.

Morgan looked at him the way you look at a gnat on your sleeve.

"That's enough."

"Oh, now it's enough?" His voice cracked—too loud. "I built your entire backend infrastructure. I protected your vendors. I gave this airline deniability. And you're going to crucify me because some *suicidal* pilot didn't like being monitored?"

He sneered—eyes on Izzy now, full of venom.

Izzy didn't move. Her breath stayed shallow, her eyes locked ahead.

She stood there while a man with a loosening tie and a failing career questioned her will to live in front of a room full of power.

The word hung there. Not said to her—about her. Like she wasn't even in the room. Like she was already gone.

Her pulse hit the base of her skull. She clenched her teeth. If she spoke, it would shake. And she would rather swallow glass than let him hear it.

That's when the door opened.

Two men walked in. Nordic as hell. Built like custom cabinets. Both in matte black suits, carrying the dead-eyed calm of people trained to separate idiots from billion-dollar spaces.

Russell froze.

The taller one reached for his elbow.

"Don't fucking touch me," Russell snapped, jerking away. "I'll walk out when I'm ready."

"You're ready," the man said, in clean, unaccented English.

Russell tried to twist free. It wasn't even a fight. One guard took his wrist, the other lifted his laptop bag. Within seconds, he was being walked backwards toward the door, still yelling.

The door shut behind him.

Silence,

Morgan smoothed the front of her blouse like she'd just swatted a fly. Then turned back to the room, her voice flat.

"Captain Ventura. As I was saying."

This time, her voice wasn't performance. It was human.

"You saved this airline. You saved lives. And you did it while being watched, doubted, and betrayed by the system that was supposed to protect you."

A pause. A promise.

"I won't let it happen again."

And then she walked out. No glance back. Just the sound of her heels on engineered wood, a woman who did not need to stay in the room to own it.

Izzy stood where she was, blinking once.
Then she sat.
Not because she was told.
Because the war was over.

42

Outside, the pilots looked like they'd just witnessed a particularly satisfying public execution and were pretending not to celebrate.

Most had already peeled off. When Morgan stepped out and said simply, "She's fine," they'd taken the cue. No one wanted to linger too long or make it weird. They hadn't shown up for applause—they'd shown up so she wouldn't walk in alone. Mission handled.

A few remained. Quiet. Present. Watchful.

Delaney was still posted by the wall, arms folded, sunglasses on indoors like always. When Izzy passed, she slapped her on the back hard enough to knock the wind out of her.

"You should come up to the homestead next summer," Delaney said. "Alaska interior. Closest neighbor's a glacier. Good air. No Wi-Fi."

Izzy froze. That was basically a marriage proposal, coming from Delaney—a woman who once walked out of a fleet event mid-speech because someone used the word 'synergy.'

"Yeah," Izzy said. "I'll think about it."

Delaney nodded once. Then left.

Down the hall, Morgan stood with her back against the wall, half-tucked under the arm of a tall man who was pretending not to be all over her. He murmured something low. She rolled her eyes but didn't move.

Captain Kieran O'Hara. Still wearing the same well-worn flight jacket and stainless steel pilot's watch he probably had at his first command checkride. His hair had gone mostly salt and pepper, but not in a way that suggested aging—more like refinement under pressure. Izzy would bet her savings that he wasn't going to retire until someone pried the sidestick from his hands—and even then, there would be paperwork.

Izzy hadn't seen him before she went into the meeting. Which was probably the point.

When he noticed her watching, he stepped away from Morgan with the air of a man who thought he was being subtle. He wasn't.

"You held the line," he said. "Nice work."

No sentimentality. Just a fact, stated like a weather report.

And in that moment, she knew.

He brought them. Or pulled the first thread. The ones who showed up. The quiet crowd outside that door. Kieran was old school. Heavy metal. Loyalty over everything. If anyone could marshal a ghost fleet of senior pilots into showing up for a woman most of them had never spoken to, it was him.

Izzy gave a shallow nod. No words. Just enough to say *I see you.*

He tipped his head. Then turned back to Morgan, who resumed pretending he was an inconvenience while tugging his collar back into place like she hadn't just been hanging off him like a scarf.

Izzy exhaled.

Near the elevators stood Freja Lindström—tall, bone-pale, and tailored to lethal precision, with cheekbones sharp enough to trigger a metal detector and the kind of platinum hair that wasn't dyed, just inevitable. Her slate-blue suit fit like it had been engineered, not tailored, and the way she stood—arms folded, one hip cocked just slightly—radiated the kind of calm usually reserved for apex predators and exiled royalty.

Izzy hadn't seen her in years.

Freja had been her boss, back before the split—when LUMA was still small, boutique, barely holding its own against the legacies. She'd founded the airline. Personally interviewed every captain in the early days. Back then, Izzy saw her constantly. Knew her walk, her espresso order, the exact rhythm of her heels in the hallway.

After the reorg, Izzy signed with LUMA US. Freja stayed with the parent company. And now she was global CEO.

Izzy hadn't seen her since.

Until now.

"Captain Ventura," Freja said, voice smooth, unhurried. "Do you have a moment?"

She didn't wait for a reply.

Izzy followed her without a word. Down the hall. Through a keycarded door that opened into a private office —clean, brutal, modern. Marble desk. Framed photo of her with some Airbus board members. No clutter. Not a single personal item, unless you counted the sixty-thousand-dollar coffee machine hiding in the corner like a war crime.

Freja gestured for her to sit. She didn't.

Instead, she opened a drawer. Took out a slim black folder. Handed it over.

Izzy flipped it open. Investment packet. High-tier equity. Vesting schedule included. Very serious numbers.

She looked up.

"You're serious."

Freja gave the faintest nod. "I am. And I trust you'll continue to show the good judgment you're known for."

Izzy just stared.

Freja folded her hands neatly on the desk, voice steady and smooth, like reading a weather report.

"Captain Ventura, you could've gone public. You didn't. That says something. And while we're confident in your professionalism, it's always wise to ensure alignment—especially when there's so much at stake."

The words were soft. The meaning wasn't.

The door opened.

Morgan stepped in, her presence the punctuation to Freja's subtle threat.

"Just take it."

Izzy looked down at the folder again. Then back up.

She thought about the gym. About Rey, about the girls training on borrowed gloves and taped-up shin guards. About that busted water heater. About the outreach programs they wanted to launch. About the space they could build if they had real money. Security. Ownership.

She rolled her eyes.

"This is bribery," she said flatly. "You shaved three years off my life and now you're handing me a folder like it's a spa voucher. What's next—a fruit basket for not suing you?"

Freja didn't blink. Morgan didn't react. The silence was smooth and plausible.

Izzy snorted once, without humor.

"Fine."

Morgan smiled. "Knew you were smart."

Neither woman moved to shake hands. But Izzy took the pen.

43

1 month later

Doha International gleamed—curated to an inch of its life. Immaculate floors stretched like a mirror. Glass walls stood flawless, untouched. The lounge lighting stayed cold and constant—not harsh, just insistent. Designed to keep you alert, restless, eyes forward.

Izzy hadn't moved in half an hour.

She sat near the back of the crew lounge with her jacket still on, the collar sharp against her neck. One leg crossed over the other. Her bag was zipped, her phone sat screen-down beside a paper cup of mint tea gone cold. A single dry date sat on the napkin in front of her, half-bitten.

She'd cut her hair.

It used to fall to her waist at home, always tied back at work, and braided like control was something she could wear. Now she just let it drape just past her shoulders—straight, clean, undecorated.

She wasn't angry. Not like before. This didn't feel

personal. It was just the system doing what it always did—breaking things that didn't matter enough to protect.

Her flight to Lisbon had been pulled. Aircraft reassigned for a corporate repositioning. VIP onboard. She'd been replaced by a standby crew and left in the lounge like a placeholder.

A message from Ops had arrived five minutes later.

Standby for Line Check duty.

Captain I. Ventura has been reassigned.

Crew pairing update to follow.

She didn't scream.

But she wanted to.

She'd flown to Qatar plenty of times. The protocol was always the same. Keep it professional. Stay in uniform. Don't linger alone in public places. Most international crew didn't stray from the hotel compound. Izzy never had. She didn't feel unsafe.

Today, it didn't matter. Nowhere to go. No flight waiting. Just a gate that wasn't hers and a pilot who would, inevitably, be annoying. Names didn't matter.

She had more money than she could ever need now. She had distance. Her reputation was more or less intact. Her career no longer sat in her chest like an open wound. She didn't need to fly. Not anymore. She wanted to—but that was different. The fear was gone.

Whatever Ops threw at her, she could take it.

So she sat. Quiet. Tired. A little bored. She checked her email, deleted three notifications, and checked the weather in Lisbon. She let the date sit untouched. She didn't refresh the crew pairing.

She didn't care.

Not until the lounge doors slid open behind her, and

someone walked in with a crew bag, a uniform, and a voice she hadn't heard in awhile.

Nico's gate had decent light. That was rare. Usually it was fluorescent and miserable, but this was soft, natural, streaked in through curved glass. He looked like someone who had almost slept and almost shaved. Tie crooked, collar loose, hair still wet from a too-fast rinse in the crew hotel sink.

He was FaceTiming the sisters.

Or rather, he was FaceTiming the toddler.

Ahsan had just said "ammo"—*uncle* in Arabic—and Nico was still recovering. His heart was somewhere in his throat. It wasn't the first time, but this one had sounded deliberate.

"That was a fluke," he muttered. "He just likes the 'm' sound."

"Stop pretending it didn't ruin you," Layla said, voice tinny through the speaker. "Your eyes are doing that soft wet puppy thing."

They were in Brooklyn, probably in the kitchen. He could hear the drawer that always stuck and the noise Layla made when she opened the fridge with her foot. There was a crash in the background—something ceramic.

Nico checked the crew portal on his tablet without breaking stride.

Final leg.

Final flight.

One more line check. After this, he was free.

Layla kept talking. Something about sippy cups and the

sociopolitical implications of BPA. Nico wasn't listening anymore.

He was halfway through adjusting his tie when someone tapped his arm.

He turned.

Someone from Ops. Early twenties. Polished red nails. LUMA badge on a lanyard that looked freshly issued. She smiled the way people smile when they're used to being looked at.

"Captain Farrah?"

"Yeah."

She closed the distance between then and looked up at him like it was a conversation, not a checklist. "Just wanted to give you a heads-up—your Check Airman's been pulled. Injury on layover."

Nico blinked. "What kind of injury?"

She checked the screen. "Camel dismount."

"Camel?"

"Yeah. Sand dunes tour. He got tossed. Sprained wrist, maybe fractured. He's off rotation until medical clears it."

Nico stared at her. "He fell off a camel?"

"Technically it says spooked dismount, but yeah. He's done."

He scrubbed a hand over his mouth, trying not to laugh or curse. "Jesus."

"Anyway, they reassigned you." She tilted the tablet so he could see. "Captain I. Ventura. She's already here."

His mouth went dry. He looked down at the screen.

Then back at her.

"You lucked out. She's, uh...very respected. Technically certified for long-haul line checks. Not known for leniency, but the standards are solid."

He nodded once. "I know."

"She's in the crew lounge."

"Okay."

She tilted her head. "You two flown together before?"

Nico didn't answer right away.

"Once or twice," he said.

She kept standing there.

"I should head that way," he added.

"Of course." She stepped back, just a little too slow. "Well—safe flight, Captain."

He gave her a polite nod. Nothing more.

Didn't ask her name. Didn't look back.

He was already walking toward the crew lounge. Toward Izzy.

Toward whatever this was about to become.

Then he looked down. Ahsan's face filled the screen, wide-eyed and overlit, drool trailing from his chin. Layla shifted him with one arm, just enough to smirk at Nico over the baby's head.

"Go ahead, we'll mute. Just pretend we're not here watching you panic-sweat over your ex."

SHE WAS SEATED near the back of the lounge, half-shadowed by a wall-mounted TV playing muted weather loops. Blazer still on. Chin slightly tilted. One leg crossed like she was holding court, not waiting for a reassignment. A half-bitten date sat on a napkin in front of her like it had offended her personally. Mint tea. Unfinished. Probably cold.

And her hair—

He stopped moving.

Her hair was down.

Loose, unbound, free of the tight control she used to

think was necessary—military habit, cockpit discipline, the illusion of safety.

It fell just past her shoulders now. Straight. Clean. No pins. Just there. Like it had always been like that. Like she hadn't built a whole identity out of tying it back so no one could touch it.

He wanted to touch it.

He was pretty sure he wasn't supposed to want that anymore, but his body didn't care. His body wanted to sink his hands into it. Tilt her head back. Thumb the inside of her wrist. Pull her into his lap and ask her what changed, and if he was still allowed to know.

She looked different.

Not younger or softer—lighter.

She'd stopped asking permission like she no longer needed the job to prove anything. Like she could walk away from the airline and still be someone worth fearing.

It broke him a little.

He stepped forward, slow. Folder in hand. Shoulders square. Tie still uneven. He hadn't spoken to her in a couple months and now he was walking toward her like his lungs hadn't locked up the second she looked up.

No smile. Just a flicker—tight, subtle, and very fucking dangerous. She looked him over like he was just another assignment. One she already regretted.

He stopped in front of her. Didn't sit.

"I think you're my Check Airman."

She sipped her tea, slow and deliberate. Then looked up. "Don't start."

He lifted the folder between them. The front page said it. *Check Airman.* Like the FAA had never met a woman.

He held it up. "It says Airman."

"I don't write the regs."

He pulled a pen from his pocket. Scratched it out. Wrote: *Check Pilot.*

Then handed it to her.

Her eyes rolled. Her mouth twitched. Just once. Like her body hadn't gotten the memo to stay neutral.

THE WALK to the gate was uneventful in the way only aviation could make humiliating.

They didn't speak much. Just that brittle, meaningless preflight rhythm—*block time? got the ATIS?*— delivered like strangers who'd only just been introduced. Which was technically the point.

When you're in an airport and you see two pilots standing at the gate, not talking, staring vaguely in the direction of boarding group three like they've never heard of eye contact—that's on purpose. It's designed awkward. Built into the bones of the job. Crew pairings aren't supposed to be close. You're meant to be alert. Because flying is all about judgment. Decision-making. Chain of command. Clear heads. And if the person sitting next to you is someone who's seen you drunk, vulnerable, half-naked—or worse, undone—that clarity? It gets compromised. Subconsciously, emotionally, chemically. Doesn't matter how disciplined you are.

Respect and professionalism above all. Friendly, sure— but never familiar.

They were not that.

He and Izzy had seen each other wrecked. He'd held her while she muttered in her sleep, kissed her in multiple cities. She'd sobbed, silently, into his shoulder after their last time together. He knew how good her hands felt on him. She knew how his breath stuttered when he came.

And now they were standing four feet apart at Gate C7, pretending they'd never touched each other.

Accountability, he thought. *Yeah right.*

He was about to spend seven hours in a pressurized metal box, pretending the sound she made when she let go wasn't still in his head.

NICO HAD NEVER BEEN SO aware of a checklist in his life.

The cockpit felt smaller than it was. Pressurized, yes, but not by altitude. Just proximity.

Izzy was already seated, flipping through the flight plan like it might bite. Her nails were short. No polish. Her hair now tucked behind one ear, already beginning to frizz from the recycled air. He wanted to touch it so badly it was giving him chest pressure.

They didn't talk much during the first twenty minutes.

Standard flow.

Left seat: him. Right seat: her.

Final supervised leg. IOE. Last goddamn hurdle before he got to be a real boy in the eyes of the FAA.

He wasn't nervous. He was performing nervousness, because anything else would've looked arrogant.

And he needed to impress her.

Which was stupid, because she already knew him—deeply—but now she was seeing him through the one lens he couldn't afford to fuck up: professional command. Leadership. Judgment.

No kink. Just systems and tone.

They pushed back six minutes behind schedule. ATC clearance was clipped. Routing was dense and less efficient than it should've been—probably a flow restriction over Tehran airspace. There was a hold built into the estimated arrival window and the METAR for Heathrow looked like shit: overcast at six-hundred feet, gusting winds from the southwest, and turbulence already flagged en route over Ankara.

Perfect.

He called for taxi. She acknowledged. Voice neutral. Not cold, just careful.

Takeoff was smooth.

It was after the climb checklist that things started to...loosen.

"Route's uglier than I expected," he said, once they'd passed FL180. His voice felt too loud in the cockpit.

Izzy didn't look over. "It's Doha. They're always passive-aggressively overprocedural."

He smiled. That was familiar. That was hers.

By FL340, they'd hit cruise and the FMC was stable enough that she finally leaned back, crossed her arms. Not hostile. Just resting in her authority.

He glanced over.

"You look different," he said.

She didn't look at him. "I cut my hair."

"I noticed. It suits you."

Silence.

Then: "I stopped wearing it up after Copenhagen."

He glanced at her, careful. "Why?"

She shrugged, quiet. "Didn't feel like it anymore. Some days I braid it, some days I don't. No one's counting."

That lodged somewhere in his ribs.

Thirty minutes passed. Routing brought them across southern Turkey. Beneath them: dry mountains, dust valleys, streaked ridgelines in slate and rust. They'd see the Black Sea by the edge of Bulgaria. Then come up over Vienna. Then Brussels. Then the Channel.

"Have you flown this leg before?" he asked.

"Plenty. But not recently."

He nodded. "I like this one."

"Because of the route?"

"Because it's just long enough to feel like something but not long enough to get emotionally weird."

A pause.

Then she huffed a laugh. Low. Almost unwilling.

He let himself look at her fully, just for a second. Her mouth was bare. No lipstick. She looked lighter. Not softer. Just less contained. She looked like she'd survived something. And maybe that was why he still wanted her more than air.

They hit turbulence over Belgrade. Light at first. Then moderate chop. He took the controls manually—partially out of instinct, partially because he wanted her to see it. His hands were steady. Control input was clean. Pitch adjustment precise. No overcorrection.

Izzy didn't comment.

She didn't have to.

They flew on.

Over Western Europe, cloud cover thickened. The sun vanished behind a milky haze. The airspeed indicator fluctuated. It would be bumpy through descent. ATC gave them a runway change—27L, instead of 09R. More crosswind. More challenge.

Fine.

Let it be hard. Let it demand something.

He landed it clean.

Not perfect. But intentional. Firm. Within limits. No bounce.

And when he called for flaps up and she acknowledged

it, something in her voice cracked—barely—but enough to keep him breathing.

They didn't speak much during taxi. Ground gave them a remote stand, far side of Terminal 5. A long roll in silence.

The logbook stayed open on her lap.

When she finally turned to him, her voice was level, but her eyes weren't.

"You passed."

He nodded. "Thanks."

"You didn't need to impress me, you know."

"Yes I did."

She blinked once.

He added, quieter: "I still want to."

There was a pause that could've held an entire confession.

But she just closed the logbook. Looked out the window.

They sat in silence, surrounded by 250,000 pounds of aircraft and history, pretending the sky hadn't just reminded them who they were to each other.

They deplaned like strangers.

Out of the cockpit, it all reverted.

The shared air, the memory of her laugh over Ankara, the ghost of her thigh brushing his hand during descent—all gone. Stripped away the second the cabin door opened. Just two senior crew walking off a jet like they hadn't once fallen apart in a hotel room and put each other back together the wrong way.

She handed in the release paperwork at the crew desk. No ceremony. Just a strike through the line check section and her signature beneath it.

Released to Line.

Captain N. Farrah.

Evaluator: I. Ventura.

His name. Her writing. It shouldn't have felt like a scar.

"You're official," she said, not looking at him. "Congrats."

He nodded. "Thanks."

There was so much he wanted to say.

Instead, he followed her through the crew corridor, past Heathrow's brutalist terminal walls, through the backstage tunnels that only pilots and rats knew.

Neither of them said a word in customs. She presented her badge like she'd done it a thousand times—because she had. He stood beside her, silent. Present. Devoted like an idiot dog.

She didn't ask him what he was doing later.

She didn't glance at him once.

He had no right to expect anything, but he still felt something in his chest buckle as she walked ahead of him, toward the car pickup zone like this was it. Like this was the last time.

His stomach dropped.

He was going to let her go. Again.

He told himself: *Don't follow her. Don't be a freak. Don't say something you can't take back.*

And then she stopped. Turned.

Her face didn't give anything away. Just a half-second flicker of something unreadable—sharp, internal, reluctant.

"The girls at The Mat miss you," she said.

He blinked.

"There's a demo tomorrow," she added. "We're expanding—knocking through the wall and taking over the shop next door."

He frowned, because the phrasing caught him off guard.

"Wait, seriously? That's huge, Izzy." He grinned, open and proud. "You're building it out. That's—fuck, that's amazing."

She looked away too fast.

And then it happened—barely there, but real. A flush rising beneath her skin, high across her cheekbones. Not heat from sparring. Not sweat.

A blush.

His brain short-circuited.

She was blushing. *Blushing.*

He didn't say a word. Didn't dare. Just held still, like if he moved, he'd scare it off. But inside? He was screaming.

"Anyways," she huffed. "It starts at seven."

He swallowed. "You'll be there?"

Her eyes dropped to his mouth, then back up.

"Yeah," she said. Quiet. "I'll be around."

Then she turned again. No smile. Just that.

But she'd said it.

And for the first time in weeks, he let himself breathe.

44

Nico took the long way to the gym. Circle Line to Wood Lane, then cut through the side streets like a coward. The air was damp, light still hanging around the edges of sunset.

He told himself he wasn't nervous. That the detour had nothing to do with her.

By the time he reached the gym—tucked between a Polish bakery and a vape shop, the sign still half-falling off —his palms were sweating.

The windows glowed. Warm light. Movement behind the frosted glass.

He adjusted his jacket and stepped in.

The smell hit first: eucalyptus spray, old sweat, and feet. Not bad. Just honest.

This place had seen blood and breakdowns and whole-ass lives turned around. It had held him once, too—when she let him in. When they trained together in silence.

He took off his shoes and walked in barefoot, bag slung over one shoulder.

He'd dressed with exactly her in mind—black joggers,

low on his hips, hugging his thighs. A grey t-shirt that clung a little too well. A lightweight track jacket, unzipped just enough to show collarbone. No logos. Just him, unarmed.

Clean-shaven. Sleeves rolled up. Intentional.

He was there to help. He was there for her.

He looked like bait and he knew it—tailored to her taste: clean, soft, a little undone. She always looked twice when he tried too hard. He hated himself for leaning into it. He hated how badly he wanted her to notice.

Izzy was across the room.

And he—he was done for.

She wore that loose-cut white tank she used for mobility drills, hair down around her shoulders, black leggings hugging her like a death wish. She was barefoot, grounded, pure command. Teaching a takedown like it was scripture. Speaking low, firm, clean.

Not a hint of flirt. No softness. Just control.

And Nico, like a pervert, like a fool, watched her like she was water and he'd been crawling across the desert.

Not as his ex. Not as the woman who stopped texting him.

As the force that made the room safer.

He helped where he could. Held mitts. Demonstrated a few blocks. Let the Tuesday night dolls tease him about his form, about his smile, about how long he'd been gone.

He didn't care.

Not with Izzy two mats over, demonstrating ground defense with a calm that made him ache. She moved between groups like she ran the place—because she did. The new girls watched her like she was unbreakable. The ones who knew her already gave her shit.

One girl—Lina, one of the Tuesday night regulars— wandered over mid-wrap, smirking.

"Oi. Nico."

He blinked. "Hey."

"I bet she said we missed you."

He nodded once, careful.

"Yeah, that was a lie."

His stomach sank.

Lina grinned. "We didn't say shit."

Pause. Just long enough for it to cut.

Then: "But *she* missed you, bruv. So bad. It was grim."

He nearly sat down. Right there on the mat.

Lina was already walking away, whistling.

He stayed at the edge of the drills, stretching, correcting form, keeping busy. But his eyes kept betraying him.

Every time Izzy spoke, he tracked it.

Every time she raised her arms, bent her knees, rolled someone over with clean, elegant brutality, his pulse spiked like a teenager at a school dance.

Her skin glowed under the lights. Her voice landed like truth. Every time someone asked a question, she answered like they deserved to know.

And when someone froze mid-move—scared, ashamed, triggered—Izzy crouched to their level. No condescension. Just a quiet hand and words Nico couldn't hear.

Whatever she said worked. Every time.

He could've watched her forever.

He was watching her forever.

This was it. There was no out.

She called time on the last drill like she owned the clock. Told them all to hydrate. Passed out snacks like a mother who hated being thanked.

And when she looked up—caught him watching, maybe —he didn't drop his gaze.

Not this time.

She looked away, but slower than before. Like maybe she'd seen the hunger in his eyes and didn't mind the burn.

His heart was trying to break out of his chest. His cock wasn't far behind.

This was far beyond wanting her. It was closer to worship.

NICO STARTED SHOWING UP AGAIN.

He didn't say much. He didn't look for her. He held mitts for whoever needed them. He kept his hands steady and his mouth shut. He wiped down mats. Rewrapped gloves. Picked up energy drink cans that didn't belong to him and folded towels without being asked.

Rey didn't greet him. She didn't kick him out either.

That was as close to permission as he was going to get.

The gym had changed. It was still rough around the edges—scarred walls, sweat-heavy air—but there was a new finish to it. The ceiling had been raised. The lights were cleaner. The ring had been replaced. The heavy bags were new. He caught someone calling it the Mat like it was a real place now, not just a nickname. The mats themselves were pale grey now, with pale pink edge tape. The locker room walls had been repainted. The sound system was better.

Someone had built this with care. Someone had rebuilt it for permanence.

He kept coming back. No one asked him why.

The first time he saw Izzy after demo night, she was finishing a circuit. She didn't stop when she saw him. She didn't speak. Just walked past him, hair tied low, face unreadable, sweat sliding down her spine.

He didn't stare. He just went back to work.

By the third week, she nodded at him once when she came in.

That was it.

He nodded back.

It stayed that way for a while.

He never tried to linger. Never stayed late. Never asked for drills. Never cornered her for a moment she didn't offer.

He trained. He worked. He listened. He left.

At some point—two months in, maybe more—she let him hold pads for her.

No eye contact.

No small talk.

Just stance, weight, sound.

He kept his hands right where she needed them. He didn't flinch when she hit.

When the round ended, he stepped back without a word.

More weeks passed.

The gym started holding more community sessions. People from outside the fight world started showing up. Teens. First-timers. A few older girls from youth shelters. Some of Lina's friends from further out, who didn't say much, but came back week after week.

Izzy ran most of it on days when she wasn't flying. Rey handled the rest. Nico helped where he could.

No one mentioned what had happened. He was just there. A pair of arms. A fixed point. Reliable.

One night, after a demo, Izzy touched his hand.

They were standing by the storage closet, checking inventory. No one else around. She reached for the clipboard and her fingers brushed his—and then didn't move.

She didn't look at him.

But she left her hand there.

He didn't say anything. He just let it sit.

She walked away ten seconds later. Didn't explain. Didn't look back.

It took everything in him not to follow.

December came. They decorated the gym.

It wasn't elaborate, but it was real. Rey found a four-foot fake tree that leaned slightly to the left. The girls taped paper snowflakes to the mirrors. Someone brought battery-powered fairy lights. Even Izzy got dragged into it—hooked tinsel over the front desk with a look of deep judgment and exactly one eye roll.

She didn't stop them, though.

Nico spent most of the holiday in New York with his family. But he came back early for the first annual Christmas party and member appreciation event. Rey called it a "soft gathering." Lina brought a glittery sheet cake that said Punch Your Way Into The New Year. Someone made cocoa. They didn't train that night. Just played music. Sat on the mats. Laughed a little too loudly.

Izzy stayed longer than he thought she would.

Another month passed. The gym got new signage.

The front desk was rebuilt. Branded towels arrived. There was a shoe rack now. Nico found himself restocking protein bars like it was normal.

Izzy came in late one afternoon. He was taping the corner bag.

She walked past him. Paused. Looked back.

And smiled.

Small. Unsteady. Real.

It wrecked him.

He didn't ask for more.

He just kept showing up.

45

Nico turned thirty, and every off-duty pilot and flight attendant in London with a grudge, a crush, or flexible morals showed up to celebrate.

He hadn't planned anything. He'd mentioned it once—offhand, in passing, to no one in particular—and somehow it had turned into an op. The group chat lit up. Schedulers were blackmailed. A gate agent's cousin who was apparently an up-and-coming DJ got booked. A senior purser secured a private mezz at some overpriced club in Soho through her ex-boyfriend's sister. Someone printed fake boarding passes that said N30 GATE CLOSED and passed them around like drink tickets.

It spiraled fast.

By 22:00, there were fifty people there for him, all in varying stages of clubwear and employment risk.

Flight attendants. FOs. A couple off-duty captains. A cluster of LUMA crew from the Barcelona base who had clearly pre-gamed on the train.

Someone brought a tray of jello shots shaped like aircraft.

Someone else brought condoms branded with "Captain's Cockpit."

It wasn't classy, but it was deeply, unrepentantly for him.

Cy was already parked in a corner booth with his husband, Mas, both sharing a fishbowl margarita.

André was circulating with three separate groups, somehow louder than the music.

The DJ had just started playing a remix of Come Fly With Me that made two pursers scream.

Nico was holding someone else's vodka soda and considering an early exit when he saw her.

Izzy.

Walking in behind André, hair down, black dress, expression unreadable. She looked stunning. She also looked like she wanted to disappear.

She found him near the bar. Didn't smile. Just handed him a box wrapped in brown paper like this was a staff meeting.

"You brought a gift to the club?"

"I mean, I can take it back if you don't want it."

"No! That's mine!"

He opened it right there.

New mitts. Matte black. Custom-stitched.

Inside the lid was a keychain. Bright red. I BRAKE FOR TURBULENCE.

He laughed—out loud, no warning. A short, full-body noise that caught him off guard.

"Thanks," he said, suddenly unsure what to do with his face.

She shrugged. "Didn't think you needed anything fancy. Just something that works."

They didn't leave each other's side all night.

It wasn't announced. It wasn't theatrical. He just kept

finding her again, and she didn't move away. They danced. Light touches, nothing crude. Her hand on his shoulder. His palm against her hip. The music was too loud to talk, which helped. No confessions. Just rhythm and heat and proximity.

People gave them space.

She didn't drink much. Neither did he.

At some point, the cake appeared—"DADDY MATERIAL" spelled in icing across what looked like a Tesco sheet tray. A flight attendant from Glasgow shoved it in his face, and Izzy actually laughed. Not a smile. A real, full sound. He would've kissed her right then if they hadn't been surrounded.

By two, the place was thinning out. The DJ started playing songs with actual lyrics. Someone tried to start a conga line. André vanished in the direction of a rooftop smoking area. Cy and Mas waved goodbye with a nod and a raised glass.

Nico offered to walk her home. She didn't argue.

Outside, the city was wet and quiet. Her heels clicked on the pavement.

Neither of them said anything until they reached that glass and steel lobby.

She turned. Looked at him like he was still on probation.

"Happy birthday," she said.

Then—so fast he almost missed it—she rose onto her toes, pressed a quick kiss to his cheek, and vanished inside before he could even think to move.

He didn't follow.

He just stood there, hand halfway raised, stunned and blinking like someone had thrown a flashbang instead of affection.

They were two weeks and ten years apart. His party was chaos. Hers would be silence.

TWO WEEKS LATER, Izzy turned forty and didn't pretend to care.

She took the week off. She wasn't flying. Her out-of-office reply was curt and specific and legally bulletproof. She didn't need to prove anything anymore.

These days, she used her vacation days like someone who meant it. She booked facials and forgot the dates on purpose. She spent mornings at the gym and afternoons in silence. She slept better. She'd stopped drinking coffee after two p.m. Not because it made her anxious anymore—just because she liked sleeping.

Cy had quit the airline last year. Came in third on Bake Off, sold a pitch for a cookbook, and now lived in an upgraded flat like a smug little house-husband. They hung out more now. He had time. She'd forgotten what that looked like in a person.

André was still flying. Still loud. Still cosmically cursed in love, but in a more philosophical way now. He'd done a month in India after a breakup with someone who never actually deserved him. Came back glowy and dangerous. Didn't chase anything for once. Just showed up. Said he was single and "full of gods." No one questioned it.

The gym was still the gym.

On Tuesday, Rey casually warned her.

"Don't have a meltdown Thursday night," she said, stretching out her shoulder with a resistance band. "We're doing a thing. No bullshit. You don't have to say anything."

Izzy looked at her. "What kind of thing."

Rey didn't answer. Just adjusted the band tension and said, "Wear something nice."

So Izzy wore a dress. One with sleeves. Simple. Velvet. Not feminine in the traditional sense, but fitted enough to feel deliberate. Boots, of course. The same ones she'd had resoled three times. Hair down. No makeup.

She walked in like she didn't know, but they knew she knew.

The lights were low—someone had replaced the gym's harsh fluorescents with string lights, soft and golden, like it was sacred instead of sterile.

The playlist was at forty percent.

Someone had brought her favorite champagne—Billecart-Salmon, because they had taste.

No one said "surprise." No one yelled. There was no banner.

It was perfect.

There were maybe ten people total. Lina. Two of the new girls who never missed a session and never smiled unless Rey was on the mat. André brought two full bags of doner kebab from the place across the street—like he was feeding a family reunion, not ten people—and a sparkler candle that refused to stay lit. Cy sent flowers that made the whole front desk smell expensive. He was doing a book signing early in the morning and couldn't make it, but had sent the three-tier cake.

It was absurd in a way only Cy could get away with.

The top tier was black cake, Trinidadian-style, soaked in rum and port and clove-heavy enough to stun a man. The middle tier was Earl Grey sponge with lemon curd, because she'd once said tea cake was "fine, I guess," and he'd never let it go. The bottom tier was some light, tropical thing with coconut and passionfruit, delicate and beautiful and entirely too much.

The whole thing was finished in smooth white fondant with brutalist piping and a sugar plaque that said, FORTY & VIOLENT in gold lettering. No candles. Just presence.

Izzy narrowed her eyes at it. "He's insane."

Rey handed her a fork. "And he loves you."

Nico was already there when she arrived.

He didn't come up to her. He didn't hover. He was wearing a clean tee and jeans, helping move chairs. She didn't look at him for more than a second. But he looked good. Still tan. Hair a little longer. Still quiet. Still here.

Someone started music. No one danced. She sat on the floor with her back to the ring and let herself exhale.

Later, when half the room had filtered out and Rey was pretending to mop, Nico came up to her with a package.

Wrapped—not by him, obviously, but by someone at Harrods or somewhere worse. The paper was matte, the fold lines surgical. No card. Just intent.

Inside: a logbook.

Leather-bound, hand-stitched, likely by some lunatic in the Alps with a title and no internet. Her name was engraved on the cover—discreet, unshowy, permanent. The pages were heavy. Archival. The kind of thing designed to survive fire.

He didn't look at her when he spoke.

"Pretty sure you were down to your last few pages."

She didn't thank him—just ran her thumb along the spine like she was checking for a blade.

He just nodded. Then walked off, leaving her with three hundred blank pages and no excuse.

By ten, it was down to a few stragglers. She reached for the broom.

Rey clocked it instantly.

"Nah. I think the fuck not," she said. "You're not working today."

Then she kicked them both out like it was her flat, not the gym they co-owned together.

They walked out. She didn't wait for him. Just turned east and started walking, heels sharp on wet pavement. He caught up by Hammersmith. She hadn't spoken since they left the gym. The get-together was still clinging to her—glitter on her collarbone, candle smoke in her hair.

They walked in silence to the station. Piccadilly to Green Park. Jubilee to Canary Wharf.

She didn't sit. He didn't push it. At the platform, she didn't look back. He followed anyway.

Canary Wharf hit different at night.

Glass and silence. No piss-streaked concrete, no fried chicken bones on the curb. Just cold light, river air, and buildings that looked like they didn't want to be touched.

She didn't slow down. Just led him through the polished quiet, toward that curved white tower that scraped the sky like it was trying to leave.

When they were outside her door, she didn't say much. Just looked at him.

"I want you to come in," she said. "Not to fix anything. Just to stay. If you wanted to."

He exhaled—slow, like it didn't matter.

Like he hadn't just heard her say the one thing he'd been waiting for.

"Yeah," he said, too casually.

Then he adjusted his jacket for no reason at all.

She didn't smile. Just watched the way his mouth went taut, like he didn't trust it not to break.

.   .   .

SHE OPENED the door with one hand and left it swinging behind her. He caught it. Stepped in.

He followed her in silence, hands in his pockets like that would do anything to hide the fact that he'd been half-hard since she'd invited him in.

Izzy's flat looked like her mind: precise chaos. No curated calm this time, no fake tidy for guests. Just life. The real kind.

There was a Tupperware lid under the table like it had given up on being useful. A bunch of workout towel samples were draped over a chair, shades of charcoal and wine-red and brutalist beige, all tagged with neon post-its. Boxing shorts in three cuts, two of them clearly hand-altered with pinned seams. Her rolling whiteboard was pushed crooked against the kitchen wall—covered in gym expansion sketches, supply chain notes, half a business plan. One corner just said "PUNCH GIRL SUMMER?" in black marker.

She didn't explain any of it.

And he didn't need her to. He read the place like terrain. A woman who lived hard, moved fast, forgot to rest. Someone with too many missions and no goddamn time to recharge.

She was clearly home more now—but barely. And every surface screamed the same thing: she needed someone who'll worship her and do the laundry.

It hit him square in the chest. Made him want to clean the whole flat on his knees in silence and then eat her out on the kitchen table until she forgot why she was ever alone in the first place.

Instead, he stood there. Quiet and respectful.

She kicked off her boots, didn't look to see where they

landed. Walked to the kitchen, cracked the fridge. "You want something?"

He almost said water. Then she held up a bottle—thick glass, label in Japanese, the kind of whiskey you overnight to people you respect too much.

"It's from Captain Sato," she said, voice casual, almost bored. "The card says, "The thing you pulled off with the data leak deserves top shelf."

Nico snorted. "I hear no lies."

She nodded. Poured two fingers of it into a glass, held it out.

He took it, stared at her like she was the last honest woman alive. "How are you still surprised when people show up for you?"

She raised an eyebrow. "What does that mean?"

"It means you could ask any pilot in this fleet to take a bullet and half of them would thank you for the hole. You're a legend."

Izzy snorted. Looked away like she didn't know what to do with that. Typical.

They didn't sit. Didn't toast. Just stood there, shoulder to shoulder, backs to the living room, looking out the window like the city might start confessing next. It was quiet enough to hear her ice crack in the glass. The air was dense. Hot. Months of restraint coiled in the silence.

She didn't reach for him. Didn't even turn to look.

But when she finally did, it was slow. Measured. Like she'd decided.

Like maybe the test had already started.

She had one hip to the glass, the city laid out below like it was built for her and didn't even know it. The lights caught the edge of her dress—black satin, low neckline, slit up the side—and he felt something behind his ribs actually give.

Forty. She had just turned forty and looked like a fucking threat.

She brought the whiskey to her lips, took a measured sip, throat moving slow, deliberate. Nico watched it like it was porn.

Izzy nodded once. "Captain Sato has taste."

"He has fear," Nico said. "You make grown men want to be useful."

She gave him a side glance for that. Cool. Sharp. But her lip tugged, barely, like the start of a smirk. And that tiny twitch almost ruined him.

He took another sip, throat dry, blood unmanageable. The whiskey was excellent—warm, sharp, unapologetic. Kind of like the woman who handed it to him. It was unbearable, standing there next to her, knowing the weight of her was right there, a reach away, and not touching her.

Then—without looking at him—she said, "All that discipline."

Like she was only just seeing it for what it was.

She tipped her head to the side, slow and deliberate. Not coy. Just clean, like a page turning under a steady hand.

Then her eyes found his and held.

"Show me what it was for."

He didn't speak. Didn't smile.

For a second, nothing moved—except his pulse, sharp and stinging in his chest, like it wanted out.

This wasn't a dream. She was letting him in.

He stepped in behind her like he couldn't help himself. One hand brushed her hair aside, slow, deliberate, exposing the clean line of her neck like it was something sacred. He bent down and kissed the skin there—hot, open-mouthed—

and she arched back toward him like her body already knew what was coming.

His hand found her waist, the other slid under her jawline, and he turned her to face him. Their mouths met. At first, it was slow—soft enough to be mistaken for restraint—but it bled into something messier almost instantly. Desperate. Her breath hitched and turned into this quiet moan that vibrated against his lips. She wanted more. She wasn't shy about it.

He pulled back just far enough to smirk against her mouth.

"Already?" he muttered, voice full of that cocky disbelief that only half-covered his own unraveling. She said something smart in return, all challenge and heat, then added:

"You have my consent. Don't play gentle."

So he didn't.

He scooped her up without ceremony—grip tight, control total—and carried her to the table like he had one mission. It was a beautiful table, expensive, covered in all the chaos of her life: binders, post-its, scattered pens, a roll of measuring tape, fabric swatches half-unfurled like petals. He didn't care. They didn't care. He laid her down across the surface and everything clattered to the floor in a rain of chaos. The noise was loud, but not louder than her breathing.

The dress came off in one clean motion, like muscle memory. She was bare underneath. No underwear. Waxed, perfect, like she knew this exact moment was coming and planned for it. The scent of her hit him then—heady, warm, unreal—and he let out a low, involuntary curse.

His mouth dropped to hers again, slower now. Intentional. Then down—jaw, neck, collarbone—tracing the shape of her like a map he was relearning. He'd had her before, but not like this. His hands slid up to her breasts, and yeah, they were still everything he remembered: full, heavy, too good for her frame, too good for him, and the first time he saw them he'd actually gone lightheaded. He wasn't proud of that.

Now, he gave them his full attention, mouthing at the skin, sucking at the swell, worshipping like a man who'd stumbled into a second chance and wasn't about to waste it.

Then he laughed. A sharp, disbelieving bark that came from somewhere deep in his chest. It wasn't mockery—it was awe, it was hunger, it was *finally*. He ducked his head and let it rumble against the soft flesh of her chest.

"What?" Izzy asked, breath hitching, trying to sound annoyed, but her voice was syrupy and unfocused. Her eyes were half-lidded, pupils blown wide, mouth slightly parted like she'd already taken three shots and a hit off something stronger. She looked ruined. Beautifully so.

"I've missed these," he murmured, almost reverent, before biting down hard enough to make her jolt.

His hands were greedy, unrepentant. He groped and pulled at her breasts like he owned them, like they'd been haunting his fucking dreams, like maybe they had some kind of spell on him. He sucked one nipple into his mouth, then the other, as if trying to memorize them again with tongue and teeth. She hissed.

"Fuck's sake, Nico," she growled, moving as if to finish herself off.

"Oh, absolutely not," he said, that devil-smile cracking wide across his face.

Before she could get up, he grabbed her wrists and dragged her arms down to the table, pinning them flat. Then, with casual brutality, he shoved her legs up and out with one shoulder so her knees bent and her ankles lined up perfectly with her restrained wrists—offering everything and giving her nowhere to hide.

She was glistening. Wet. He could smell her arousal, thick and heady, flooding the air around them like perfume —rich and dark and sweet and utterly hers. His mouth actually watered.

He leaned in slow, hovering just above her inner thigh.

"You smell like fucking heaven," he muttered. "Like honey and sweat and some expensive shit I couldn't afford even if I tried." His breath dragged over her skin, hot and merciless. "You think I'm gonna let you rush me? After all this time? No. You're gonna take it."

She let out a sound caught between a moan and a scoff.

And then he buried his face between her legs.

This was the part he didn't joke about. The part where he turned monk-level devout. He loved going down on her —loved it the way some men loved cars or drugs or money. It was his favorite sin. Her taste was complicated and specific: sweet with a salt edge, a tang of clean sweat, and something faintly floral. It coated his tongue like nectar. He groaned against her, loud and low, because why bother pretending to be cool about it?

His tongue moved like he had a blueprint, like he'd spent hours drawing up the exact geometry of her body and knew every angle by heart. He licked with long, flat strokes at first—teasing—and then circled and sucked with increasing focus until she was writhing. But she couldn't move. Not really. He had her wrists pinned to the table, legs bent and open, his raw strength holding her exactly where he wanted her.

"Fuck," he muttered into her, voice sticky with praise and ruin, "You taste so good. I could die here."

She cried out when the first orgasm hit—sharp and fast

like a snap. Her whole body arched, tried to twist away, but he just pressed harder, held her still, made her take it. Her thighs trembled. Her hands flexed against his grip. But he didn't stop.

He didn't want to stop.

He kept licking, relentless, cruel in his devotion, driving her into a second, then a third wave. He lost count somewhere after that—each time her moans blurred into gasps, then sobs, then broken whimpers. He preened under the sounds, drunk on them. No drug came close.

And then—then—he slipped two fingers inside her, curling them in perfect sync with his mouth.

That was when it got obscene.

The rhythm he found was punishing and precise. A little savage. Every nerve in her body seemed to be singing some cracked, chaotic hymn and he was the choir and the preacher and the damn altar.

When she came again, it wasn't explosive. It was deep. It cracked open from inside her, a seismic thing that turned breath into broken sound. Her whole body convulsed once —and then it gushed. Her thighs spasmed, her breath stopped, and the flood hit his mouth in a rush of slick heat.

They both froze.

For a second, neither of them said anything. The room was silent except for her ragged breathing, the soft drip of liquid on the table, his tongue still lazily lapping at her because he couldn't stop himself.

"Holy shit," he finally said, voice hoarse, grinning like a man who'd just seen God and tasted her.

Her eyes were vacant. Not dumb—just erased. Like someone had reached inside her skull and short-circuited everything that made Izzy sharp, calculated, untouchable.

He stared, caught in it. The empty, dazed look on her

face—soft lips parted, brows slack, pupils blown—was so far removed from her usual razor-edged self it actually stunned him. This was a woman who could cut glass with her words. And now? Now she blinked up at him, dazed, almost confused.

"What?" she murmured, genuinely lost, like she'd woken up in another dimension.

He didn't answer. Just scooped her up like she weighed nothing.

Her legs wrapped around his waist, arms looped around his neck, and their mouths crashed together—sloppy, uncoordinated, furious. She tasted like herself, like sex and sweat and the kind of wild desperation that lived in the space between lovers who'd waited too long. They stumbled into the bedroom still kissing, hands clawing, teeth grazing.

They hit the bed hard. She landed on top of him, straddling his hips like it was instinct.

Her fingers were already tugging at his clothes, fumbling with his fly, dragging his pants down like she needed him now and couldn't quite remember how buttons worked.

"Can I?" she asked, voice pitched high and breathless. "I want to ride you."

He was already groaning, helping her, lifting his hips so she could strip him bare.

"I got the implant," she said, cheeks flushed with heat, voice cracking on a whimper. "I haven't been with anyone else."

His eyes snapped to hers, sharp with need.

"Of course you haven't," he said, his voice low, ragged. "You think I've been fucking anyone else? I can't even get hard unless I'm thinking about you."

She let out a strangled laugh, half-disbelief, half-drunken pleasure.

"I'm serious," he growled. "I can't even jerk off unless I picture you on top of me, looking like this. You ruined me."

She guided herself over him, slow, deliberate. He held her hips, steadying, worshipping. And then he helped her slide down onto him—inch by inch, agonizing and perfect.

Her mouth fell open.

She whimpered, body stiff for a second, thighs trembling with the stretch. But he saw it—that gleam in her eye. That flicker of pain-turned-pleasure. That sick twist in her brain that re-routed agony straight into desire. She loved it. Craved it. Her hips jolted, shuddering against him.

"Oh fuck," he moaned, head falling back into the mattress. "That's it. That's my good girl. Take all of it."

She started moving—slow at first, then faster. Her hands braced on his chest, and the rhythm turned filthy. She slammed down on him like her life depended on it, making those noises he lived for—soft gasps and sharp cries, punctuated by the filthy slap of skin on skin.

He met every thrust with a sharp grind of his hips, fucking up into her while one hand locked around her waist and used it, dragging her down harder, faster. The other hand came up to her breast, pinching her nipple, rolling it between his fingers until she was cursing and clenching around him.

"Look at you," he panted, voice dark with hunger. "Bouncing on my cock like it's your job. Fuck. You feel so good."

And God help him—he meant every word.

She felt too good. Unreal. Like slipping into warmth after frostbite, like returning somewhere he didn't know he'd been missing until he was buried inside her again. She clenched around him—tight, pulsing, alive—and for a second it knocked the breath out of him. His vision stuttered. His grip on reality wavered. It was almost out-of-body, like his soul tried to leave his chest and got stuck somewhere around her hips.

"Fuck, Izzy," he gasped, voice raw. "You feel like home."

She was riding him like a force of nature—grinding, gasping, clenching hard enough to make him stutter under her. And then she came. Again. Still moving, still fucking through it. Her whole body shuddered in slow, rippling waves that never quite stopped. It was relentless. She didn't give herself time to breathe.

He snapped.

In one fluid motion, he flipped her—pressed her down into the mattress on her stomach, dragged her underneath him like something he owned. His torso crushed against her back, nearly his full weight holding her down, and she let out this broken little sound like she loved it.

He grabbed her wrists, moved them above her head so her fingers just barely touched the headboard, and locked them in place.

And then he started fucking her.

No finesse now. Just raw, brutal, ragged thrusts that shook the bedframe. He used every muscle, every inch of strength like he was trying to brand her from the inside. She took all of it. Moaning, sliding up the sheets with every slam, letting him use her however he wanted.

Her walls kept rippling, again and again, like her body didn't know how to stop coming. It was endless. He barely registered the number anymore—just the way she kept clenching, kept gasping, kept giving.

And in the middle of it all, he had the dumbest fucking thought: *she is letting me do this to her. Letting me wreck her like this.*

She turned her head to look back at him, eyes so far

gone they were almost translucent. Glazed, unfocused, but still watching him, seeing him like he was hers.

That was it.

He bent down and kissed her—deep, possessive, a thank-you and a surrender and a promise—and came inside her with a groan that sounded like it was torn out of his spine. It was long. Messy. Like relief. Like he'd been holding it for years.

He stayed inside her, still pushing, small thrusts that kept wringing every last drop out of both of them until his muscles failed. Even when he started to soften, he didn't pull out. Couldn't. Didn't want to. Their bodies were slick, sticking together. Sweat soaked the sheets beneath them. Her hair was damp, clinging to her neck and temple.

She lay there, cheek to the mattress, flushed and quiet, the soft light from the city catching the edges of her face. And she looked beautiful. Wrecked. Completely and utterly his.

When he finally pulled out, it was shameless.

Even in the dark, he saw it cling to her inner thighs like a signature. It glistened in the low light like something holy and filthy all at once. He knew it would haunt him. That exact image. Burned into his brain, branded behind his eyes.

He exhaled. A low, shaky breath. His whole body ached with the kind of satisfaction that didn't come often. And even still—his first instinct was her.

He moved to get up, to grab a towel, to clean her, to do something. But before he could fully stand, she reached out and tugged him back down, pulling him into the heat of her body like gravity itself had shifted.

She laid on his chest, her face pressed to the spot over his heart, breathing slow, deep, almost heavy again. His arms came around her without thinking. One hand in her hair. One across her bare back, tracing the curve of her spine with idle fingers.

They didn't say a word. Didn't need to.

There was something loud and unspoken between them, buzzing just under the surface. Some instinctual understanding vibrating through their skin, humming in the air between every breath:

Whatever the hell this is...we need to figure it out. Because I want this. Over and over. Every night. Always.

But saying it out loud would ruin it. It would shrink it down. Make it mortal.

So instead, they stayed like that. Quiet. Still. Breathing together. Sticking to each other with sweat and release and something bigger.

Eventually, they moved—limbs slow, joints aching. Rinsed off under soft water, hands gentle, eyes lowered.

Her shower was ridiculous. Jets coming from angles he didn't know were legal, steam control, some kind of digital panel that looked like it belonged in a cockpit. One button said "Recovery Mode." He didn't ask.

She blinked up at him, hair slicked back, voice low.

"I want to soak. I'm sore."

He chuckled, low. "Can I come with?"

She gave him a look that was somehow both indulgent and dangerous. "Obviously."

And then, like it was nothing, she led him into a second bathroom—one she hadn't even mentioned. The lights flicked on to reveal the most ridiculous, luxurious tub he'd ever seen. Sleek, deep, minimalist. Japanese soaking-style, pristine stone. Of course she had this. Because Izzy never did anything halfway.

They slipped in together once the tub filled. Water up to their shoulders, steam curling into the air. Her back against his chest this time, arms resting on his, and the kind of silence that wasn't awkward. Just heavy. Intimate.

Eventually, they started talking.

Not about what just happened—not directly. Not yet.

But about them. About time. About how long it had been. About everything they'd tried to convince themselves they didn't want.

And under the fog of heat and the softness of her skin against his, Nico found himself thinking—not for the first time tonight—*I'm not letting this go. Not again.*

Some time passed.

They were pruny. The kind of warm, floaty, over-steeped soft that only came from sitting in hot water for too long with someone who had peeled you open. The steam had begun to cool around the edges, and Izzy was reclined against his chest like a cat that had finally decided not everything needed to be fought. Nico's arms draped lazily around her, fingers tracing little circles on her forearm.

They were quiet, but not awkward. It was the kind of quiet that held weight. After what they'd just put each other through—physically, emotionally—it made sense that words needed time to find their footing again.

Then she sighed and tilted her head back slightly. "We probably shouldn't fly together anymore."

He blinked. Of course. Of course they shouldn't fly together again. That's the whole design—rotations, short pairings, no permanent partnerships. They don't even encourage friendships in the cockpit, let alone whatever the hell this was going to become.

He grinned against her hair. "That's fine. Captains don't usually fly together anyway."

That made her laugh. Real, throaty. The kind that came from her gut and left her breathless.

She let the quiet settle again, more reflective this time. "I think I'm always gonna hate you a little bit," she said eventually.

He didn't stiffen. Just waited.

"Not like... hate hate. Just a little. For how some things were easier for you. Not because you asked for it. Just because it was there. Just because you got to be charming, and golden, and allowed to fuck up without the world ending." She shrugged, small and tight. "I won't take it out on you. But I'm telling you now. When I'm hungry or tired or sad, it might show."

He nodded. "So you're human? Wow. Didn't see that coming."

She rolled her eyes. "I'm serious."

"I know. I hear you." He shifted a little behind her, adjusting his hold. "You're giving me a user manual. I like it. Like a care label sewn into the lining."

"I'm warning you," she said again, quieter now. "I come with fire exits. And maybe a little hazard tape."

He paused. Then: "You okay with me being a little crazy?"

She snorted. "Define crazy."

"Dominant. Possessive. Obsessive. A little..." He searched for the word. "Sociopathic."

"Please," she said, with a lazy smile. "Did you forget I knocked your ass to the ground once?"

He kissed her shoulder, teeth grazing skin. "How could I forget? I tasted the mat. Had burn marks on my ego for a week."

They went quiet again. But this time it was heavier. Softer.

The kind of quiet that invited slow hands and the return of heat between them. He turned her gently, and the way she looked at him—unguarded, almost tender—wrecked him all over again.

They fucked in the water. Slow this time. No chase, no edge—just that pull, that ache, like their bodies had been waiting to get back to this. To her.

His hand cradled the back of her head. Her fingers dragged down his spine. Their mouths barely left each other's.

It wasn't perfect. It was real. Messy, grounding, human in all the places they used to avoid.

Afterward, they toweled off in silence, heavy-limbed and half-drunk on exhaustion and heat. Crawled into bed still damp. Twined together like seaweed on the shore.

And for the first time in months—maybe longer—they slept. Really slept.

Neither of them stirred until noon, when sunlight had already spilled across the sheets and the city was already hours deep into its day. They woke tangled. Her cheek on his shoulder. His hand cupped against her hip. The kind of sleep that felt like forgiveness.

No alarms. No roles to perform.

Just them. Finally.

EPILOGUE

One year later.

She woke up feeling like her soul had been flattened and left in an unclaimed baggage cart.

Local time meant nothing anymore. She was pretty sure her body thought it was 3 a.m. in Bogotá or maybe mid-afternoon in Seoul. Her last pairing was something foul—LHR to GRU to JFK to CDG and back to Heathrow with a three-hour turnaround and a red-eye slot they only gave to people too senior to bitch publicly. Pilot shortage was real, and apparently she counted as reliable.

Didn't help that one of the most capable captains on the damn roster—the one currently alphabetizing their spice rack—had taken himself off long-haul, multi-day pairings for good.

She blinked against the morning light. Or maybe it was afternoon light. Whatever. The flat was quiet, warm, still holding onto the heat of a man who left the bed a few hours ago and had no guilt about it.

From the kitchen: music. Low volume. Something jazzy, minor key, probably Arabic. Not a playlist. A mood.

And the smell—garlic, herbs, olive oil. Smugness.

He was cooking again. Probably had already gone for a run. Probably reorganized their Tupperware lids by circumference.

Izzy sat up slowly, hair in her face, body disoriented but fed up with rest. She padded into the kitchen barefoot—and nearly turned back around.

He was at the stove: shirtless, in gray sweatpants slung low on his hips, plating eggs and fruit like he was auditioning for some tactical-lifestyle cooking channel. His back was all clean muscle and former-military discipline, shoulder blades moving like choreography. His forearms flexed as he gripped the pan, veins raised, hands steady, like even breakfast required control.

The kitchen windowsill—where once there'd been nothing—was crowded now. Little ceramic pots. Fresh herbs. A trailing philodendron. Some cactus thing she hadn't bothered to identify. Signs of him. Spreading. Taking root.

She hated how good he looked in her space. Like he belonged there. Like he knew it.

He looked up. Smiled like it was easy.

"Morning, killer."

"Ugh," she muttered.

He handed her a glass of cold water like he'd anticipated the attitude.

"I made shakshouka."

She eyed the plate like it had wronged her. "One day, I'm gonna sedate you just for the peace."

He kissed the side of her face. "I'll let you if you wear that nurse outfit and keep the heels on."

She flushed, opening her mouth but nothing came out. Just leaned against the counter while he set the food down in front of her—eggs soft-poached in blistered tomatoes, herbs, and harissa, mint over Greek yogurt like it was normal. A bowl of strawberries and orange slices on the side.

He sat across from her and poured himself coffee.

"I reorganized the pantry," he said, like it was nothing. "Turns out you can do that when you're not hopping from Seoul to Lima every week."

Nico still logged flight hours. Still made the standard pilot's salary. Just did it from time zones that let him sleep in her bed.

She took a bite, chewed slowly, and said around a mouthful of food, "You're turning into a housewife."

"I'm a house husband," he corrected. "I cook, I clean, I give you orgasms. Order may vary."

She made a noncommittal sound.

He leaned forward. "You mad about it?"

She didn't answer. Just took another bite and let the silence stretch until it softened.

She wasn't mad. Not really.

Maybe a little humiliated about how much it turned her on.

Breakfast was over. Her plate scraped clean. He was still shirtless, still smug, rinsing dishes like a man who'd just gotten praised by God for his egg technique.

She stayed in her robe. Coffee in hand. Leaned against the counter like it was nothing.

Big mistake.

She heard the shift before she saw it—his steps quiet, deliberate. A second later, he was behind her. No announcement, no showboating. Just that quiet, anchored weight of his chest near her shoulder and his hand ghosting her hip.

"If you're gonna stand like that," he said, voice low, voice dangerous, "I'm gonna touch you."

She didn't turn. Just sipped her coffee. Then, flatly:

"You've got forty minutes."

He blinked. "That's it?"

"I have a to-do list. Your sisters land at six. The towels aren't folded. And I want this place looking like no one's ever fucked in it, even though—"

"Too late," he muttered, already hooking two fingers into her robe belt.

She let him. Let the mug hit the counter. Let her head fall forward just slightly as he peeled the robe open, slow, reverent, like unwrapping a weapon.

Then he dropped to his knees.

He didn't say anything. Didn't have to. His hands came up to grip her thighs and pull her back toward the edge of the counter, and she gasped—not from surprise, but from muscle memory. From knowing exactly how far he'd go.

She braced herself on the counter as he licked, sucked, groaned like he was starved. It was filthy. Unapologetic. He hadn't shaved that morning—she felt the scrape of his jaw in flashes of sensation that made her legs threaten to fold.

"Ah, Nico," she groaned.

He just hummed in agreement. The vibration shot through her like a jolt.

She came fast. Tried not to. Failed. Her head hit the cabinet with a dull thud, her breath shattered, and he kept going. Another wave hit before she could even recover from the first, and she gasped out his name—annoyed, unsteady, half-laughing, half-ruined.

When he finally stood, her knees weren't doing much.

He caught her by the waist. Pulled her in. Kissed her neck like it was a thank-you.

She glared up at him. "I was gonna nap."

He shrugged, unbothered. "So nap satisfied."

She tossed a dishtowel at his head. He caught it one-handed, grinning like a man who'd just won something.

She narrowed her eyes. "I still have shit to do."

"I'll fold the towels," he said, already walking toward the linen closet. "You do what you need to do."

She tried to focus. She really did. There was a to-do list somewhere—digital, color-coded, possibly sentient by now—but she couldn't remember where she'd left it.

Probably under the binder, which was currently open on the dining table, mocking her with tabbed dividers and branded flyers for the second gym. The second gym.

She'd been tricked. This was supposed to be a passive investment. Show up. Punch things. Approve some flooring. Smile vaguely at contractors. Now she was fielding supplier drama at 2 a.m. and googling VAT thresholds while sleep-deprived.

Lina's handwriting was scrawled across a neon pink sticky note on the cover:

"I'm not moving to Newham forever. Don't get smug."

She wasn't smug. She was panicking.

Lina was technically running the new location, but Izzy was the one losing sleep over invoices and punch bag suppliers.

Nico's sisters were arriving in six hours. Layla. Samira. And the toddler—Ahsan—who she last saw sitting in first class eating ice cream out of a champagne flute.

Izzy pulled her hair into a loose bun, tried to find mascara, gave up, then started folding towels like a psychopath. The flat still smelled like sex.

Meanwhile, Nico was in boxers. Wandering around the living room barefoot, coffee mug in hand, humming like he didn't have a single survival instinct.

She glared at him. "Do you ever panic?"

He took a sip. "Not when you're this sexy in crisis mode."

"I will stab you with this butter knife."

"Knife play, babe? I'm into it."

She turned back to the kitchen island. The gym flyers were askew. There were water rings on the wood. She needed to reply to an email about lease renewals. She needed to hire a third assistant manager.

Then the doorbell rang.

Izzy froze.

Nico finally looked nervous. "What the fuck. That can't be them."

She checked her phone for the first time in sixteen hours.

Samira: Hey we are taking the earlier flight. Layla got done with her taping early.

Of course.

She glanced down at her robe, at the cluttered table, at Nico's bare chest and criminally unbothered posture.

"Open it," she snapped, already halfway to the bedroom.

Nico opened the door with zero urgency. Izzy was still zipping up her jeans in the hallway, heart rate somewhere between pilot emergency checklist and social anxiety nosebleed.

"Hi," he said, entirely too casual.

Layla blew past him first, oversized sunglasses, three tote bags, and the aura of a woman who had already insulted a train conductor this morning. Samira followed, composed as ever, carrying what looked like a very expensive toddler-sized tactical backpack. Ahsan came last—

toddling fast, sticky hands out, eyes scanning like he was on a mission.

Izzy barely had time to say hello before Ahsan made a beeline for the coffee table and immediately reached for the one sharp decorative object she'd forgotten to move.

"Ahsan!" Nico said sharply, already intercepting. He handed him a wooden toy and slid the offending object across the table with two fingers like it might be radioactive.

Layla, meanwhile, stopped just past the threshold. Sniffed the air. Narrowed her eyes.

"Did you two just fuck?" she asked, like she was inquiring about the weather. "You're gonna traumatize my son. And me, for that matter."

Nico didn't even blink. "We thought we had time."

"Great. His first long-term memory is going to be your kitchen and the smell of za'atar and boundary violations."

Samira didn't even look up. "I hope you pay for his therapy."

Izzy wanted the floor to open. Or maybe the ceiling to cave in. Anything dramatic enough to erase the look on her face, which she was certain was hovering somewhere between mortified and braced for impact.

Before she could open her mouth, Layla turned, elbowed her lightly in the ribs, and grinned.

"Relax, Captain Sexy. We're just giving you shit."

Then she pulled Izzy into a hug. Not polite, not tentative. Just arms around her like they'd done this before. Because they had. Because now they texted all the time. About gym leggings. About assholes on the internet. About everything.

Izzy exhaled into it, just enough to admit—only to herself—that it felt good.

Across the room, Samira had zero interest in emotional moments. She was already opening her laptop.

"Give me the Wi-Fi," she said.

"No," Nico replied immediately. "Absolutely not."

"Coward," Samira said.

"Name-calling? You set a bad example for our nephew."

"I'll figure it out in five minutes anyways."

Layla flopped down on the couch, kicked off her boots, and shouted, "Someone better be making tea!"

Izzy was already standing there with the tray.

Silver-plated. Heavy. The one she'd shipped home from Beirut after that long weekend with Nico, swearing it was just for show. On it: delicate gold-rimmed teacups, the matching pot still steaming, a small dish of dried apricots and candied orange peel, toasted pistachios in a porcelain bowl, and a linen napkin folded with terrifying precision.

She set it down on the coffee table with all the calm of an Emirates first-class flight attendant, then stepped back like she hadn't just blacked out and served full Arab wife fantasy.

Silence.

Then Layla screamed. "Look at her!"

Samira blinked. "Is this...from your anniversary trip to Beirut?"

Izzy cleared her throat. "It's just a tray."

"But it matches the set."

Layla picked up a dried apricot like it was evidence. "This woman decanted almonds into a porcelain dish. What did you do to her, Nico?"

Nico shot her a smirk like *Wouldn't you like to know?*

"I'm being...hospitable," Izzy said through gritted teeth.

"You're giving full auntie right now," Layla said, popping a pistachio. "Like one more tray and you're gonna start asking if we've eaten and why we're not married."

Izzy sat down, crossed her legs, and took a sip of the mint tea like she wasn't burning alive inside.

Samira clinked cups with her. "It's good tea, though."

"Obviously," Izzy muttered.

From the kitchen, Nico called out, "She made me do a test pour last night."

Izzy turned to glare at him, murderous.

Layla wiped a tear. "God, I love this family."

AFTER TEA, they got up and went to work. Like the sisters had lived there for years.

The flat had two extra bedrooms. Nothing was ready. One was half-full of storage bins and gym merch. The other had a stack of flattened boxes and Nico's spare uniforms still in dry cleaning plastic.

No one cared.

They made a nest on the floor for Ahsan first—toddler bed, fresh sheets, something vaguely soft with cartoon animals on it. Nico handled it with clinical efficiency while Layla acted like her son was being crowned prince.

Izzy dragged out a tote bag from the coat closet and dumped it on the bed—two dozen LUMA-branded designer amenity kits she'd stolen from the ground crew over the past six months. Face masks, sleep socks, hand lotion, gold-trimmed everything.

Layla screamed. "These are full size! You're a criminal."

"Probably, yes," Izzy said.

They made plans for dinner around the chaos. Rey was coming—after a quick hiring meeting with Izzy to get more bodies into the second gym. She still couldn't believe she was saying things like "second gym" and "our people" and meaning them.

Cy and Mas were bringing wine. André was coming late, but he'd promised to bring the new guy. No one knew much yet except that he had shoulders and a job and hadn't run off screaming, which made him a front-runner.

"We need to starve ourselves before then," Layla said solemnly, staring at the counter. "It's going to be too much food."

Samira nodded. "I support that."

Nico brushed past Izzy in the kitchen, hand skimming her back like it was instinct. She didn't flinch. Didn't pull away. Just leaned into it slightly. Let him. He didn't say anything. Just looked at her like she was the only thing that mattered.

And that's when it hit her.

That she'd once been a lonely girl in a crumbling house on a naval base in Jacksonville, Florida. That her parents hadn't done their job. That she'd learned early how to save herself and assumed that was the whole story—that getting out was the goal, that survival was all she could ask for.

She never thought there'd be more.

She didn't dare hope to be loved.

But here she was.

Here he was.

Here was her family—messy, loud, early when they said they'd be late, and somehow exactly what she needed.

Some families were chosen. Some were stolen.

Hers walked in early and stayed for dinner.

ABOUT THE AUTHOR

Kim Serrano lives in Chicago, where planes fly past her window and there's usually a rescue dog nearby. She's worked more jobs than she can list, which helps when writing about people in high-pressure situations making bad decisions.

Hold Control is her second novel, after *Burn Rate*.

Find her at kimserrano.com, or on Instagram and TikTok @kimserranobooks.